WILLOW
and the boys

The Rise of a Georgia Family
During the 1800s

RICK MAIER

Willow and the boys
The Rise of a Georgia Family During the 1800s

Copyright © 2023 by Rick Maier. All rights reserved.

Published by Scribblers Press
9741 SW 174th Place Road
Summerfield, Florida 34491
Published in the United States of America

Printed by Trinity Press
3190 Reps Miller Road, Suite 360,
Norcross, Georgia 30071
Book cover and inside page layout designed by Bridgett Joyce
The opinions expressed by the author are not necessarily those of Trinity Press.

Paperback ISBN: 978-1-950308-60-6
Kindle: ISBN: 978-1-950308-61-3

Library of Congress Control Number: 2023921526
Rick Maier 11/30/23

Ordering Information
For ordering this book visit www.scribblersweb.com

ALL RIGHTS RESERVED – No part of this book may be reproduced in any form without permission in writing from the author. This book is a work of historical fiction. The story and characters are fictitious, and any resemblance to actual people is unintended. References to geography, historical events, and historical people are intended to be factual to serve as a context for the story and background for the characters.

Books by Rick Maier

- *Bone Dust*
- *Exit South*
- *Orange Terrace*
- *The Tunnels Below St. Edana*
- *Fire and Faith (nonfiction)*
- *Alaska Awakening*
- *Willow and the Boys*

www.rickmaier.com

Chapter One

1833

Roy Bowers remained seated at the table as his management team stood and exited the room. The loud banter of the men could be heard slowly drifting down the hallway as they chided the comptroller for focusing on rising expenses when they had just set another record for monthly revenues.

Roy sat reflecting, absently rubbing the red oak table as he glanced around his office walls at the many architectural drawings of construction projects his company had completed. The weekly project review meeting had gone well. Bowers Builders was now a well-run and successful organization. Why wasn't he thrilled?

He wasn't bored, depressed, or unhappy about anything. Every day was busy, but he missed the excitement. In the 1812 War, he built bridges and fortifications and then fought the British in the trenches in New Orleans. After getting discharged in 1815, he started his own construction company outside the stockade of Fort Hawkins on the western frontier of Georgia. When the Creek Indians ceded the land west of the Fort, Roy moved across the Ocmulgee River to build more homes and businesses, even before the official founding of the town of Macon in 1823.

Roy searched for a word to describe how he felt. Melancholy? Anxious for a new adventure? A desire to feel more needed?

Buck, his oldest son and crew manager, strolled back into the room toward the stove. "You want some more coffee, sir?" The stove in the corner provided warmth on this chilly March morning as it kept the coffee pot hot.

Roy waved his hand over his cup, staring at nothing in particular.

"Something bothering you?" Buck asked as he refilled his mug.

"I'm fine," replied Roy. "Just thinking about how things are going."

"I'd say things are going really well, don't you agree? Our projects are on time and on budget, and more requests for proposals arrive every week. Everybody's busy and in a good mood."

"Things are great," agreed Roy, nodding and looking up with a forced smile. "And I'm impressed at how you and the other managers are stepping up to the tasks." Roy stood from his chair and went to the window. "You might not remember, but ten years ago, the view of town from here was nothing but a collection of wood shacks and makeshift tents along the river. More of a camp than a town."

Roy looked over and waved, inviting Buck to join him at the window. "Look at it now. Flocks of people out shopping, smoke spewing from the chimneys of businesses, and neighborhoods of nice homes. Macon is taking off!"

"I know! And we've built a bunch of those structures," replied Buck, putting one hand on his dad's shoulder. "I'm proud of the contribution our company is making." Buck turned and faced his father. "So why the long face?"

"It's hard to explain how I feel. I'm proud, really proud of all we've accomplished. This may sound like an old geezer talking, but y'all are doing such a good job that it makes me wonder about my role here." Roy slowly nodded and pursed his lips. "Maybe it's time for me to step aside."

"Step aside?" exclaimed Buck. "Are you kidding? You're the heart of this company. Maybe you haven't hammered a nail in a while, but things wouldn't get done without you."

"I hardly said two words during our meeting."

WILLOW *and the boys*

Buck rubbed his beard as he gathered his thoughts. "Have you ever noticed how, when any of us say something, everyone looks to you to see your reaction?"

"You don't need to butter me up, Son," said Roy kiddingly, continuing to stare out the window.

Buck continued. "Do you remember when Grandpa kept falling, and he would complain about living too long? You told him to get up and dust off, that we needed him around to keep us all on track.

Roy stood quietly. He was listening but didn't know what to say without sounding whiny.

"Grandpa was in his sixties," continued Buck. "You'll only be fifty next year." Buck had only known Roy and Roy's father between the time his mother and Roy married in 1816 and when the wise old rancher died in 1827.

Roy stretched his arms and raised his head. "I'm not upset. I'm fine. I'm excited about what's happening. We've been very successful, and it's new ground."

"Like Grandpa used to say, the test of a man is not how he deals with failure, but with success."

"Grandpa never had—"

Roy's assistant, Pauline, entered the room abruptly. "Sir, the sheriff is here to see you. He says it's urgent."

Roy and Buck looked at each other, surprised by the sudden interruption. "Please invite him in," replied Roy.

The sheriff walked into the room, hat in hand. He hesitated to speak as if searching for the right words. "Roy, there's been an accident involving your wife, Helen. I'm afraid it's bad."

"Is she hurt? What kind of accident? Where?"

"Her carriage overturned up on the road to Smarr, and she was thrown off into the trees." The sheriff paused and grimaced. "I'm afraid she died from a blow to her head."

Buck slumped and groaned. Roy stood with his eyes and mouth wide open. He patted his son on the shoulder and walked closer to the sheriff.

"Are you certain it's Helen? Are you sure she's not just unconscious?" asked Roy. The sheriff stood quietly to give Roy time to react to the news. "Did this just happen? Where is she now?"

The sheriff looked to Buck and then back to Roy. "Mrs. Rose came up on the accident and rushed to my office to report what she found. My deputy and I rode out there and found Helen lying a few feet from where the carriage had broken down on the road. The wheel had come off the axle, and she was lying on the side of the road up against a pine tree. Her head must have hit that tree pretty hard. There was a good bit of blood. She wasn't breathing, and there was no heartbeat. It must have happened a good while before because her skin was bluish when I arrived."

"Did Mrs. Rose see the accident?" asked Roy. "Did anyone?"

"Mrs. Rose told me she hadn't seen anyone else along the road going in either direction, and no one else has reported anything to me."

"And where was this?"

"A little over a mile north of town, where the road to Smarr bends left to cross the creek. Not many people live up that way or travel that road."

"And where is my wife now?"

"We haven't touched anything. I've got one deputy taking a wagon up there, and another deputy is still at the scene. I came here as quick as I could, and I'm fixin' to ride back up there."

Roy thought for a moment. "I want to go with you." He turned to Buck. "Son, I need you to go to the house and tell everyone what happened. We'll bring your Ma back home."

Buck didn't answer but looked up at his father and slowly nodded. His eyes were full of tears.

The two men galloped on horseback from Roy's office on Fourth Street north up Walnut Street, where it became a narrow dirt lane through the woods. Having known the sheriff socially for a few years and hearing only positive things about his performance, Roy was confident that a good man was handling Helen's accident.

Though the road was muddy from the overnight showers, they didn't let that slow them down. When they arrived at the scene, the deputy was walking along the side of the road searching the ground, and the carthorse was tied up to a tree.

"This morning at breakfast," said Roy as they dismounted and walked past the broken-down carriage toward the body, "Helen said she was going to the farm right after I left for the office. Something about looking after. . ." Roy stopped dead in his tracks at the sight of his Helen lying on the ground. He bowed his head and groaned, breathed deeply, and continued walking.

"So, there was nothing unusual about her being out here in the country today?" asked the sheriff.

Roy shook his head. "No."

"Did she come out this way often? She knew the road?"

"She traveled this road at least twice a week. We have a farm less than a mile north of here."

"And she was an experienced wagon driver?"

"Excellent," said Roy, then he turned toward the crippled carriage. "A couple of years ago, she had me buy that carryall carriage because it has a top for the rain and plenty of space for cargo. She loved that carriage, and my stable man, Samuel, took good care of it. I can't imagine how it failed like this."

Roy kneeled beside his wife's body. "No one has touched her," said the sheriff as he backed away to give Roy some space.

Roy had seen many dead bodies in the 1812 War, but never one he loved so dearly. He reached over in the dirt, picked up the bonnet she always wore at the farm, and brushed it off. Roy tenderly pulled her crumpled body away from the tree and reverently repositioned her to lay supine. Her limbs had stiffened, and dried blood stained the left side of her hair and face. There was a deep, raw gash above her ear where she had hit the tree. Helen's eyes were cloudy, and her eyelids were too rigid for Roy to close.

He went over to feel the impression on the tree and saw the caked blood on the bark. Standing upright over his wife, he bowed his head, closed his eyes, and quietly recited Psalm 23. Then he wiped the tears from his cheeks. "I'm so sorry, Helen. I don't know how this could have happened, but if someone was responsible, they will face justice."

Roy walked over to inspect the wagon wheel, which lay a few feet from the carriage. The sheriff returned to his side. "There's nothing wrong with this wheel," said Roy. "The spokes are intact, and the iron rim looks fine."

They looked closer at the wrecked carriage. "And I don't see anything wrong with the reaches and axle," observed the sheriff. "Best I can figure, the one thing missing is the linchpin," he added, referring to the wedge of steel sculptured to fit tightly into the hole at the end of the axle to secure the wheel. "The pin on the right side is fine, but we can't find the left one." He called the deputy over. "Have you found any sign of that linchpin yet?"

"No sir," replied the deputy. "I've been up and down the road. I looked in the brush but haven't seen a thing."

"If the pin came loose in this turn in the road," continued the sheriff, "it would be lying nearby. It must have come off somewhere further down the road."

"If it had loosened," observed Roy, "the wheel would have started wobbling, and Helen would have had some warning."

"You're right. But why aren't we finding it?"

"I guess we need to keep looking," replied Roy. The three men walked further along both sides of the road until the wagon driven by another deputy arrived. The officer pulled a stretcher off the wagon as Roy and the sheriff wrapped a sheet around Helen's body. The four men carefully lifted Helen's body onto the stretcher and the stretcher into the wagon bed.

"Take her to your house?" asked the sheriff.

Roy nodded. "I'll lead the driver there."

Roy had been focusing on why the carriage had failed, probably to take his mind off the reality that his wife was gone. But the priorities of the situation became clear. He patted the sheriff on the back. "If you'll push the carriage to the side of the road, I'll get some men to come get it. Right now, I need to go be with my family."

Roy stood to take one more look around the scene, slowly shaking his head in disbelief. The deputy tied the reins of the carthorse to the back of his wagon as Roy mounted his horse. "Sheriff, I appreciate all the attention you're giving this. I hope you and your men will keep trying to figure out how this could have happened."

"We certainly will, Roy. And I'm deeply sorry for your loss. I know the whole town will be praying for you and your family."

Roy rode off to lead the wagon down the road. When they arrived at the house, his sons and several servants gathered to stand on the front porch. Roy's youngest son, Tim, ran out and clutched his father in a tearful embrace. Tim was the sensitive Bowers, more like his mother than his father in showing his emotions.

Roy saw his stable man standing on the porch. "Samuel, come here!" Samuel shuffled to stand before Roy. "You heard about the carriage wheel coming off?" Samuel nodded. "We need to talk later."

Roy, Buck, the deputy, and Tim carried the stretcher to the master bedroom, removed the sheet, and laid Helen on her bed. Roy asked everyone to give his sons a few minutes alone with their mother.

After the boys had said their goodbyes, Roy entered the room alone. Helen's skin was cool to the touch as he put his hand over hers. "God, Helen, we are really going to miss you! I don't know how we're gonna deal with this, but I know you will be watching over us." Roy bent over and kissed her on the forehead. "Sleep in peace."

Roy went into the hallway and asked Atha and another house servant to tend to Helen, cleaning her wound and changing her into an appropriate outfit.

Atha, who had served Miss Helen for many years, nodded as she sobbed. "I can't believe this, Mr. Roy. Miss Helen was so beautiful and full of life. Her passing is so very, very sad. But I'll fix her up in her Sunday best."

Roy told his sons he needed to stop by the office and would return soon. At the office, he asked his assistant to contact the company's general manager to take over the business for a few days, the local carpenter to make the funeral arrangements, and his minister to arrange a service.

"Don't you worry, Mr. Roy," replied Pauline. "I'll talk to each of them right away. We will take care of everything. You just take care of your family."

Chapter Two
1833

By the time Roy arrived home, friends and neighbors were gathering on the porch of the family house. Three thousand people lived in Macon, but news traveled fast. Roy handed his reins to Marcus, the chief servant, who was manning the entrance. Samuel wasn't in sight. He thanked those who had gathered for their support. Each expressed shock and sadness and asked what they could do for the family.

Roy entered the house and found Buck and Tim in the study.

He embraced each of his boys with a mighty bear hug as if to express his sadness with strength and then looked them both in the eye with a nod to express the hope that together, they could get through the tragedy. Following the embraces, no words were spoken. None were needed.

The three Bowers men sat quietly in chairs facing each other. Roy slowly shook his head as he ran his fingers through his graying locks. Buck sat solemnly, staring out the front window. Young Tim had his elbow on the chair armrest, an open palm barely keeping his head from collapsing onto his knees. His body shuddered, and whimpers escaped his effort not to break down and cry.

"How can we get word to Jeremy?" asked Buck of his father. Jeremy, the middle son, was studying at the University in Athens.

"I asked Marcus to get word to Kitch to fetch him," replied Roy. "It's a full day and a half of riding, so he might not get here for the funeral."

"And the minister? Will he be here soon?"

"I've asked Pauline to send word, but he may be traveling. Hopefully, he can get here tomorrow. He's probably out riding his circuit."

There was more silence when the family dog, Jax, strolled into the room and put his head on Roy's leg. "What are you doing in here?" asked Roy, reaching out to pet the four-year-old setter and collie mix. The dog was happy to live outside but occasionally wandered into the house to check on things.

Sary, the cook, came into the room following the dog. "Sorry, Mister Roy. He was scratching at the back door, so I let him in."

"That's okay," replied Roy. "Let him be for a while. He knows things aren't right."

The dog made his rounds to Tim and Buck for a quick back scratch. "Jax knows Ma should be here, that something's wrong," said Tim.

"Buck, have you told Abigail?" Roy asked. Buck and his wife Abigail had a son and three daughters and lived two blocks away on Spring Street.

"I stopped and told her," replied Buck. "She's going to have a tough time breaking the news to the children." Buck took a deep breath. "Have you thought about the funeral arrangements?"

"Pauline is contacting that carpenter who people say handles funerals as well as making coffins."

"Should we close the business for a few days?" Buck followed up.

"Just on the day of the funeral," replied Roy.

"What are we going to do, Pa?" asked Tim. "Ma was the glue in this family. She kept us all on track."

Roy nodded his head slowly. "You're right. We all counted on her a lot, but now she's gone. This is going to be tough, but between the four of us, we will be all right. It's just gonna take time. We all need to make some changes and pitch in at the house, and the business, and the farm." Roy paused to gather his thoughts. "Your mother and I raised you boys to be independent, but now we got to be a team to support each other." Roy sat up, putting his hands on his knees. "You boys have full lives. I think I'm the one who will miss your mother the most. Most every big decision I've made, I ran by her."

Roy stood and walked to the window at the sound of hoofs on the gravel driveway. "Looks like the sheriff is here. I need to go see what he wants."

Roy greeted the sheriff at the door and invited him to come and join his sons in the study.

"I won't intrude on you long," replied the sheriff. "I just wanted to make sure everything was okay here."

"Did you find that linchpin?" asked Roy.

"We found one along the road a good distance from the accident. But it doesn't match the pin on the other wheel. It's too small for the hole in the axle."

"I can't imagine any other carriage or wagon losing a pin there on the road," added Roy.

"I agree. And that bothers me."

Roy filled the boys in on how they thought the carriage wheel had come loose, hurling Helen into the tree on the side of the lane.

"I was wondering," inquired the sheriff, "if I could talk to the man you mentioned who takes care of the carriage."

Tim spoke up. "That would be Samuel. I'll go fetch him."

Tim was the free spirit of the family; he spoke openly and from the heart. At sixteen, he was more interested in the operations of the carriage house and the livestock at the farm than working in his father's business or going to college like his older brothers. Tim's dream was to join the throngs of men prospecting for gold around Dahlonega, but Roy and Helen insisted that he help out with the family operations, at least until he was eighteen. He was good buddies with the Black stable hand, Samuel, and had no problem locating him in the carriage house working on a saddle that didn't appear to need any work.

"I am really gonna miss Ms. Helen," said Samuel as Tim approached. His eyes were red and glistening with tears. "She was a mighty fine lady."

Tim patted Samuel on the arm. "We all will, Samuel. But right now, please come with me. The sheriff is here and wants to speak with you."

They returned together to the study.

The sheriff greeted Samuel and began his questions. "Do you remember prepping the carriage for Mrs. Bowers early this morning?"

"Yes, sir. I check that carriage first thing every morning in case Miss Helen needs to go somewhere."

"Did you check the linchpins on both wheels?"

Samuel stood erect, hat in hand, but looked down periodically. "Yes, sir. I looked that carriage over good. It's a fine carriage."

The sheriff explained how the accident occurred and how they found a linchpin along the road that was the wrong fit. "Look at me, Samuel. How could that pin not be the right fit for that axle?"

"You're talking to him like he's somehow responsible, sheriff," interrupted Tim. "Are you accusing him of something?"

"Let the sheriff do his job, Son," injected Roy.

The tension in the room settled down after a moment, but Samuel was visibly uneasy. He shuffled slowly in place and stood with his head down.

"Take your time, Samuel," said Roy, trying to calm the man's nerves. "Just tell the sheriff what you know to be true."

"I was up early feeding the horses when Mrs. Bowers left in the carriage. But I knows the wheels of that carriage were in good shape."

Roy knew that Samuel was honest and able to speak for himself. Despite being indentured, the family encouraged their servants to read, write, and speak up. But there was something a little off in the way Samuel was acting. Maybe standing before the sheriff made him nervous.

The sheriff continued. "Mr. Bowers has told me that you're an experienced hand. If you have any ideas about how that wheel came off the wagon, I hope you will let me or Mr. Bowers know."

The sheriff turned to the Bowers men. "I apologize for intruding at this terrible time. We're all praying for your family." He turned to leave. "I can see myself out."

Marcus came into the room as the sheriff was leaving. "Mister Roy, a man out front would like to know about the arrangements for Miss Helen."

Roy walked to the foyer with his sons to greet the carpenter, Mr. Thompson, who would oversee the arrangements for the wake and funeral. Roy introduced his sons.

"We need to pick out a place for the casket for the reception," said Thompson as he scanned the rooms. "I'm sure there will be friends who will want to sit with her tonight." He pointed toward the parlor. "That's a good spot. Do you agree?" Roy nodded. "I've already made arrangements for the service at the Methodist church and burial at City Cemetery. Is Thursday okay for the service?"

After a few moments, Roy replied, "Whatever you think is best,

Mr. Thompson."

Buck sensed that his father needed time to absorb all the sudden interruptions and decisions he had probably never considered. "I'll work with Marcus and Thompson to take care of everything, Pa," said Buck. "You go rest in the guest room. It's been a very tough day."

"I appreciate that, Son. I will rest, but Tim, please ask Samuel to come and see me in the study."

"Right away, sir," replied Tim.

Roy had purchased seven slaves over the past ten years. They all lived in a separate wing of the house with their own dining room, a bedroom for the men, and a bedroom for the women. As an experienced butler, fifty-year-old Marcus oversaw the others and general household operations. Sary, his wife, was the cook and had a young assistant. Atha was in charge of cleaning and laundry; she was thirty and came with her daughter to assist her. Samuel had experience with horses and was responsible for the carriage house. Samuel's son, Kitch, was twenty and stayed in a small cabin at the farm where they raised livestock and crops—the destination Helen never reached.

Roy greeted Samuel in the study. "Where are your shoes, Samuel?"

"Miss Helen told me not to wear my stable shoes in the house. She always said to save the stink for the stable."

"She had her rules," agreed Roy, "and I reckon we should keep following them." Roy stood to face Samuel. "I may be seeing this wrong, but you didn't seem yourself when you were talking to the sheriff. Were you holding something back?"

"I guess I'm just mighty upset about Miss Helen passing, sir."

"I don't think you were telling the sheriff everything."

Samuel looked down without saying anything. Roy waited in silence.

"I'm not sure this is anything," began Samuel, "but it troubled me a bit. After you left this morning and Miss Helen came out to go to the farm, Mr. Norman showed up. I was across the way, but they started raising their voices, and it looked like they was arguing."

Norman Hammond was Helen's brother. Norman had served in the 1812 War and spent his last months of duty with Roy at Fort Hawkins in Macon. Immediately after getting discharged, they started the building company as partners. Roy had design and selling skills, while Norman's experience was in finance and scheduling projects.

Norman introduced Roy to his sister, Helen, and they began spending time together. Roy was thirty-two years old at the time and anxious to settle down. Helen had just lost her husband in the War and was struggling to raise her teenage son, Buck, alone. Roy and Norman brought the boy into the business, and Roy was impressed with Buck's skill and hard work. The following year, Roy and Helen married, and Roy adopted Buck.

Things went well between Norman and Roy until a few years later when Roy caught Norman skimming profits from the business. Norman denied the accusations, but Roy had proof. Instead of pursuing any criminal charges, Norman was offered a settlement that left Roy with full ownership of the business and Norman with generous quarterly payments over ten years. Roy ran the details by Helen, who thought the agreement was equitable to her brother and husband.

When Bowers Builders continued to grow rapidly in the months following the settlement, Norman felt that Roy had swindled him. He demanded a significant increase in his payments or to be brought back as a partner. Roy refused, and Norman began making scenes at the shop and disparaging Roy in public. During one of Norman's rampages at a job site, Roy pinned his brother-in-law against a wall and threatened him. Helen was as mad at her brother as Roy, but when Norman continued stalking company job sites, and Roy controlled his anger, she stopped speaking to her brother.

"Did you hear what they were arguing about?" Roy asked Samuel.

"No, sir. I was in one of the stalls repairing the gate."

Roy wasn't surprised that Norman would make a scene at the house, except it had come just before the accident. "Was Norman anywhere near the carriage?"

"Miss Helen was about to leave, so yes, they were standing right next to the carriage."

"Did you see him do anything to the wheels?"

"No, can't say I did. That's why I didn't say anything to you or the sheriff. You know, it was just odd that he was here, that they was yelling, and then there was the accident."

"I agree," replied Roy. "It does seem suspicious. And I appreciate your telling me what you saw. Do you think Norman knew you were in the carriage house to see this?"

"I don't think so. Mr. Norman was pretty focused on whatever it was that brought him out to see Miss Helen." Samuel paused for a moment and then looked at Roy with tears in his eyes.

Samuel left, and while Roy wanted to pursue this new lead, he had more pressing matters to attend to.

The carpenter delivered the coffin to the house. Roy called on his sons to help him and Thompson lay Helen in the coffin and carry the pine wood box to the parlor. Atha had dressed her in a fine navy dress and her favorite pearl necklace and matching earrings. Thompson set up a makeshift stand with planks over sawhorses and draped it with a fine white cloth to match the casket's lining. Roy expressed his appreciation to Thompson for doing such a fine job so quickly.

Roy stood for several minutes over the coffin, expressing the many wonderful things Helen had meant to him: raising their three boys, helping him steer the growth of the business, and managing their joy-filled household and productive farm. Then, he helped Thompson arrange the parlor to receive guests for the wake.

Buck, Abigail, and their children came to pay their respects. Roy had to bow his head when Buck held up his youngest daughter to say goodbye, and she blew a kiss to her grandmother. As twilight arrived, Buck's family left, and several of Helen's friends came to the house to sit with her body through the night. One of Helen's closest friends insisted that Roy and Tim retire to their bedrooms to rest up for tomorrow, which was sure to be a long day of greeting the many people who would come to pay their respects.

Roy thought that Norman might have had the decency to come to the house to mourn the loss of his sister, but he did not arrive before Roy retired to his bedroom.

Roy didn't like to show his emotions, but when he entered the bedroom and saw the bed he shared with Helen, he collapsed in a chair and wept. He fell asleep in the chair—in the bedroom where he had never slept one night alone.

Chapter Three
1833

Roy was in the parlor the following day, receiving friends who came to pay their respects. He kept glancing out the window hoping his son Jeremy would miraculously arrive, when he spotted his brother-in-law approaching the house. He excused himself and hurried outside to intercept Norman before he came through the front door. Tempers might flare anytime the former partners ran into each other, and Roy wanted to avoid a scene.

"Norman! I'm surprised to see you," exclaimed Roy.

"Surprised to see me at my sister's wake?" said Norman in an agitated tone.

Roy didn't respond to his question. "Helen is in the parlor."

Norman nodded and turned to walk toward the front door when Roy grabbed his arm.

"And after you've paid your respects," added Roy, "I hope you'll come back out here so we can talk."

Norman yanked his arm out of Roy's grasp. "And why would I do that? There's nothing I want to hear from you. I'm here for my sister, not you."

"I want to hear why you came here yesterday and talked to Helen in the carriage house. Just before she went on the ride that left her dead."

Norman's face contorted into a befuddled expression, and he took a moment to respond. "What the hell are you talking about?"

Roy couldn't tell if he was surprised by the implication or that someone had seen him with Helen that morning. "Do you deny being here yesterday morning and talking to Helen?"

Norman was still off balance and thought for a moment. "I needed to ask my sister if she was coming to our house for my daughter's birthday party."

"And that led to yelling and threatening gestures?"

"I don't know what you think you saw or where you got your information, but I don't have to answer your stupid questions. It sounds like you believe I had something to do with the wheel coming off that carriage."

"So you know that the wheel came off? Who told you those details?"

"Everyone knows that. I don't remember where I heard it." Norman stood erect and pointed his finger in Roy's face. "This conversation is over. I should be blaming you for losing my sister; it was your carriage. Or maybe you need to accept that accidents do happen. And if you think there was foul play, you should let the sheriff do his job." With that final outburst, Norman turned and walked into the house.

Buck came over to his father after seeing the heated exchange. "What was that all about?"

"Your Uncle Norman has some explaining to do." Roy gave Buck the details of what Samuel had told him.

"You think Uncle Norman fooled with the carriage wheel?"

"It's worth considering. There's been a lot of bad blood with Norman ever since your mother sided with me when our partnership broke up. We gave him a generous settlement, but he demanded more. I refused, and ever since then, he's done nothing with his life but get drunk. I've heard your Aunt June kicked him out, and he's been working as a hired hand on the river barges."

"Did he say why he came to see Ma yesterday?" asked Buck.

"Some ridiculous story about a party for your cousin, but I doubt it. Hell, his own family wants nothing to do with that sad fool. And to think what a good soldier he was when we fought together in New Orleans."

"He has been acting like he's gone a bit haywire." Buck looked around to gather his thoughts. "Should we tell the sheriff what Samuel told you after being questioned yesterday?"

"I'll arrange for Samuel to meet with the sheriff again and tell him." Roy turned his son toward the house. "But today, I just want to take advantage of being with you boys."

Roy hated that neither Jeremy nor Helen's parents had arrived in time for the funeral, but it was too late to delay the many arrangements.

Respect for the many things the Bowers family had done for Macon turned the funeral into a community-wide event. People lined the streets as the wagon transported the coffin to the church, and the church was packed shoulder to shoulder. The preacher asked Tim to read scripture and Buck to thank everyone for their support on behalf of the family. Mayor Seymour spoke of Helen's efforts to begin a public library, gather food and clothing for those falling on hard times, and help with the new Methodist church expansion. The preacher knew Helen well and delivered a heartfelt eulogy.

The burial was at the City Cemetery on 7th Street. Hundreds of friends, employees of Bowers Builders, and well-wishers followed Roy and his two sons as they walked behind the wagon bearing the casket. Roy wanted to bury Helen at a larger cemetery being planned at the end of Wharf Street, where there would be more room for a family plot, but Rose Hill Cemetery wasn't ready.

As they were walking from the cemetery, Roy gave Buck a nudge. "I haven't seen Norman in the church or the procession."

"I think you got his attention," replied Buck.

Following the funeral, Roy invited close friends to the house. As the guests were leaving, Jeremy, the middle son, arrived at the house. The seventeen-year-old student at the University of Georgia had left Athens the previous day, spent the night in Madison, and rose at dawn to ride straight to the house. Kitch, who had gone to fetch him, was far behind.

Jeremy leaped off his horse and ran to his father. His hope that Kitch was wrong, that his mother was somehow still alive, was dashed with one look at his father's drawn face. "It's true? Ma is dead?" asked Jeremy in a near panic.

Roy reached for his son's arms to calm him. "Yes, I'm afraid it's true." Roy put his arm around Jeremy and led him toward the study in the house. "The funeral was earlier today. I'm sorry you missed it. A lot of people came to the service. It was a fitting tribute to your Ma. But I'm glad you are here. We're all together now."

"How are you and Buck and Tim doing?"

Roy took a deep breath. "This is going to be a big adjustment, that's for sure. But I think we'll all be okay. Tim is taking it the hardest." Roy patted Jeremy on the back. "How are you? You must be exhausted."

"I just couldn't believe the news. A carriage accident?"

Jeremy asked many questions as Roy explained everything, from the accident scene to his confrontation with Norman. He was tall, thin, clean-shaven, often dressed more formally than the occasion, and appeared more studious than his rugged-looking brothers. Roy was proud that one of his sons was going to college.

"You and I can visit the accident scene and cemetery tomorrow," Roy offered. "I hope you'll stay as long as you need, but you shouldn't feel obligated to remain here for me and your brothers. Your schoolwork is more important than you worrying about things here." Roy smiled at Jeremy. "Your mother was so proud you're studying to be a lawyer. She would always say how you will be a great governor someday."

Jeremy nodded at his father. "Thanks, Pa. I will return to Athens, but I need a few days here before I can think again about my studies."

Tim came into the study and greeted his brother. They talked until Helen's parents arrived at the house, having traveled by stagecoach from Augusta. Roy's mother in Pleasantburg, South Carolina, had probably just gotten Roy's letter about Helen's death.

The next three days were sad, gloomy times for Roy and his three boys. While it was great to be together, a rare event anymore, there was none of the typical ribbing and horseplay. Buck didn't talk about any new building projects, Jeremy didn't show off his two years of Latin, and Tim had stopped dreaming out loud of discovering a mother lode of gold up north. Helen's parents were only adding to the gloom; her mother was losing her sight, and her father was in agony over a nagging toothache.

Following breakfast on the third day after the funeral, Roy summoned his sons for a meeting in the study. "We all know that things need to change around here, and I want to start with a couple announcements."

The three sons sat up straight with anxious expressions. Usually, their mother, not Roy, called family meetings.

Roy continued. "First, about the business. Buck is ready to take on more responsibility at the company, and I'm ready to step aside to let younger minds run things. Next week, I will announce that Buck is the new president."

Tim and Jeremy nearly tackled Buck with congratulatory handshakes, back slaps, and hugs.

"The new boss man!" yelled Tim.

"Well deserved, brother!" exclaimed Jeremy. "But you can't just retire, Pa."

Roy continued when the boys settled back in their seats. "Jeremy, you need to return to Athens as soon as you're ready. The governor-to-be needs all the education and connections he can get."

Jeremy nodded with a mixture of resolve and a bit of regret that he would be far from home for months or even years.

"Tim, I'll get to you in a minute." Roy gathered his thoughts. "Do y'all remember a few months ago when I got notice of winning that lottery granting us a 160-acre lot in North Georgia? It wasn't all luck because they doubled the chances for war veterans, but the property will be reassigned if we don't make an effort to claim and improve the land."

Roy took a deep breath. "So here's what I have in mind. It will take weeks to prepare, but I plan to travel up there and check out the land. If the property is a swamp or on the side of a mountain, I'll turn around and come home. But I'm going to assume the land is worth developing and take two wagons full of supplies. The trip is over a hundred and eighty miles, so it will take many days. I'll probably spend the summer up there and won't return here until fall."

"I want to go with you, Pa," yelled Tim. "Thar's gold in them thar hills!"

"I figured you would want to go, and I would certainly appreciate the company. But there are a couple of conditions. The militia plans to round up the Cherokee in the area to move them out west. I know you have a soft heart for the Natives, so you must agree not to interfere with the effort."

"It's wrong and un-Christian to kick them off their land," stated Tim, "but if you let me go with you, I promise not to get involved. Besides, I'll be too busy building my sluice and panning for gold."

"And that's the other condition," continued Roy. "There might be time for some prospecting, but first things first. Food and shelter will be our priority. We must build a cabin, hunt and fish for food, and plant crops. I understand the property is along a river, but there won't be much time for panning."

"Understood," replied Tim, still as excited as a kid at Christmas.

"I can visit when the quarter finishes in May," responded Jeremy. "Honestly, Tim, I'm jealous. That sounds like a hell of an adventure."

"We would love to have you join us, but again, school comes first," responded Roy. He looked over at Buck, who sat silently. "What are you thinking?" he asked.

"Your absence will leave a gaping hole at the company," replied Buck. "And what happens to this house and the farm?"

"I plan to take Samuel and Kitch with us, so we may need to shut down the farm. But Marcus and the rest of the help should be able to handle things here. And you might want to think about moving your family into this house. Abigail can take care of the place just like your Ma did."

The smiles all quieted down at the mention of Helen. Buck broke the silence. "Pa, are you sure you're not acting out of grief instead of thinking clearly? It's only been a few days."

"I've been thinking about this ever since I got the notice about winning the land. And I'm not planning to stay up there permanently. I'll be back in a few months. You'll need to save me one of the upstairs bedrooms for when I return."

"But Pa, you're taking an awfully big risk traveling all that way without knowing what to expect," exclaimed Buck. "The wagons may not make it, the Indians are fighting mad, and crazy prospectors have flooded into that area. There could be trouble."

"I've thought about all those things and more, but I think it will be okay." Roy paused to make sure Buck didn't have more to say. "There are a lot of details to work out, but what do y'all think?"

"I love it," yelled Tim.

"I think it sounds great," replied Jeremy.

"Buck, we have three out of four in favor," said Roy, "but it's also important to have your honest support."

Buck didn't want to spoil the opportunity for adventure for his father and Tim. "It's a wild, crazy plan, sir, but I'm okay with it. You just have to promise to return to Macon at the end of summer. Or earlier."

"Absolutely. I promise."

Chapter Four
1833

Roy met with his lawyer and accountant to find the best way to turn his company's management—not ownership—over to Buck. But he struggled with a few issues. Buck would be younger than anyone on the management team, yet he had earned the respect of those he worked with, especially Donny, Roy's long-term general manager. Roy had seen sons ruin other family businesses, but Buck had already shown discipline and leadership. And Roy would ultimately still be in charge, so there was little risk.

And there was the well-known fact that Buck was adopted. But Roy loved Buck like a son. Besides, Jeremy and Tim took no part in the business.

Roy decided to make the move and met with Buck and Donny to explain the new arrangement. Donny was a fellow Army Corps of Engineers veteran with a real knack for design and pricing jobs. He was one of the original hires, and Roy grew to rely on him heavily.

"Buck, I want you to confer daily with Donny. Donny, I want you to let Buck make mistakes, but not big ones. I know you two will figure it out. Anyway, things won't be all that different from how we've operated for the last couple of years. I want you both to market our services and sign off on proposals. And Buck, you need to stay involved with the crews."

Roy explained the new terms he had drafted with his lawyer. "You will both get nice raises and a share of the company's profits. I also want to set aside part of the profits as bonuses for the crews. I have set the bonus criteria for this year, but I want you two to determine the goals for future years. These terms will all be in writing and signed before I leave. Any questions?"

Both men smiled brightly at each other and thanked Roy for his generous arrangement.

Roy put down his notes. "Now, here's a little wrinkle. I will have no income for the next few months and plenty of expenses. I've been building a hefty sum in the company account for surprises, but I will draw down most of that for my trip. You should have plenty of funds to operate, but if you run into slow payments or unexpected expenses, you may have to borrow some money from the bank. The company has good credit, so I don't expect problems."

"What kind of expenses do you anticipate for your trip?" asked Donny.

"There will be lodging, food, hiring help, and the cost of materials to build a cabin. Eventually, I'll need to buy some horses to start a herd. Plus, I'd like to buy a sawmill once I figure out how to power it."

"We have an unused sawmill and building materials here. Why not take what you need?"

"It's a long trip, and I want to pack as little as needed. I'm already figuring on two full wagons."

"I kinda wish I was going with you," replied Donny. "That's going to be one dadgum great adventure. But you can be sure that Buck and I will keep things rolling here." Donny put his arm around Buck's shoulders, and they looked at each other with big, wide grins.

"You two will have a big time here as well," replied Roy, thankful that the men seemed as excited about the new arrangement as he was.

Roy invited Buck and his wife, Abigail, to dinner one night. Following the meal, they discussed the next big issue that Roy had given much thought.

"I think it's time for you two to take over this place," declared Roy. "The house is too big for me alone, and I'll be gone for a while."

"That is very generous, but we're so settled in our house!" replied Abigail. She looked around at the fine design and furnishings. "Of course, it's not nearly as nice and big as this."

Roy liked Abigail. She was a terrific mother and wife. Wise, proper, and devout. A young version of his Helen. "This place started as a little cottage at the north end of Mulberry Street. We kept expanding the space as our family and resources grew. It oughta meet all your needs for a while."

"What about your other two sons?" asked Buck. "Why should I get this big prize?"

"I think you should give me what you get for selling your place, and I'll put those funds away for when Tim and Jeremy need a place of their own. Plus, this place will have higher maintenance expenses than you're used to."

"There's so much of you and Helen in the furnishings and grounds," remarked Abigail. "But if you're determined to give it up, I think it needs to stay in the family. The children would love having a live-in Grandpa." Abigail looked to her husband for some sign of agreement.

Buck looked upward and sighed. "Okay, we would be honored to take over. You just have to tell us what room or rooms you want as your own for when you return from North Georgia."

"I'll just need a bedroom. If things work out as I expect, I could be spending long summers up there for some time."

"I was afraid you were going to say that," replied Buck.

Roy began gathering the supplies they would need on the trip: camping gear, food and water, guns and ammunition, clothing, tools, maps, and grant documents. He created a secret drawer in one of the wagons to secure cash and valuable papers.

He asked his local contacts who had traveled north for details on what conditions to expect but found no one who had traveled as far north into what was recently Indian Territory. Would there be a town nearby with shops and men for hire? Where was the nearest Army garrison or state militia barracks? How different was the weather? How was Governor Lumpkin's effort to remove the Natives going?

Mapping out an itinerary for the trip was equally challenging. Roy visited with the people at the Central of Georgia Railway office in Macon to see if they would share their findings. Though it would take many years for trains to roll, the proposed route would connect Savannah to Macon to Chattanooga, creating a link from the Atlantic seaports to the Tennessee River, the Mississippi River, and the massive territory acquired in Jefferson's Louisiana Purchase.

The railway people were guarded about the land they expected to acquire but did provide Roy with maps showing rivers and towns. Part of his trip followed planned rail routes, and they indicated that he would likely meet Central of Georgia Railway surveyors in the field for updates and advice.

The day of departure arrived in early April. Roy thanked the managers at the company who had disassembled a sawmill that now fit neatly in one of the wagons. Samuel hitched two-horse teams to each wagon and filled any nooks and crannies left in the beds with produce, biscuits, jerky, and water jugs. Roy addressed the servants at the house, encouraging them to support Buck and Abigail.

As they mounted the wagons, Tim yelled to his father, "Where's Jax?" They had agreed to bring the dog, but he was nowhere in sight.

"I don't know," replied Roy, "but we need to get going." Roy climbed into the wagon seat and waved to the family and friends who had gathered at the house. With a flick of the reins, they were off.

Tim kept hollering for Jax as they rolled down the street. About a block down the road, the dog caught up to Tim's wagon and leaped into the floorboard and onto the tarp covering the wagon bed. Roy looked back from the first wagon and smiled. So far, so good.

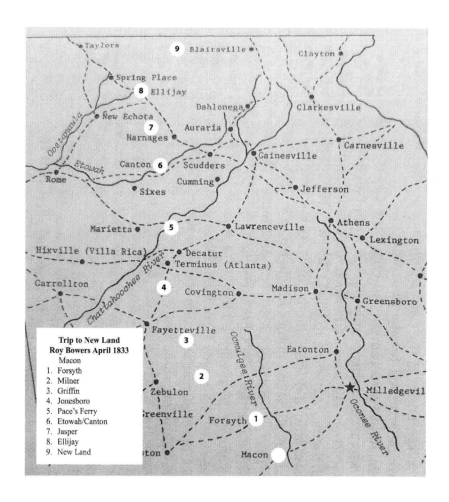

Chapter Five

1833

The journey's first stop for Roy, Tim, Samuel, and Kitch, Samuel's son, was in Forsyth, a village north of Macon and a future stop for the railroad. The road was well-worn and relatively flat, so they had no problem meeting Roy's travel goal of twenty miles per day. Once the men secured the horses and wagons at the livery stable, they found a roadhouse that provided lodging and food. The Bowers checked in at the desk.

"That will be a dollar and twenty cents each for a room. Supper and breakfast are extra," announced the woman behind the counter. "Two beds in a room."

That sounded reasonable, and Roy reached into his pocket for some money. "There are four of us."

"I see two. We don't serve Negroes."

"We want to stay together," replied Tim.

The woman looked at Roy and waited. "You want to stay here or not?"

"Is there another place in town where we can all stay together?" asked Tim.

"Not unless you want to stay at the colored barn outside town."

Tim looked at his father. "I say we continue north and find a place to camp."

Roy thought for a moment. "We've already paid for livery, and it's getting dark. We should check in here and let Samuel and Kitch stay with the wagons at the stables."

"Then I'll stay with them," said Tim.

Roy shook his head and smiled at his son. "So that's how it's going to be? Always the abolition fighter?"

"Just trying to do what's right."

"And you're making me sleep on the ground over your principles?" responded Roy. He looked at the clerk and then at his son. With a shrug, he told the clerk, "I guess you lost some business... and I will lose some sleep."

Roy walked out of the roadhouse to join the others outside. "C'mon, fellows. Let's go back and hitch the wagons and go up the road to pitch tents in the dark somewhere. Tim insists on leading the way."

They found a spot a short distance north of Forsyth to make camp. Kitch and Tim had shot a couple of rabbits along the way, which they cooked and served with corned beef and pickled beets from the wagon. Following their meal, they sat around the fire. Jax chowed down on the leftovers.

"Can I ask what happened back at the inn that caused you to abandon the plan on our first night?" asked Samuel of Roy.

"Well, ol' Tim here took a stand for Negro rights in opposition to the inn rules."

"The boy is headstrong," said Samuel.

"His virtue can get in the way of reason sometimes," replied Roy.

"The old bag was a bigot," injected Tim. "She probably hates Indians, too. And she probably voted for Jackson for president." Andrew Jackson was serving the first year of his second term and causing a lot of division over his decisions. Tim didn't care much about politics except for notable politicians like Jackson, who did not share his sense of justice for Natives and Blacks.

"Hey, I voted for Old Hickory," replied Roy, feigning offense. "He's a good man."

Tim responded, "You like him because you served under him in New Orleans, but the man is a tyrant. He's ignoring the Supreme Court's ruling that it's unconstitutional for the state to take over Indian lands."

"Jackson believes it necessary for the country to expand west," responded Roy. "And moving the Natives was the deal made years ago when Georgia gave up the land that is now Alabama and Mississippi."

"That was about the Creeks, not the Cherokee," responded Tim.

Not wanting to rehash tired political arguments with his son, Roy turned to Samuel. "What do you think, Samuel?"

"I can't vote, so I stay out of politics."

"Kitch, what do you think of President Jackson?"

"If he didn't tell the Indians to leave Georgia," replied Kitch, "I'd be chopping wood and cleaning stalls instead of sitting here at a fire with a full belly."

After the men had a good laugh, Roy announced, "We need to rise at dawn. Let's hit the sack."

The second day of travel was uneventful except for an afternoon storm that slowed their pace along muddy roads. Roy had purchased four raincoats made of this newly developed rubberized fabric that kept them dry and warm in the chilly April winds. They stopped at the general store in Barnesville, where Roy bought a smoked ham from Gideon Barnes, the owner.

They camped outside of Milner, Georgia, but soon gave up on starting a fire with wet wood. They enjoyed a feast of ham and cold beans. Roy broke out a jug of whiskey after dinner, hoping it might warm them up, help him sleep better, and divert the conversation from something other than politics. It was after six o'clock, so they had an hour or so of daylight but no light from the fire. Conserving the few hours of lantern fuel packed in the wagon was critical.

"So why do you think that wheel came off Ma's wagon?" asked Tim of Samuel as they sat under a tarp tied to trees between their tents.

Samuel began rocking back and forth, his hands rubbing the tops of his legs.

After a moment without a response, Tim asked another question. "Could the carriage have been fitted with two different sizes of linchpins, and the one coming loose was just a freak accident?"

"That's not possible, Son," replied Roy, sensing Samuel's discomfort with the conversation. "And Samuel seeing your Uncle Norman at the carriage house that morning raises another strange twist to the story."

"Uncle Norman was at the house? You don't think he had anything to do with the accident, do you, Pa?"

"I don't have any evidence, and your uncle denies having anything to do with the carriage. It's just strange that he was so angry with me and your mother, and then the accident happened on the day they had words."

"What words? What happened?"

"I wasn't there, but Samuel was. Norman says he was there to ask about some minor family issue, but Samuel saw otherwise."

Samuel explained what he had seen that morning, and Tim was visibly upset at hearing all of this for the first time. Tim downed the little bit of whiskey his father had poured into his cup, grabbed his hat and coat, and marched off into the woods. Jax followed him.

"You want me to go after him?" asked Kitch. "It's getting dark."

"No, he'll be okay. And I need to try to get some rest after waking up several times last night."

On the third day, the men traveled through Griffin and stopped near a creek where a crew of about ten men from the Central of Georgia Railway had set up camp just north of town. Roy introduced himself to the men. They were glad to have some outside company and invited Roy and Tim to join them in the mess tent. The cook provided food to Samuel and Kitch, who stayed with the wagons.

"How is the planning going for the railroad?" asked Roy during dinner.

"The line between Savannah and Macon is underway, but floods and fever among the men have slowed them down. Our group is charged with developing the route for a line that will eventually run between Macon and Chattanooga."

"That could be an economic boon for Macon," observed Roy.

"It could if the railroad doesn't run out of money. And at the pace they're moving, it could take many years for the trains to roll."

Roy explained how they were headed to North Georgia and asked if the men could share any information about their route.

"They won't let us show our map detail because speculators are already buying up land in anticipation of our route, but you can probably guess that we draw a straight line between here and there and then work around crossing rivers and hills. We have another survey team in Marthasville, a day's ride north of here, where the tracks will intersect with rails that will run east and west between Augusta and Birmingham. Stay on this road, and you might meet up with them."

Roy thanked the men for their hospitality and left with Tim to pitch their two-man tent adjacent to the camp.

On the fourth day, the Bowers men continued north on the trail as it became less traveled. The road that was fifteen feet wide and well-worn was now eight feet across, rough, and often covered by a canopy of tall trees. After about twenty miles, Roy stopped at a farmhouse along the way to inquire about the area. The owner, also a veteran of the War of 1812, was as interested in Roy's journey from Macon as Roy was interested in what to expect to the north.

After Roy provided highlights of his trip, the farmer shared what he knew about the area to the north. "You've been riding on relatively flat piedmont, but that's about to change. A day's ride north of here, you'll come to the Chattahoochee River. You'll need to find a ferry to cross. When you get north of the river, you'll leave the old Creek lands and arrive in the new territory ceded more recently by the Cherokee. Everything gets much less settled."

"And will we soon be seeing some prospectors?" asked Tim.

"Maybe further north of the Chattahoochee, but most of the claims have run out."

"And will we need to cross any rivers north of the Chattahoochee?" asked Roy.

"You'll be turning northeast toward Ellijay. You will cross the Etowah River, but that shouldn't be a problem. Your challenge will become crossing mountains, not rivers."

"Are there any military forts north of here?" asked Roy.

"Some Georgia and federal militia are patrolling throughout the area. The federal troops are based out of Fort Armstrong on the Coosa River just over the line in Alabama."

Roy thanked the man for the information and asked if they could camp on the edge of his field. The farmer agreed but declined Roy's invitation to join them for dinner around the campfire. He had sick children to take care of in the house.

In the middle of the night, Roy woke up to the sound of Jax barking wildly. He reached over to wake Tim when one, two, and then three beasts charged the tent. Fortunately, the tent collapsed, and the men lay flat beneath the stampede of tusks and hoofs tearing over the tent and its contents. Roy and Tim took a long minute to collect themselves before scurrying out of the shambles. Roy found his rifle in the little bit of moonlight. "Light the lantern!" Roy yelled to Tim.

Samuel and Kitch were now standing outside their tent in their underwear. Samuel lit his lantern. "Hogs?" Samuel asked Roy frantically.

"Yeah," replied Roy, looking out into the nearby woods where Jax was barking in pursuit. "At least three."

"You both okay?" asked Samuel, looking at the flattened tent.

"Yeah," replied Roy. "Kitch, go tend the horses. Tim, you and Samuel sit in the wagons in case they come back. Take your rifles."

Roy walked slowly toward the sound of Jax barking and stopped at the edge of the lantern light. All of a sudden, the hogs came stampeding in his direction. He backed up three steps and cocked his rifle. Tim and Samuel raised their rifles while seated on the wagon benches. Jax came running right toward Roy, followed by the passel of at least five hogs. He fired at the leader. The hog was hit, but its momentum tore into

Roy's left leg, knocking him to the ground.

Another hog came right toward Roy as he tried to scramble away. Another shot rang out, and the charging hog tumbled and lay squirming three feet from Roy. Roy got to his feet, reloaded, and put a bullet in the hog's heart. Tim finished off the first hog a few feet away."

"Thank you, Tim. That was close."

"It wasn't me. I didn't have a clear shot."

Roy went to Samuel. "Thank you, Samuel. I think you saved my life."

Samuel nodded and smiled. "But you've got a bad cut," he said, pointing to Roy's left leg. Blood was streaming down the leg through Roy's long johns. Samuel turned and went to the wagon bed and returned with a roll of gauze. "Where you hiding that whiskey?"

Roy directed Tim to the other wagon where he had stored the jug. When Tim returned, Samuel asked him to get a fresh pair of long johns from Roy's bag. He had Roy strip down and sit on his blood-soaked long johns while he cleaned the wound with gauze soaked in whiskey and wrapped Roy's leg in a bandage.

Tim returned with clean long johns and started laughing at his father sitting on the ground, fully exposed in the lantern light. "Now that's a sight that will haunt me!"

Roy scrambled to his feet. "Give me those!" Roy barked as he snatched the drawers out of Tim's hand. "Go on and reload. Go find Jax."

Tim roamed the area, yelling for Jax. Roy and Samuel stood over the dead hogs. "Must be a hundred and fifty pounds a piece," observed Samuel. "Big male with mean-looking tusks."

Tim and Kitch came over to admire the kill. "Wow, that was something!"

exclaimed Tim. "But I hope Jax gets back here soon. I don't hear him or see him anywhere."

"Want me to dress 'em out?" asked Samuel of Roy, still admiring the hogs. "That's good pork."

"No," replied Roy. "There's no time to cure the meat, and getting our sleep is more important. Get the boys to drag them into the woods, please."

Roy and Tim spent a few minutes fixing their tent and belongings when Jax walked up with his tail wagging, quite pleased with himself. "I'm not sure if Jax drove those hogs our way or rescued us," observed Roy.

"At least he survived the chase," Tim said as he fussed over the dog. "Way to go, buddy!"

Roy woke up with a bloody, stiff leg. Samuel redressed the wound, and Roy found comfort in lying in the wagon bed alongside Jax as Kitch drove the team on their fifth day of travel.

The trail eventually led them to a small village on the lower bank of the Chattahoochee River. Tim met the proprietor in the general store, Hardy Pace, who also owned the surrounding farm, gristmill, tavern, inn, a ferry to cross the river, and dozens of slaves. Pace came over to meet Roy and convinced him to have his medical man treat his injury. The man cleaned the cut with salt water and whiskey, applied several stitches, spread butter mixed with honey over the wound, and wrapped a clean cloth around his leg.

"How much do I owe you, doc?" asked Roy when he finished.

The older Black man shook his head.

Roy slipped him a silver coin out of sight of Pace.

Roy insisted on renting a room with a bathtub, and, this time, Tim did not object to being separated from Kitch and Samuel, who stayed in a nearby shack. Tim found a raw cow bone for Jax to keep him occupied while spending the night tied to the wagon at the livery.

Clean, shaven, restocked, well-fed, and rested, the Bowers crossed the river on day six to continue their journey north. After several hours, they reached Etowah, an old Cherokee village now part of the Gold Belt region in Georgia. Houses built with lumber by settlers stood in contrast to the Native dwellings built with vertical logs and thatched roofs. Tim spoke to prospectors walking along the road who explained how they were moving west from the overcrowded claims around Dahlonega but were having little luck. Their soiled, torn clothing, long hair, and shabby beards betrayed those who exaggerated any prospecting success. While thousands of miners had quit, thousands of others were determined to keep searching for their fortunes along other creeks north of the Chattahoochee River.

Tim would have spent hours talking to the prospectors, but Roy kept hurrying him along. "I know you have this fancy image of prospectors," said Roy to Tim at a stop to rest the horses, "but as you can see, they are a ragtag lot. They don't look like they're having fun or finding a fortune."

Tim replied, "I'm not looking for a fortune. I want to make it on my own and learn to live off the land."

Roy put his hand on his son's shoulder. "Then you'll probably find what you need where we're headed!"

"I sure hope so," replied Tim. He scanned the horizon. "This is the first time I've ever seen mountains. They're magnificent!"

Roy looked out to share the view. Rolling foothills stepped up to taller mountains in the distance, all covered in new green foliage shimmering in the setting sun. "They are, but hopefully, the trail follows the creeks between them, and we won't have to climb any." Roy rubbed his chin. "The day is about spent. Let's go another mile or so and camp. We need an early start in the morning."

They pitched tents in a clearing on the side of the road. Roy wasn't comfortable sleeping close to a prospector camp, so they took shifts guarding the wagons overnight. Between Jax barking at the occasional prospector passing in the distance, coyotes howling nearby, the chance of bears sniffing around the wagons, or another feral hog attack, each of the men taking their two-hour shift had no problem staying awake.

Day seven took Roy's troop to a collection of tents and shacks that some called the town of Jasper. The climb over the foothills of the southern Blue Ridge Mountain range taxed the teams and slowed their progress. The trails were getting rougher, and the weather was cooler with spotty showers. They made camp in a thunderstorm and ate the jerky and canned vegetables they had brought from Macon without the warmth and comfort of a fire.

Roy's leg was stiffening up. Samuel changed the dressing after breakfast and dinner, using more of the honey butter he got at Pace's. There was no sign of infection, but Roy hobbled around in some pain.

"Tomorrow, we will arrive in Gilmer County," explained Roy. "It will take us all day to get there. I'll need to find the courthouse in a village called Ellijay to record our claim to the land. We'll camp there, and it will probably take us the best part of the next day to reach the property."

"What if there are no trails leading to the land?" asked Tim.

"There may not be," said Roy. "We'll have to load our supplies onto the horses and make our way by foot."

"Do you expect any problems with Indians?" asked Samuel.

"I'm not sure," replied Roy, "but if we find a friendly Cherokee who speaks English, I'll hire him to lead the way."

On day eight of their journey, they followed the trail for several miles along creeks in valleys between tall, green mountains. As they crossed one of the deeper creeks, Roy's wagon got stuck on some rocks. The men got out and tried to help push the wagon, but it wouldn't climb out of the creek.

"Samuel, see if you can hitch your team in front of mine," Roy asked. Samuel chocked the wheels of his wagon and hooked his team to the front of Roy's team. The four horses gave it all they had; the wagon rocked back and forth but remained stuck.

Roy asked Tim to get the heavy rope and two pulleys out of the wagon bed. "Samuel, let's unhitch the teams and get them up the bank to level ground." Samuel knew what to do; he had done this before.

"Watch and learn, boys," said Roy to Tim and Kitch.

Roy attached one pulley to the stuck wagon frame, and Samuel attached the other pulley to the left doubletree of the rear team. Roy tied one end of the rope to the tongue on the wagon and threw the loose rope back up to Samuel, who ran it through the pulley on the team and threw the rope back to Roy. Roy ran the rope through the pulley and back to Samuel, who tied it to the right doubletree on the team.

"We just tripled the power with pullies," Roy explained, then muttered, "Let's just hope the rope doesn't snap." Roy gave Samuel the signal, and the teams pulled the wagon steadily out of the creek and up the hill.

Samuel untied the rope and pullies and brought the teams back to the wagons. "I don't know how, but it works!" he quipped to the boys. The men re-hitched the horses to the wagons. Samuel took a different route through the creek, and the wagons continued through the hills.

They soon arrived in the Cherokee village of Ellijay. Many of the houses were deserted, and they saw many more Natives than whites along the road. No one was unfriendly, but everyone seemed to have somewhere to go or no interest in doing anything at all.

Roy found the makeshift courthouse and went inside to record his land grant. The clerk gave him a deed and a plat drawn up by state surveyors showing the metes and bounds of his land. Roy signed the documents and paid the fees.

Roy asked the clerk, "I want to hire a guide, ideally a Native who speaks some English. Do you know someone?"

"You might ask the locals who hang out at the store down the street."

Roy and Tim walked to the store, where they found several Natives sitting under a clump of trees to the side of the building. The men wore shirts and trousers. The women wore muslin dresses that looked handmade. There were no feathered headbands, war paint, or tomahawks. The group resembled farmers more than hunters or warriors.

"Hey there! Do any of you know someone who could lead us to our new land?" said Roy, holding up his plat and pointing to the lot.

The men looked at Roy, then at each other, and said nothing.

Tim spoke softly to his father, "They don't look happy about a white

WILLOW *and the boys*

man coming up here wanting help to claim their land. Imagine that."

Roy announced: "I will pay in silver coins if someone would tell us the best way to get there."

No one jumped at the opportunity until, finally, one older man came forward. He studied the plat and then motioned to a teenager to join him. They spoke briefly in Cherokee, pointing to places on the paper. The young man said, "I know the way."

Tim asked, "Can you take us there?"

"The way I know is a day there and a day back. How much do you pay?" The teenager's English was surprisingly clear.

Roy thought about it for a minute. He knew work and money were scarce in the area, yet he needed to make a generous offer since the others had shown little interest in the task. "Three dollars. A dollar when we start and two dollars when we get there. And we'll provide you with food and bedding."

The young man looked to the older man, who studied Roy for a moment and then nodded. "When do we go?" asked the teenager.

"In the morning. We'll meet you here." Roy held out his hand, and the teen shook it with a smile. "What is your name?"

"Attakullakulla, but settlers call me Atta."

Roy introduced himself and Tim. "We'll see you in the morning, Atta!"

As they returned to their wagons, Roy told Tim, "Three teenage boys may be trouble. One white, one Black, and one red. Make sure you are the peacemaker in the group."

Chapter Six

1833

Their guide, Atta, rode in the lead wagon with Roy and Kitch as the group departed Ellijay in the morning.

"You speak very good English," remarked Roy as they rode along a surprisingly well-traveled trail.

"My father insisted that we learn the white ways."

Roy asked, "Was that your father looking at the map back there with you?"

"Yes. He and I have traveled all over the Territory. He fought in the War and gets odd jobs with the Army."

"What were you two discussing as you were looking at the map?"

"Your land is next to our friend named Waya Madstone. We know the family."

"So, if you know how to get to his place, finding my property will be simple, right?"

"Madstone property is on this side of the river. Your land is on the other side. We need to find a place where the wagons can cross."

"And this Waya Madstone is a good man?"

"He is rich. He has a white wife and a farm with many slaves. Like you."

"It's true that Samuel and Kitch are slaves that I purchased. But they can read and write and are both good with horses. If you ask them, I believe they'll say I treat them kindly." Roy thought about what Atta had said. "Madstone is Cherokee?"

"Full Cherokee. He and my father were scouts for General

WILLOW *and the boys*

Jackson's Army."

"I was an engineer in Jackson's Army," added Roy. "We built bridges on the way to New Orleans and earthworks once we got there. Then we fought the British and won."

"My father and Waya Madstone fought the Creeks and then stayed in Alabama to guard the ones they captured and put in stockades."

"The Cherokee sided with us in the War. Our country owes a lot to the Cherokee." Roy thought for a moment. "Does your family expect to be forced west or be allowed to stay in Georgia?"

"Talks continue, so I do not know. What do you think?"

"I don't know," sighed Roy. "Georgia has granted all of the Cherokee land to settlers in the lottery. But the settlers must allow Natives living on their land to stay. It's a mess."

"Waya Madstone says he owns his land and will stay no matter what happens. Having a white wife must make him special."

By mid-afternoon, they reached the Toccoa River. The water was wide and rocky, and the depth was difficult to gauge from the bank.

The men stood on the smooth gray rocks along the bank, studying the situation as Atta waded into the river. He stepped carefully, using a stick to test where to take his next stride.

"Is it too cold?" Tim yelled to Atta. In April, the air temperature could be eighty in the afternoon and thirty a few hours later.

"Cold, but okay," replied Atta, wet to his hip. He waded just past midstream and turned around. "The horses would have no problem. Horses and small wagons cross here often. But your wagons are heavy, and the water is high."

"There are ruts where wagons have crossed recently," observed Tim, pointing to the bank.

"In summer, after the rains, it would be no problem," added Atta, "but it is early spring."

"If we crossed here, how much farther would we have to go?" Roy asked, studying the map.

"Not far. We are close," replied Atta. Then he thought of an idea. "If you want, we could go to Waya Madstone's farm. That trail we just passed goes to his place. He might have a raft."

Roy looked at the map again. "Are we near Madstone's?"

"Yes." Atta pointed north. "Right over there."

Roy studied the map further and said to the group, "Well, let's meet our new neighbors!"

The trail leading to the Madstone farm passed along newly tilled fields on gently rolling hills. Men were busy working the soil, driving mule-drawn plows, and hauling provisions. Some were Native, some Black. Soon, a big, blood-red barn with fenced pastures appeared on the right and the Madstone mansion to their left.

"This is amazing," observed Roy. He hoped his land had the same terrain. He looked across the river, but all he could see were trees.

The wagons followed the circular drive to the front of a large, white, two-story frame house. They stopped at the steps leading to a massive porch with tall Greek columns. A Black servant at the front of the house greeted them and returned inside.

Moments later, a man came through the front door. He was about Roy's age, portly, clean-shaven, and had a full head of hair peppered with gray. "I am Waya Madstone. Welcome there, Atta." He walked down the steps to face the Bowers. Samuel and Kitch stayed on the wagons. "Please introduce me to your friends."

Roy moved toward Madstone with an outstretched hand. "I am Roy Bowers, and this is my son Tim. We have been awarded land from the state directly across the river from you. We had doubts about crossing the water back on the road and hoped you might recommend a way to reach our lot."

"Ah, welcome, Bowers! I look forward to being neighbors! Where do you come from?"

"We have traveled from Macon and hope to make this our home."

"You have had a long journey! How did you know the land would be any good?"

"We didn't," responded Roy, "but we had faith. And from what I can see, we are in luck!"

"It is good land!" Madstone exclaimed, then motioned toward the house. "Why don't you come inside, and we can get to know each other."

Madstone led Roy and Tim inside. "Thank you for your hospitality, Mr. Madstone," said Roy as they were seated in a parlor off the main lobby.

"Please, call me Waya."

"I understand that you served under General Jackson in the War!" said Roy. "I also served in Jackson's Army and fought in New Orleans. I think that may have had something to do with winning our land in the lottery."

"Yes, serving with General Jackson has its rewards. But I was here long before the state seized the Territory, and I am expanding my lands by buying lots from lottery winners. You didn't hear from me because I'd rather stay on this side of the river." Madstone looked out the window. "I'm sure you are anxious to explore your property, but there's not much daylight left. You are welcome to stay here tonight, and I will help you cross the river in the morning."

Roy could see from Tim's expression that they shared a reluctance to stay with a man they hardly knew.

Madstone continued, "I'd like to show you around my place, then we can have dinner, and you can sleep in our guest rooms. You will be well rested for your adventure in the morning."

Roy saw no alternative. "We accept your generous offer, Waya."

"Well then," responded Madstone, "Let's take a walk, and I'll show you around."

Madstone talked as they strolled past the barn toward the river, pointing out his beef cows in one pasture and dairy cows in another. Chickens roamed freely around them as he paused and pointed toward his fields.

"I grow the three sisters. We are planting about two hundred acres of corn. In a couple of weeks, when the corn grows a few inches tall, we'll plant bean seeds. When the beans come out of the ground and start climbing the corn stalks, we'll plant squash. The squash leaves will shade the soil in the dry months before harvest. My family has followed this process for generations, but I'm doing it on a scale that probably has never been done before." He waved his arm across the fields. "I've tried cotton and tobacco, but these three sister crops provide the most revenue, considering the cost of getting the yield to market."

"Very impressive, Waya," remarked Roy. "But where do you find the labor?"

"I buy slaves wherever I can find them. In Athens, Augusta, or Chattanooga. And I hire Indians to supervise."

"And you are Cherokee?" asked Roy.

"Full-blooded."

"And you're not afraid of losing your land?" asked Tim.

"No. I have an agreement blessed by the county," said Madstone proudly, then his expression became more reflective. "I'm one of the lucky ones. The state surveyors worked around my farm in carving out the lots given away in the lottery."

Madstone continued, "But if there were any justice in this country, no Cherokee would be forced to leave their home. For years, I encouraged the people of my village to learn from the settlers and adopt their ways. We helped the trappers and welcomed the early settlers. We fought with the Army. Then a bunch of greedy outsiders came searching for gold, and the militia is forcing my people to leave our homeland."

"I'm sorry how things have turned out for your people," said Roy. "But you have certainly made the best of a bad situation in looking out for your family."

Madstone's mood lightened after a moment. "So, what do you plan to do with your land, Bowers? Do you plan to bring more slaves up here to work?"

"No, I will not hire slaves if I can find men to work."

"You're one of those abolitionist people?"

Roy saw the risk of conflict coming. "I'm not an abolitionist, but I do not favor slavery, either. I just do what's right for me given the times we live in." Roy moved to change the subject quickly. "And as far as what we plan to do with the land, I guess I'll have to survey the place first. I grew up on a ranch, so my first thought is raising horses and maybe cattle."

"I think you'll find your land to be like mine, rolling hills. There's plenty of room for horses and cattle; maybe you should also consider mules. I'm glad you didn't say you were planning to raise pigs. They stink." Madstone slapped Roy on the back to lighten the mood. He turned to lead the men further down toward the river until they came to the side of a good-size pole barn. "This is my money maker," said Madstone, pointing to a sizable still. "We've got plenty of fresh water and corn, and I buy barley from up north to make the finest whiskey in North Georgia. I want you to try some." He went to a cask with a tap and poured a couple of ounces into three cups. With one toss of his arm, Madstone downed his sample.

Tim looked to his father for permission, and Roy poured all but a taste from his cup into Tim's. Then he switched cups. Roy took a sip and smiled. "That is excellent sippin' whiskey!"

Tim drank the little bit in his cup and opened his eyes and mouth in shock. "Wow, my throat is on fire!"

The two men laughed. Madstone went to a locker and pulled a quart jug of whiskey from the shelf. "Here, put this on your wagon for those nights you feel like celebrating on your new land!"

"Thank you, Waya!" said Roy.

Madstone reached into his pocket and pulled out a pouch. "Tobacco?" He put a chaw in the side of his mouth and offered the open pouch to the Bowers.

Tim shook his head, but Roy took a pinch. "Thank you! Homegrown?"

"Yes. I cure the leaves and soak them in my whiskey."

The men returned to the house, and the manservant showed Roy and Tim to their rooms. A warm bath had been prepared for each to clean up before dinner. Samuel and Kitch had been shown to the servants' bunkhouse. Atta was assigned to the Indian quarters, where he was content to stay for the extra dollar that Roy offered him for spending an additional night to cross the river.

Madstone invited the Bowers to the parlor, where they sat and talked. Soon, three people appeared at the door.

"Oh!" bellowed Madstone. "Let me introduce you to my family." The Bowers stood as he introduced them to his wife, Eleanor, teenage daughter, Willow, and her younger brother, Hawk. Hawk was about fourteen, medium height, dark, and lean. Eleanor was younger than her husband and not just white but had a pale complexion and blue eyes. Willow was about Tim's age, slender, and medium height. Her long curls of brunette hair had been lightened by the sun.

Willow was one of the prettiest girls Roy had ever seen, combining the best features of her Native father and white mother. Light reddish-tan skin, welcoming eyes, thin nose, chiseled chin, and full lips. She wore a long, patterned blue tear dress with colorful ribbons sewn into the shoulders, sleeves, and skirt. He watched as she tilted her head slightly downward and smiled at Tim. Tim's jaw dropped as he stared back at her. This was going to be trouble, thought Roy.

Eleanor must have also sensed the forces at work and placed Tim and Willow on either side of Roy at the dinner table. Following the meal of roasted chicken, vegetables, fresh bread, and apple cobbler, the adults retired to the parlor. Eleanor assigned Hawk to stay with his sister while the three teens went outside to occupy themselves.

Roy complimented Eleanor for a fine meal. "Is there a store around here to buy salt, sugar, coffee, and such?" he asked.

Eleanor began to answer, and Madstone cut her off. "There's a little village downstream on your side of the river. A man named Galloway owns a store in the little community that he named after himself. He's a bit disagreeable but carries a good range of goods in his store. And he handles the mail and stocks my whiskey for sale."

"How far away is Galloway?"

"You cross the river on the main road, turn left at a crossroads in a mile or two, and you'll see the store in another couple miles."

"Do you think I could have crossed the river with my wagons?"

"Depends on the water level, but one of the traders from Ellijay that stocks Galloway's store has a big wagon like yours, and I don't think he has any trouble. The Army put some rock in the riverbed so their wagons can get to a new barracks they're setting up in a village east of here called Blairsville."

Roy appreciated all of Madstone's information and was anxious for more. "Are there other land grant owners settling nearby?" he asked.

"Some. On the way here, you may have seen a trail to your right that leads to the Walker land. Ezra is some kind of Tennessee mountain man; as best I can tell, he still lives in a shack. He and his boy do a lot of trapping, hunting, and fishing. If there's a wife or more young ones, I haven't seen them. I've made him a generous offer for his land, but he hasn't replied. I'm not sure he can read. And I'm not sure he owns the land."

Madstone took another swig of whiskey and paused momentarily to collect his thoughts. "To the south of your lot is the Morgan family. They seem nice enough. Fairly young with small children. They haven't done much with their land besides grow a small garden and build a tiny cabin. He fishes a lot. They cleared a trail to their place from the main road that you can probably share to get to your place. Other than the four of us, there's no one else nearby. The county or state is going to have to cut some new roads to encourage more development and build a bridge so that it's safer to cross the river."

"Does the river have a name?" asked Roy.

"Toccoa is the Cherokee name, meaning 'beautiful'. It flows northwest to the Tennessee River."

"Is it navigable?"

"In a canoe or flatboat, but depending on the rains, there might be spots where you'd have to portage." Madstone stopped and yawned. "It's getting past my bedtime, and I'm sure you want to rest up for your big day tomorrow."

Roy stood on Madstone's cue and offered a handshake. He thanked his hosts again for their hospitality. "You and your family will have to come over to our place once we're settled so that we can repay the favor."

"Oh, I'm sure we will be seeing a good bit of each other," Madstone said with a smile. "Two war veterans with two teenagers the same age, living out in the middle of nowhere."

Chapter Seven

1833

Roy had trouble sleeping that night despite the comfortable bedding and feeling as clean and nourished as he had been since leaving home. Plus, there was the satisfaction that this thoroughly risky trip to North Georgia was nearly complete. The journey had absorbed his every thought, and now that they were almost there, he realized once again how much he wished Helen was by his side.

He thought about Madstone as well. Despite being a Cherokee during a period when anti-Indian fervor was high, he and his family were prospering. They had each other, which was all Roy ever wanted and was now missing. Madstone probably didn't appreciate how good he had it.

The Bowers and Madstones had breakfast together early the following morning.

"So what did you young ones do last night after dinner?" Madstone asked his son, Hawk.

"We played horseshoes, then cards on the porch, and then walked down to the barn. That's where they ditched me."

Waya slowly shook his head and smiled. Eleanor glared at her daughter, and Willow returned the scowl with raised eyebrows and a shrug of her shoulders. Roy stared at Tim until he looked back and then turned quickly away. They had talked about women, urges, and babies years before, but a follow-up discussion was in order.

Following the flapjacks, eggs, and deer sausage, the men went to the river to plan the wagon crossing. Samuel was already at the bank with the horses and wagons. Kitch and Atta were busy clearing brush and rocks along the bank. They had unloaded the heavier equipment and supplies near the bank to lighten the weight of the wagons.

"Atta has walked across the river, and we think we have a plan," announced Samuel. "If we could use that lumber lying on the side of the barn, we can build a raft with a few pine logs. This spot is deep enough for a wagon to float across. The current is not too strong for the horses to cross. It's plenty cold but not too bad as long as the sun stays out to dry things."

Madstone nodded with approval. "That's one smart boy you have there," he said to Roy.

"He's a man with a lot of experience around horses and barges," replied Roy proudly. "Before I knew him, he worked on the river in Macon with horse-drawn flatboats."

Madstone had a couple of his slaves cut down two pine trees near the bank while the others brought boards and tools from the barn. The logs were notched and strapped together, and the boards were nailed onto the logs. Within a couple of hours, the raft was ready.

Roy approached Atta. "We're ready to cross, so I guess this is goodbye." Roy extended his hand. "You've been a big help, Atta, and we thank you!" Roy handed him silver coins. "I hope you will return to help us cut the trees and build a cabin."

"You are brave to come all this way. I need to get back to my family, but I hope to return." The Native smiled and turned to go home.

Kitch took one end of a heavy rope in one hand and the harness of a two-horse team in the other and carefully waded through the thigh-high water. The horses dragged the raft across the ground to shallow water where the wagon could be loaded. Kitch tied the rope to a tree on his side of the river as Samuel pulled his end taut and secured it to a tree at a slight angle upstream to account for the current.

Roy and Tim secured the wagon on the raft and used the taut rope as a guide as the horse team pulled them across the water. Once the wagon was on Bowers land, Samuel switched the rope to a tree upstream, and the men returned the raft to the west bank to repeat the process.

"What do you want to do with the raft?" asked Roy once they had transported both wagons and were about to make a third trip loaded with equipment and supplies.

"Keep it over at your place," replied Madstone. "It may come in handy. We have canoes if we need to cross."

Roy shook Madstone's hand. "I can't thank you enough for letting us stay with you and helping us get the wagons across. I hope you will come to visit us soon."

Roy stood on his riverbank with the men. "Well, we did it!" he exclaimed as he shook each of their hands with a pat on the shoulder. "Let's give thanks." They bowed their heads as Roy thanked God for a safe journey. "The long days of riding in wagons are now over, and the hard labor begins. Let's check this land out."

The men walked into the woods. The pine trees were sprouting new cone seeds covered in yellow pollen that swirled through the air in the slightest breeze. Pine straw covered the ground in a soft, brown blanket. The tall oak, hickory, and other hardwoods had recently leafed out to produce a bright green canopy that sparkled between patches of sunlight. Roy scanned the terrain as far as he could see into the woods. Hills and ridges rose in the distance, and he was pleased with the gentle rise of the bank above the river. It was anything but the swamp or steep side of a mountain he had feared.

Roy walked up and down the property along the river, looking for a good place for their camp. He wanted to stay within an easy walk to the water's edge and above the flood plain. He found a spot he liked and addressed his team. "What do y'all think about this site for our camp? It's relatively flat and shouldn't flood." Everyone agreed.

As the others cleared the trees and ground for the camp, Roy looked for a place along the riverbank where water could be diverted through a race to turn a waterwheel to power the sawmill. Once the men had pitched the tents and gathered wood for a fire, they followed Roy for a hike south to establish a path to the main road.

"Should we try to find Morgan's place that Mr. Madstone told us about?" asked Tim.

"Maybe another day. It's time to rustle up some dinner."

For many days, the Bowers team cleared dozens of trees to make room for the house, mill, and wagon access to the road. The logs were cut to eight-foot lengths to supply wood for construction. The Bowers team was delighted when Atta reappeared one day, ready to work.

One afternoon, Roy called on the Morgan family living on the lot below them on the river. As Madstone had reported, they had made little progress on clearing the woods for crops or livestock, and their cabin was quite primitive. Roy found the family fit and friendly but wondered how they would survive the next winter living on fish and an occasional deer or turkey.

Tim did his share of the labor but used the longer daylight hours to explore the land before and after the workday. He found the stones marking each of the corners of the lot and crisscrossed the property, looking for anything interesting, from wildlife habitat to signs of squatters. The Georgia law that authorized the creation of lots on Cherokee land also prohibited new owners from evicting any Natives living on the land—until they left voluntarily or were forced to move. This was primarily a problem in the gold belt, but finding no Natives living on the property was a relief.

It was on a hill in the northeastern corner of the lot that Tim found what he thought was a remarkable rock outcrop. He had never seen anything like this formation and rushed to get his father to take a look.

"Here it is!" announced Tim, leading his father through the trees to his discovery.

Roy was wondering what his son thought was so unusual. In front of them was a treed hill, a bit steeper than the nearby hills but nothing special. When they reached the hill's far side, Roy understood why Tim was so excited. A cliff of rock rose twenty feet straight up above the surrounding ground. It was as if some giant force had sliced the hill in half. The stone was layered in thin, even sheets and streaked in gray, black, and reddish patterns, with embedded crystals that sparkled in the sunlight. At the base of the cliff was a pile of stones that had fallen from the vertical wall.

"Wow, this is unusual!" declared Roy on seeing Tim's find. "You did good discovering this place! I've never seen anything like it before." Roy picked up one of the stones at the cliff base. "This looks like slate." He walked around observing the wall of rock. "It forms in these unique sheets." The stone Roy held was only a half-inch thick yet perfectly flat and hard. "They use this on roofs and floors because it's easy to cut into thin pieces but is as hard as marble."

"If I remember from my geology lesson," observed Tim, "where there's slate, there's quartz. And where there's quartz, there could be gold."

Roy chuckled. "I don't know about that. There may be a better chance of finding coal than gold around here. In any event, this is certainly worth inviting an expert to have a look." Roy patted Tim on the back. "Thanks for finding this, but let's agree to keep your discovery to ourselves until we learn more about what we have."

One day, as Tim continued to explore the land, a white hunter approached him in the woods. Tim's first thought was that the guy would be tough to lick in a fight, but he appeared to be friendly. The hunter looked about Tim's age and carried a flintlock rifle. They walked within a few feet of each other, and he introduced himself as Zeke Walker. Madstone had described the father, Ezra Walker, as a mountain man, which fit Zeke as well. He was tall and fit, hadn't cut his hair or shaved in months, and wore a leather vest, coonskin cap, and leather moccasins.

As they talked, Zeke explained how he spent his days hunting game for meat and pelts. "You're welcome to join me hunting and fishing around here," Zeke told Tim.

"That would be great, but my father and I are working on our new land," replied Tim.

"I've seen you and other men cutting down many trees. Don't you have any regard for the forest and the wildlife that lives here?"

"Sure, I love the land, but if it wasn't us, it would be someone else clearing the trees. And we're going to raise livestock on the land."

"Yeah, farm animals inside fences."

"This whole area has been granted to settlers by the state. If you and your family arrived here more than a year ago, you may be living on someone else's property. So, your problem is with them, not my family."

Zeke stood silently. Tim couldn't tell if he was upset or just thinking.

"Well, I gotta go," said Tim. "It was good to meet you, and I hope we meet up again soon."

As Tim went on his early evening hikes around the property, he tried to stay within sight of the river. He could not get the image of Willow out of his head and hoped that she might appear close enough on the far bank to get her attention.

One early evening, as Tim wandered through what was probably Morgan property, he spotted Willow through the trees. She wore a blousy blue top gathered at the waist with deerskin leggings and long boots. Her hair was in a ponytail. Her Tom-boyish appearance was quite a contrast to how he remembered her at her house. Tim was surprised to see her on his side of the river. But then he saw another figure. She was walking and holding hands with Zeke Walker!

Tim raced toward them and stopped close in front of Willow. "It's good to see you again, Willow!" After a moment, he turned. "Hello again, Zeke. Mind if I join you?"

Willow let go of his hand, and Zeke looked less than happy about the intrusion. But Willow smiled and said, "Sure!"

"Pardon my looks. I've slaved all day on our land." Tim combed through his hair and rubbed his face. "Do you two know each other pretty well?"

Willow replied, "Yes. We met a couple of years ago. My father nearly shot him one time for trespassing on our property."

"I was chasing a wild hog that crossed the river and plowed through his fields," clarified Zeke.

"What do y'all do for fun around here?" asked Tim.

"Hunt and fish," replied Zeke.

"My father has me doing chores around the farm most mornings," added Willow. "Then, on the weekends, he invites Cherokee boys to the house, hoping I will find one I like. So far, no match. So, my mother has me helping her with cooking and sewing. They threaten to send me to some finishing school if I don't marry and have babies soon."

"How old are you, if you don't mind my asking?" Tim asked Willow.

"Seventeen. Same as Zeke. And you?"

"Sixteen," replied Tim.

"It's getting late, Bowers," said Zeke with a scowl. "Shouldn't you be back at your camp scraping the bark off logs?"

"I do need to head home. It's getting dark," replied Tim. "Willow, can I see you home?"

Zeke stepped between the two and faced Tim. "Back off, farm boy!" he snarled. "If she needs help, she can count on me."

Tim had learned from his older brother that it was always best to strike first and quickly. He reared back, punched the taller boy in the gut, and then brought his knee up to meet the boy's chest to send him tumbling.

Willow looked at Tim with a look of shock. "Why'd you do that?" she yelled.

"He called me a farm boy! You live on a farm, too, so he insulted us both!"

Willow went over to see that Zeke was okay, then grabbed Tim's arm and turned him around to walk toward the river. "That was foolish! I appreciate you offering to see me home, but your problem is that you made an enemy of the wrong guy."

"He does seem kinda crazy, but facing him again will be worth it if you'll agree to see me sometime soon."

Zeke had recovered and was now racing up behind them. He launched through the air to tackle Tim in the back. They both hit the ground on their sides and quickly stood to face each other.

"Stop! Stop it!" yelled Willow as she stepped in between them. "There's no need for anybody to get hurt!"

The two boys stood facing each other with fists cocked, huffing and staring at each other as if to dare the other to strike first.

"That's enough!" declared Willow. "Zeke, turn around and go home! Tim, you, too! It's late, and I'm leaving!"

Willow marched toward home, and since Tim was heading in the same direction, he walked alongside her on the path along the river. They soon reached the riverbank where Willow had left her canoe to cross.

She turned toward Tim. "After all that fuss, I don't know if it's still possible, but I want the three of us to be friends. That means you and Zeke need to get along." She looked toward her house and back at Tim, and her tone changed from demanding to inviting. "This doesn't mean you won, but I'm going to ask my mother if you can come to dinner sometime soon. I'll be at the river about this time tomorrow night and let you know what she says."

Tim smiled. He wanted to sneak a kiss but lost his nerve. "Okay! I'll see you tomorrow night!"

The Bowers team spent the next day gathering rocks from along the river to line the race they had dug to divert water from the river to power the mill's waterwheel.

Roy noticed that Tim was behaving oddly. "Why do you keep looking around? Something out there spooking you?"

Tim hoped that Zeke wouldn't do anything crazy, but he couldn't be sure. "I'm looking out for a big buck," he replied, not ready to tell his father about his fight and the possibility that the battle wasn't over. "I'm always hungry for a good venison steak."

That evening, Tim was on the bank of the river looking out for Willow when he spotted Zeke Walker approaching in the distance. Zeke had his rifle slung over his shoulder but gave a friendly wave as soon as the two were close enough to make eye contact. Tim walked in Zeke's direction, deciding that a fight was better than flight, especially on his home turf. To his surprise, Zeke smiled and began the conversation.

"I've been thinking about yesterday," said Zeke, "and I just hope there are no hard feelings."

"I wouldn't blame you for being mad at me for sucker punching you like that," replied Tim, "but you did provoke me."

"Maybe I would like to settle the score, but there is no sense in creating some kind of feud. Friends are hard to come by around here."

Zeke extended his hand, and Tim took it. "I'd like to be buddies!" said Tim. "I think we could teach each other a lot. If you're interested, my father's trying to hire some help to clear the land and build a cabin and barn."

"Real money?"

"Of course!"

"I'd like that. I hesitated because folks around here are more likely to barter than pay. I don't need any more…" Zeke was interrupted by movement across the river. "Well, looky there," he said, pointing to Willow as she strolled through the field toward the river.

"But we have a problem," continued Zeke. "We both like the same girl. What are we going to do about that?"

"We do the only fair thing," returned Tim.

"Shoot pinecones from fifty paces?" offered Zeke.

Tim laughed. "No. We let her decide." Tim nodded toward the river, and both boys rushed to the bank, took off their socks and boots, and waded across.

"You fellas aren't going to start fighting again, are you?" asked Willow as they waded through the cold, thigh-high current.

"Nah," replied Tim. "We're allies now. And we both want to see more of the prettiest gal in Gilmer County." Willow looked gorgeous in her patterned long shirt, white cotton blouse, and navy vest.

Willow looked at both boys to see if they were serious. "You're talking about me?" asked Willow, feigning a Southern sweetness that she picked up from her mother. "You both want to see more of me?"

Tim and Zeke both smiled and nodded, and Willow thought for a moment. "Let's go sit on that log over there and talk about this." They made their way over to the trunk of a fallen maple tree, and Willow sat in the middle.

"Before I forget, Tim, you're invited over to the house for dinner Friday night."

Zeke grimaced. "Sounds like you've already made your choice of beaus."

"No," replied Willow, "he asked, and I was just getting back to him. Besides, I've known you for years and just met Tim." Willow cupped her hands on her lap and sat upright. "My father wants me to marry a Cherokee boy, but I don't think he would disown me if I didn't. So, I have a question to ask you both. If you got married someday, how would you support a family? Something beyond shooting rabbits or sawing up trees."

Tim went first. "My father plans to return to Macon at the end of the summer, but I intend to stay here to keep working on the place. I told him I want to be a rancher and raise livestock, and he liked the idea. And if things don't work out with that, my family owns a successful contracting company in Macon, and I could become an owner with my brothers there. And then there's always a possibility that as I pan the creeks around here, I just might discover the biggest vein of gold this side of Dahlonega."

"Wow," remarked Willow. "You've given this some thought!" She patted the top of Tim's thigh and then turned. "Zeke?"

"I don't have all the particulars, but as more people settle around here, I'm ready to grab whatever opportunity comes my way." Zeke paused for a moment. "Besides, supporting a family is more about raising the children right and showing them how to live off the land. And as far as finding gold, I've tried panning all along the banks of this river, and all I've found is pyrite . . . fool's gold."

"Dang, Zeke! I didn't know you did any prospecting," declared Tim.

After a few minutes of animated but boring stories about searching for gold, Willow wanted to return to the discussion she had started. She put her finger and thumb under her tongue and produced an ear-shattering whistle. "Here's the deal. I like both of you guys. What do you say we build something where we can meet regularly? Just us three. Maybe a little shelter over there." She pointed to the nearby woods and then extended her arm, palm down. "You in?"

Zeke and then Tim put their hands over hers. "To helping each other!" exclaimed Zeke.

"And to tell each other if we find any gold around here!" said Tim.

Roy was on the other bank, wondering why Tim had not yet come back.

He soon heard the whistle and laughter from across the way and saw the three teens sitting there having a good time. At least Tim wasn't alone with Willow. He turned toward camp, glad to know that his boy was making the best of their adventure.

Early one morning, Tim and Atta took to the woods to hunt for a turkey. Atta liked to follow the deer trails through the woods to quicken their pace and make less noise. He came to a spot and stopped suddenly.

Atta pointed to a tree several yards in front of them. "You see that tree, how it is crooked?" The trunk was more than a foot in diameter. Four feet off the ground, the trunk turned left at a near-perfect right angle. A few feet further along the trunk, the tree made another sharp, right angle skyward.

"Yeah," replied Tim. "Looks like a tree fell on it when it was a young sapling."

"No. It is a trail tree created by Cherokee. It points to something of interest along the path."

Tim didn't know whether to believe Atta or not.

"You find trail trees all along Cherokee paths. When the tree is young, you bend it to run just above the ground. You strap the trunk and stake it. In time, the tree will bend again toward the sun. The tree grows as it is trained."

They went closer, and Atta pointed to the elbow of the trunk. "See that scar in the trunk? That's a piece of the tree inserted under the bark as a sign that this is a Cherokee trail tree."

Tim studied the tree. "So, what does this one point to?"

"I'm not sure. Maybe to the gold field."

Tim perked up, and Atta started laughing. "It really is a signal tree, but I don't know what it points to. Maybe a village that no longer exists or a good place to cross the river."

Tim slapped Atta on the shoulder. "Well, let's go where it's pointing. I'm sure that's where the turkeys are hiding."

Chapter Eight
1833

Once they had cleared the trees on the trail to the main road, Roy had Tim drive the wagon to the Galloway store to get supplies and any mail while the others worked on constructing the sawmill building. Sawing logs by hand would take too long, so getting the mill up and running was a priority.

Sleeping in a tent was getting old for Roy, but the weather was pleasantly cool, the insects were tolerable, and the drainage was good when it rained. Jax kept the reptiles and other wildlife from invading the area. They built a makeshift outhouse and a table under a tarp near a fire pit equipped with iron cooking racks to make the camp quite comfortable. Roy had even thought of packing the parts of a barrel to use as a makeshift bathtub.

Roy's middle son, Jeremy, arrived in late May. He first traveled from school in Athens to Macon, then to what the Bowers now referred to as Galloway, Georgia. Roy had mailed directions that helped Jeremy make the trip in only four days on horseback, counting on good weather and the stamina of a seventeen-year-old.

Roy introduced Jeremy to Zeke, Hawk, Atta, and a friend of Atta's who had arrived to help. The crew now included Blacks, Cherokee, and whites, all sharing the load equally to accelerate their progress. Willow began coming over with jugs of sweet tea and lemonade, but Roy had to delicately ask her to limit her visits because she was too big a distraction to the all-male crew.

"Were you able to find somebody at the University?" Roy asked Jeremy, out of earshot of the others. Roy had written to Jeremy to see if someone at the school might be available to check out the rock outcrop

Tim had discovered.

"Yes. This fellow is an assistant geology professor who grew up in Wales around slate mines. He should be good and his fee reasonable. He came to Georgia to prospect in the summers, and he was excited at the possibility of discovering new minerals other than gold. He should be here within a week or two."

"And when you talked to Buck, did he have any new information from the sheriff?"

"Yes. The sheriff searched the carriage house and found the linchpin that fit Ma's carriage. It was lying under a workbench. And they figured out that the pin his deputy found on the road was for Ma's old carriage. That doesn't explain how the wrong linchpin got on the carriage, but it does explain why the wheel broke down."

"And has the sheriff pressed your Uncle Norman?"

"He still strongly denies ever touching the carriage that morning. He's furious at you and Samuel for insinuating that he could have been responsible for the death of his own sister."

Roy looked down and shook his head slowly. "Lord, we may never have closure on how your mother died. Either Norman was so drunk or angry at us that he sabotaged that wheel, or Samuel didn't inspect the carriage like he said."

Roy shook off his sudden sadness. "And your brother? How are he and his family and the business doing?"

"Everyone is great! Abigail has taken over the big house, and the business is going strong. Not to say that they don't miss you!"

Roy patted his son on the shoulder. "I hope you can spend some time here."

"Only a couple weeks. This law firm in Athens offered me an apprenticeship. I'm excited about the opportunity, and I figured you would want me to accept."

"Of course I do! That is great news! And I hope once you become a lawyer, you consider practicing around these parts someday. From what I hear, there are plenty of disputes to settle and not enough lawyers and judges to handle things. I'm not sure where I would go for help if we had a legal problem."

"The best lawyers are still in the cities, but this area is bound to grow quickly once these tens of thousands of land grants get developed."

Willow named her trio of friends the Unalii, or "friends" in Cherokee. They met most evenings in a lean-to built with logs from the woods. She commandeered her father's canoe to allow the boys to keep their feet dry crossing the river. They explored nearby tributaries of the Toccoa for potential areas to pan for gold. Tim had plans to build a sluice, but there never was enough time to do any serious prospecting.

Tim was now far ahead of Zeke in the competition for Willow's affection. On occasion, when Zeke was unable to meet, the two would hold hands. Despite the desire, Tim and Willow agreed to take things slow, and neither wanted to exclude Zeke from the Unalii they all enjoyed.

One night, when they were alone, Tim remarked, "I'm surprised your parents let you come out here by yourself. Don't get me wrong; I think it's great. It's just that in Macon, the girls I knew were always under the watchful eye of their mothers."

"My mother and I have talked about how men are and about the consequences. And my father thinks I should be married by now. I guess I've earned their trust. Maybe it's different with Cherokee people than your town friends."

Tim leaned into Willow and laughed. She leaned in as well until their noses were an inch apart. "You smell wonderful, like a field of flowers!" Tim remarked. Then he kissed her on the cheek. Willow stood abruptly as if repelled by his bold move.

"I'm sorry, I didn't mean anything by it," said Tim, slowly standing to face her and bracing for a rebuke and possibly a slap in the face.

Willow wrapped her arms around his neck and smiled. "Well then, kiss me like you mean it!"

Tim pressed his lips to hers, holding the kiss for several seconds. Then Willow pushed off his chest with a sly smile. "I'll see you tomorrow, townie."

On another rainy evening, when Zeke wasn't with them, Willow and Tim got carried away. Holding hands transitioned to roaming hands, the kisses became much more passionate, garments were loosened or removed, and the bodies joined together as nature intended. After the fireworks, they continued to snuggle as if they had no regrets. But little was said as both considered the risk they had taken.

Zeke had been noticing a change in the relationships for some time— the subtle touches, extended glances, and lack of curiosity about their shared activities and plans. But after seeing them joined together from a distance that night in the lean-to, he was heartbroken. And angry.

One day at the cabin under construction, Roy assigned Zeke and Tim to glaze some windows when the glass slipped and shattered on the ground. Tim blamed Zeke for losing his grip, and Zeke blamed Tim for not working fast enough. Tempers flared, and fists were raised before Roy could get between them.

"It's not a big deal," said Roy. "We have more glass."

Still, the boys were ready to face off.

"What's this really about?" asked Roy.

"Your boy stole my girl," replied Zeke.

"I can't help it if she likes me more," said Tim. "It's not like you two were engaged when I showed up."

"We were serious! And you're a sneak and a liar. Just because your family has money, you think you're entitled to everything."

"Whoa, Zeke!" injected Roy. "That's not fair. You're a good worker, and you get paid generously. I think we've treated you fairly. Now, you boys need to settle down." Roy thought for a moment, searching for a resolution. "Tim, you go work with Samuel at the mill and send Kitch up here to work on the cabin."

"I ain't working alongside no slave," declared Zeke. "My father told me I was better off hunting snakes than working with slaves and redskins." He gritted his teeth and held his fists to his sides. Then he relaxed with a sigh. "Actually, I don't need this crap. Just give me what you owe me, and I'm done."

Roy reached into his pocket and handed Zeke some coins. Zeke turned and walked off the property.

Noah Lewis, the geology professor and part-time prospector, arrived at the camp as expected and toured the Bowers property with Tim, Jeremy, and Roy. When they arrived at the cliff of gray rock, he was quite impressed.

"I shouldn't be surprised that slate exists in these old mountains, but I've not seen anything like this in Georgia. There's probably plenty more rock like this that runs deep in the ground, but it's remarkable to have a crop exposed like this on the surface."

"What are the gold speckles in the rock?" asked Tim.

"That's pyrite. And the clear speckles are bits of quartz."

"Is it practical to mine this and sell it commercially?" asked Roy.

"Yes, of course. There are all sorts of markets. Water runs off the tiles, which makes them great for roofing and flooring. The roof tiles can be brittle, but you could walk on a floor of thicker slate for a hundred years, and it would look like new." Noah picked up one of the thinner slate pieces at the base of the cliff and tapped it with his knuckles. "Hard as steel." He struck the tile over a rock, and it snapped in two.

"Anything unique about getting it out of the ground?" Jeremy asked.

"Not particularly. Slate has been mined for centuries in Northern Europe. And I understand there are successful mines in New England. It's kind of like coal mining, labor intensive and dusty, but you can make a lot of money because people value good slate."

"Do you find gold where you find slate?" asked Tim.

"That's a good question. Gold and slate both exist in this area. But gold doesn't come from slate, or vice versa. Both minerals tend to be pushed up to the surface from deep in the earth in the same general areas. The same with coal and shale."

"Are there varying grades of slate?" asked Roy. "Are these stones good quality?"

Noah studied the rocks exposed on the side of the hill. "I'd say so. See how these thin layers of rock run in straight, parallel sheets? It's called foliation, and these layers are linear and consistent. That's a good sign. And the blue-gray coloring is good. The rock I tapped with my knuckles sounded dense, but it will take testing in a lab before we know the grade of hardness."

"The biggest challenge would be getting the rock from here to market," said Roy.

"That, I know nothing about," said Noah. "But as far as getting the rock processed, you will need a facility close by to split, cut, and trim the large slabs you extract from the ground. Each step of the process is a real art, so you'll need to find men with those skills."

The men continued discussing the mining process as they returned to camp. Samuel had cooked stew for dinner. Noah spent the night and left in the morning to resume his summer prospecting endeavors near Dahlonega.

Jeremy was excited about what they had discussed. "What do you think, Pa? Are you ready to get in the mining business?"

"I thought I'd come up here and retire on a horse ranch, not be a miner."

"It's got to be worth exploring," exclaimed Jeremy. "I know it would take a sizeable investment to get started, but this could be even bigger than the contracting business."

"Maybe, but we don't know anyone who knows anything about mining slate," said Roy. "Unless you think we could hire Mr. Lewis as a consultant."

"I don't see why not," replied Jeremy. "He doesn't make much as an assistant professor. Do you want to make him an offer?"

Roy nodded.

"I'll ask him," said Jeremy. "It will be weeks before I see him again, but I think he will jump at the opportunity."

"And then we would need to find the skilled men to work the pit and cutting process," said Roy. "And find buyers and a way to transport the tiles."

"Maybe you could visit other slate operations up in Virginia or Pennsylvania and find the people we need," suggested Jeremy. "As far as sales go, how about developing connections with the store's suppliers in Galloway, where you buy all your building materials? The same boats that bring those goods here could take the slate back up the river to Chattanooga."

Roy replied, "I like your ideas, Jeremy. I can do the research, and if Noah Lewis agrees to help, we'll have a big head start. But you need to stick with becoming a lawyer."

Tim was preparing to drive the wagon to Galloway one day when he spotted Jax walking slowly toward the cabin. He was wobbling and favoring his front leg. Tim ran over and coaxed Jax to lie on his side. "Ol' boy, what's wrong?" asked Tim. Jax was panting as if he were exhausted. When Tim pet his head, Jax snapped at his hand, something Tim had never seen him do before. Tim carefully picked him up and carried the dog to the front porch.

Roy was at the mine, but Samuel was nearby and came to help.

"He's acting very strange," complained Tim. "Something's really wrong."

Samuel began inspecting the dog's body. Jax yelped when he touched his right front leg, and Samuel looked closer. "I'm afraid a snake got him. His leg is swollen, and you can see blood around two fang marks on his fur."

"What can we do?" asked Tim frantically.

"Not much we can do. If it was a rat snake, he'll limp around for a day or two and get better. But if it was a copperhead or rattlesnake . . ."

Suddenly, Jax tried to get to his feet. Tim reached to restrain him, but Jax quickly collapsed and lay panting heavily, whimpering between breaths.

Tim lay down on the porch floor next to Jax. "Come on, boy, hang on!" Tim looked back to Samuel. "There must be something we can do!"

"Some say to cut the fang marks with a knife and suck the venom out, but we can't do that on his leg. And we don't know how long ago he got bit, so I don't think a tourniquet like you'd put on a man's arm would work. I think you're doing all you can."

"He's messed with snakes before," said Tim. "I thought he'd know better than to get bit."

"I hate snakes. I just leave 'em alone. But old Jax might not have even seen what bit him."

Tim lay on the porch floor with his arm over Jax for over an hour as Samuel stood nearby. Slowly, the venom reached Jax's heart and lungs, and his labored breathing stopped. "He's gone, Samuel," declared Tim, shaking his head as his eyes filled with tears. Tim sat next to his dog while Samuel went to get two shovels.

"Come on, Tim," said Samuel. "Let's give him a proper burial."

Tim found a good spot near the river where they dug a hole between the trees. Samuel said a prayer, and Tim said goodbye. They piled a dozen big river rocks over the mound of fresh dirt.

Roy arrived home to the bad news and stood over the grave for a while. He walked over to Tim and put his arm around his shoulders. "I'm so sorry, Son. Ol' Jax was a good dog, and he had a good life. I wish he could have stayed with us longer."

Tim visited that pile of rocks often. He thought about getting a pup, but replacing a good dog like Jax might not be possible.

Roy was more excited about the slate mining opportunity than he led on, but his primary focus was getting the cabin completed. The structure was framed out, including a big front porch, but there was still much work to do. Roy had chosen to lap the milled pine siding, so it wouldn't be an authentic log home, but the natural finish would make it a fine cabin in the woods. He ordered a new tin sheeting material for the roof, and the rock foundation and chimneys would provide handsome accents.

The cabin was laid out with a spacious living and dining area, two bedrooms, and a large loft that could hold several beds. There were plenty of windows and two fireplaces, and Roy planned to build lots of cabinets and storage along the walls. The back of the cabin could be expanded if needed. Roy and Samuel would get their own bedrooms, leaving the nightly ladder climb to the loft for Tim and Kitch. The tents in the existing camp would stay to accommodate the hired help.

They built a primitive lean-to to serve as a temporary barn and lined the footpaths with pebbles to improve the footing and minimize tracking mud. A cistern collected rainwater from the roof, and a well was under construction to provide drinking water.

The sawmill was also a resounding success. Samuel and Kitch became experts at cutting and planing the logs from the scores of trees cut down for the pastures and driveway. Atta, his friend, and Hawk became good at working the big bow saws to drop the trees and drag them down to the mill with horses.

"So, how do we get rid of all the stumps?" Tim asked his father.

"At this point, it's too much work. We need a couple of oxen to pull them out of the ground, but I haven't had any luck finding any bulls nearby. Next year, they'll be easier to pull out, so for now, I'm willing to put up with the unfinished look."

On the days Tim drove the wagon to Galloway to pick up building materials, Willow rode at his side. They seldom made the five-mile trip without pulling off into the woods to cuddle together in the wagon bed.

"You're staying here when your father returns to Macon, right?" asked Willow one day.

"Yes, I intend to live up here for the rest of my life."

"Good, because I don't know what I'd do if you were gone all winter." Willow rested her head on his shoulder.

"I want to spend every day with you," exclaimed Tim.

"Is that your way of proposing?" asked Willow in a playfully accusatory tone.

"No. I mean, yes, I would propose if I thought you would consider it, but I wasn't thinking of doing it today." Tim winced at his own awkwardness.

"Then you are asking me to marry you?"

Tim stopped the wagon, turned to Willow, and reached for her hands. He had visions of marrying this woman he idolized, and now that she sounded open to the idea, he was thrilled. "Willow, will you marry me?"

Willow wrapped her arms around him. "Yes, Tim Bowers, I would love to marry you."

They kissed and held each other until Willow gently pushed away. "But you know we can't say anything to anyone or get engaged until you ask my father for permission," cautioned Willow.

This was all moving fast for Tim. He got the wagon moving again. "Do you think he will agree? I need to talk to my father, too."

"I'm pretty sure he will, but you must be ready for the questions he might ask. Like where we will live. Do you want children? How will you provide for us?"

"I think he would love having his daughter and grandchildren living next door. As far as making a living, the ranch will be up and running in the spring, and there's the possibility of working the slate mine. But my father doesn't want me to tell anyone about the mine."

"Maybe he will want my father as a partner."

"Having a business partner hasn't worked well for him in the past, but I will mention it."

They arrived at Galloway's store, loaded what they needed, and headed home.

"Are you thinking about a wedding next spring?" asked Tim. "When my father returns from Macon?"

"I was hoping we could do it right away!"

Tim was taken aback by her response. "I thought it took months to plan a wedding. Won't your mother be upset at rushing things?"

"I thought you were sure about this," questioned Willow. "Why wait?"

Tim knew his father would have concerns, but he didn't want to dampen the excitement of the moment. "Okay! Whatever you think is best!"

They continued to plan their future together playfully. Tim wanted a house of their own. Willow wanted at least four children. He hoped they would have a school and church to attend someday.

"Do we invite Zeke and his family to the wedding?" asked Tim.

"You didn't hear? Zeke joined the Army."

"He did? How did you find out?" asked Tim, surprised that she knew before he did.

"He came over a few days ago to tell me."

Tim was a little troubled. "Are you sure you're over him?"

"Tim, he's joining the Army."

The next day, Tim discussed the wedding plans with his father. "No!" exclaimed Roy. "You're too young, and this is too quick! I like Willow, and you two make a good couple, but you need to give this more time. You've only known each other for a few weeks."

"Are you going to disown me if I do marry her?"

Roy knew he had to be careful. Tim was emotional and determined, and this was the kind of issue that could rip apart their relationship. "Of course not. You're old enough to make your own decisions. But this is a big commitment, and I think the timing is all wrong."

Tim looked down, shaking his head and cussing under his breath. "I'm in a tough spot here, Pa. You're mad at me, but if I go back on what I said, Willow will be really upset. She was so excited, and I am, too."

"I understand. But you both need to give this time. If you're right for each other, waiting a few months will go by quickly."

"I don't see the point in waiting, Pa. I love Willow, and I'm certain she's the woman I want to marry. I'm sorry if you're disappointed in me."

Roy took a deep breath and ran his hand through his hair. "You'll probably run into more resistance from Willow's parents. Waya Madstone will probably make the decision for you both."

"I'm going to have dinner with the Madstones tomorrow night. I don't know what to expect when I ask his permission." Tim shook his head and changed the subject. "Do you care if I mention the slate discovery to Mr. Madstone?"

"I don't see the need," replied Roy, still trying to get over Tim's sudden choices. "That's rushing things as well."

Tim nodded and excused himself to take a walk. The victory of winning Willow's hand had become far more complicated than he expected.

The Madstones had Tim for dinner, as they did every few days, but the conversation during the meal was stilted. Tim figured that Willow must have told her parents about their engagement plans, and they were not happy. After eating, Madstone asked Tim to join him privately in the parlor. Tim braced for a strong rebuke, the second in a day.

As soon as they were alone, Madstone clenched his fists and got right up in Tim's face. "I ought to slay you where you stand, boy!" yelled Madstone.

Tim was stunned. He backed up, but Madstone stayed right in front of him. "You have sullied my daughter and brought dishonor to my family!" he yelled.

Tim wondered why he was so upset. Delaying the wedding was not a big deal. He had come to ask for Madstone's permission, not to be threatened.

Eleanor and Willow came running into the room. "Father, stop!" yelled Willow. "Tim doesn't know what I've told you."

Now Tim was alarmed. He saw their troubled expressions, but no one was saying anything. He shook his head quickly and held out his hands. "What don't I know?"

Willow walked over to Tim, and her father backed away. She grabbed his hands. "Tim, I'm going to have a baby. Your baby. When I told my parents about getting married right away, they said no. So I had to tell them. And now you know."

Tim counted the days in his head since that night in the lean-to. It hadn't been four weeks. "Are you sure?"

"I'm positive," replied Willow.

Tim's shoulders slumped, and he exhaled loudly. He looked at Willow, first with a look of despair and then with calm resolve. He squeezed Willow's hands. "And you still want to get married?"

"Of course I do, dummy!"

"We need to talk this through," said Eleanor as she walked closer. "Waya and I agree that the wedding should be as soon as possible, but have you talked to your father about all this?"

"Yes, ma'am. He thought we were rushing into this. Of course, I didn't know to tell him that a baby was on the way."

"Well, at least it looks like you're stepping up to your responsibilities," said Madstone, having calmed down considerably. "Now you need to explain this all to him and everyone else who notices how quickly this baby will come."

Tim thought for a moment before speaking. "Mr. and Mrs. Madstone, I'm sorry about how this all turned out, but I love Willow. I will be a good husband and father."

Madstone abruptly left the room. Eleanor came closer to Tim. "Don't mind him. Deep down, he is happy to see Willow get married. He likes you, and I know he will love a grandbaby. This just isn't happening the way we were expecting. But he's a practical man and will calm down. You'll see."

Tim, Willow, and Eleanor sat in the room discussing plans for the wedding. The mood had lightened considerably when Madstone returned. "I need to talk to Tim alone," he barked. As Eleanor exited the room with Willow, she tenderly patted Madstone on the arm and smiled.

Tim and Madstone sat facing each other. "I don't like the way this has happened. I don't like it one bit. But it's done. Now, we need to speak man to man."

"I came here tonight to ask your permission to marry your daughter," responded Tim.

"Of course, you must marry her, but my permission has conditions," stated Madstone. "You need to know what you are facing. Willow is half Cherokee, and I fear you are not prepared to have mixed-breed children in this hateful and prejudiced white world."

"I am prepared, sir," replied Tim. "I would be proud to raise my sons and daughters right here in their native land and native ways."

"I have my doubts. You have had a privileged upbringing in a good, Christian family, and I'm not sure you have seen the way a lot of other whites treat Natives."

"I have seen plenty of bigotry. And I see your example. You have had a very successful life married to a white woman."

"Yes, but it has cost us both dearly. We have lost touch with many of my Native family and friends. I've never met any of my wife's family. We are often not accepted by either whites or Cherokee."

"My family and I respect you," replied Tim.

"Maybe so, but you reject the idea that I own slaves. You might try, but you still judge others just as we are judged."

"Even though some in my family own slaves, I still love and respect them. I may not accept the idea of people owning other people, but I respect you and your family. And I love your daughter."

Madstone sat deep in thought for a couple of moments. "I believe you truly love Willow, and I approve of your marriage. I just want you to brace yourself for how people will treat you."

"I believe I am ready, sir. With that condition, do I have your permission?"

The two men stood and shook hands. It was more a resolution than a celebration.

Later that evening, Tim explained things to his father. Roy threw up his arms and stomped his foot. "Goddammit, Tim! We talked about this! I warned you to be careful, but you couldn't control yourself!" Roy turned in place and shook his head. He took a deep breath. "I am disappointed in you and mad at myself for not limiting your activities. Certainly, you and Willow should have been more disciplined in your choices. People will talk when Willow starts showing weeks after the wedding." Roy sighed and looked off into the distance.

"I accept responsibility for all this chaos, but I hope that, in time, it won't matter," replied Tim. "I love Willow, and she loves me. We will make it work."

Roy looked at Tim with an expression of surrender. "Okay, Son. You better make it work."

Chapter Nine

1833

The day of Tim's wedding came on a warm, breezy day in August. Only their parents knew for certain why Willow and Tim had arranged the event so quickly. Others must have suspected, but no one said anything because the couple was so well-matched and clearly in love.

As Roy was waiting outside the cabin for Tim and the other men to get ready, he spotted a group of six Cherokee men rambling through the woods beyond the pasture. As he approached them to see what they wanted, they jumped the fence and rushed toward him. Roy had picked up a bit of Cherokee from his workers and yelled to the group, "Let's talk."

The men were dressed in native garb of linen and deerskin, and each wore a similar necklace of colorful beads. They carried long knives in their belts but had no guns. As they approached, the leader, who appeared to be in his twenties, yelled something that Roy did not understand. He charged Roy, grabbed him by the arm, and turned him around. The other men surrounded Roy as they marched him toward the cabin. The leader kept yelling at Roy in a tone that sounded threatening.

The group made enough noise to alert the men inside the house. Tim, Samuel, Kitch, Noah, Atta, and Atta's friend rushed out onto the front porch to confront the gang. Not only were the marauders matched in number, but Tim and Samuel carried rifles. The Cherokee were surprised by the appearance of such a force and stopped in their tracks several yards from Roy's posse. Still grasping Roy's arm, the gang leader pulled his knife from its sheath and yelled something in Cherokee. Samuel and Tim raised their rifles, ready to shoot.

Atta moved toward the leader and yelled something back.

"Who are these men?" Roy asked Atta in a calm tone.

"They are bandits. They raid settlers, take their things, and try to force them off their property."

"Tim, Samuel, lower your rifles," ordered Roy. "We don't want bloodshed. Atta, tell these men that they made a mistake. Tell them to turn around and get off the property."

Atta and the gang leader exchanged words that seemed to calm the tempers. After a few moments, the Cherokee began to back away, using Roy as a shield. A few yards further, they released Roy, jogged back where they had started, hopped the pasture fence, and disappeared.

"Thank you, Atta," said Roy, exhaling deeply. "That coulda gone sideways."

"Those men are not good Cherokee," replied Atta. "They cause problems for all of my people."

"It's certainly understandable that they are angry at losing their land," said Tim.

"Yes, we are all angry and sad," responded Atta. "But a few thousand Natives cannot resist tens of thousands of whites moving into this land. And those men learned nothing today. They will continue to make trouble until they are dead."

Roy joined the men on the porch as he gathered his wits and let the adrenaline rush fade. "Thank you for settling this without bloodshed," said Roy, shaking Atta's hand. "Thank y'all for showing restraint. I guess we all learned a lesson that things around here are still a bit dangerous and unsettled."

The men calmed down and finished getting ready. Atta volunteered to stay at the cabin; he would fire a shot if the marauders returned. As the men crossed the river on the footbridge, Waya and Hawk Madstone greeted them with big smiles and handshakes. Hawk led Tim to the house to meet with the minister, Madstone led Roy to the house, and the others went to take a seat in front of the house.

"You spared no expense, Waya!" remarked Roy, admiring the preparations around the farm. Tables and benches for nearly a hundred guests were set up under tarps to shade the sun and provide cover in case of rain.

Waya pointed to one of several fire pits where a pig was roasting on a spit. "That hog has been cooking since yesterday."

"I've sent over several jugs of wine," said Roy. "I figured you would have the whiskey. Is there anything my boys or I can do to help?"

"No, sir. Let's go inside and relax."

Roy and Madstone sat in the parlor. "So, what's this I hear about you mining rock?" asked Madstone.

Roy was a bit surprised that Madstone knew about the slate. "We're trying to figure out if this outcrop we found is worth anything. It looks like good quality, but we're not sure about the density or how deep the vein runs."

"I've heard about slate but didn't know you could find it around here."

"We were surprised as well. Most of the mines in this country are north of Virginia."

"If the vein of slate crosses over your property line, you know that I own the lots to your north and east, right?"

Roy could almost hear the wheels turning in Madstone's mind. "The rock we've seen so far is well within my boundaries. But yes, I am well aware that you own the lots on three sides of me. It will take a lot of men and expense to build a mine of any scale, but I'm hoping that steam engines and other new equipment will reduce the number of men we must hire and let us go down into the vein instead of creating a wide pit."

"You might have no choice but to buy slaves."

"I'd rather hire men from outside the area than buy slaves. What I really need are men experienced in working the stone, and the best come from Europe."

"I'm just glad you found slate and not gold. The last thing we need is to turn this area into another gold belt."

Eleanor Madstone came to the doorway. "It's time! Waya, come see your beautiful daughter! Roy, please go to the foyer to meet with Tim and the minister." Tim had asked his father to be his best man.

Roy regretted that Buck and Jeremy couldn't attend; they would have needed more notice to plan the many days of travel. He regretted even more that Helen was not here to see her youngest son settling down and getting married.

Roy and Tim went out through the front door to find scores of people sitting on benches in rows facing the front porch. A few were Madstone's Native friends from as far away as Ellijay, but most were farm workers and their families. Flower bouquets lined the porch deck, and the preacher's wife played hymns on a piano borrowed from the music room. The two Bowers men stood together quietly with the preacher.

The crowd hushed and turned as a covered carriage came from the back of the house to make a wide circle around the people seated and stopped at the back center aisle of the benches. Waya Madstone stepped out and helped Willow down the carriage steps in her long gown. She looked like an angel in her light-colored dress trimmed in lace. Her hair was curled and adorned with several miniature roses.

The preacher's wife played *Love Divine, All Loves Excelling* on the piano as Waya and Willow walked toward the porch. Madstone had agreed to a Christian wedding to please his wife and Roy. The ceremony was elegant and went without a hitch.

The meal served after the wedding was as fancy as the ceremony. The roasted pork, vegetables, and desserts were delicious, and Roy was glad to see that Madstone allowed his farm workers to eat with everyone else under the tarps.

Having agreed to the Christian ceremony, Madstone insisted on some Cherokee wedding traditions following the meal. He got everyone's attention and thanked them for coming. Madstone welcomed the union of his and the Bowers families as a holy man instructed Tim and Willow on their roles in the ceremony.

Tim and Willow were given torches, which they carried to three stacks of wood cut from seven different kinds of trees. Tim lit his fire on the left as Willow did the same with her fire on the right. They sprinkled a mixture of sage, tobacco, corn, and grass onto the fires as the holy man chanted a Cherokee prayer. Once their fires were burning brightly, they each took the torch from their fire and lit a third, much larger stack of wood in the middle.

As Willow and Tim stood on either side of the fire, Eleanor and Roy carried blue blankets to drape around their respective child's shoulders. As another Native prayer began, the couple walked to the front of the fire to stand side by side. Willow grasped the corner of Tim's blanket and neatly folded it. Tim did the same, and they turned to face each other. Then, Madstone, Eleanor, and Roy draped a large white blanket around the couple, and everyone cheered.

Following the ceremony, Hawk and two friends played fiddle and guitars to their version of mountain music and invited everyone to dance. After several numbers, Roy convinced Samuel to join them with his harmonica. As Samuel began to play, a commotion in the distance caused everyone to stand and stare as several mounted militiamen rode up to the gathering.

The leader dismounted, and Madstone went out to meet him. Roy followed.

"I'm sorry to disturb you, but we're looking for a group of Cherokee men on foot." The leader kept looking over Madstone's shoulder as he spoke. "They've been robbing and terrorizing citizens around here."

"I haven't seen . . . " Madstone started to say when Roy interrupted.

"I saw those men! It was hours ago at my place across the river. They were poking around, but we scared them off."

"Which way did they head?"

Roy pointed past his property. "Due east. They were on foot and keeping to the woods."

"I appreciate that information," the man replied as he scanned the people gathered under the tents. "Some kind of party you're having?"

"My daughter just married his son," replied Madstone. He thought for a moment. "Would you and your men like to get something to eat? We have plenty of food."

The officer didn't hesitate. "Yes, sir! We would appreciate that!" He spoke to his men, and they dismounted to help themselves to a late afternoon meal.

Samuel played a couple of songs on his harmonica, and then Willow and Tim served wedding cake to each of their guests. After a while, the officer came over to Madstone. "We certainly do appreciate your hospitality. The bride and groom are a handsome pair! We need to get back to our chase, but let me give you a couple of friendly reminders. Nigras are not to be dancing with whites, and it's illegal to serve alcohol to Injuns."

Madstone took a deep breath. He knew better than to make a scene. He said nothing, and the officer and his men finally turned toward their horses and rode off down the lane.

Roy walked up to Madstone, sensing that something disturbing had happened. "What was that about?" asked Roy.

"Nothing. Just another ignorant white man in a uniform."

Roy wanted to pursue it, but Madstone turned and walked back to the party. Whatever was said could not have been good. But as Roy watched the militia ride out of sight, he was relieved to see for the first time that some law enforcement was active in these parts.

Chapter Ten
1833

Cool winds and dryer weather marked the end of August. Noah Lewis had agreed to serve as a consultant in developing plans for the mine, and the first step was to accompany Roy on a trip north to Virginia to visit existing slate operations and explore how to hire the skilled men they would need.

Before leaving on the trip, Roy stopped at the Morgan's house, their neighbors to the south. Jasper Morgan had offered to sell two riding horses with saddles at a price that led Roy to believe things were getting desperate for his neighbors.

"If you sell these, you'll be down to one horse. What if something happens to that one? How will you survive the winter?"

"I'm not sure we can," replied Jasper. "My bum leg won't let me get around much, so I'm unable to work the land. We pretty much live off fish and venison."

"I'd like to share an idea with you," offered Roy. "I believe we will see a lot of growth in our area over the next few years, and I want to be ready for that opportunity." Roy took out a map he had drawn to point out different features. "Here's my lot and the lane we cleared that connects our properties to the main road. All this land between your house and the road is untouched woods that would make a great area to subdivide for homes and shops. It borders the river and the road and represents an ideal spot for the next town between Ellijay and Blairsville."

Morgan was still listening, so Roy continued. "Here's my offer. I will buy your two horses at a fair price so you'll have some money to make it through winter. Then, I want to hire you to make a weekly run to the store in Galloway to buy supplies for your family and my crew. I'll pay you five dollars a week to make the runs, and you can use my wagons and horses. My objective is to help your family hold on to your land because I think you and Miriam would be great at running the store and tavern we will need to get this village started. If you're interested, I'll be back in the spring with more details."

Miriam Morgan came into the room. "I couldn't help overhearing your conversation." She looked at her husband, who was just blankly staring ahead. "Mr. Bowers, I like what you're saying. We accept your offer." She walked over and shook Roy's hand vigorously. "God bless you, Mr. Bowers."

Roy rode to Athens to meet Noah. Jeremy joined them for dinner and gave his father a quick tour of the University campus. Roy and Noah left the next morning, and it took the pair nine days of hard riding to reach the small mining town west of Richmond. The countryside surrounding the mine was very similar to the landscape of the Bowers property – hilly, wooded terrain with a nearby river.

They met with the owner and asked for a tour, explaining that they might be interested in becoming partners in the operations. The owner wasn't completely sold on their motives but agreed to walk them around the facility.

The rock had been mined for years, producing a broad, deep open pit. Men drilled holes by hand in the face of the rock several feet above the bottom of the pit. Tubes of black powder were inserted in the holes, and the blast caused large chunks of rock to tumble to the pit base. Stones any larger than what two men could carry were broken apart. The slate was transported in small wagons pulled by oxen to a building near the pit. The slate was split with chisels to produce slabs about four inches thick. The slabs were cut into squares with a hand-operated saw wheel and then split again with a chisel into thin sheets no more than a half-inch thick.

"Slate rock separates easily if you know how to work it," explained the owner. "The key is finding men with the skill to read the layering of the rock in the wall to know where to blast and finding others who can split the rock into smooth, thin tiles." He took a tile from one of many tall stacks of finished slate lined up all along the side of the building to let his visitors appreciate the unique qualities of his product.

The owner invited the men to his office, an unorganized mess covered in thick dust from the plant. He whipped a towel across his visitor's chair seats, sending dust everywhere. "You say you are considering an investment," began the owner, pouring whiskey into three glasses and offering one to Roy and Noah. "Now that you've seen one of the finest slate mines in America, what is your proposal?"

Roy took a moment to reply; he had no intention of even tasting the whiskey. "I am impressed with your finished product but equally unimpressed with how you produce it. The men in the pit and those processing the ore are all Welshmen, and none look very happy to work here. The men doing the lifting and hauling are all slaves, and their motivation is about equal to how much you pay them. Zero. You use wagons to transport the rocks where I would expect to see trams on rails and steam engines to power the trams and the machines in the shop."

"You don't mince words, do you, Bowers," replied the owner. "Much of what you say is true, but they all require a great deal of money. That is why I even entertained giving you a tour of my operation. I thought you were going to make me an offer."

Roy continued. "I also wonder how much effort you make in marketing. You produce a quality product that should be in high demand. So why is there so much finished inventory stacked everywhere?"

"You're right! There is high demand, but our customers don't have the cash. Most builders use wood products that might last a decade. Slate lasts for centuries."

Roy looked to Noah, who nodded. "Mr. Daniels, we thank you for showing us your facility, but I'm afraid this is not something we can invest in."

The owner reached into the drawer of his desk, pulled out a revolver, and waved it at his visitors. "Okay, then. This little show is over. Get the hell off my property!"

Noah nearly jumped out of his chair at the sight of the gun. Roy rose slowly from his chair and extended his arm toward Noah. "I think it's time we go, Noah. No need to waste our time talking to a man with such a short fuse." Roy turned toward the miner. "Good day, Mr. Daniels."

Roy and Noah next rode to Washington to see what support might be available from the government. As they made the three-day trip, they agreed that recruiting the craftsmen they saw in Virginia would be the quickest way to get the Bowers mine up and running.

Their first stop on arriving in D.C. was the headquarters of the Army Corps of Engineers, where Roy used his past service to get a meeting with an officer with some clout.

"We thank you for your past service, Mr. Bowers. What can the Army do for you?" asked the major.

Roy explained how he planned to open a slate mine on newly acquired land in North Georgia. "If you plan to evict the Indians, the Army will need a presence. I wonder what forts and roads you plan to build in the area."

The major called on an engineer who worked in that area to join the meeting and bring his drawings. They studied the maps, and Roy pointed to the existing road near his property.

"Right there," exclaimed Roy, pointing to the map. "You show the road, but there is no bridge across the river. When the water is high, wagons cannot safely cross."

The young officer replied, "That road connects our barracks between Alabama and Blairsville. We are aware of the issue, but it is not considered a priority."

Roy asked, "Can you elevate it to a priority? Not only does the Army depend on the road, but there is an increasing volume of commercial development along that corridor."

The major responded, "We appreciate hearing from citizens like you, but we typically work with state engineers. Officials from Massachusetts and New York are in here all the time, but I can't remember the last time we heard from anyone from Georgia."

Following more discussion, the major ended the meeting by thanking the visitors for coming and promising to see what he could do. Roy left, cussing under his breath.

Roy and Noah's next stop was the Capitol to meet with the congressman representing the North Georgia counties. The congressman assured Roy that President Jackson was already making plans to have the U.S. Army remove the Cherokee from Georgia—just as large Native populations had been removed from all other states east of the Mississippi River. It was not the news Roy wanted to hear, but it did provide clarity for what to expect.

Roy explained his plans to open a slate mine to the congressman. "The success of our mine will depend on rail access, and I was hoping you could tell me which route the government favors. Will the lines go through Dalton or up through Ellijay?"

"Certainly, I would favor tracks through Ellijay because it's in my district, but you shouldn't expect to get details like that from Washington. Most people in this town are more interested in expanding the Underground Railroad than laying track in Georgia."

"A major at the Army Corps told us they routinely work with engineers from the northern states but not Georgia. Can't we step up the pressure?"

The congressman sighed. "See, that is the problem I have all the time. People from the northern states are always in Washington with their hands out. The southern states operate like independent little countries, expecting nothing from Washington except to be left alone. I wish I had more resources to get things done for North Georgia, but I feel like David fighting Goliath."

Roy realized that he was getting nowhere. "You remember that David was victorious, right?" The congressman didn't reply. Roy looked at Noah. "Come on. I think it's time to head home."

It took Roy and Noah nearly twelve days to travel from D.C. to Georgia, and in that time, they continued to discuss their detailed plan to develop the slate mine.

"We need to divvy up the tasks," Roy suggested to Noah. "You're still okay spending the winter at the mine?"

"Yes. After what we saw in Virginia, I want to find the best way to cut and split the tiles and determine what equipment we will need."

"I'll be in Macon, but I'll be developing some contacts to determine how to market the tiles and the best way to transport the loads. Will you need help?"

"I might need a man or two."

"Hire what you need," replied Roy. "Tim and Kitch will be focused on clearing pastures, but they can assist you with finding some helpers."

Once Roy was back at the cabin, he and Samuel prepared for their trip to spend the winter in Macon. Tim was living with Willow at the Madstone house. Kitch and Noah would have their own bedrooms in the now-finished cabin.

Roy was greeted with open arms when he arrived in Macon in early October. Abigail had his room ready in the big house, and Buck had arranged for them to attend the dedication of the Methodist church expansion on Mulberry Street. Buck's managers and several local officials participated in the event, so it was a rousing welcome home.

Roy's first priority in Macon was visiting Helen's gravesite. City Cemetery was filling up rapidly, and the small, four-acre property was now a green oasis in the booming industrial district. Roy tried to tune out the noises and other distractions as he stood at the granite headstone. He was there for some time because it took that long to tell Helen all that had happened to her family over the past months—Buck and the business, Jeremy and his law apprenticeship, Tim's marriage to a wonderful young woman in the mountains, and his ventures into the mining business. Roy imagined Helen beaming with pride at how well her boys were doing. He knelt at the grave and prayed, asking God to watch over their family.

Roy found that he had plenty of time on his hands in Macon. Outside of family and business activities, he had little contact with others. Helen would have had their evenings booked full of dinners with friends, social events at church, and evenings together to take a stroll, dine out, or simply sit under the stars. Buck and Abigail included Roy in some of their activities, but it felt awkward. It just wasn't the same. He missed his Helen.

Roy met with the sheriff at the new county building on Mulberry Street. The sheriff had nothing new to report—no confession from Norman or an explanation for the switched linchpins.

Roy tracked down his brother-in-law working at the wharf. He was surprised to find Norman working in the office and not on the docks. Norman was not happy to see Roy but agreed to meet with him outside the building.

"I know you are looking for closure," offered Norman in a calm and conciliatory tone. "I am, too. But you have to accept that I had nothing to with that wheel coming off."

"You were the only person there before the accident," replied Roy. "Samuel said your conversation with Helen was heated. I don't believe that you were discussing some birthday party."

"You're right. I came, once again, to ask her to let me back into the business. I had been drinking and got mad, and she was upset with me for wrecking my life and not moving on." Norman faced Roy. "I am trying to rebuild things. I'm taking my job here seriously. I stopped drinking. I'm spending time with my family. And I've cooperated with the sheriff."

"But you admit to being drunk that morning," stated Roy.

"Yeah, but I wasn't so drunk to want to kill my only sister!" Norman looked around in frustration. "Look, I've tried to put myself in your shoes in needing to understand what happened. But I don't know anything about carriages. I don't know a linchpin from a spoke. And why would I or anyone switch instead of loosening the thing and then throw it under a workbench where the sheriff said he found it?"

Roy was taken aback by Norman's new soberness and composure. Maybe Norman had nothing to do with the death of his sister. Perhaps he was putting his life back together. Maybe it was time they both moved on.

Chapter Eleven
1834

Roy was fascinated with the new science of steam engines, not so much about the workings of the motors but how the new technology could be applied. While many in the industry focused on powering ships and trains, Roy's interest was in applications for construction, sawmills, and mining. Horsepower could replace manpower, and things once thought to be beyond reach could now be achieved.

During the early months of 1834, Roy read everything he could find about the development of engines. He visited engineers in the railroad, shipping, and cotton mill plants around Macon to see how they planned to apply the new technology. He developed plans to use small engines in his building business in Macon as well as the prospective mine up north. But there was one big problem.

The most efficient fuel to power steam engines was coal, and the nearest coal mine was in the northwest corner of Georgia. In other regions of the country, coal was being delivered to plants by train, but rails were not yet running to Macon, let alone to the mountains. Wood to fire the boilers was plentiful, but cutting, hauling, and seasoning firewood was inefficient. Roy's plans were just many years ahead of the times.

Noah was also researching the latest mining techniques. He met Roy once over the winter in Decatur, splitting the distance between them, to continue planning the layout of the mine. To be successful, they needed a layout that could be easily expanded. Noah had mapped out the elevations around the slate outcrop to identify a good location for the processing plant, and together they worked on a system of mule-drawn mine cars on rails to transport the ore from the pit to the plant.

Roy spent several hours a week at the construction company to help

Buck and Donny with new building projects. The business was growing steadily, partly because they ran a good operation and partly because Macon was quickly becoming an industrial hub. Since Eli Whitney invented his gin to separate the cotton seeds from fiber, mills were popping up all around Central and South Georgia. Macon was not only in the center of the state but the northernmost point on a river navigable to the ports in Savannah and Brunswick.

However, the growing demand for cotton also fueled the need for slaves. While Congress outlawed the importation of slaves to the U.S. in 1808, hundreds of slaves were still being bought and sold near the courthouse in downtown Macon.

Roy was against slavery but was a businessman, not an activist. He had bought slaves in Macon for his company and home, not to save money, but because he couldn't find help for what needed to get done. Helen had taught Atha, Samuel, and Marcus to read and write and encouraged them to study the Bible and attend church services on Sundays. She celebrated their birthdays with cake and a present. Those who could read and write were paid an allowance to teach others. They did so in secrecy because Georgia law made it a crime, but the law was unenforceable.

Roy negotiated with each servant that, in exchange for their labor, they would receive meals, lodging, education, a small allowance, and one or two days off per week. The act of manumission, granting slaves their freedom, was outlawed in Georgia, so while they were not legally free, Roy treated them more like employees. These men and women were good souls, certainly not property.

Buck and Abigail were well aware of how Roy and Helen dealt with their slaves, and Roy was glad to see that they continued to treat the slaves in the business and household kindheartedly.

Jeremy received his degree from the University of Georgia in December. The law firm where he had served as an apprentice hired him immediately. A year or two working as a clerk in the Athens firm would hopefully allow him to join the bar association. Once a member of the bar, he could practice anywhere in Georgia.

One aspect of Jeremy's life that trailed the progress of other men his age was dating. All of the students at the University were male, all the attorneys were men, and he had little spare time for social activities. But there was one young woman who worked as a secretary at the law firm that he found particularly appealing. Miss Emma Randolph. She was smart enough to be an attorney and quite attractive; her father was one of Jeremy's favorite professors who taught economics at the University.

The law firm had a strict policy against nepotism, but that didn't stop Jeremy and Emma from having lunch together and sneaking out on a date. When Emma invited him for dinner at her house, her parents gave them a generous amount of space to be alone after dinner. She was a working girl of twenty and beyond the age of being chaperoned at every turn.

They took long walks around Athens, named for the Greek city of culture, and then cuddled on the porch swing at her home. Emma wore her sandy blonde hair curled on top of her head, and her medium build fit nicely into the hollow of the dapperly dressed Jeremy's shoulder. Jeremy introduced Emma to fishing in the nearby Oconee River, and Emma taught Jeremy to play gin rummy.

Emma's older brother worked at the cotton mill on the river. He was married with two children. Her older sister was married with four children. The family got together every Sunday for church and lunch at Grandma's. Jeremy enjoyed the camaraderie of the big family, but he soon realized that if he and Emma were to marry and his career required relocation, she would be quite reluctant to leave her loving, joyful family in this budding community.

That winter, the town of Athens was consumed by an influenza outbreak. Many people became ill, but most survived. Unfortunately for Emma's sister, caring for her sick children left her so weak that she died of pneumonia. Emma's mother was also ill and unable to care for the grandchildren, so the responsibility fell to Emma. She took a leave from the law firm and spent her days teaching lessons to her motherless nieces and nephews and her nights ensuring they were fed and bathed.

Jeremy tried to help Emma in the evenings but became busy with work. One of his cases was a family battle over the estate of a father who had built a successful store in Athens and had died from influenza. The two sons had taken over the business and shut out their mother and sister. The sons claimed that the company barely supported the two of them. The mother claimed that the business was hers, though she had never been involved in the day-to-day operations. Her goal was to employ everyone in the family to provide a good living for all.

The brothers retained a lawyer, and the mother asked Jeremy's firm to represent her and her daughter, Hannah. The attorney who took the case had more important work to do than get bogged down in a domestic dispute and turned the job over to Jeremy.

The biggest challenge of the case was determining the profitability of the family store, which was made more difficult during this period when the town's economy was still struggling to recover from the epidemic. The two sons became hostile, making the task even more complicated. Jeremy's objective was to provide evidence that the store could support all four family members, just as it had when the father was alive. Already apparent was that the two sons were spending money generously on their own families while the mother and Hannah began selling their possessions to buy food.

As they met at the family's two-story brick home to discuss the case, Jeremy was drawn to Hannah, especially her sense of humor, good looks, and beguiling personality. Her amber eyes and dark brown hair made her quick, bright smiles even more flirtatious. He understood that she was putting on the charm, but he couldn't help finding her appealing. He was loyal to Emma, but his commitment was waning. Hannah needed to be rescued from a family splitting apart at the seams, while Emma needed support to rescue four young children in need of a surrogate mother.

Jeremy gave the situation a lot of thought over the next few weeks. Both women seemed bright and responsible. Both appeared to be as interested in him as he was in them. He had known Emma longer, but he wanted the chance to get to know Hannah better. In time, he could see proposing to either one, but he didn't have much time before he hoped to have an opportunity to move back to Macon.

He decided to have a frank discussion with Emma. "I admire the sacrifices you are making taking care of your nephews and nieces, but it comes at the expense of us having time together."

"Are you saying you don't want to see me anymore?" asked Emma with an expression of both sadness and anger.

"I don't know. It's not that I want to break up. It's just that our circumstances have changed so dramatically. Do you see a time that we can get back to what we had?"

Emma sighed. "I just don't know. My mother is getting stronger, and she wants to help. My brother-in-law might remarry, but I don't see that happening anytime soon." Emma was now in tears. "I just didn't think that you were the kind of man who quits when things get bad. Is it another woman?"

The look on Jeremy's face gave him away. Emma responded, "Okay, we are not engaged or anything, and you don't owe me an explanation. Let's just agree to take a break. You are certainly free to explore other relationships." Emma began sobbing. "I can't blame you. My sister's death had nothing to do with you. I just don't know how I'm going to tell my father and family." Emma was hardly able to say the words. "They love you as much as I do."

Jeremy didn't know what to say or do. He wanted to hug Emma and say he was sorry, but that wouldn't be honest. He felt awful, like some kind of bully or heel. He wished he had never initiated this conversation. But then, he had been forthright and honest. He hadn't just moved on without having a conversation.

"Please don't cry, Emma. You are a terrific person for helping your family. But I expect to be moving to Macon as soon as I join the bar, and I know that your loyalty to your family would, or should, prevent you from joining me." He gave her a quick hug and left the house.

Over the following weeks, the relationship between Jeremy and Hannah heated up. Hannah helped him on the case by watching the sales activity at the store and staying in touch with her sisters-in-law to track how they spent their time and money. Jeremy called on Hannah nearly daily to work on the case or to be together to ride horses around town and the surrounding countryside.

Jeremy and his senior attorney won the family dispute in court, restoring the mother as the sole heir of the store. The senior attorney was impressed with how Jeremy's research and investigation convinced the judge that the store could support the entire family and how his coaching of the mother provided persuasive testimony that she alone could bring reconciliation and harmony to the family and business. The attorney nominated Jeremy for the Athens bar, and he was accepted.

One night, as they strolled through the University campus in downtown Athens, Jeremy got down on one knee and asked Hannah to marry him. She accepted. They considered having a quick ceremony, but Hannah's mother wanted a big wedding, and Jeremy wanted to give his family time to attend. Her uncle offered to host the wedding in June at his Milledgeville plantation, where Hannah had spent a few weeks each summer growing up. The house was built for entertaining scores of guests, and her uncle insisted on providing the food and drink.

A few days after they had agreed on their wedding plans, Jeremy received an offer letter from an attorney in Macon asking him to join their firm. It was the same firm his father used for the building business and probably the most prestigious group in Macon. He accepted the offer proudly. Hannah and Jeremy reconsidered their options: get married right away so that they could go to Macon together or take turns traveling to see each other until the wedding.

They agreed to stick with the big wedding plans.

Jeremy said goodbye to the attorneys and staff at the Athens law firm. He stopped by the University to let Emma's father know he was leaving town. Jeremy packed his few possessions in a crate to be shipped to Macon by stagecoach. After a long farewell with Hannah and her family, he rode out of town. Jeremy made overnight stops in Madison and Eatonton, then arrived at the family home in Macon.

The ache of being away from Hannah and all the good memories of life in Athens was soon replaced with the joy of seeing his father, being near Buck and his family, and returning to all he had grown up with in Macon.

Chapter Twelve
1834

The weather turned warmer by the middle of March as Roy prepared to make another journey north. The concerns and doubts of his first trip a year ago faded, and he was now confident and excited about the expedition. Buck was doing well with the business, Jeremy was now a lawyer bound for success, Tim was going to be a father, and Roy had sufficient funds to invest in what might become a prosperous slate mine. While he missed Helen dearly and wished she were by his side, all these activities dulled the emptiness of life without her.

Roy had acquired a smaller wagon that could make better time and three horses that he would bring along to the ranch in addition to the two draft horses pulling the wagon. He had purchased and packed the hammers, chisels, saws, and other masonry tools that Noah told him they would need to begin producing slate tiles. He counted on Noah to bring the black powder, fuses, and other supplies required to blast the rock.

By mid-April, Roy and Samuel arrived at the ranch to a rousing welcome by Tim and Kitch. Noah was at the mine.

"Wow, y'all did a great job taking down all those trees," observed Roy as he looked around the area. "The place is starting to look like a ranch."

"We hauled the logs down to the mill, ready for Samuel and Kitch to produce the lumber we'll need for the new barn," replied Tim. He took a closer look at the horses that made the journey. "And those are fine-looking Quarter Horses you brought. I hope that stallion gets busy soon."

The boys had done a lot of work improving the grounds. More importantly, they each looked healthy and fit. "How has the weather been?" asked Roy.

"A lot colder and rainier than Macon, that's for sure," responded Kitch. "We had some snow back in February."

"And you've eaten well?"

"We had plenty of venison, turkey, and fish," added Tim, "and Jasper Morgan brought us dried fruits and vegetables from the Galloway store every week."

"I brought some seeds so we could start a small garden here soon," said Roy. "Which reminds me. We're going to have to hire some help. Tim, can you ride down to Ellijay and see if Atta can round up some strong men? I couldn't find him when I rode through there."

"I'll go in the morning," replied Tim. "And I talked to Hawk about working this summer, but he can't. His father needs him on their farm."

"And how is Willow?"

"She's great! She'll probably be over soon." Tim intentionally left out mentioning the baby. "Kitch and I started to build a bigger bridge over the river, but a storm knocked it out. We'll need your engineering skills to design something that will last."

"I'm happy to work on that, but I must focus on mining that slate. We need to figure out if it's worth pursuing."

"And you're going to Jeremy's wedding?" asked Tim to confirm the message in his letters.

"Yes. It sounds like it will be a fancy affair! I brought a suit for you."

Roy was about to ask more about Willow when he spotted her crossing the old footbridge. "Oh, my Lord! Look at that!" he exclaimed. Willow was holding a baby in her arms. Roy rushed toward the bridge, and

Tim followed.

Roy kissed Willow on the cheek. "Can I hold her? Or him?"

"Baby Carrie, meet your grandpop!" said Willow as she held out the baby swaddled in a blanket.

Roy gently held her in his arms. "When was she born?"

"Eleven days ago," replied Willow. "So far, so good!"

Roy did the math in his head, confirming that Willow was pregnant when she and Tim married the prior August. "And how are you feeling?"

"Great!" replied Willow. "My mother and Tim have been so helpful."

Roy gently poked the baby's nose. "You and I are going to have some terrific adventures together, Carrie!" He gently caressed her head. "And all that dark hair. Thank goodness you resemble your mama!"

Tim smirked and shook his head, then put his arm around Willow as he admired his father gently swaying with his new granddaughter. "You said in a letter that Jeremy's Hannah came to Macon. Do you like her?"

"Oh, yeah. Hannah is another bright, gorgeous belle like your Willow."

"If I go to Jeremy's wedding in Milledgeville, it will seriously cut down on the time we'll have to get things done around here. I wanted to ask what you thought."

Roy handed the baby back to Willow. "You're thinking about not going?"

Willow interrupted, "We'll see you later. I need to get Carrie out of this cool weather." She headed back to the Madstone house.

Tim responded, "It's just with the baby and all of the projects we have going on, I don't know how we can both go." He began counting on his fingers, "Improving the cabin, building a barn, fencing the pasture, operating the sawmill, and working the mine. There's a lot to do."

Roy recalled the listlessness he had felt in his last months in Macon. That feeling was now long gone. "We will need to get some good help and delegate."

"Do we have enough money for everything?" asked Tim.

"Yes, the company had another good year, but the mine may require me to tap into what I had saved to retire, so we won't have a penny to waste. And as I spend more time at the mine, I want you to focus on getting the ranch up and running. We have enough money to buy a few more horses to build a good herd. I brought some plans for you to start on the barn, and we'll need some corrals. You do that while Samuel and Kitch run the mill, and Noah and I concentrate on the mine." Roy thought for a moment. "Maybe it's best that you don't go to Jeremy's wedding. Your call."

"I'll remain here," said Tim, "though I hate to miss seeing everyone. There's much to do, so let's get moving!"

Tim drove the wagon fifteen miles to Ellijay the next morning. He found Atta at the store and asked him to recruit some able-bodied men. Tim checked into the inn overnight and, the next morning, returned to the cabin with Atta and four other Natives.

Noah and Roy got right to work on the outcrop of slate, a fifteen-minute walk from the cabin. They built a wood scaffold to reach high on the face of rock and used a special masonry hand drill to bore a hole in a seam. Noah carefully filled the hole with a tube of gunpowder and inserted a fuse. They lit the fuse from a safe distance and watched as a large chunk of rock separated from the cliff and fell to the ground. They chiseled the big chunk into pieces small enough to carry and brought them to level ground away from the cliff. The rock was flat on the top and bottom but jagged in width and length.

"I've only done this with the screwdriver and hammer I had," said Noah as he studied the masonry saw, chisel, hammers, and other tools Roy had brought from Macon. "These ought to make things go much quicker!"

Noah scored the seam twice with a chisel, and the stone split in two. "It's a miracle how evenly it splits."

"The art will be getting it down to tile size," responded Roy.

After several hours of cutting and splitting, they produced a few tile-size pieces. "We need to build the kind of hand- or foot-powered machinery they had in Virginia to make this go much quicker," Noah observed. "But I think the color and density look quite good," he added, wiping off one of the pieces with a wet rag.

"I'm impressed," replied Roy. "I like the purple and blue hues, though the tiles do look fragile."

"You want them thin. If the density tests come back okay, we'll be in business!" said Noah.

The next day, Noah left to take the tile samples to the University in Athens. While Noah was gone, Roy and Noah's helpers built a large shelter for working on the stone and assembled a foot-powered table saw Roy had brought from Macon. They also mapped out a wider trail from the mine to the house and a shortcut to the main road.

Tim and his helpers began building the barn as Samuel and Kitch produced the needed lumber at the mill.

WILLOW *and the boys*

The longer days of summer allowed the men to make good progress with their work. Roy, Noah, Samuel, and Kitch slept in the cabin while the hired men slept in tents. They took turns cooking their favorite meals and enjoyed eating together. Tim joined them occasionally but spent most evenings with Willow and her family. After dinner, they hunted and fished. After dusk, they often sat together around a big fire pit that Tim had built. Each group, Cherokee, Black, and white, shared their favorite songs and stories. Life in the mountains.

Roy began preparing for his trip to Jeremy's wedding in Milledgeville. He was ready to ride the two hundred miles alone after they had agreed that Tim would stay at the ranch. Willow, however, began nagging Roy to let her join him.

"I want to meet my new family!" she insisted. "And I've not traveled much outside the Cherokee Territory. Please, let me go with you."

"I can't afford the time it will take to drive you in the wagon," argued Roy. "It will take two or three times longer than riding to Milledgeville."

"Wagon?" exclaimed Willow. "I want to ride horseback!"

"Carrie and Tim will be lost without you. And it's only been a few weeks since you had Carrie."

"I feel fine, and I need a break. My mother wants to watch Carrie, and Tim likes the idea. And my father found a wet nurse among his field hands."

"It doesn't look right, a young woman traveling with a graying old man. There will be nights spent in boardinghouses or tents along the way."

"I'll pay for my own room if it makes you feel better. You're my father-in-law. A trip like this will give us a chance to get to know each other better."

There was no convincing Willow otherwise. Roy agreed to the plan on one condition: that she call him Grandpa.

Hannah and Jeremy's wedding in Milledgeville was a grand affair. Jeremy had reserved rooms for Roy and Willow at the Franklin Hotel, where dignitaries stayed while visiting the state capital. The bride and groom made everyone feel welcome. Hannah fussed over Willow and made an extra effort for Roy to visit with her well-connected uncle. The mansion was decorated with lots of flowers, and music played throughout the home and gardens. Roy felt a little guilty at only buying the alcohol for the reception while Hannah's uncle spent a fortune on food, music, dresses, and decorations.

Roy loved hanging out with Buck and Jeremy for two days, touring the town and catching up on family news. He grinned with pride at how Abigail, Willow, and Hannah bonded like sisters in no time.

When the trip ended, and Roy dropped Willow off at her home, she hugged him and kissed his cheek. "Thank you so much for taking me to the wedding, Grandpa. I knew you were a good man, but now I have even more respect for the way you raised three outstanding sons."

On his return in early July, Roy was anxious to see how Noah was doing at the mine. The geologist turned miner had hired two additional men from an ad he placed at the store in Galloway, and together, they had milled two wagons full of tiles.

Roy drove a wagon of slate to Galloway after the store's supplier agreed to ship the load to his warehouse in Chattanooga and peddle the tiles to his local builders. Roy told the wholesaler that he could keep all the proceeds, hoping the wholesaler would return with new orders.

This first load might not be enough to roof a house, but it was a start in establishing market connections.

Noah kept producing the tiles, hoping for good news. Two weeks later, the wholesaler reported that he stopped taking orders because the demand was so great. If only the supplier's flatboat could haul more than two wagon loads of tiles down the river at a time.

They were now ready to hire the craftsmen. Roy made the week-long journey alone to visit the small shanty town near the mine he had previously toured with Noah in western Virginia. He found the tavern where the men would meet after work. It was a loud, rough place, the kind of establishment the mine owner was unlikely to frequent. Roy sat quietly drinking a beer until he spotted the one Welshman who seemed to connect with all the others.

"Can I buy you a beer?" Roy asked the man. He agreed and introduced himself as Owen.

"I'd like to make you a business proposition, Owen. I need a crew of about six men skilled in mining and finishing slate. You and your friends are just the kind of men I'm looking for. My mine is in the mountains of North Georgia, and we plan to open in the spring."

Owen was fully engaged, and Roy continued. "I can offer you and your crew a good raise and much better working conditions, living accommodations, and weather." Roy provided more details.

"I'm impressed," said the Welshman, "but we just met. How can I trust you?"

Roy pulled several bills out of his pocket. "This should cover your time and expenses to come and check out my operation in Georgia in the next few months. There will be no hard feelings if you don't like what you see. Just let me know."

The Welshman accepted the bills, and Roy gave him a map with directions and his address for exchanging correspondence. The men shook hands.

The next challenge was making good on his promise of good living conditions for the crew of mine workers. When Roy returned home, he visited his neighbors, Jasper and Miriam Morgan. They talked about the success of the past winter's arrangement. The small amount Roy paid Jasper to make runs to the store in Galloway helped sustain the family, but barely. And Jasper's bad leg was not getting better.

"As I mentioned last fall, I have a proposition for you," Roy announced. "I don't think the area around Galloway's store will attract enough people to become the next town between Ellijay and Blairsville. It may be near the river, but it's too far off the main road. Your property, on the other hand, is on both the river and the road. You have an ideal spot to develop town lots. You need a steady monthly income, and I need a place to house a group of men coming to work on my property."

Roy pulled out a map he had drawn of the area. "This is what I have in mind. Between your house and the road, I've drawn thirty single-acre lots that could produce a good bit of income for you. We could build houses on them to rent or sell, or you could sell the unimproved land. Or maybe a combination of each."

Roy let this sink in and continued pointing to the map. "See this two-acre lot here on the river? I want to convince Mr. Galloway to move his store there. He can build a dock for shipping and construct a store facing the main road."

Miriam asked, "Would that land flood in a bad storm?"

"I guess anything's possible, but the land sits high above the river. I don't think there is any more risk of flooding than at my house or yours. Galloway will have to make that decision."

WILLOW *and the boys*

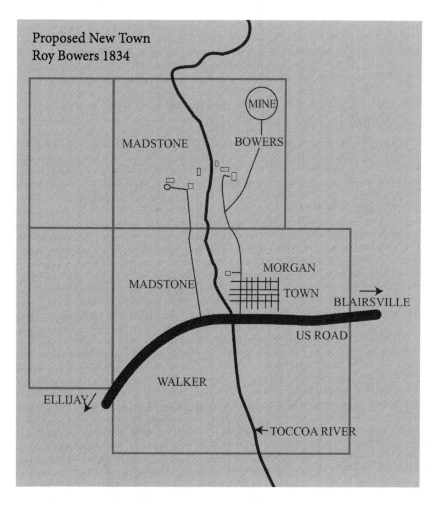

"Do you know how to get all this done?" she continued.

"This all needs to get written up and recorded with the county, and I know a good lawyer who could do it right. Once that's done, I want to buy these three lots and build houses on them immediately. If you give me a good deal, I'll front the legal costs for the whole project."

"Mr. Madstone has offered to buy our property," said Miriam. "It's a stingy offer, so we've held off. Why don't you make us a better offer for the whole lot?"

Roy was taken aback. "I thought you enjoyed living here! Where else would you go? And when this town takes off, you'll be in the middle of everything, making a bucket full of money." Roy could see Miriam was considering the possibilities. Jasper just sat there.

"Mr. Bowers," she said, "I think this is a grand idea. Let's do it!"

Roy returned to the ranch and asked Samuel, Tim, and Noah to meet with him. "I've told you about hiring a crew of men in the spring. They will need a place to live, close enough to walk to work. I just met with the Morgans, and they agreed to subdivide part of their land to start a village that would include lodging for our new employees. I've written to Jeremy, and he says he can take care of the paperwork."

Tim spoke up. "That is a fantastic idea! A village right here! We could call it Bowersville!"

"You're getting ahead of yourself, Tim," replied Roy. "So, the Morgans agreed to sell me three of the lots where we can build two boardinghouses for the mine workers. They will need a place to eat, so we should build a tavern on the other lot. Samuel, do you think we can mill enough lumber for these houses? And, Tim, do you think you have enough men to build them?"

"The lumber for the barn and corrals is just about ready," said Samuel. "Yes, I think we can handle more."

Noah asked, "What about windows, nails, and other building supplies?"

"I'll place that order with Galloway after he agrees to move his store here." Roy pulled out his map and pointed to the large corner lot. "I figure he will like having his store facing the road and an adjacent dock on the river."

"One big issue," inserted Noah. "Don't we need a bridge over the river to make this work?"

"Good point," responded Roy. "We need to put pressure on the county or state to build that bridge, and I think they'll be agreeable once they've seen our plans for a town. But even if we don't get the bridge right away, we can make this village a reality. Horses can cross the river."

Everyone agreed to the plan. Now, they needed to work the plan.

The summer months were busy, and Roy was pleased with the progress. Galloway agreed to buy the lot from Morgan and build a store. The Morgans were delighted because selling just a few acres was more than a third of what Waya Madstone had offered for their entire 160-acre lot. Jeremy was working in Macon on getting the lots surveyed, deeds written, and documents recorded. Samuel and Kitch were busy producing lumber and glad to have new help to do the heavy lifting.

Noah was excited that Galloway's new dock would be much closer to the mine. Tim was relieved that the bridge between the Madstones and Bowers was just high enough for boats to pass—if they were loaded down and the river wasn't high.

One day, Waya Madstone came over to visit Roy. "I understand you bought the Morgan lot out from under me."

Roy couldn't tell if he was mad or just chiding him a bit. "I agreed to buy three acres from the Morgans. And they sold two acres to Galloway to relocate his store."

"Well, they won't be selling to me, but that's okay. I've got all the land I need. And if your village idea works out, land values will increase greatly."

"Sounds as if you like the idea of a town," suggested Roy.

"Sure, I like it! I just bought the lot that lies on the other side of the road from the Morgan lot. The poor guy jumped at my offer. He had no idea he was sitting on the other side of a new town."

"Well, that puts you and the Morgans in business together to promote the town, and competitors in selling lots. That should keep the land prices reasonable. I'm focused on building a couple of boardinghouses in town to clear out the workers camped outside my cabin."

"Maybe Tim and Willow will want to build a house in this new town. It will get them out of my house."

"That would be great! A big house with room for lots of grandchildren!"

Noah Lewis worked every day supervising the extraction and processing of the stone on a relatively small, start-up scale. Roy often came by to help and discuss things with Noah. Roy took regular trips to Galloway's store and to Chattanooga to expand the supply lines and customer base. And he kept abreast of the latest mining technology by subscribing to journals and corresponding with industry engineers.

One builder in Chattanooga told Roy that his slate roofing tiles were good but that there was a much greater demand for larger, thicker flagstone for flooring. He indicated that if Roy's flagstone had the same attractive gray, sand, and purple coloring as the tiles, which they should, he would be a much bigger customer. Roy checked with other builders and found similar feedback. Slate tile roofs had more of a northern appeal, whereas every homeowner in the South wanted fine flagstone floors.

Roy's design for the new barn came from growing up on a farm in

WILLOW *and the boys*

Pleasantburg, recently renamed Greenville, South Carolina, in former Cherokee territory. His father raised horses and taught Roy how a ranch should operate. The new horse barn was an improvement on the barn of his youth, with a dozen stalls, a saddle room, and hay storage. Outside the crimson-stained barn, the team built two pastures enclosed with this new iron wire and a training corral with pine posts and rails. Tim had borrowed two oxen from the mine to remove those tree stumps too large to dig or chop by hand.

Jeremy completed the paperwork for the town lots and arrived at the ranch to get signatures and visit his family. While he was at the county offices to record the documents, he met with the county commission to discuss building a bridge over the river. They were impressed with the need, but there were not sufficient funds to pay for construction. They did agree to fund a work crew to improve the rock bed to facilitate wagon crossings.

The county executive asked Jeremy to meet privately. "We desperately need lawyers in this part of the state. The prospectors are fighting over claims, settlers are arguing over land boundaries, and the state is gearing up to send the Cherokee out west. Much of this will be settled in court, and we don't have enough attorneys to carry the load. You seem to be a fine lawyer, and your family has a stake in bringing peace and prosperity to the area."

The idea was one that Jeremy had been considering for some time. He loved the frontier spirit in North Georgia and saw the opportunity to make a difference. The cool weather and mountain landscape energized him. He could be closer to his father and younger brother. There was one big problem: his wife Hannah loved the city life of Macon.

Jeremy replied to the official, "I agree that there is a great opportunity here, and I find the area quite appealing, but I'm newly married and just months ago joined a law firm where I can gain a lot of experience.

Maybe I can make a move in a few years, but I need to return to Macon."

Roy and Tim were riding one evening after dinner when they spotted a band of soldiers at Madstone's place. They rode over and joined Waya and his family as they stood before four mounted Georgia militiamen.

"I have a deed to this property!" barked Madstone at the leader. "We have no intention of leaving this land."

"These men are telling you to leave your home?" Roy asked Madstone incredulously.

"We are not commanding; we are suggesting," replied the officer. "All of the other Southeastern tribes have already moved west, and it's only a matter of time before the Cherokee are forced to leave Georgia." The officer looked around the property. "I understand you have served in the Army, married a white woman, and put the land to good use. But if I were you, I'd be selling while the getting is good."

"Lieutenant," asked Roy, "do you have orders to harass all Indians, or are you picking on Mr. Madstone for some reason?"

"I don't know who you are, but it's clear that you don't realize how much tension is rising around these parts. My orders are to keep the peace, and trouble is already brewing." The officer stared at Roy for a long moment, then turned his horse and rode away, followed by his men.

"That's the third group in two weeks," said Madstone as he went over to console his wife, who was in tears. Tim dismounted to stand by Willow, who stood shuffling her feet and mumbling curse words.

"I know they will continue to try to force the Cherokee to leave our lands like the other tribes," said Madstone. "But I don't think my rights should be beneath those of the ragtag prospectors and trappers moving into this land. Our tribal leaders are in Washington right now trying to work out a solution that's fair to all."

Tim spoke up. "This isn't right, Pa! What can we do?"

"Forcing people from their homes is wrong," responded Roy, "but I don't have a good solution. I support westward expansion, and, at the same time, I support the rights of Natives. I try to stay out of politics, but this situation requires a compromise to be worked out in either Washington or the state capital in Milledgeville."

"Jackson and Governor Lumpkin don't compromise on anything," said Tim. "They get their power from the plantation owners and the hordes of prospectors that now want free land. The Cherokee are terribly outnumbered."

"I don't know exactly how," replied Roy, "but we need to get more involved."

Over the following weeks, Roy wrote to state and federal lawmakers urging them to visit North Georgia to see the conditions and meet with the Cherokee leaders. Roy met with John Ross, the principal chief of the Cherokee, at their headquarters in New Echota. He asked Jeremy to familiarize himself with the legal issues surrounding the current turmoil to help the family support the cause of the Cherokee.

Being in Macon, once the land of the Creeks, Jeremy found little support for Natives. In contrast to the Cherokee, the Creeks had massacred and kidnapped settlers and sided with the British in the War of 1812, only to be roundly defeated and sent west. But he agreed with Roy and Tim that forcing the Cherokee from their lands, peaceful people who had tried to assimilate, was wrong.

Roy was most concerned for Willow, who walked her father's farm fields every day to monitor the crops and rode bareback around the ranch. She stood in the water catching fish with a spear and shot game with a bow in honor of sport over invention. Roy admired Willow for how she loved the land and wildlife. He respected the fact that she was quite outspoken on the issue of removal, as was Tim.

Would she be included in the government intrusion or get hurt battling the injustice?

Chapter Thirteen
1838

Four years later...

Roy loved being a grandfather to Willow and Tim's children. Carrie was now four years old and full of unbridled vigor. She was getting into everything and talking up a storm. Willow had miscarried twice, so everyone was jubilant when Adam came along the previous year.

Tim had bought two of the acre plots from the Morgans in town and constructed a frame house for his family, designed and funded by Roy from the proceeds of selling Buck's house in Macon. Willow insisted on putting some distance between their lot and the two mine worker bunkhouses; the men could get rowdy at night and wake the children. The walk from their home in town to Roy's cabin and the Madstone's house was a little over a mile or about twenty minutes.

Everyone gathered at the Madstone house on Sunday mornings for Bible study and prayer, followed by lunch. They all pitched in to prepare and clean up the meal because it was too much for Eleanor to do alone. The Madstone home was now operating more like a farmhouse than the big house on a plantation since the Natives that Waya Madstone had employed were gone, rounded up like cattle, and sent west to the Indian Territory in what would become known as the Trail of Tears. The slaves who had worked around the house were now working in the fields.

Waya Madstone was spared from removal, confirming his claim in an Ellijay court against a prosecutor who knew far less about the law than the attorney that Jeremy had referred to Madstone. Willow and Hawk were never challenged because their birth mother was white. The Madstones were some of the very few Natives left in the area.

The mine was operating at total capacity. The Welshmen from Virginia brought a wealth of experience to the operation. They appreciated that Roy was reinvesting most of the profits from slate sales into new technology that reduced much of the hard labor. Roy and Noah had engineered a tram system powered by steam to bring the heavy ore from the base of the pit to the finishing facility. They had also built hand- and foot-powered machines to chop, trim, and drill nail holes in the tiles. The two steps that still required the skill of the Welsh artisans were knowing where to blast and splitting the slate into thin sheets.

Noah sorely missed Atta and his Native friends who had performed much of the hard labor at the mine. After learning that the state had hired a crew of workers to build a bridge over the river on the main road, Noah went to observe the progress. Months later, when the project was completed, he hired the best men to work in the mine and to haul finished goods to warehouses in Blairsville and Ellijay.

Sales of the slate and flagstone were adequate to pay the men well and offer quarterly bonuses. Noah was earning far more than he could make teaching geology at the University. A portion of the mine's profits went to improve worker housing and ensure the company tavern offered good food and drink at reasonable prices.

Jasper Morgan had retired from driving wagons and began running the tavern. In reality, his wife Miriam provided most of the organization and energy to provide their patrons with a clean, fun atmosphere. They purchased a piano for entertainment and built horseshoe pits outside the building. Their core customers were the mine workers, but they also welcomed travelers who stopped for a meal along the road. On Sundays after breakfast, Miriam held a church service and invited the Methodist circuit rider preachers to come when they could.

Tim spent his days at the ranch while Willow tended to the children. He bought and sold Quarter Horses and a few mules and oxen. With the Cherokee gone and more settlers developing their lots in the area, he had little competition and a steady demand for his stock.

Roy now lived in the cabin with Samuel and Kitch. Kitch was only twenty-four but had already learned a hard lesson the previous year.

Kitch had always dreamed of going north to live in freedom. Roy tried to discourage him from going but made it clear that the decision was his. Once Kitch chose to go, Roy gave him a paper that Jeremy helped draft declaring Kitch a freeman. It was not valid under Georgia code, but the law was loosely enforced. Samuel thought the venture was too risky, but his son was determined. The slaves at the Madstone farm quietly suggested that Philadelphia was a good destination and offered advice on finding the Underground Railroad aid stations as he made his way north.

Kitch set off one day with a sack of supplies. He stayed to the rugged Appalachian Mountains terrain through Tennessee, Virginia, and Maryland and then hiked east to Philadelphia. In the weeks it took him to make the journey, he ate fish, rabbit, and squirrel. Once in the city, he felt truly free, unlike many runaway slaves who had rewards posted for their capture and bounty hunters in pursuit.

But in time, Kitch became discouraged. The only work he could find was menial labor for little pay. Food and clothing were expensive, and medical care for free Blacks was nonexistent. The housing was dirty and unsafe. During the cold, harsh winter, he began preparing to return to the Bowers ranch that spring. He may have been free in Pennsylvania, but life with his father and the Bowers in Georgia provided him with contentment and purpose.

Roy often had dinner at his son's house. Willow was an excellent cook, blending recipes from her mother, the slave woman who helped raise her, and Native friends of her father. That evening, she cooked a turkey

Tim had shot, plus fresh corn, beans, and squash that accompanied most summer meals.

"They're building another house down the lane," remarked Tim. "Someone that Galloway hired to help manage the store. It's starting to feel like a real town around here."

"It is," replied Roy. "Pretty soon, we need to find a doctor, a schoolteacher, and a lawman. And then a blacksmith and a barber. And maybe our favorite lawyer might be ready to be a big fish in a big pond."

"I would love to have Hannah and Jeremy here," added Willow. "Having another young woman around here might keep those mine workers from spitting tobacco and piddling anywhere they please."

Roy laughed. "Some of them plan to bring their wives and children here now that they feel secure in their jobs."

"I hear that Galloway plans to close his original store," said Tim. "That's where our mail goes."

"Then it should begin coming here," assured Roy.

"But it goes to the village of Galloway. Can there be two towns called Galloway? Don't you think it's time to name this place and maybe incorporate the town?"

Roy responded, "Jeremy said we need at least a couple hundred citizens plus a mayor and marshal before the state approves things. We're not there yet. But I do like the idea of naming our village something other than Galloway."

"How about Bowerstone?" suggested Willow.

"Clever!" replied Roy. "You've given this some thought! But I'd rather leave my name out of it. If it were up to me, I'd name it Helen."

"That's good, Pa!" exclaimed Tim. "Or how about Blue Mist? Waya says that's what the Cherokee call the mountains here because they have that smokey blue hue."

Roy clapped his hands on his knees and moved away from the table. "I have to head home, and I don't think we'll come up with a final name tonight. Probably the best way to do this is to create a town council. I nominate you two, Waya and Miriam. If the four of you can agree on anything, it's got to be the right choice."

"I nominate you as Mayor!" exclaimed Willow.

"I decline your nomination, but I greatly appreciate dinner. Thank you!" Roy turned to head home. "I'll see y'all tomorrow!"

The Madstones invited Roy to dinner at their home for the second time in a week, which was unusual. He enjoyed the meals and company but felt bad because he couldn't properly reciprocate. The cabin had no China, linens, silver, or glasses of different sizes. He, Samuel, Noah, and Kitch usually ate stew or meat cooked on a spit with beans and coffee, all served in tin bowls and cups.

When Roy arrived at the Madstone house, Eleanor introduced him to her sister, Catherine, who was visiting from Birmingham, Alabama, a town about two hundred miles to the west. She and her husband had a farm there, but he had been killed in a skirmish with some Creeks. Catherine tried to run the farm on her own, but it was too much. She sold the property and now wanted to live near others in a community.

Roy immediately saw what was happening when Eleanor began pointing out her sister's accomplishments in glowing terms to Roy and Roy's to her sister. Catherine was attractive, personable, and independent, all traits he admired in a woman, but the thought of courting a woman at his age terrified Roy. And Roy wasn't eager to be a stepfather to Catherine's three daughters, although they had all married and lived in Tennessee.

Catherine and Roy joked about her sister's matchmaker efforts as they sat alone in the parlor after dinner. It became clear that Catherine was no more interested in getting remarried than Roy. And he found that strangely attractive. She was not some needy widow.

"My sister thinks that I cannot survive without the protection of a man. She forgets that I slayed the savage that killed my husband." Catherine spoke like a warrior but in a cultured tone.

Roy laughed. "She thinks I cannot live without a woman to cook and clean for me."

"Eleanor said that you lost your wife in a tragedy that remains unsolved."

"That is true. Helen was always careful and a darn good buggy driver. They can call it an accident, but the circumstances have never made sense to me."

"It sounds like you miss her very much. I wish I could say the same, but my husband's temper damaged my and our daughters' lives."

"And now you can start over. But why don't you go live with one of your daughters?"

"They have asked me, but I don't want to be a burden. They should raise their own families without my interference."

"So, what are you thinking? What are your plans?"

"I have always enjoyed teaching children. People say that I would make a good schoolteacher."

Roy's wheels were turning. He did not fully understand the shift in his feelings, but he now wanted to learn more about this woman. "Maybe I can show you around our little village sprouting up on the river tomorrow. We may soon be in need of a schoolteacher."

Roy organized the first town council meeting to include someone from the Madstone, Morgan, Galloway, and Bowers families. He asked Tim to represent the Bowers, but Roy also attended this first session to ensure things got off to a good start. Mr. Galloway insisted on leading the meeting, considering himself the most invested citizen in the community. Roy could easily argue, but he let Galloway have his way.

"We are here to voice our concerns about the organization of our town," began Galloway. "I'll get things started. We need more signage to direct travelers where to turn off the main road. And I'd like the town to issue permits so that we can restrict others from selling what we already stock on our shelves."

Everyone groaned, and Roy spoke. "Before we start spending money and restricting things, we need to lay down some basic policies. Who should be on this council? When does it meet? Who will lead the meetings?"

Miriam Morgan spoke next. "I agree that we need a council, and the first order of business should be to hire an expert to lay out the streets. We need a town square with public buildings and spaces. Without some kind of plan, we will keep selling lots to whoever shows up with the money, and soon, we'll have a mess on our hands."

"I agree with Miriam," said Roy. "We need to set aside spaces for a courthouse, a public park, a school, and such. And I'd like to see space set aside for a train station someday. Hopefully, we will soon have enough demand for a stagecoach to come through here, and they could use that space in the meantime to pick up and drop off passengers."

Miriam responded, "If we all agree on a planner, who's going to hire and pay them?"

"That's easy," exclaimed Waya Madstone. "You're the one selling the land, so you pay for it."

"That's not going to happen," Miriam replied. "We're doing this for the good of all, so everyone needs to contribute. But Jasper and I will donate four acres for a town square and public building to get things going. And that's in addition to the many acres we've already contributed for public streets."

A lively discussion of ways to raise revenue followed. Tax by the acre. A poll tax on each adult. An income tax. A tax on sales. Again, Miriam settled the group down and offered a solution. They agreed that each of the four families represented in the room would share the expense of a planner equally. Roy offered to do the search and supervise the work.

Next, the group agreed to form a town council comprised of a representative from each of the four families that would meet monthly at the tavern. The meetings would be open for anyone to attend. Miriam was selected to be the first leader.

"What are we going to call this town?" asked Tim.

"I think we should call it Galloway," yelled Galloway.

"We can't have two towns with the same name," replied Tim.

The meeting erupted with a variety of suggestions for a name.

Miriam, in her booming voice, got everyone to quiet down. "Most of the names I've heard are about your people. I think we should center on our Creator. I say we name the town Glory. Glory, Georgia."

Not everyone was thrilled with Miriam's choice, but no one objected, and it had become clear that there would be no consensus for other suggestions. The group agreed.

Two hours had passed, and everyone was exhausted. The first meeting of the Glory Town Council adjourned.

The meeting got Roy thinking about features he liked in the towns he had visited. The streets were laid out in a grid to fit the landscape, with a courthouse and spacious park at the center. Clean water and sewer systems were crucial but out of sight. Some areas were designated for residences and others for industry. Land needed to be set aside for churches, a cemetery, and a firehouse. Indoor gatherings could be held in the churches, and outdoor events in the park.

Tim told Willow about the meeting and the discussion about their new town. She was excited that their children might have the best of both worlds—a community that met everyday needs, set in the mountains by a river.

Roy shared his thoughts for a town with Catherine as they rode horses in the evenings. Catherine liked the idea of at least three wide streets with medians for trees and benches. She favored a view of the river from downtown, which required careful planning to avoid manmade obstructions. She thought there should be a statue in the park honoring the Cherokee history of the grounds and hoped the business of buying or selling slaves would be prohibited.

Roy enjoyed spending time with Catherine. They talked as they sat on the rocks along the river, hiked trails through the woods, and visited with the Madstones. One night, he invited her to his house for some of Samuel's venison stew. She enjoyed the stories about Samuel's life in Macon and Kitch's adventures in Philadelphia. Roy saw her home to the Madstone's house, and she held his arm tenderly as they walked. At the bottom of the porch steps, they turned to each other to say good night, and Catherine kissed him.

"Wow, that was very nice," exclaimed Roy.

Catherine turned and walked to the front door. She turned back to see Roy standing there watching her. "Sweet dreams!" she said and went inside.

Chapter Fourteen
1838

Weeks later...

Roy and Catherine spent a good bit of effort fixing up the cabin's interior in anticipation of the big day. Jeremy and Hannah were coming with their three-year-old son, Billy. They purchased some linens, pillows, spreads, and curtains to gussy up the rugged, unfinished wood furnishings and make the place more inviting. Samuel and Kitch agreed to sleep in tents during Jeremy's visit.

Jeremy had purchased a carriage with steel springs and plenty of room for luggage. He followed the itinerary Roy had sent him with places to eat, sleep, and care for the horses. The railroad between Macon and Atlanta—formerly named Terminus, then Marthasville—was still under construction, and there were no stagecoaches north to the cabin. So, the only option was to make the nine-day trip in their own carriage.

Roy intended to show off the area to impress Hannah with life in the mountains. He believed Jeremy was ready to move, but Hannah might be holding onto life in the city. She had agreed to visit, so there was hope.

It was pouring rain when Jeremy arrived at the Bowers' ranch. The welcoming committee of Roy, Tim, Willow, and their children stood waving and yelling from the porch. Jeremy carried Billy in his arms under his cloak. As Hannah made her way to the cabin, her shoe came off in the mud. She tried unsuccessfully to reattach the shoe, balancing on one leg, and nearly fell into the mud. Roy ran out, grabbed the shoe, and helped Hannah hobble to the cabin.

Hannah tried to smile as she greeted the group, but she couldn't stop grimacing and gritting her teeth. "I don't know how ya'll do it, making that trip every year. I'm dirty and exhausted, and now my toes are caked in mud." She fluttered her arms and stomped her feet to shake the rain off her coat.

Roy wanted to ask her why she wasn't wearing tall boots but held his tongue. "You're here now, and that's all that matters," he said. "It's terrific to see you! Come on inside and freshen up."

Willow hugged her sister-in-law, "It's great to see you again, Hannah! Welcome!"

Roy gave Jeremy a big mountain hug and took Billy in his arms. "You are going to love your visit here, Billy!"

"Yeah, Billy," said Carrie, "We can go fishing in the river and visit the mine!"

Hannah reached over and removed Billy's coonskin cap that his father had purchased on their journey. "I don't think he needs to be around any mine," said Hannah.

"Oh, it's fun!" replied Carrie. "They blow up rocks and have big oxen."

Willow winced, and Tim changed the subject. "Hannah, let me show you this shower contraption that Pa rigged up on the side of the cabin. We have a tub for baths, or you can take a shower! If you want, Samuel and I can boil up some water for you to try it out."

Hannah looked at Jeremy as if she had just gotten a whiff of manure. "Is their privacy?" asked Jeremy.

"Of course! It's fully enclosed," replied Tim. "There are hot and cold water vats above that sprinkle down like rain. It's quite clever!"

"I think I just need a basin and a couple of towels, thank you," replied Hannah.

WILLOW *and the boys*

Samuel had a meal ready after Jeremy had brought in their luggage and Hannah had freshened up. Jeremy provided highlights of their trip. Then, Willow, Tim, and Roy took turns explaining the details of their new town. Jeremy was fully engaged, while Hannah doted on Billy. She was less than interested in talking about the town and didn't dare ask what was in the stew.

The next day, Roy drove Hannah and his three grandchildren around in the wagon. They had breakfast at Tim's house, visited the mine from a distance, and had lunch at the tavern. They returned to the cabin in the afternoon for Billy to nap and Hannah to relax. Jeremy and Tim spent most of the day reviewing Roy's maps and notes about the town as they walked the area. Jeremy agreed to represent the town when they were ready to send their incorporation plan to the State Assembly, which could be months or years away.

Willow helped her parents host dinner for all the Bowers one night. The children had a lot of fun with the barnyard animals and running through the tall rows of corn. One of the servants was tasked with keeping them safe, but Hannah made frequent trips outside the house to check on her son.

Willow made an extra effort to spend time with Hannah over the next few days. The two moms, each married to Bowers boys, should have had much to talk about, but Willow later warned Tim privately that Hannah did not want to make the trip, was not having a good time, and had no intention of moving to the mountains. The two women held quite different perspectives.

"Is there no doctor nearby?" asked Hannah.

"He's about a three-hour wagon ride away."

"And there's no church here?"

"A preacher comes at least once a month," answered Willow, leaving out the part about holding services in the tavern. "Having a doctor and a church are priorities in our plan to grow the town." Willow looked up and around and smiled. "But don't you love the cool breeze, the sound of the river, and the green mountain views?"

"Those are nice," Hannah responded, "but so far, Billy has told me about this horse that had five legs and tried to ride another horse. He's gotten poison ivy all over his hand. He caught a lizard that he had to show me. And he says he wants to marry Carrie."

Willow laughed. "He's having a good time here!"

"Yeah, but where would he go to school?"

"I'm teaching Carrie along with some of the miners' children. We think my Aunt Catherine will be a wonderful teacher once more families move to town and we build a school."

Hannah just shook her head. "I guess I just miss living in a city where everything is settled."

One night, the three Bowers men sat around the fire pit sipping Madstone whiskey. "Hannah doesn't seem to be enjoying her visit here," remarked Roy.

"It took some convincing for her to make the trip," replied Jeremy. "She can be difficult about things. I told her I was going and taking Billy with me. She didn't like the idea, so she reluctantly agreed to come along. I'm sorry that she doesn't seem to appreciate your frontier hospitality. I certainly do. I'd join you here in a heartbeat if she weren't so dead set against it."

"I guess she has it pretty easy at home," offered Tim.

"Oh yeah. Servants, stores, concerts, and her set of friends. And she thinks this area is full of wild Indians, runaway slaves, and desperate prospectors hiding behind every tree."

"Well, not every tree," quipped Roy. He took another sip. "Maybe you could come up for long visits with Billy. We can certainly use a good lawyer around here. Before long, you'll be a judge, and they're talking about making this a new county. The problem is that we don't yet have a town big enough to be the county seat." He grinned widely. "Maybe that could be Glory someday!"

Jeremy nodded and then winced. "It's just so hard to visit when it takes so long to get here."

"That's why we need a railroad between here and Atlanta," replied Roy.

"If the area keeps growing, that could become a reality," offered Jeremy. "It's quite something how you've got that slate operation up and running so efficiently, Pa."

"The credit goes to you for finding Noah Lewis. He's the one that makes things happen." Roy went to take another sip, but his cup was empty. "I guess it's time to call it a day. You boys have wives to attend."

Jeremy stood. "Speaking of wives, tell me more about you and this Catherine lady we met the other night at the Madstone's house."

Tim added, "Yeah, you two seem to be getting closer every day."

"We're friends," answered Roy. "I like her, and she puts up with me."

"So where is that going?" asked Jeremy. "You two going to live together soon?" Tim and Jeremy were having a good time razzing their old man.

"I don't know where it's going. Catherine is just visiting and could up and leave at any time."

"It doesn't look like she's going anywhere soon," said Tim. "She's been staying at Madstone's a lot longer than what I'd call a visit."

"I'm kind of set in my ways, and she probably is, too. We're friends, good friends."

A few days later, Jeremy and Hannah packed their carriage for the trip back to Macon.

"Sure you can't stay longer?" asked Roy, holding his grandson in his arms. "We've enjoyed having you!"

"And we appreciate all of your hospitality," replied Hannah. "But Jeremy has work, and I have a hundred things to attend back home. We'll see you in Macon."

"I had fun, Grandpa!" remarked Billy as Roy handed him to Jeremy. "Daddy, can't I stay?"

"You have lessons and church, Billy," said Hannah.

"I'll miss you, Billy," expressed Roy with a tug at his heart.

Carrie came up to stand near the carriage and waved. "Bye, Billy. Next time, I hope you can stay at my house longer."

The carriage went down the lane.

Willow remarked, "That's the happiest I've seen Hannah all week. As she's leaving."

"Yeah," said Roy. "Jeremy's got his hands full with that one."

Roy traveled to Macon that November to spend the holidays with Buck's and Jeremy's families. He enjoyed celebrating the last Thursday of November as a day of thanksgiving and prayer, something quickly becoming a popular American tradition. As the days became colder and shorter, Roy spent his time helping at Bowers Builders, visiting the railway and cotton mills to see the latest use of mechanical power, and working with Jeremy on the plan to incorporate the city of Glory.

Samuel Morse introduced the telegraph, and Roy searched for everything that might bring this breakthrough to North Georgia. Implementing the system between cities would take years, but the implications were exciting.

The subject that captured the headlines in all the newspapers, however, was the suffering of the Cherokee, Choctaw, Chickasaw, Creek, and Seminole tribes as they were forced west from their Southeast homelands. They were dying from exposure, disease, and starvation. Unnavigable conditions on the Tennessee River foiled the plan to transport the Cherokee primarily by boat. The winter was the coldest and snowiest on record. And to make matters worse, the federal and state militias shepherding the Natives often treated them harshly.

Back in Macon, Roy was disappointed that the Central of Georgia Railway was again delayed in constructing the line north from Savannah and had no immediate plans to build a bridge over the Ocmulgee River to downtown Macon. His hope of rails north of Macon might take many more years.

After a few weeks in Macon, Roy was getting restless. There was so much to do at the ranch and mine and so little to challenge his energies in Macon without interfering with Buck at the construction company. The banks were lending freely to meet the rising demand for expansion, and Buck had increased the company workforce by fifty percent in the four years he had been in charge.

At their annual company meeting, Buck asked, very gingerly, if there was a way that Roy would consider an orderly transfer of ownership. Buck had arranged for a loan from the state-owned bank to buy the company from Roy. It was a fair offer, and Roy was seriously considering the matter. He would be paid a significant sum upfront but lose his annual distribution of earnings.

Unfortunately, things began to unravel in the next few days. After several years of prosperity, panic swept the national and local economies. Cotton prices on the international markets fell twenty-five percent in one day in February. There was a run on the New York banks, and hundreds of banks around the country soon closed. Timber, land, crop, and livestock prices tumbled after years of speculative increases. People began demanding payment in silver and gold instead of U.S. currency.

Roy remembered the bad economic times following the 1812 War and the panic of 1819. He understood that a recovery could take years, but things would eventually improve. The plans for Buck to buy the business were shelved. Fortunately, the company had a backlog of work to keep the core of its workforce employed, and the Bowers had sufficient reserves to weather the storm. And Roy knew that it was in these times that men of means and little debt expanded their wealth.

Jeremy and Buck would be okay in Macon. It was time for Roy to get back to Glory. Despite the risk of rain, snow, and cold, he packed up his wagon and headed north.

Chapter Fifteen
1842

Four years later...

Roy was leaning against the corral fence watching Willow train a new horse when Jeremy suddenly appeared in a wagon coming up the road toward the cabin.

"What a great surprise!" exclaimed Roy. "What brings you here? I had no idea you were coming!"

Jeremy climbed down and gave his dad a big bear hug. "You didn't visit this winter, so I thought I'd come see how y'all are doing."

Willow came over and greeted her brother-in-law. "It looks like you have a full wagonload. I hope that means you can stay a while."

"Where's Tim?" asked Jeremy.

"He's been grading the roads in town," replied Roy. "We're down to twenty horses, and it keeps him busy."

Young Carrie, now eight, came out from the barn, trailed by her little brother, Adam. "Uncle Jeremy!" screamed Carrie, leaping into his arms. "Look, Adam, it's your Uncle Jeremy!"

Jeremy had to put Carrie down to pick up Adam for a hug. "You're both getting so big!"

Carrie moved about, looking all around the wagon. "Where's Billy?"

"He's home with his mama," replied Jeremy, trying to smile.

They went into the cabin to visit. Roy put on a pot of coffee as they sat at the table.

"You're hobbling a bit, Pa. You feeling okay?"

"Just getting old. It takes a while to get moving in the morning, but I feel fine." Roy pointed toward a bedroom. "I'm fortunate compared to Ol' Samuel. Poor man's so sick that he's having trouble getting out of bed."

They all walked into Samuel's bedroom. He was not only bedridden but also struggling to breathe. He could barely speak or keep his eyes open. After visiting for several minutes, they heard Tim enter the cabin. "Anyone here?" Tim yelled.

Jeremy came out to greet his little brother.

"I was wondering whose wagon was out there!" bellowed Tim as he playfully slugged Jeremy's arm. "It's great to see you! What brings you up here?"

Jeremy's expression turned serious. "Well, now that y'all are here, let me tell you my news. Carrie, could you please take Adam out to the barn?"

Everyone took a chair around the dining table. "I'm sorry I didn't send you any warning, but Hannah and I are separating. I can't live with her any longer. It kills me not to be there for Billy, and I'll continue to fight hard for custody, but I'm considering coming here to live."

Willow, Tim, and Roy glanced at each other. They were not surprised that Hannah had worn him out.

"We're thrilled to hear you're joining us, but sorry about your marriage, Son," said Roy. "I hope Billy can come for long visits and maybe join us when he's old enough to decide."

"Just bring him up here," argued Tim. "No one's gonna take him away."

"I can't kidnap him," replied Jeremy, shaking his head. "I lost the state senate election in Bibb County after Hannah gave the other candidate some personal dirt on me. That was the last straw."

"If there's dirt on you, I'd like to hear it," chided Tim.

Jeremy stared at Tim and took a deep breath. "She claimed I was unfaithful to our marriage." Jeremy looked around the table, knowing they wanted to hear more, but left it at that. "And then the law practice is suffering in this economy, so I decided it was a good time to make a change. If you'll help me get settled, I'm ready to be part of the northern family!"

"Hell, yeah, we'll get you settled right quick!" said Tim. "We have ourselves a new town attorney!"

"Of course, you are welcome here, Jeremy!" exclaimed Roy. "What did Buck say when you told him?"

"He understands completely. He said he would do the same if he were in my shoes. And he'll help me make sure that Billy is okay. Hannah is in our house with no debt, and I'll send her support every month."

"Does Buck think the company will be okay?" Roy followed up.

"Things are slow. They've cut back a lot, but I think he'll be okay. Macon is still suffering from low cotton prices."

"My Daddy is hurting from low corn and grain prices," added Willow. "He's thinking of going back to tobacco. Demand for tobacco and whiskey never seem to suffer."

Just then, Catherine walked through the door carrying a sack of groceries in each hand.

Jeremy looked at his father with wide eyes and a big grin. "Well, I'll be!" He jumped up to greet her. "It is great to see you, Catherine! You remember me?"

"Jeremy, of course! What a surprise! I had no idea you were coming!"

"Looks like he's moving up here to God's country!" exclaimed Roy. "I had no idea either until he pulled up in his wagon."

Catherine put her bags on the counter. "It's wonderful to have you here. I only wish I had bought more food at Galloway's."

"Old man Galloway died last fall," Roy explained to Jeremy. "With his death and the depression, we were afraid the store would go bust. But Jean Galloway is doing just fine. We took over the dock and barge to make things easier for her. And we keep paying their high prices to keep them in business."

"And how about the mine?" asked Jeremy. "Have you had to cut the payroll?"

"Noah had to let a few laborers go," replied Roy, "and we made a deal with those who stayed on. We cut their pay, but we stopped charging rent for the bunkhouses, and they eat in the tavern for free. When the inventory got too high, we cut back to four workdays. On their off days, we provide hunting and fishing equipment, and the tavern buys whatever they bring in. They seem to love the arrangement!"

"We've been eating a lot of turkey and trout around here for the past couple of years," added Tim.

"Pa said you were out grading roads earlier?" Jeremy asked Tim.

"A surveyor staked a bunch of the lots in town, and I've been cutting down trees and chopping up stumps in the roadbeds. We got a steel blade that I attach to a log and drag behind a team. It levels the dirt out really well. Noah said we should patent our invention."

"It sounds like we can propose incorporating the town soon," said Jeremy.

WILLOW *and the boys*

"And we now own the lot across the road from town," said Roy. "Waya sold it for cheap after Willow badgered him for months. That gives us more space for town lots once the economy recovers."

"Father needed the cash for seed this spring," said Willow. "Things are tough."

"Catherine has been teaching in our new school building!" announced Tim.

"I wish Billy could go there," replied Jeremy. "Maybe I could teach the kids this new game called baseball they started playing in Macon." Jeremy looked at Catherine standing behind Roy, her hands massaging his shoulders. "Did I miss something? Are you two getting serious? Did I miss a wedding invitation?"

Roy laughed. "We've both had weddings."

"That's not what I asked," barked Jeremy as if he were interrogating a witness. And then he smiled.

Roy reached up and patted Catherine's hand. "That's the best answer you're going to get, counselor."

Kitch had been sleeping on a cot in Samuel's room since his father became bedridden, so Jeremy moved into Kitch's bedroom in the cabin.

One morning, Kitch told the group that his father was having trouble drinking water. He hadn't eaten anything for days. Catherine checked on Samuel and confirmed that the end was probably near. "He asked for you, Roy."

Roy went into the bedroom and sat on the bed beside Samuel. "How you doing, old friend?"

Samuel had difficulty speaking, and his eyes filled with tears.

"You want me to help you into that fancy shower room we built?" asked Roy in jest. "It will make you feel better."

Samuel smiled, and the words came out slowly. "No ... hurts ... to move."

Roy reached for the glass of water beside the bed. "Well, at least drink some of this."

Samuel took a sip, and Roy leaned his head back down on the pillow. "You... good friend, Boss." Samuel winced and then spoke again. "Need to tell you." Samuel gasped for air. "I..."

"Tell me what, Samuel?"

"Day before ... accident ... I greased the wheels ... Can't remember ... putting pin back ... I may have ..." Samuel sobbed. "I mighta . .. killed ... her." Samuel grimaced in pain, and Roy patted his hand.

The day of the accident had become a distant memory to Roy, but Samuel's words brought back the mystery and pain. Roy sat for several moments with his eyes closed, trying to recount the events of that morning. Samuel had pretty much accused Helen's brother, Norman, of causing the accident. And now, as he's dying, he admits that he may not have reattached the right linchpin? But he's not sure he did or didn't. And he kept that guilt inside for all these years?

Roy's emotions were racing. Disbelief. Closure. Anger. Sympathy. He looked down at Samuel, who had tears streaming down his cheeks. "You have been a great friend, Samuel. I remember the day I brought you to the house. And when your wife died and how you raised Kitch to be a good man like his daddy." Roy took a moment to reflect. "I'm glad you told me about the accident. If you did mix up the pins, I'm sorry you've been carrying that burden all these years. It was an honest mistake because I know how much you loved Helen. If she were sitting here, she would slap your arm and tell you to forget it. She would forgive you, and so do I."

Roy wiped the tears from his cheeks and worked up a smile. He reached again for the glass of water and turned to Samuel. But his body was still. He was breathing, but each breath was fitful and shallow. Roy pulled the covers up to his old friend's chest. "Rest now, Samuel. Just rest."

Two days later, they buried Samuel. His was the first Black grave in the new cemetery in downtown Glory, and Roy made sure he had a fitting stone grave marker from the mine.

The town of Glory began to come alive that summer of 1842. Slate sales began to rise, giving Noah the resources to hire new workers. Tim sold more horses, and Willow nurtured new foals and trained some of the young mares and stallions. Madstone was optimistic that the summer's crop would bring higher prices. He raised the price of his whiskey. Galloway's store was stocking more new items. More travelers on the road stopped at the tavern, and Roy and Tim considered adding some rooms for overnight guests. The Morgans stayed busy running the tavern and showing available lots to prospective new residents.

Kitch decided to stay after his father's death to run the lumber mill. When he had time, he worked at Madstone's distillery to learn that trade. He moved back into Samuel's bedroom at the cabin but dreamed of owning his own home one day. Roy and Catherine discussed getting married, but Catherine insisted they get married in a church, not the tavern's meeting room. Roy began drawing plans and raising the funds to build a church on a lot near the courthouse square.

Roy helped Jeremy build a new house on a town lot where he could practice law in a downstairs office and live comfortably upstairs. As the only attorney in town, he handled various issues—a restraining order for one of the mineworker's wives, closing land sales, and bad debt collections for Galloway's store.

One of Jeremy's cases involved the property that Ezra Walker claimed to own. Ezra had been squatting on Indian land for over fifteen years, and now the people who won the lot in the lottery wanted him off their land. Tim worried how Zeke might react to finding his father gone—if he ever did return. Roy didn't want to see an original pioneer lose his home. Jeremy worked out an arrangement to give Walker three years to vacate his cabin. Ezra signed with an "X."

But Jeremy's real interests were in public policy, and he was ready to get involved.

These were dynamic times in the development of the United States, requiring decisive political leaders. The country was embroiled in the abolition of slavery and Manifest Destiny, the drive to expand U.S. territory to the Pacific coast. Texas had won independence from Mexico in 1836, but the battles over the Southwest were not finished.

Martin Van Buren followed Andrew Jackson as president in 1837 but lost his reelection effort to Virginian William Harrison. When Harrison died thirty-two days after taking office, Vice President John Tyler, also a Virginian, served the balance of the term. The institution of slavery would continue as long as Southerners occupied the White House.

In Milledgeville, there was momentum to move the capital to a more northern site to better serve the bustling new railroad hub of Atlanta and the annexed Cherokee territory. With the recent growth of North Georgia, the state was also considering subdividing Gilmer County to reduce travel time to the nearest county seat.

Jeremy made it a point to network with political officials in Ellijay whenever he needed to appear at the county courthouse. He also tried to connect with state senators and representatives who might help with his hopes to run for state office one day. Those connections could also be helpful to the town of Glory.

Jeremy also joined Tim in looking after their father. At nearly sixty years old, Roy's mind was sound, but years of climbing roof rafters and lifting heavy lumber had taken a toll on his back and legs. Jeremy noticed that when they took their walks, Roy periodically stopped to point out something that required a few moments of rest to discuss. He often found some reason to drive the wagon instead of riding horseback, but he could still shoot a rabbit and throw horseshoes as well as anyone.

Catherine was a considerable help to Roy, though she wasn't much younger. Every summer in past years, she had taken a few weeks to go to Chattanooga and Knoxville to visit her daughters and their families. This year, however, Catherine insisted that they visit her in Glory. She promised a big surprise if they would arrange to visit together. All three planned to arrive the same week in July.

The Bowers and Madstones agreed to sponsor a big Independence Day celebration on the square downtown. Madstone supplied the chickens and pig, Willow cooked gallons of baked beans, Catherine made the slaw, and the Galloways brought a collection of desserts. Everyone knew to bring along their own plates and utensils. Tim provided trail horses for every rider size and skill, and he marked a route in town for foot and riding races for later in the afternoon.

The entire town showed up for the celebration. Owen, the Welsh miner Roy had recruited from Virginia, had developed into an informal chaplain for the miners. Owen agreed to bless the meal once everyone had filled their plates. But before asking everyone to join him in prayer, he spoke in his thick Welsh accent. "Today, we honor America's birthday. This is my new home. I look out and see my neighbors, all of different races, nationalities, genders, and ages. This is a country like nowhere else on Earth."

Everyone clapped, and Owen continued. "And it was one man who had the vision to bring us all together. I want to take this opportunity to thank you, Mr. Roy Bowers."

Everyone stood and applauded. Roy stood and waved, and the applause got even louder. "I thought he was supposed to give the blessing," he said to Catherine, standing at his side.

"Now you need to say something," she replied.

Everyone sat back down except Roy. "Thank you, Owen. Thank you all for being here today to celebrate Independence Day, and many thanks to those who put this event together. You know, I'll take some of the credit for recognizing what this patch of land might become, but it is all of you who make this a community of people who take care of one another. I'm thankful for the hard work you have invested in this town. God willing, this is just the beginning of something very special." Roy paused to make sure he had covered things. "Now, Owen, bless this meal so we all can eat!"

Chapter Sixteen
1842

Catherine's three daughters arrived from Tennessee and settled at the Madstone house. One brought her teenage children without her husband, and the other two brought their husbands without their children.

"So, Mother, what's this big surprise you promised?" asked one daughter as the family met together in the parlor.

Catherine stood and turned to the side, extending her arm. "Well, I want you to meet the man I will marry the day after tomorrow!"

Roy walked into the parlor from the back hallway and stood beside Catherine. After the initial shock of the announcement, Catherine's family cheered and came over to greet Roy. It was all pretty awkward, but Catherine wanted to make an impression. And that she did.

"I guess that went pretty well," observed Roy as he and Catherine later walked outside together.

"You were a major hit!" Catherine replied. "They love you!"

"I think they are all happy that you're happy," said Roy, putting his arm around her waist. "I'll be their new stepfather, and they're just relieved I don't breathe fire and have horns growing out of my head."

Catherine kissed him on the cheek.

The new church was not complete, but it was tidy and safe enough for the family to gather for the wedding. Buck had surprised everyone when he arrived the previous day, and the traveling minister made sure to be in Glory for the big event. Catherine wanted to invite only family and close friends to the wedding, but everyone in town knew that this was Roy's big day.

Catherine had her three daughters by her side, and Roy had his three boys at his side as the minister had them recite their vows. There was no music without a piano, and the service didn't take more than fifteen minutes. Roy drove the wagon from the church with Catherine at his side and a gaggle of his and her grandchildren frolicking on hay bails in the wagon bed. They rode to the Madstone house for the reception. Tim had attached an old sheet across the back of the wagon that read "Just Married".

Instead of buying wedding gifts for each other or taking a fancy honeymoon, Roy and Catherine gave Kitch the money he needed to build a home downtown. Not only did this fulfill a dream that Kitch had spoken of frequently, but it also removed the last boarder in the cabin.

Kitch would be the first Black man to reside in Glory, Georgia. The purchase may not have complied with current Georgia law, but Jeremy made it work, and no one in Glory objected.

As the economy expanded, the mine, store, and tavern hired more staff, which elevated the population of Glory over the requirement. Jeremy now had a petition signed by ninety percent of adult citizens who favored incorporating, minutes of monthly public meetings, and professionally prepared land surveys. He rode to Milledgeville to deliver the documents and speak with the Secretary of State officials. They assured him the General Assembly would approve the new charter when they met in the spring.

Roy decided to have the slate mine fund the cost of materials to build a stately but modest-sized town hall. The other merchants in town agreed to contribute to the cost of furnishings and landscaping, and a team of townspeople agreed to volunteer their labor. A new tax on private property would fund the cost of a part-time mayor, marshal, and public works manager.

There was a steady demand by the townspeople to bring other skilled professionals to town. Volunteers stepped up to recruit their respective special interests. Mrs. Galloway wanted a deputy marshal, Miriam wanted a doctor, Willow wanted a new schoolteacher to allow Catherine to retire, Catherine wanted a full-time minister, and Tim wanted a blacksmith. Jeremy helped the effort by using his contacts at the University of Georgia and running ads in the North Georgia newspapers.

The rush of prospectors seeking their gold fortunes in the Dahlonega area had just about run its course by 1842, and the Bowers slate mine represented a good employment opportunity for those interested in remaining in North Georgia. But competition for workers intensified when copper was discovered in nearby Tennessee, just thirteen miles north of Glory. A fledgling community called Copperhill began growing where the Toccoa River crossed into Tennessee to become the Ocoee River.

The weather in Glory during the winter of 1842-1843 was frigid, with sleet and snow keeping everyone bundled up. A few of the workers at the tavern came down with serious colds accompanied by fever and severe lung congestion. They each recovered after a few days in bed, except for one older woman who died in her sleep. Soon, the mine workers were all getting sick, and one child of a miner died.

Just as it became clear that the sickness was contagious, Roy came down with the same symptoms. Catherine reached out to others, hoping to find some remedy, but no one knew what to do except pray. It seemed that young children and older adults were the most at risk.

Catherine took care of Roy but soon came down with the same dry cough, muscle aches, and chills. They lay together in bed, barely conscious. After two days, Catherine awoke and felt better. She reached for Roy, but he didn't respond. His skin was cold. He wasn't breathing.

Two weeks before his sixtieth birthday and seven months after their wedding, Roy Bowers was gone.

Catherine was too weak to go to town for help. She could barely bring firewood in from the porch or use the outhouse. She did what she could to clean her husband's body and change the sheets. It took another day for anyone to come to the house, but finally, there was a knock at the door.

Catherine opened the front door just a crack and was relieved that Jeremy had come to see how they were doing. She asked him to step back, fearing that vapors from the house might infect him.

"I've already recovered from what's making everyone so sick," responded Jeremy. "How are you and Pa?"

Catherine began sobbing. "Jeremy, I'm so sorry to tell you that your father has passed away. In his sleep. He couldn't fight off this godforsaken sickness."

Jeremy reached for the porch post to steady himself. He had been shocked by the news of other deaths in town, but this was so unexpected.

"Oh, God, no!" muttered Jeremy. He stood quietly, shaking his head and trying to grasp the news. His father was strong and unshakable— but not immortal. "Where is his body?"

"In the bed. I'm not strong enough to move him."

Jeremy pushed through the front door and into the house.

"No, Jeremy, don't go in there. You will get the sickness!" pleaded Catherine.

"I don't care. We can't leave him in the house." Jeremy entered the bedroom and was surprised to find his father's body covered with a sheet on a neatly made bed. He slowly removed the top of the sheet to see his father's face. He wished he hadn't. His jaw had dropped to leave his mouth wide open, his eyes were droopy and half open, and the greenish-blue skin on his face was drawn. Jeremy stood back to collect himself, then pulled the sheet up to wrap it tightly over his father's face.

Catherine stood at the bedroom doorway. "I put on the outfit that he wore when we got married. I didn't know what else to do." She started sobbing again.

"You did fine, Catherine." Jeremy stood at his father's side for several long moments and then turned and grasped Catherine's shoulders. "You did everything you could. Thank you." He led her to a kitchen chair. "Now you rest here, and I'm going to go get some help."

Jeremy rode into town to tell Tim the bad news. Then he went to Kitch's house and Noah's house. Noah was sick in bed, but on hearing the news, asked Jeremy to find Owen at the boarding house. He found Owen, explained what happened, and asked him to recruit some help to dig a grave at the cemetery.

Tim and Willow went to the house to say goodbye to Roy. Jeremy warned Tim not to unwrap the sheet, but he did anyway and had the same unpleasant experience as his brother. They insisted that Willow stay with Catherine and remember her father-in-law as he was the last time she saw him.

Tim met Kitch and Jeremy at the mill and quickly constructed a coffin they carried to the cabin. Willow and Catherine lined the box with blankets and stood reverently as the three men placed the wrapped body in the coffin.

It was now getting dark and beginning to snow as the group gathered to decide what to do next.

"I do not want any kind of service right now," insisted Catherine. "So many people are sick, and those who are not ill should not be exposed to the disease."

Jeremy and Tim agreed. "Then we should bury him immediately, in the dark, to avoid drawing attention," added Jeremy.

"And we will hold a memorial service once the sickness has passed," said Catherine.

"That will give Buck a chance to get to Glory," added Tim.

The men carried the coffin from the house to a wagon Tim had hitched from the barn. Jeremy and Tim led the way to the cemetery with lanterns as Willow and Catherine sat in the wagon, and Kitch drove the team. As they approached town, they saw a glow in the distance. Once they neared the cemetery, they saw about forty men, mostly mineworkers, holding torches as they stood in a semicircle around a freshly dug grave.

The eyes of the tough, rugged miners glistened as the wagon drew near. Owen came forward to help Catherine off the wagon. She was so weak and overcome by the assembly that Willow had to help her stand. As Owen, Jeremy, Tim, and Kitch carried the coffin, four other men held ropes across the grave to slowly lower Roy's body into the ground.

Owen recited some scripture and said a prayer. Then, each of the dozens of men took a shovel full of dirt to fill the grave. When the task was complete, they began singing *Auld Lang Syne*. Their voices rang out into the night sky, and when the last verse was sung, they turned and quietly drifted into the darkness.

Tim and Jeremy thanked Owen and stood together at the foot of the grave to say their last goodbyes. They hugged each other and then Catherine. Willow invited her to stay at their house, but she insisted on returning to the cabin. She wasn't well and preferred to grieve alone.

WILLOW *and the boys*

Kitch drove everyone to their home in the wagon along the streets of Glory—Roy's vision for a new community.

Chapter Seventeen

1852

Ten years later...

The influenza epidemic and the death of Roy Bowers were a dark period in Glory. However, as had always happened, bad times were followed by better days, and the town was again flourishing. The slate mine was expanding rapidly, and with it, the population of both miners and merchants to support them. Downtown Glory now had Baptist and Methodist churches, a hotel, a livery, and multiple shops providing everything from haircuts to medicines and from dry goods to a butcher shop. And there was now a telegraph office in town, powered by wires on poles that ran along the main road.

Jeremy campaigned and easily won election to the State Senate, which met for forty days starting each January. Serving in office left ample time to oversee the staff now working in his law practice. The Georgia Assembly approved the creation of Fannin County, and Glory was named the county seat. Jeremy Bowers was instrumental in getting the bill approved, including naming the new county after James Walker Fannin, a war hero from Georgia.

Tim and Willow, now in their mid-thirties, stayed busy with the ranch operations and raising two teenagers. Tim was still Mayor of Glory and helped Noah at the mine when needed. Willow was frustrated that her son, Adam, did not take his studies seriously. He did, thank goodness, take an interest in horses and was becoming a skilled trainer.

Waya Madstone passed away in 1851 from a heart attack. Willow and Hawk helped their mother, now in her late sixties, manage the farm.

Catherine Bowers' failing health forced her to move to Knoxville to live with her daughter's family. Tim and Kitch used Roy's vacant cabin as storage for the horse farm and lumber mill.

Tim and Willow's daughter, Carrie, was now nineteen and finishing her sophomore year at Wesleyan College in Macon. The liberal arts institution for women, the oldest in the country, was founded in 1836 by the Methodist Church. Carrie lived in the residence hall on the College Street campus and spent a good bit of time at her Uncle Buck's house, located just blocks away. Aunt Abigail was thrilled to have her in town, Tim was impressed that she took classes in economics and geology, and her mother was happy that she was getting exposure to life in a city. But Carrie was itching to return to the mountains and decided not to re-enroll for the fall semester.

Carrie returned home at the semester's end and announced her decision. Willow and Tim were not happy with her news.

"Bowers aren't quitters!" howled Tim. Deep down, he had missed his daughter and was glad she was staying home, but there was also the critical lesson of persistence to impress on her.

"I've done my time in a city, and it makes me miss everything about living here. I don't need Latin and European history to help run the ranch or the mine. And Grandma and Hawk need help with the farm."

"You seemed so happy in Macon," said Willow with a puzzled squint. "This is about a boy, isn't it?"

Carrie hesitated. "Maybe. Partly."

"So, who is he?" asked Tim.

"His name is John. He has a good job at a company in Macon. We met at a school social."

"So you decided to quit school to get away from him?" Tim asked.

"No, I had already decided to come home, and John is looking for a new start. He thinks there's a lot of opportunity up here in North Georgia."

"Are you two pretty serious?" asked Willow. "How long have you known each other?"

"Yes, I think we're serious. We've been dating since last fall."

"So what's next?" asked Tim.

"He plans to come up here for a visit in the next few weeks. He wants to look for a job and see what our town has to offer."

"Where's he going to stay?" asked Willow.

"He has his own money saved up. He can stay at the hotel."

Tim and Willow looked at each other, both slowly shaking their heads. Tim was holding back a smile; Willow was holding back a thousand questions.

As mayor, Tim Bowers answered to the town council that included Jeremy as the town attorney. The two brothers often sparred over taxes and spending in the budget. When Tim asked the council for authority to borrow money to fund the chronic operating deficit, Jeremy rallied the group to turn him down.

Tim invited Jeremy to dinner one night. "Why did my own brother sabotage me on the borrowing? How will the town grow if we don't get the money?"

"I guess you'll have to raise taxes," responded Jeremy.

"You know I can't do that. Businesses in town threaten to leave because our taxes are already too high."

WILLOW *and the boys*

"They are too high!"

"Then what the hell am I supposed to do?"

"Cut spending!" replied Jeremy. "Expenses are the only thing you can truly control."

"Oh, Lord, not that old worn-out song! Cut what, street maintenance, the marshal's office, or support for the school?"

Jeremy took a moment to let his brother calm down. Willow asked Carrie and Adam to help her clear the table to give the brothers space. "Tim, you just have to recognize the limits of what the town can provide. We can't be all things to all people. The town must live within its means. You've got money in the budget for festivals, planting flowers around town, and a huge increase for assisting the needy with food, shelter, and medical care. And now you want to pay interest on new debt? They may all be nice things to do, but . . ."

"So, you would turn your back on people down on their luck? And those festivals bring people to town from all over! And cancel the Independence Day celebration?" Tim hemmed and hawed. "Our father would turn over in his grave."

"There are ways to pay for those things other than raising taxes. When people ask the town to provide something, ask them if they will pay the cost. See if the merchants and wealthier citizens will sponsor things in exchange for the recognition. The mine can sponsor Independence Day. The Galloways can donate the plants for landscaping. Members of the churches have been very generous in requests to help the poor."

"Maybe wealthier people should pay more in taxes."

"Wealth means valuing businesses like the slate mine, which is difficult. Do you know how much you are worth? Do you keep a personal balance sheet? And who's going to check it? The town already gets too many appeals on real property valuations."

"I waived receiving payment for being mayor, plus I work my ass off. I give generously to the church. I do enough."

"You do! You are a good man with a big heart, but the next Mayor may not be so generous or trustworthy. No one resents paying for marshals, roads, and fire equipment, but you budgeted a lot of money for discretionary items. That's where the cuts need to be made. The key is finding a balance and making the tough judgment calls."

Willow was in the kitchen overhearing the brothers argue. When she heard Jeremy's argument, followed by a long silence, she and Carrie returned to the dining room with coffee and cake.

Carrie split her time between helping at the Madstone farm and activities at the Bowers horse ranch. But whether she was weeding between the rows of corn or exercising the horses, her thoughts were centered on John. Was he serious about coming to Glory?

Carrie had met John at the Wesleyan bookstore, where she worked part-time as a student. He was a salesman for a local company that furnished the store with tablets, pencils, and a variety of other supplies for sale to students. John was well-dressed, well-spoken, and quite handsome. Carrie was then eighteen years old; he was twenty-two. There was an attraction from the start.

Their first date was a dance sponsored by Carrie's Alpha Delta Pi sorority at the college. They enjoyed each other's company and started seeing more of each other. John joined Carrie for lunch at Uncle Buck's house one Saturday, and both Uncle Buck and Aunt Abigail later said they liked John.

When Carrie told John that she wasn't returning to Wesleyan after the spring semester, he was pretty disappointed. Then John indicated that he wasn't thrilled with living in Macon either and would like to visit Glory to explore the opportunities there. Carrie was delighted with the idea.

Willow had Carrie do the food shopping for the family at Galloway's store. It seemed they were often out of eggs, and Carrie spoke to Mrs. Galloway about the issue.

"Yeah, my supplier is undependable," she responded.

"Where is your supplier?"

"This side of Ellijay. I think he makes more money selling eggs at his farm stand than selling them to me, so I only get his leftovers."

The conversation got Carrie thinking that she needed to get into the business of raising chickens. The hens and a rooster at the farm barely provided enough eggs and meat for the Madstone and Bowers families. Carrie asked her father and uncle if they knew anything about raising chickens. They didn't but encouraged her to pursue the idea. There was plenty of land, and they loved eating eggs and chicken.

Carrie spent two nights in Ellijay visiting the farmer who supplied the Galloway store. The old guy was easy to talk to and willing to share his experience raising chickens. She bought several hens and a rooster, and he advised her to let the hens lay eggs for several months and then slaughter them for meat.

Back at the farm, Carrie learned a lot about raising chickens in short order. The roosters often crowed at each other but could coexist without fighting if enough hens and space existed. The hens would lay a clutch of eight or so eggs and sit on them for about three weeks. Soon, Carrie had plenty of chicks, and her attention turned to keeping predators away. She asked Tim and her brother Adam to help her build some pens.

"Why do you need fenced pens?" asked Adam. "The chickens won't go anywhere."

"To keep them safe from predators, especially the young chicks. I've seen foxes, raccoons, hawks, and an occasional snake go after the eggs and chicks."

"Why don't you just bring our dog out here?" Adam asked.

"I've brought Sadie here a few times, but she just lies around or wanders off."

"She's not the guardian breed of dog you need," added Tim, remembering how Jax would be more suitable for the task.

"Plus, I must keep the roosters apart and separate the layers from the broilers."

"Broilers?" asked Adam.

"The chickens you raise for a few months and then eat," replied Carrie. "As opposed to the layers that produce more eggs and must be separated from the roosters."

Tim laughed. "You've learned a lot in a few weeks!"

"There's a lot to learn. There are so many techniques and different breeds!"

"And you slaughter them yourself?" Adam asked.

"I can, but I made a deal with the butcher in town who comes and collects the ones ready for slaughter. He also takes the eggs I collect to Galloway's store."

"Do you feed them anything special?" asked Adam.

"They prefer bugs on the ground but will eat just about anything. I've been giving them a lot of corn, but I read where I need to start giving them more wheat and barley, especially the broilers."

Tim looked out over the fields. "Well, you've got a lot of acreage to grow a variety of crops."

"Half the fields have grown wild with shrubs and weeds. Most haven't been plowed since Eduda died," Carrie said, referring to her grandfather, Waya.

"I've got some plow horses if you can find men to do the work," offered Tim.

"I don't know. Right now, I've got my hands full raising chickens and growing enough crops to feed them."

"You going to raise fighting cocks?" asked Adam.

"Hell, no!" replied Carrie, upset at the thought. "Daddy, you're the mayor. Will you please outlaw cock fighting?"

Tim laughed and shook his head. "I'll see what I can do, honey."

Carrie showed the men where she wanted the pens, and the work began.

John arrived in Glory in June. He checked into the hotel near the tavern to reserve a room and clean up after his long journey from Macon. He knocked at the door of the Bowers' house, and Willow answered. They introduced each other, and Willow invited him into the parlor.

"Carrie is out at the farm but might return in an hour or so. Then we're all going to my family's house for dinner. Was Carrie expecting you today?"

"Give or take a day or two, yes. I guess my arrival here has come at a bad time."

"No, it's fine. Let's sit and chat."

Willow asked John about his trip from Macon, his work, his family, and his experience in the Army. She told John about her time growing up on the farm, marrying Tim, and how the town was expanding. Adam came home from working at the ranch and chatted with John for a few minutes. Carrie had apparently decided to stay at the farm until dinner.

Soon, it was time for Willow and Adam to leave. The visit had gone well, so Willow asked John, "Would you like to have dinner with us? You'll get to meet everyone at once."

"I would be honored to join you!" exclaimed John.

They rode a carriage to the Madstone house. John marveled at the scenery along the way. They walked through the front door and entered the parlor. Tim was in the middle of telling a story when he stopped cold and joined the others who stood to meet the dashing stranger. Carrie ran over to John and hugged him. She introduced him to Eleanor, her father, and her brother Hawk.

Eleanor served dinner, and after some pleasant small talk, Tim began his interrogation.

"Tell us about yourself, John," requested Tim. "Things you don't want us to know."

"I was born outside of Gainesville, joined the Army at seventeen, worked in Atlanta for a couple of years, and then moved to Macon to find a better job."

"Sounds like you move around a lot."

"I would like to settle down, but I'm still exploring my options. Macon is too hot, Atlanta is all about the railroads, and the way Carrie described Glory made it sound like paradise. Do you think I'll be able to find a good job here?"

"What are you good at?" Tim asked.

"I'm good around horses from being in the cavalry. I've taken some courses at a business school in Macon to learn finance and accounting. And people tell me I'm a born salesman."

Carrie nodded, impressed. John had not previously mentioned anything about business school.

"You are pretty slick," responded Tim.

"Daddy, be nice!" pleaded Carrie. "Do you know of any jobs at the mine or ranch that John could apply for?"

"Isn't Noah looking for someone to run his office?" asked Willow.

"I don't see any calluses on those hands, so that might be a good match," responded Tim.

Carrie slapped the table and stared at her father. He smiled and stared back at her.

But Tim wasn't finished. "How old are you, John?"

"I'm twenty-two."

"I'm surprised a good-looking boy your age isn't already married," said Tim.

"Well, I've never met anyone as smart and pretty as Carrie before," replied John.

Tim was about to say something when Carrie put her hand over his. "John," she said, "would you like to see our ranch across the river?"

Tim was again about to speak when Willow put her hand over his.

"Anyone else want to join us?" asked Carrie. No one spoke up, and the two went outside to stroll alongside the farm fields, past the distillery, over the footbridge, and to the old cabin. One of the hired hands was closing up the barn across the way.

"Maybe my father will let you stay here," said Carrie as they stood in front of the cabin. "No one lives there anymore."

"It sounds like your father would rather I left town."

"Don't mind him. He likes to needle people." Carrie put her arm through his. "I think you handled yourself very well. Believe it or not, I think my father likes you. And so do I," said Carrie as she turned to John and lightly touched the tip of his nose.

John cupped her face in his hands and kissed her. It wasn't their first kiss, but it was packed with more passion and commitment than any before. Several weeks apart will do that to a kiss

Chapter Eighteen
1852

New Englander Franklin Pierce won the 1852 election to be president of a deeply divided nation. He planned to appease both the North and South by focusing on expansion to the West. However, the country was still split over growing government control in Washington, the abolition of slavery, and the cultural differences between the industrial North and the agricultural South. A Northerner was now in the White House, and states like Georgia threatened to secede if the North continued to bully their way on policy matters.

Just as the nation debated these fiery political issues, Jeremy and Tim discussed their different perspectives on the threat of secession.

"The notion of slavery is barbaric," argued Tim.

"We agree, but your father, brother, and father-in-law were owners. If the welfare of your family depended on slaves, you might feel differently."

"I would never depend on slaves, and I've argued with Buck over this many times."

"And he would say that he's dealing with the economic realities," responded Jeremy.

"There can't be much difference in the cost of owning slaves versus paying a man a wage and letting him support himself. Except one is evil, and one is good."

"My dilemma," stated Jeremy, "is having to choose between the immorality of slavery and loyalty to my home state. I'm against slavery, but I don't think Massachusetts and New York should be bossing Georgians around. It's almost as if they envy how much wealth cotton has created in the South. And if they were serious about seeking compromise, they would offer to compensate owners who freed their slaves. But instead, they're pushing the country towards a war that will ruin our economy and lead to the death of thousands."

"But Georgia won't compromise over abolition if it's left up to the people in Milledgeville. The cotton farmers have too much clout."

"They do have clout but represent a small percent of voters. We need to start changing the hearts of Georgians, but it will take time. It took many decades for the northern states to abolish slavery, and it wasn't that long ago. New Jersey still hasn't made it illegal."

"Only a minority of Georgians own slaves, so how do we do that, change hearts?"

"I plan to start by making my voice heard in the State Senate. I want them to understand that most of us in North Georgia do not support slavery. These rolling hills don't lend themselves to growing cotton. And just as the states in the North are trying to rule over Georgia, South Georgia shouldn't be bullying North Georgia into starting a war over something we don't believe in."

Tim thought for a moment. "If war broke out tomorrow, would you fight for Georgia against the North?"

Jeremy didn't hesitate. "You're damn right I would."

Noah Lewis continued doing a fine job running the mine. He ran the place like an owner because he now was. Roy's Last Will and Testament stated that ownership of the mining company was to be divided equally between Noah, Tim, and Jeremy. Buck owned the building company and family home in Macon. Tim owned the family land in Glory, including the mine, which paid a token amount in rent.

When Tim had first heard Jeremy read the will, he wondered why his father would bequeath the family business to his stepson and not his biological sons, but then he realized the fairness in the decision. Buck had done well to grow the company, while he and Jeremy had never been involved in the operations. And it was Bowers Builders that provided the capital needed to start up the ranch and mine. Jeremy received the least value in the distribution, yet he was the son who had advised his father on estate matters and drafted the will document.

Tim owned the ranch, he and Jeremy controlled the mine, and Jeremy had his law practice. The brothers were doing just fine.

Tim asked Noah to interview John for the open office manager position. "He could be my future son-in-law. I know the dangers of hiring family; sometimes they're a disaster, but sometimes they become the company's most loyal producers. I'm just asking you to talk with him. The decision is yours, and there will be no hard feelings if you don't think he's the right fit."

Noah set up the interview with John, ready to provide Tim with a list of reasons why it wouldn't work—inexperienced, not persuasive, indecisive, too expensive, bad chemistry. But John far exceeded Noah's expectations, and he hired him on the spot.

Jeremy visited the mine every few days and was amazed at the growth. The pit was now over thirty feet deep. Water was drained from the base by a steam-driven pump. Noah had rigged a lift fitted with buckets attached to steel cables to haul the rock from the pit to the finishing plant, powered by a steam engine.

"What do you think about those copper mines opening just over the line in Tennessee?" Jeremy asked Noah on his next visit.

"We haven't lost any workers to them, but hiring is a bit more challenging. I wouldn't be hiring except that we need to go further and further for wood to burn in our engine boilers. Thank goodness Willow lets us cut down trees on her eastern lots, but it's a long haul. What we need is rail service to deliver coal and ship our product."

"I agree," responded Jeremy. "Georgia may be leading the nation in rail miles, but they're missing an opportunity if they don't expand in North Georgia soon. I will make a special effort to make the point with the state legislature." Jeremy looked toward the mine office. "How is John doing? I didn't see him in the office."

"Once a month, he takes a few days to sell our products in Atlanta. He's on the road right now. He's brought us a few new accounts and increased the orders with existing accounts. He's doing great!"

Jeremy nodded and grinned. "Imagine what John could do if he had a train to ride to open new markets!"

Carrie invited John to the house for dinner often. Willow seemed drawn to John because he was well-mannered and helpful around the house. She wished Adam and Tim were as attentive. John and Tim were getting along well, especially when it came to talking about the mine and politics. After weeks of John paying daily hotel charges, Tim suggested that John move into Roy's old cabin, and he assigned one of the horses at the ranch for his use.

Carrie and John saw each other nearly every day. He had been in Glory for three months and often remarked how much he enjoyed life in the mountains. Carrie heard her father praise John for his initiative in traveling to sell slate products in his hometown of Gainesville as well as Atlanta. That kind of praise was hard to come by. Tim invited John to join him and Jeremy on their occasional turkey shoots, something her father seldom offered to others.

One Sunday afternoon, they were out riding, and John brought up the subject that Carrie was waiting to hear. "Carrie, I really like you," he said in a nervous, out-of-character manner. "I mean, I love you. Do you love me?"

"Of course I love you."

"Do you think we should spend even more time together?"

"John, if you're proposing, you can't do it sitting on a horse. You need to look me in the eye. And before you do any of that, you first need to talk to my father." Carrie smiled slyly at John. "But if I had to guess, I think you will be pleased with the response you get from us both."

"Yeehaw!" yelled John as he leaned forward, loosened the reins, and took off in a gallop. He quickly circled back to ride alongside her. "You have made my day, Miss Bowers!"

After dinner one night, John asked Tim for a few minutes to discuss something in private. Tim knew immediately what the boy wanted by the unusual request and the awkwardness of his tone. Tim prepared himself as they went to the parlor. He liked the boy, but no one was good enough for his daughter.

"Sir, I ask your permission to propose marriage to Carrie."

"It's too early, Son. How long have you known each other? Two or three months?"

"If you include our acquaintance in Macon, it's been more like a year. We have spent a lot of time together, and whenever we are apart, I only think about seeing her again. I believe she feels the same way about me."

"You joined the Army, lived in Atlanta and Macon, and only recently came up to Glory. What makes you think you're ready to settle down here?"

"I love this town! I like your family, enjoy my job, and I love your daughter. Why would I leave?"

Tim didn't have to ask how John would protect and support a family. He did a good job and was great with a rifle. Without another challenge, he went to a more threatening tone. "You know that if you don't treat her right, you'll answer to me, right?"

"Yes, sir. I know how much you love your daughter and want to protect her. If I receive your permission, she'll have two men to make sure that she's safe and happy."

Tim burst out laughing. The boy had a way with words. But he couldn't just roll over, so he got serious again. "You going to have a family and raise your children in the church?"

"Yes, sir. Sunday school and church every Sunday. And I told Carrie that we need to get the minister's blessing before getting married."

"So you've already asked her to marry you before talking to me?"

John hesitated. "Well, we kind of discussed the possibility, sir. I think she brought it up."

Tim sat quietly for a moment and then popped out of his chair. "You got my permission, boy!"

John leaped up and extended his arm for a rambunctious handshake. "Thank you, sir! You will not be sorry!"

John went to join the others and gave a big smile and subtle nod to Carrie.

A week later, John and Carrie sat by the fire pit outside the cabin where John now lived.

"Are you okay?" asked Carrie. "You seem a bit quiet tonight."

"I can't hold it in any longer!" John got down on one knee and looked Carrie straight in the eye. "Carrie, I love you. Will you marry me?"

"I love you, too, John. Of course, I will marry you!"

John reached into his pocket, removed a wooden band, and put it on her finger. "I made this myself from cedar. I hope it fits."

Carrie held her hand up to her face. "It's perfect! Thank you, sweetheart!"

They stood together and embraced. John kissed her passionately. "Thank you for helping me turn my life around," he said.

Carrie thought that was a strange thing to say, but in the next second, he wrapped her in his arms and kissed her again. The passion rose, and he led her by the hand into the cabin.

Willow and Tim were still up when Carrie arrived home. She ran to them excitedly, holding out her left hand. "We're getting married! John proposed!"

Willow jumped up from her chair and hugged her daughter. Tim stayed seated. "Yay," he said without much enthusiasm. "It's about time the boy settled down." Then he rose from his chair and hugged Carrie tenderly. "I am glad for you, honey. You deserve to be happy."

"We will have so much fun planning the wedding!" said Willow. "When are you thinking?"

"We talked about this spring."

"That sounds lovely!" replied Willow, reaching to fasten one of the buttons on Carrie's blouse.

"Just be careful between now and then," said Tim. "I think I'll start chaperoning your late nights out."

John spent a lot of his time after work at the Bowers house. Willow perked up when he mentioned plans to travel to Gainesville to talk to slate resellers the following week. She thought that this might be an opportunity to meet John's family. Plus, Willow had heard good things about the town and was anxious to see it herself.

Willow suggested that she and Carrie accompany John on the trip, and he agreed.

Gainesville, Georgia, was established in the early 1800s as a trading post at the intersection of two major Cherokee trails. The village became one of the northernmost settlements in the North Georgia frontier bordering Cherokee Territory. The gold rush that began in 1828 brought a frenzy of prospectors, settlers, and businesses to the area. Though the gold rush ended in the 1840s and a fire destroyed much of the town in 1851, the residents rebuilt the county seat into a bustling town of more than a thousand people.

The trio took a buggy sixteen miles to Ellijay, spent the night in a hotel, and rode to Gainesville the next day. After spending the second night in an inn, they followed John's directions to his parents' home east of town. When they arrived, no one was home, and the small frame house looked as if it had been vacant for some time.

"I told you not to expect anything like your house in Glory," said John, "but I don't know why they're not here."

"Can we check with some neighbors?" asked Carrie.

"I wouldn't know the neighbors anymore, but we can try."

"When was the last time you heard from your parents?" asked Willow.

"It's been months since I've received a letter from my mother."

They stopped at several nearby houses to see if they had any information. The neighbors said they hadn't seen anyone at the home for many months. None of them seemed to recognize John.

Willow wanted to ask how long the neighbors had lived there and if they knew people with John's last name, Roberts, but she didn't want to sound like a detective. It was starting to rain, so they rode back to town, where Willow and Carrie did some shopping while John called on local rock merchants. The next day, they headed home.

"Don't you think that's strange?" Tim asked Willow after hearing the story.

"I'm disappointed I didn't get to meet his parents, but it's been years since he left Gainesville for the Army. You know how boys are about staying in touch with family."

Tim rolled his eyes and shook his head. "Well, I don't like it."

At their next session, Jeremy made a speech on the floor of the State Senate expressing the need to seek compromise over slavery to avoid the risk of armed conflict with the North. The jeering was so loud that he had no opportunity to explain what he meant by compromise or express the views of most North Georgians. The president of the Senate pounded his gavel for order, but the chaos did not end until Jeremy left the chamber.

Jeremy was taunted and threatened by several of his Senate colleagues for the remaining weeks of the session. He did not regret making the speech but was alarmed at the viciousness of the reaction. It was clear that Georgia was now utterly opposed to abolition, even if it meant joining other Southern states to form a new nation.

When the session ended, Jeremy rode from Milledgeville to Macon to see Buck and his family. It had been years since he was last in Macon, and the changes in the town were impressive. The railroad from Savannah to Macon and north to Atlanta and Athens had positioned the city as a hub, with lines in all new directions being planned. With new rail service, sawmills, gristmills, and cotton mills could acquire more efficient equipment and ship their finished products to the port in Savannah. Being in the state's geographic center and an inland port to the Atlantic provided Macon with unlimited growth opportunities.

Bowers Builders was thriving with the demand for grand homes, downtown shops, warehouses, and mills. Cotton farms were expanding, and the trees removed from the fields helped meet the high demand for lumber. The need for construction was so great that Buck had to purchase slaves because he could not find enough white men willing and able to do the work.

Jeremy stayed at the family home where he grew up, now his brother's house. Abigail had a wonderful meal prepared, and Jeremy was able to catch up on the adventures of his nephew and nieces, now all young adults raising families of their own. Following the meal, Buck invited Jeremy to join him in the parlor for cigars and brandy. Jeremy passed on the cigar and asked for a whiskey instead.

"I'm glad to see that you, Abigail, and the children are doing so well," Jeremy said.

"We are," responded Buck, "but I miss Pa and seeing you and Tim. I keep hoping to find the time to visit Glory, but work and family keep me busy. Buck Jr. is in his thirties and doing great, so maybe that opportunity will soon come."

Jeremy updated Buck on Carrie's engagement, the mine, and the town. "I guess you heard about my speech to the State Senate," Jeremy added.

"Oh yeah, I caught a great deal of hell about that, especially since I own slaves." Buck shook his head. "Did you really think anyone would support you?"

"You don't mistreat slaves, separate families, or keep them from learning to read."

"Of course not!" Buck exclaimed. "I hate the concept of slavery, but I can't find men to work, and I can't change how things are in Georgia. Up north and out west, they have hordes of immigrant workers they treat like dogs and then try to tell us here in Georgia how we must live. I don't like it."

"That book, *Uncle Tom's Cabin*, is causing a real firestorm around the country," observed Jeremy. "The issue of slavery is splitting the country in two. Literally. And the North will not let the South walk away to form a new country."

"Those Yankees need to read the Constitution!" declared Buck. "The states have all the power not given to the federal government. It was the states that formed this country as a republic, not a democracy. As Ben Franklin said, democracy is two wolves and a lamb deciding what to eat for lunch. We can't let that Republican mob rule. Every state has two senators, and we elect presidents with an electoral college, not by popular vote. Each state is different and should be governed in a way that is best for their citizens."

The two men sat quietly for a few moments to give Buck a chance to calm down. "If it comes to war, what will you do?" asked Jeremy.

"I'm fifty-five years old. I don't think they will want me wearing a uniform. But I will support my state. I could probably do the most good by building things for the Army. But if it comes to it, I will fight."

"What do you think Pa would do?"

"I think he would feel the same way. Georgia first.

Jeremy slowly shook his head. "Tim asked me that question, and I told him I would fight, too. But now, I'm not sure how I feel. It makes me sick that it has come to this, that our country has become so divided."

"So you made a speech to seek compromise with the North."

"I'm trying to prevent a lot of men from dying," said Jeremy.

"At least you don't have to worry about getting reelected to the State Senate."

"That's not true!" exclaimed Jeremy. "Most of my constituents feel the same way I do. Very, very few own slaves, and they hate the idea of going to war to protect the property of wealthy plantation owners. The same is true in the hills of Tennessee and Alabama."

"Maybe so, but your chances of ever becoming governor have gone up in smoke." Buck put his hands together, quickly spread his fingers, and jerked his hands apart. "You have abandoned your sweet Mama's dream for her middle son."

Jeremy's other objective in visiting Macon was to see his son. Billy would be eighteen years old, and the only way Jeremy knew to find him was to track Hannah down. Since moving to Glory, Jeremy had sent Buck cash to deliver to Hannah at her Macon address. But Hannah left the house they shared some years earlier, and Buck lost contact with her.

Jeremy had lost his custody battle when Hannah convinced the judge of his infidelity. The years away from Billy were hard. Having Billy visit Glory wasn't practical since he was too young to travel alone. He never received a reply from the scores of letters he had addressed to his son.

Jeremy did his own investigation and found that Hannah now lived on a plantation owned by a man who had lost his wife to smallpox. Jeremy visited the house west of Macon but was turned away by the servant at the door. Not to be denied, he sat on the front steps of the house. In about thirty minutes, a man came out and confronted Jeremy.

"What are you still doing here?" asked the well-dressed gentleman about ten years older than Jeremy.

"I'm Jeremy Bowers, and I've come to see my son Billy."

"You have no business being here. Leave now, or I'll have you thrown off my property."

"Does Hannah Bowers live here? Can I talk to her?"

The man motioned to his butler, and three servants came from the house to surround Jeremy.

"Did Hannah tell you we're still legally married?" Jeremy asked.

The man did not appreciate the comment. "Escort this man to the front gate and make sure he rides off!"

The servants did as they were told, and Jeremy offered no resistance. "I guess I'll see you in court, Mr. Kendall."

Jeremy slowly walked his horse toward the gate, escorted by the servants. He kept looking back at the house, hoping Billy or Hannah might come outside or to a window to shout something his way. There was no such response, but Jeremy was confident that he had the right house.

Chapter Nineteen
1853

A few months later...

The wedding took place on a sunny afternoon in April. Carrie asked her Uncle Jeremy to instruct the usher team to seat her family and friends on both sides of the church. They were unable to reach any of John's family or friends, so no guests of the groom were expected.

As Tim stood arm in arm with Carrie at the back of the sanctuary, he whispered in her ear, "Soak this in, sweetheart; all of these people are here for you today and always." Tim began his measured stride on cue from the preacher, knowing he needed to hold Carrie back from cantering toward the altar.

Willow sat in the front pew of the church with tears in her eyes as Tim arrived at the altar, kissed his daughter, and surrendered her to John. He took his seat next to Willow, who gave him a pat on his leg. "Good job, Daddy," she whispered.

John had asked Adam to be his best man, but learning that he should make a speech at the reception, he gladly relinquished the role to Jeremy. Adam, Noah, and Kitch served as groomsmen, and Carrie asked three girlfriends from town to be her bridesmaids. The ceremony went without a hitch, and the crowd of about two hundred walked to the fellowship hall for finger sandwiches, sweet tea, and wedding cake.

Willow circulated throughout the reception to greet everyone and thank them for coming. She noticed one man standing to the side on his own. He was dressed nicely and had a long but neatly trimmed beard. She asked Tim if he recognized him, which he didn't, so she walked over to say hello.

WILLOW *and the boys*

The man smiled brightly when she approached. "You don't recognize me, do you, Willow?"

Willow closely studied his face. "Forgive me, but I don't believe I do."

The man extended his hand. "I'm Zeke Walker."

"Zeke!" Willow almost screamed, shaking her arms and beaming from ear to ear. Her childhood friend and first kiss by a boy had returned! "What a great surprise to see you! Oh, my lord!" She turned and looked for Tim, but he was occupied. "It is so nice of you to come today! Where do you live now?"

"My home is in Atlanta. I have a butcher shop there."

"How wonderful! How did you hear about Carrie's wedding?"

"Well, besides selling meats, I import and sell wine. A customer by the name of Bowers ordered two cases of champagne to be shipped to a town at the intersection of the Toccoa River and the road to Ellijay, and I thought it must be you. So, I brought the cases up myself."

"Oh my! Tim will get such a kick out of this! You must come to our house after the reception!"

Zeke looked around, scanning the room. "No, I just came to see you. Carrie is such a beautiful young woman! She seems to have your features and spunky personality. And what a sight to see this new town that has popped out of my old hunting grounds!"

Willow sensed that Zeke might be harboring some old feelings and did not persist. "Do you have a family back in Atlanta?"

"Yes. The children are now off on their own. My wife and son help run our store."

"Please come to the house later. We have so much to catch up on."

"No, I don't know a soul here and don't want to distract you from your guests. Now that I know you and Tim are doing so well, I'm going to go check into the hotel and get ready for the long ride home in the morning."

"Well, at least come meet Carrie!"

Zeke winced and then looked down. "No, I really don't have time. I'm just going to sneak away. But tell me, how long have you known John?"

That came out of nowhere, thought Willow. "It's been several months. Carrie met him at college in Macon, and they seem to genuinely love each other."

Zeke hesitated before replying, "It was so great to see you again!"

"I wish you wouldn't rush off! Promise that you will return to Glory soon so we can get together. We need to toast the reunion of our Unalii trio! I'll order the wine if you promise to deliver it!"

Zeke smiled and patted Willow's shoulder. Then he turned and left the hall.

Tim wasn't about to let his only daughter get married without a real celebration, so he invited the wedding party and some close friends to his house for the after-party, where they served champagne, whiskey, and barbeque in abundance.

Tim got everyone's attention to toast his new son-in-law. "Son, let me tell you what I've learned in twenty years of being married to your wife's mother. Whenever you're wrong, admit it. Whenever you're right, keep your dadgum mouth shut!"

Jeremy followed up. "John, I also want to offer some advice on your marriage."

"Maybe you're the wrong guy for that," bellowed Tim.

"Maybe I am," replied Jeremy. "But I want John to appreciate what he's getting into." He walked over and put his arm around his niece.

"This woman rides, fishes, and shoots with the best of us. She is part farmer and part rancher during the day, and then prepares a wonderful meal and plays the piano by candlelight. She is a force, and you are one lucky man, John."

There was quiet for a few moments until Tim raised his glass. "Here's to Carrie and John! May you grow old together and bear many children!"

After a while, Carrie and John said their goodbyes and left to stay at the Madstone house. But the party continued for hours.

Ten days after the wedding, Willow received a letter from Zeke Walker. He gushed about how wonderful it was to see her again and the development of Glory. He suggested they meet in Atlanta if she had other business there or in Canton, Georgia, which was halfway for them both. Zeke had some important information to share with her and hoped they could meet at her first opportunity.

Willow thought the request was odd. Why couldn't he provide more information in the letter? And why wasn't Tim invited?

Willow discussed the letter with Tim, who had already thought it odd that Zeke didn't come to the house after the wedding reception. "But it is kind of intriguing that he wants to meet," responded Tim. "Why don't we both go to Canton and see what he has to say?"

Willow agreed and wrote back to Zeke, agreeing to meet the following week. Canton was a fifty-mile trek on horseback.

They checked into a hotel in Canton and met for dinner at a tavern. The first few minutes were full of joyful greetings and stories between old friends, but Tim was anxious to hear what Zeke had written that was so important.

"Okay," Zeke started, "let me get right to the point. I know Carrie's new husband, but I know him as Robert Sawyer. He's not who he says he is, and I thought it was important for you to know."

Tim sat back in his seat with a heavy sigh. Willow winced and rubbed her neck.

Zeke continued, "As I told Willow, I have a butcher shop in Atlanta. More than five years ago, this young man named Robert Sawyer applied for a position I was hiring for the shop."

"And you're sure this Robert Sawyer and our John Roberts are the same man?" asked Willow.

"I am positive. And that's why I acted so rudely at the reception. I didn't want him to see me. When I first realized it was him, I ducked out of the church and hung around until I could find one of you alone. I didn't want to ruin the day, but I felt compelled to tell you what I knew. And it's why I didn't want to meet with you again in Glory and take a chance of him spotting me."

Willow and Tim sat listening intently, and Zeke continued. "So, Robert, or John, made a good impression, and I hired him. He was good with customers and a hard worker, but I began to think there was something off about the boy. It was months later that the marshal came to my shop and arrested him. A machine shop owner in Atlanta had accused him of stealing, and they took him away."

"Was he stealing from you?" asked Tim.

"Not that I knew off, but I stayed up with his case. I even thought about helping him until I learned more about his background." Zeke took a deep breath. "Here's the awful part. I'm glad you're sitting down. Sawyer was married to the shop owner's daughter and stole cash by not recording sales when no one was looking."

"Oh Lord," moaned Willow. "He was married before?"

"Goddamn!" Tim exclaimed in an angry, muted voice.

"He sure deceived us," Willow said. "He even took Carrie and me to meet his parents in Gainesville, though we never did find them. Do you know anything about his parents?"

"I think he told me they died of cholera years ago." Zeke changed the subject. "How old is Carrie?"

"She turned nineteen recently," replied Willow.

"Has John told you how old he is?"

"He said he was twenty-two," replied Tim.

"That can't be," declared Zeke. "He was at least twenty-two or twenty-three when I hired him, and that was five years ago."

"What a liar!" exclaimed Tim. "He is such a fraud!"

Willow just shook her head. "Carrie met him in Macon. How did he get down there?"

"He was convicted of theft and spent at least a couple years in prison in Atlanta. After that, I lost track of him."

"Do you think he's after our money?" Tim asked Willow.

"Carrie made it sound like their meeting at the college was completely random," replied Willow.

"But he does handle cash at the mine," said Tim, "and that worries me."

Zeke injected, "The boy talks to anyone and charms almost everyone, but he has an evil side. It would be best if you were very careful in dealing with him. I've never seen him get violent, but he's young and strong."

"Do you think the marshal in Atlanta can help us get rid of him?" asked Tim.

"He did his time in prison and divorced that other woman. I imagine that the Atlanta marshal is done with him. Have you noticed anything missing or unusual about him?"

"Not really," said Tim after thinking for a moment. "He's been a decent fellow so far, wouldn't you say, Willow?"

"Yes. He seems good to Carrie."

"Maybe he's changed, or maybe he's just waiting for an opportunity, I don't know," said Zeke. "I just knew I had to tell you all of this. And I'm sorry it's happening to such great people."

"We are grateful that you did tell us, Zeke," said Willow. "What a blessing that we reconnected after all these years, even if it did involve this terrible news."

"Rest assured that that boy is gonna face justice if he tries to hurt Carrie or our family," added Tim. "Do you want to be part of the firing squad?" Tim asked Zeke, trying to lighten the dark mood of the meeting. "I know one thing. When this is over, you have got to come up to Glory to let us thank you for being such a good friend."

"That would be wonderful!" said Zeke. He pushed away from the table. "Well, it was a long journey today and has been an exhausting evening for us all. I think I'm going to turn in. Want to meet for breakfast?"

"I'm going to visit some local customers of the mine in the morning," Tim responded.

"I'll be here for breakfast," said Willow. "Seven o'clock?"

"I look forward to it!"

"Before I turn in," said Tim, "I'm going to settle for dinner and your lodging. We really appreciate you, Zeke."

Zeke nodded with gratitude as he and Tim shook hands.

Willow gave Zeke a hug. "The Unalii strike again! Thank you, Zeke."

The next morning, Zeke and Willow met for breakfast.

"Well, that was a fun dinner conversation last night," Willow said in jest.

"I still feel bad about burdening you with all of that," replied Zeke.

"You did us a great favor, and we are grateful!"

"I also feel bad about how we parted all those years ago. What's it been, twenty years?"

"Yes, I guess," replied Willow. "But we've all had such good lives. No sense in fretting about something so long ago."

"Last night, you said that Carrie was nineteen. I left for the Army about twenty years ago."

Willow quickly understood where this was going. "Are you thinking that Carrie might be your daughter?"

Zeke raised his shoulders, pursed his lips, and slowly nodded.

"Zeke, Carrie is Tim's child. Trust me. I know we knitted the needle a couple of times that summer before you left, but that ended before Tim and I got serious. I know it sounds like I'm some loose woman, but I was young and naive. I remember being very open with you about wanting to go with Tim, hoping we could still stay friends. That was very hard for me to say, and I know you were upset because you soon ran off and joined the Army."

"So, you and Tim were knitting the needle, as you say, at the same time as you and me?"

Willow wanted to run from the room, but Zeke was such a good friend, and she wanted to keep it that way. "No, Zeke," replied Willow in a stern but civil tone. "Of course not. Just believe me when I tell you that Carrie is Tim's daughter."

"I know it's best for us all if I accept what you're saying. But there's something else I need you to know. I never stopped caring for you, Willow. And to see what a wonderful mother and wife you have become doesn't help me shake the memories."

Willow's anxiety turned to sympathy. "I have fond memories of you, too, Zeke. But you must get over this, or we can't be around each other again. My relationship with Tim is all I could ask for, and now we have this crisis with our daughter to work through together."

There were a few moments of silence. Willow reached over and patted the table near Zeke's hand. "Now, tell me more about your children."

On the train ride home, Willow and Tim discussed what to do next about John.

"I don't think there's much we can do unless we catch John, or Robert, or whatever his name is, doing something stupid," suggested Tim.

"We must tell Carrie," said Willow, "but it will break her heart!"

"Or make sense of strange things he has said or done that only she knows."

"But will she believe us?" asked Willow. "Do we confront him?"

"Confront a born liar? A con man? No, at least not right away," replied Tim. "We need to set him up. If he likes to lie and steal, we need to give him that opportunity."

"You have something in mind?" asked Willow.

"No, but I'll come up with some kind of trap."

Jeremy was shocked to hear the stories about John. "Is this Zeke fellow trustworthy? Is he sure John is the Robert Sawyer he knows?"

"I've known Zeke since I came here with Pa," replied Tim. "I believe him. And I've had a sneaky suspicion about John all along. He's just a little too fancy."

"So, what do you have in mind?" asked Jeremy.

"I talked to Noah about all this," replied Tim, "but he says he hasn't seen anything unusual about John at the mine. But then he's had no reason not to trust him or watch him closely. So, here's my plan. Let's get someone we can trust to order a wagon full of flagstone and pay in cash. We'll see what ends up on the books."

"And if everything goes through the books okay, what do we do with a wagon full of stone?" asked Jeremy.

"We'll return it to the mine at night, and you get your money back."

"My money?" questioned Jeremy.

"Yeah. I was hoping you could arrange this. I would foul it up."

Jeremy just rolled his eyes. "And do we try this more than once if necessary?"

"If we have to. At least give it two or three tries."

"Okay," replied Jeremy. "I'll talk to the sheriff so he knows what we're doing."

Chapter Twenty
1853

Jeremy had a client who lived on a subsistence farm a few miles outside Glory. He had represented the man in purchasing his property three years earlier, and the guy never paid him his fee. The man was educated and had a nice family, but he kept apologizing for not having the cash to pay. Jeremy rode out to see if the man was willing to perform a simple task in exchange for having his debt forgiven.

"I want you to go to the mine and order a wagon load of flagstone," began Jeremy. "It's important that you talk to a man named John." Jeremy described John in detail. "He's going to give you a price and ask for fifty percent down, with the rest payable on delivery. This should cover the deposit." Jeremy handed the man a wad of bills. "Now, here's what's important. If it's just you and John, pay him the deposit. If he asks if you want a receipt, say no. If John isn't there to take your order, or if there is anyone else in the office within earshot, leave and tell them you'll be back with the money."

"You're giving me the money to get a wagon full of stone?" asked the man. "What's the catch?"

"You don't get to keep the flagstone; I do."

"So why get me involved?"

"It's complicated. John, and only John, must write up the order and take the cash. Otherwise, you'll need to go back. And no matter what happens, I need you to stop by my office and tell me exactly what was said."

"I don't know. This is all very strange. Are you asking me to do something illegal?"

"Absolutely not. You're just acting as my agent, so they won't know it's me who is really buying the stone."

The man shrugged. "Okay. When do you want me to do this?"

"Can you do it Thursday morning, about eleven o'clock?"

"Yeah, I can do that."

Jeremy thanked the man and said farewell. As he mounted his horse, he looked back at the farmer standing in his doorway, looking perplexed as he counted the stack of bills in his hand.

Jeremy informed Noah that the sting was set up for Thursday morning. Noah's job was to ensure that John was alone in the office at that time.

The farmer entered the mine office on Thursday morning as instructed. The man Jeremy had described as John was alone at the office counter.

"What will you use the flagstone for?" asked John.

"To pave my porch floor."

"If you're doing this work by yourself, will you need pieces light enough for one man to lift?"

"My wife can help me," answered the farmer.

"And where do you want this delivered?"

The farmer began to give John directions to his place, but in the middle of doing so, he realized that he was about to give this man he had never met the address where his family lived. He was never comfortable with his role in performing this stunt and began to tremble.

"Are you all right?" asked John. "Come sit over here and take some deep breaths."

"No, I'm okay. I just don't think I can place the order today."

"Okay, that's fine," said John. "Come back when you're ready, and we'll finish the process."

John watched as the man hurried out of the office and later relayed the strange encounter to Noah. The farmer went to Jeremy's office to report how things went.

"I don't give strangers directions to my home," said the farmer.

Jeremy was disappointed but thought it was worth another try. "There is no risk to your family. Can you go back in a day or two?"

"No. Here's your money back, and I scraped together five dollars to put against my debt to you. I don't want anything to do with this."

Jeremy met with Tim and Willow that night for dinner at the tavern. He explained the whole failed attempt.

"Do we know someone else we can get to place an order?" asked Tim.

"I don't think it's a good idea," replied Jeremy. "There are too many things that can go wrong."

"I think we should just confront him head-on," said Willow.

"You know he's just going to lie and deny everything," replied Tim.

"Maybe so, but we're not trying to lock the guy up," Jeremy responded. "We simply want him out of Carrie's life."

"It would be great to have Zeke here to confront him," said Tim. "Do you think he would do that?"

"I can write him," said Willow. "It's a lot to ask."

"Either way, we need to get this done before something happens. He may already be stealing the mine blind."

"Noah told me he's started numbering all the sales tickets and accounting for each one," added Jeremy. "And he's reviewing all orders."

"That will only make John more suspicious," suggested Willow. "We need to confront him as soon as I hear back from Zeke."

Zeke agreed to make the long journey to Glory again, and Willow offered to have him stay at their house in town. When Zeke arrived, Willow arranged for Jeremy to join them, and Tim asked John to stop by the house after work to discuss mine business. Willow didn't want Carrie to be there because she still hoped that this was all some big mistake that they could iron out with John alone.

John couldn't hide his look of bewilderment when he arrived at the house and first saw Zeke.

"I believe you know our friend Zeke," said Tim.

Everyone was anxious to see how John would react. After recovering from the initial surprise, he reluctantly accepted Zeke's extended hand in a greeting. "Yes, I remember working at his shop in Atlanta." John looked nervously around the room to see if there were any other bombshells. "But how do y'all know him?"

"We grew up together," replied Willow. "Zeke's family was among the original settlers here in Glory."

Everyone sat around the dining room table, and Jeremy got things started. "John, we wanted to talk tonight because we've learned some things about you that really concern us. We don't think you've been completely honest about your background and want to clarify things."

WILLOW *and the boys*

"First, I'd like to know," began Willow, "where are your parents? You took Carrie and me on a trip to Gainesville to meet them, but we never did. So, what's the story?"

John had his hands on his knees, looking down at the floor as if to buy some time. "I took you to the house where I grew up, but I knew they wouldn't be there. I'm sorry about that." John looked out and took a deep breath. "I was quite impressed when I met you and Mr. Bowers and saw how you lived. I didn't want you to know that my parents were nothing but trash. My father was a drunk. My mother took me away from that house in Augusta when I was young, and we moved to Gainesville. She became a prostitute, but at least we had food to eat, and the beatings stopped. As soon as I could, I joined the Army."

"I'm sorry that you had a bad childhood," replied Willow, "but you could have just told us the truth or said you didn't want to talk about it. To take us on some trip to nowhere was plain wicked. What makes you lie like that? Why should we believe anything you say?"

Before he could answer, Tim hit John with another question. "Have you been married before?"

John looked shocked. He glanced at Zeke with a sneer. "Yes, I was married. I had just gotten out of the Army, met this girl, and we got married. It turned out to be a big mistake. She and her family were not good people."

"And this girl's family owned a shop?" asked Jeremy.

"Yes, and I worked there."

"And did you ever steal money from the business?"

"It's not stealing if you own the business."

"But you didn't own the business, did you?" Jeremy followed up.

"The old man didn't pay me enough for us to live on. I just settled the score."

"But you were convicted for stealing and spent time in prison, didn't you?" continued Jeremy.

John grinned and slowly shook his head as he turned to Zeke. "Happy, old man?" he asked with contempt. "You're a goddamn snitch."

"And you are a goddamn liar!" yelled Tim even louder.

The room went quiet.

"How old are you, John?" asked Jeremy.

"I'm twenty-eight."

"Why did you tell Carrie you were twenty-two?"

"Does it really matter?"

"Did you take classes at a business school in Macon, as you told Carrie and her parents?" Jeremy was in full attorney mode.

"I'm not answering any more of your questions," replied John, breathing hard and fast.

"Is your name really John Roberts?" asked Jeremy.

There was no response. John rubbed his face and neck with his hands and took a moment to collect himself. "Look, I've done many stupid things in my life, but I was trying to start over after getting out of prison. I got a job at that company in Macon and took some classes at the business school. And then I happened to meet Carrie, and she invited me to this town that her family practically built. I realized that I could start a new life here!"

"Should we just accept your word that you haven't been stealing money from the mine?" asked Tim.

"I told you, I wanted to start fresh. Why would I steal anything? You have all been very good to me."

"One thing's for sure. You are a good talker," said Tim. He stood in place. "And now you're trying to turn this bloody mess into you being the victim." Tim took a deep breath. "I know people can change. But here's the thing. I don't think I could ever trust you again. You could have told us the truth from the start. But instead, you lied or at least failed to tell us things that were mighty important for us to know. Now we hear it all from an old friend who just happened to attend your wedding!"

Zeke had been quiet the entire time. His mere presence had served the purpose, but he spoke now. "Have you been more honest with Carrie? Does she know more about your past than you've told Willow and Tim?"

"I think she would say I've been a good husband."

"You're not answering the question!" shouted Tim. "Does she know any of this?"

John put his head down. "No. I don't think so."

"She is going to hear it all," said Willow. "You can either tell her in our presence or..."

"You can ride your ass out of town tonight, and we'll tell her everything," interrupted Tim.

"I will tell her," said John. "However you want me to handle it. All I want is another chance."

"That is asking a lot, but it's not up to us," said Willow. "It's up to

Carrie. Either way, this is going to break her heart." Willow tried to hold back a sob. "Damn you, John or Robert, or whatever your name is."

Willow became concerned about how John would react to all of this. Would he go home and confess everything to Carrie, or would he wait until he was confronted again by the family? Would he leave town or do something belligerent?

Tim arranged for the family to meet at Jeremy's house the following afternoon. But Willow couldn't wait until the meeting to get a sense of how Carrie was feeling. She found her daughter the next morning at the chicken house gathering eggs.

"So, how is your morning going?" Willow asked.

"Great!" replied Carrie, smiling and in a cheerful mood. "How are you doing? Come for some fresh eggs?"

"I'll take half a dozen if you don't need them for the market." Willow began picking eggs to take home. "Is John okay? Did he mention anything about the meeting last night?"

"He said it was about the mining operations. Nothing unusual."

Willow was disappointed that John had said nothing to Carrie. She should have just waited until the meeting, but curiosity got the best of her. "Does John ever seem a little off, as if he's not happy?"

"He gets tired of me nagging him about being messy, and he can be a bit moody sometimes. But I guess I'm not the easiest person to live with either."

"Do you remember your father and I talking about Zeke, the man who grew up here decades ago?"

"Yes. He sounds like a nice fellow. Why?"

"Well, it turns out he knew John back in Atlanta."

"What a small world! How did that even come up?"

"He came to town yesterday to visit," Willow fibbed.

"And did he say good things about John?"

"Sweetheart, I need to tell you some things, but you can't say anything to John. Can you do that?"

"Mama, you're beginning to scare me. Did Zeke say bad things?"

"Nothing awful, just concerning. We want you and John to come to Jeremy's house as soon as he gets home from the mine. We can discuss everything then."

Carrie stood face to face with her mother. "Mama, what is this all about? Should I go talk to Zeke myself?"

"He left for Atlanta this morning." Willow wrapped her arms around her daughter, careful not to do or say anything that would upset her even more. "We can talk about all of this later this afternoon. Just please don't say anything to John about this conversation."

Carrie stood looking quite perplexed. "Why don't you just tell me what Zeke said? How did you think I would react to saying these things without giving me any details?"

"I'm sorry I have upset you, but we can have a full conversation this afternoon." Willow patted her daughter's arms. "In the meantime, you must take care of your chickens. That one over there looks like she's trying to steal an egg from the other hen."

Willow walked away feeling terrible and knowing the worst was yet to come.

That afternoon, Willow, Tim, Carrie, and John gathered in the conference room at Jeremy's office. Jeremy said that he would join them after dealing with some urgent business.

Tim started the conversation. "John, I believe you have a few things to tell Carrie. Why don't you start with your real name?"

Carrie broke into a look of shock with her eyes and mouth wide open. "Your real name?" she yelled.

John went from fidgeting in his seat to clenching his shoulders and fists. He had prepared to tell his story from the start, not with a part of his past that was hard to explain and that Tim had taken out of order. "Carrie, I've made a lot of mistakes in my life. I want to tell you about them. The most important thing is that I love you, I really do, and even before I met you, I decided to make a clean start. Changing my name was part of my commitment to being a better man."

"So, what is your name?" asked Carrie.

"Robert Sawyer. But hold on. Let me start at the beginning." John started with how he was raised by parents who were not good people. He admitted that the trip to Gainesville to meet his parents was a ruse.

"Oh my lord!" exclaimed Carrie, trying to put the pieces together and then getting angry. "How could you? You lied about your parents and wasted our time and money on a wild goose chase?"

"There's more, honey," said Tim. "Tell her about being married before."

"What?" yelled Carrie. "Is that true?"

"I'm sorry, Carrie," said John sorrowfully. "It was a big mistake, and we're divorced."

"Yeah, divorced after you got out of jail!" said Tim sarcastically.

"Tim!" yelled Willow, "let the man tell his story."

But Tim was fired up. "No, I won't let him try to fast-talk and charm his way out of this. Carrie, the man was convicted of stealing from his wife's family business, and then he spent time in prison."

Carrie started crying, and Willow went to her side. "Tim, you need to settle down!"

"This asshole has caused our daughter a lot of pain. How do you expect me to act?"

A few minutes passed, and Carrie settled down. "So, our meeting at the college store in Macon, that was all a setup?"

"No, no!" exclaimed John. "As I've said, I was committed to starting a new life before I met you. I had worked for that company for many months. Meeting you was completely random."

"You could have told me these things before we got serious. Did you think your past wouldn't catch up with you?"

"That's why I jumped at the chance to live with you here in Glory. It gave me a clean start. And then time passed, and there was never the right time to tell you about all those stupid things I had done."

Carrie sat with her hands tightly clasped above her knees, trying not to scream and run from the room. "What do you expect from me? To just accept all of this, and life goes on as usual? It would have been easier to hear that you're sleeping with another woman." She rubbed the back of her neck.

There were footsteps, and Jeremy entered the room. "You're just in time to join the party!" said Tim. "John here is about to explain to

Carrie how he understands why she's shocked and angry, but if she gives him a chance, he will prove how much he loves her and that he has turned a new leaf."

"Tim!" yelled Willow. "Stop making things worse than they already are!"

Jeremy went over and patted Carrie's back. "Do you want me to stay or go?"

"Please stay," replied Carrie. "I just don't know how to feel. So many lies. So much deceit. And I guess it all comes as such a shock because I never saw any of this evilness in the months we've known each other."

"It might be good to take your time to absorb all of this," said Jeremy.

The room was quiet for many moments.

"I didn't get a chance to say this," said John to Carrie, "but I beg you to give me a chance. I really have changed. You just said you've seen how I've been since we met. If Zeke hadn't brought up all of these things in my past, we would be making dinner right now and planning our future together. If you reject me, I don't think our lives can ever be as good as they would be if you give me a chance to prove how much I love you."

"Nice speech, snake charmer," remarked Tim.

"Tim!" said Jeremy. "Carrie doesn't need your two cents. We need to let these two have some time together. It's nice outside. Let's go sit on the porch."

"What would you do, Uncle Jeremy?" asked Carrie.

"You know I can't answer that," replied Jeremy. "This isn't a trial, but you alone are the jury. Everything depends on what's in your heart. And whatever you decide, I know you'll make it work."

Jeremy stood and walked toward the porch. Tim wasn't following until

WILLOW *and the boys*

Willow pulled him out of his chair and led him outside.

John just sat there in a daze.

"That damn idiot," said Tim as the brothers and Willow sat on the porch. "He's made a total disaster of things now."

Tim patted Willow's hand. "What do you think will come of this?"

"I don't know," replied Willow. "Judging by how John handled things tonight, even with you losing your temper and butting in all the time, I think she may just give him a chance."

"I agree," added Jeremy. "The boy does seem convincingly remorseful."

"He's a snake," said Tim. "I hope she kicks him out. We don't need him around." He sighed and shook his head. "If she does let him hang around, I could never trust him again. And he no longer has a job."

"The boy has faced the consequences," said Jeremy. "He spent time in prison and has now made an enemy of his father-in-law. I don't know which is worse."

"Whatever our daughter decides," added Willow, "you must support her, Tim."

"Yeah, with one eye on the cash drawer."

"Did you notice how Carrie asked her uncle for advice and not you?" observed Willow.

"Yeah, the uncle who defends the guilty in court."

"I heard that," said Jeremy. "I'm sitting right here, you old fart."

That brought some much-needed levity to the group.

"I'm going for a walk," announced Jeremy. "I hope you'll let me know tomorrow what happens."

A few minutes later, the door opened. John walked straight out of the house and down the road.

Carrie soon joined her parents on the porch. "Can I spend the night with you?"

Tim rushed over and hugged Carrie. "You know you can. Anytime you want for as long as you want."

Willow joined in the embrace as they swayed in the cool evening air. "So what happens next?" she asked.

"I asked John to leave, to pack his things and be gone by morning."

Tim and Willow stared at each other.

"In three months, I'd like him to return. We'll have a discussion and take it from there."

"I'm proud of you, honey," said Tim.

"You know we will support you all the way, whatever you eventually decide," said Willow.

They walked home, and Willow prepared some leftovers for dinner.

Tim let out a big yawn and a stretch. "I need to go to bed. I don't think I slept a wink last night."

John left town without a fuss. Carrie moved on without much change to her daily routine. She tried not to think too much about her marriage because the revelation of John's past was just too shocking and humiliating. Why was he not honest about his past? Their courtship was short, and the marriage was still in the honeymoon phase, but some things he did or said should have raised suspicion. How could she have been so blind as not to see his true character? How could she trust any man again?

Chapter Twenty-One

1853

Carrie found that she was content despite John's absence as long as she could stay busy and remain close to her family. But she couldn't help dwelling on what she might say to John when they met in a few weeks.

She once adored his sense of humor and charming ways. But right now, the betrayal overshadowed any love she had once felt. She could forgive his past and give him a chance to prove that he had changed, but the deception of that trip to Gainesville stuck in her claw. Her reaction, if the meeting were today, would be that he stay gone. But she needed more time to consider her options.

On a trip to Galloway's store one day, Carrie found they had no apples for sale. She spoke to Mrs. Galloway, who complained about her supplier. It was the same old problem as the egg shortage months earlier. Carrie had fixed the egg problem and was now determined to attack the apple crisis.

The apple farmer who supplied the store was also in Ellijay, so Carrie made another overnight trip to visit his orchard. But instead of the collaborative, kind ways of the old chicken farmer, the apple farmer was gruff and kept insinuating that she was too young and naive to grow apple trees successfully. She followed him around as he did his business, asking him questions in a way that let him show off his experience and knowledge.

And Carrie soon learned that growing apples was far more complicated than she had imagined. Apple blossoms were both male and female but could not pollinate themselves. Apple seeds do not necessarily produce the variety of apples of their parent. Trees take at least six years to produce fruit and require a certain number of chill hours each winter. There were thousands of apple varieties; some were good for eating off the tree, others for cooking, and the rest for making cider. Did she want to produce sweet cider, hard cider, apple brandy, or vinegar? Were there bees present to pollinate the blossoms? Had she ever grafted a scion to rootstock?

The farmer was impressed that, despite overwhelming her with information, Carrie still followed him around, asking questions. "Look, if you are serious about growing good apples, you should work at an orchard for a few seasons. But I'll give you a little gift for being so persistent. Follow me."

He went to the door of a root cellar dug into a grass-covered hill and ducked inside. Carrie peeked in to see bushels and bushels of apples in cold storage.

The man came out and handed her a cloth bag that was cool and damp. "There should be about six germinated seeds in here," he said. "Plant them in small pots with good soil, and when they sprout, plant them in a field with good sun and drainage about fifteen feet apart. In a few years, you should have some Stayman apples, which are good for eating and cooking."

"You are so generous!" exclaimed Carrie. She held the bag like fragile treasure. "Thank you! I will do as you say and return to let you know how they do!"

The farmer watched as Carrie carefully stored the bag and rode off, then shook his head and smiled. He doubted the pretty girl would ever return, but if she did, he would cut her a little more slack.

Between her new dedication to raising chickens and starting an apple orchard, memories of her failed marriage were fading for Carrie. She received a letter from John pleading for another chance. She replied that she would not be available to meet as they had arranged and that he could expect a visit from Jeremy to sign papers for an annulment of their marriage the next time her uncle was in Atlanta.

Weeks later, when Jeremy had legal business in Atlanta and found an open afternoon, he arranged to meet with John Roberts, or Robert Sawyer, after tracking down where he worked and lived.

"Why should I sign your papers?" John asked Jeremy.

"Because you misrepresented yourself to my niece, and your marriage is over. For starters, you used a false name on your marriage certificate."

"Carrie said we would meet to reconcile. She's the one who lied."

"There is no need to meet. Carrie has made her decision."

"I will sign, but I want alimony."

"Men don't get alimony. It's for women raising children. And this is an annulment, not a divorce."

"I helped the family develop more business for the mine. I found new customers in new towns worth tens of thousands of dollars in sales. Give me two thousand dollars for those services, and I'll sign."

"You were already compensated generously for your service. We will pay you nothing more."

John sat there silently.

"You're not going to sign?" asked Jeremy as he gathered his papers. "Fine. We'll see you in court in Ellijay. I hope you can afford a good attorney because I know the judge there. He does not suffer fools like you."

Jeremy left thinking that he probably could have gotten John to sign the agreement for a hundred dollars or less, but getting the judge to sign the decree would only take an hour of his time.

The man most impacted by John's sudden departure was Noah, now short an office manager and salesman. While he was glad to no longer worry that all sales were recorded properly, he missed how well the boy had managed the office. Tim asked Noah to consider his son Adam for the position. Adam had worked at the mine in different capacities but never impressed Noah as a hard worker. In fact, other employees reported that he often acted like his father owned the place. But there was some chance that Adam could be more effective in the office than working alongside rough-and-tumble miners, so Noah gave him the job.

Within a week, Sally, the woman who worked in the office, came to Noah, ready to quit. "The boy is worthless. His friends come by often and hang out. He has me doing all the work. He takes two-hour lunch breaks. I can't cover the office by myself. Either he goes, or I go."

Noah trusted Sally's story. Adam was not cut out to lead others.

"I hate to upset your father," said Noah when he met with Adam, "but I can't have you managing the office anymore. The men don't want you back in the pit or the plant. So, what do we do?"

"I thought I was doing fine in the office," replied Adam.

"You weren't. Sally threatened to quit, and I can't spend my time supervising you. Either you start pulling your weight, or you're fired. There are plenty of men in town who need a job."

"I'll patch things up with Sally."

"No, things have to change. From now on, you will work for Sally. I'm giving her the power to dock your pay and to fire you if necessary."

"I'll make it work," said Adam sheepishly. "My father's going to kick my ass if I lose this job."

"Well, you're sixteen years old. Maybe it's time you learned that your last name only goes so far."

Within three days, Sally fired Adam, and Noah promoted her to office manager in charge of a new assistant. Tim was furious with Adam and put him to work at the ranch cleaning stalls. He threatened to turn him out of the house if he failed to do the work properly or missed his nightly curfews.

Tim's rebuke got Adam's attention. Within a few weeks, he was reassigned to help train the horses, a task he found interesting and took more seriously.

Chapter Twenty-Two

1861

Eight years later...

Tensions that had been rising for years reached a fever pitch after abolitionist John Brown raided the arsenal at Harper's Ferry. While Abraham Lincoln won only forty percent of the popular vote, his election as president in November 1860 was the last straw for the Southern states. The years of compromise over slavery were over. The North now had the power, and the South refused to abide by their autocratic rule. In December 1860, South Carolina voted to secede from the United States.

A month later, the citizens of Georgia were asked to elect delegates to represent them in a special convention to consider secession. State Senator Jeremy Bowers was chosen for the north-central counties of Georgia. He was one of a small minority of moderates within a crowd that was hell-bent on immediate action. Surprisingly, the delegates were slow in deciding how to hold a special election for citizens to vote up or down on secession.

The convention never completed its process; a vote was never held. It wasn't necessary. At 4:30 a.m. on April 12, 1861, the South Carolina militia began bombarding the federal forces at Fort Sumter in Charleston Harbor. After 34 hours of shelling, the Union forces surrendered. The War Between the States had begun.

Jeremy left the capital in Milledgeville and returned to Glory. Mayor Tim organized a town meeting to have Jeremy update everyone on what happened at the capital and the implications of a potential war. Jeremy explained how the Governor had immediately asked for volunteers to join the militia and authorized the fortification of defenses around Atlanta, now the largest industrial center in the state and the hub of railroads throughout the Southeast. Union naval forces had begun blockading the port of Savannah, so the Governor wanted all resources focused on expanding the production of military supplies within the state, including the powder works in Augusta, the naval works in Columbus, a munitions factory in Macon, and textile mills throughout Georgia.

"I want to fight!" yelled Hawk Madstone, Willow's brother. "Where do I sign up?"

"A recruiter should be visiting here in the next few weeks," replied Jeremy. "But it will take months for any fighting to begin if it does. Most of the U.S. Army is out west fighting Mexicans and Indians, and it will be months before the two armies can get organized. I, for one, hope we can somehow work this out without going to war."

Owen, the fifty-one-year-old Welsh foreman at the mine, spoke. "I think I speak for many of us in saying that we don't understand all of this talk of war, and we sure don't want to be forced to take up arms to fight for something we aren't a part of."

"I understand, Owen," responded Jeremy. "No one is being required to fight, at least for now. The state is just asking for volunteers. But life will change for us all if there is war. Everyone will be impacted."

"And I don't see our town being directly involved if there is conflict," added Tim. "We are not close to Atlanta or any other town of military significance. There is no railroad near here. The Yankees probably don't know we exist and couldn't find us if they wanted to!"

The comment brought a cheer and a bit of levity to the dark, frightening prospect of war.

Over the following weeks, the economy of Georgia transitioned from private industry to preparations for war. A state official visited the businesses in Macon to assess the current resources and ask industry leaders to redirect their equipment and manpower to war production. Foundries in the city would soon be producing iron and metal for weapons, textile mills would fabricate uniforms and knapsacks, and construction companies would build wagons and coffins.

Buck finished the projects near completion and began taking orders from the state. But it was soon apparent that his downtown shop was too small for large-scale production. He met with his lumber supplier, who had a rail siding and acres of open land around his mill. The two owners worked out the joint ownership details, and Buck began building a structure that was high, wide, and long enough to handle any orders they received from the military.

Georgia was one of the original seven states to form the Confederate States of America; four more slave states would soon join, while five other slave states remained loyal to the Union. Initially, Governor Brown resisted some of the directions of CSA President Jefferson Davis, who wanted to command all troops from Southern states. The Governor wanted Georgia men to defend Georgia, but he soon capitulated. Every Southerner revered Davis's choice to lead the CSA Army, General Robert E. Lee, especially after Lee had turned down Lincoln's offer to lead all Union forces.

One hundred thousand Georgians volunteered to fight in 1861, and over six hundred fought in the first Battle of Manassas in Virginia in July 1861. One of those men was Hawk Madstone of Glory, Georgia, who would serve under General G. T. Anderson, Commander of the Army of the Shenandoah. The South named their armies after land areas and battles after nearby towns, as opposed to the North naming their armies and battles after bodies of water.

Jeremy hosted the visit of a state official to Glory in the late spring of 1861. They toured the ranch with its forty trained Quarter Horses, the lumber mill run by Kitch, and the mine run by Noah. Most slate customers had canceled their orders, so the mine was operating well below capacity and approaching the point of shutting down.

"Are you familiar with the copper mine in Copperhill, Tennessee?" asked the official on his tour of the Bowers mine.

"I know of the operation," replied Noah.

"The CSA wants to expand the operations at that mine, including the rolling mill west of Copperhill in Cleveland, Tennessee. Would you and your men consider working up there? It would be a great service to the war effort."

"Would working there exempt my men from active service if there is a draft?"

"I believe so, but I can't say for sure."

Noah checked with his foreman, Owen, while Tim discussed his possible role in the move with the official.

"We will purchase all of your horses that pass our standards, Mr. Bowers, and would like you to join your crew in Tennessee."

Tim found that agreeable. The CSA needed everyone to contribute to the cause, the price for the horses was fair, and his family would no longer need to care for the herd in his absence.

Noah returned from the meeting with Owen and his crew. "My men and I agree to work at the copper mine and mill, but we fear there may be a problem. The owner is a German with a reputation for being a real tyrant. Plus, he employs a bunch of Brits, and many of my men are Welsh. The Welsh and Brits don't get along."

"I can assure you," replied the official, "President Davis will not allow quarrels between men to jeopardize our efforts. If the owner resists your help, we will make the necessary changes. Which might mean putting you in charge."

Noah looked at Tim, and they both nodded. "I guess we're going to Tennessee!"

Tim discussed the events of the day with Willow at dinner.

"I don't like you being gone, especially if the war comes to Georgia, but I'd rather you work to produce copper for the cause than fight on the battlefield. The children and I can take care of things here, and you'll only be fifteen miles away, so I hope we will get to see each other frequently."

"They wouldn't want me if there was a draft. I'm too old. I just hope I can find a meaningful role at the copper mine. The only thing I know about that mine is that the smelting process to extract the copper from the ore is filthy and smelly."

Willow wrapped her arms around her husband. "You are a leader, and it won't take long for them to recognize that. They aren't going to put the Mayor of Glory on some menial task."

While Buck and Tim had resolved what role they would play in the new era of war, Jeremy was thoroughly conflicted. He wanted to support his family and the state he had sworn to protect. But this war was all wrong.

Jeremy stayed in touch with a university classmate who had worked his way through the federal bureaucracy to a position on the Secretary of State's staff in Washington. The classmate wrote to Jeremy to emphasize how intolerant the Northern legislators in Congress were of the South's obstinacy over slavery. As a member of the Georgia Senate, he hoped Jeremy could influence his fellow legislators to find a compromise. The classmate also shared the poorly kept secret of how the Union would deal with the South if it came to war. The strategy was the same as the one used to defeat the Mexicans: blockade the ports and starve them of goods they could not produce internally. The Union was already blockading the southeastern Atlantic seaports and beginning to control the Mississippi River.

Jeremy understood the Union Navy was superior to anything the South could muster. And he also understood that the men of the South were fighting for deeply held ideals that they would die to preserve. And eventually, they would die. By the tens of thousands or more. The North had more men and resources. They would not let the Confederacy secede or succeed.

Jeremy wrangled with the issue for weeks: fight or flight. In the end, he chose flight.

Jeremy decided to go to Washington and do what he could to mitigate the losses. He would not take up arms with or against his brothers because it would only prolong the inevitable destruction.

Kitch went to talk to Jeremy after hearing of his plans. "I want to go with you!" he announced.

"I'd like your company," replied Jeremy, "but you've been up north before and returned. Are you sure you want to go back?"

"This is different. My people deserve to be free. Slavery is wrong, and I want to fight to end it!"

Jeremy and Kitch began their trip in September 1862 when the weather was mild. Union forces had control of central Kentucky and western Tennessee following the Battle of Shiloh in April 1862. The route through Knoxville and Lexington to avoid Confederate forces would take many days longer but should keep them clear of both armies.

Jeremy and Kitch arrived in Baltimore in October. The Union had recently declared victory in the Battle at Sharpsburg despite heavier casualties, which caused celebration in the city. Lee's Army of Northern Virginia was indeed vulnerable. But the reports that hundreds of Georgians were among the nearly four thousand that died that day in a cornfield so far from home broke Jeremy's heart.

Jeremy and Kitch parted ways in Baltimore. Kitch wanted to fight for the Union. Jeremy wanted to go to the capital to work within the government to find a way to end the fighting.

The Baltimore recruitment office on Charles Street turned Kitch away. President Lincoln opposed enlisting Blacks because he feared it would push the border states of Maryland, Delaware, Kentucky, Missouri, and West Virginia over to the Confederacy. However, by December 1862, it was clear that the Union needed more men, and Kitch was assigned to a Negro regiment.

Jeremy stayed at the Washington home of his college classmate. It would be weeks before the classmate could arrange for Jeremy to meet with one of the Assistant Secretaries of State, but he finally made the connection. Jeremy was treated with great suspicion at the first meeting.

"You are from Georgia, and yet you are meeting with us. Why?" asked the Assistant Secretary.

"I want to help end the conflict," answered Jeremy. "Surely, we can find some compromise to stop the bloodshed."

"So you come representing the State of Georgia?"

"No, but I was a State Senator and a lawyer. I want to find a way to help."

"But you have no real authority. The best path to quickly end the bloodshed is for you to provide us with details about Georgia's capabilities so that we know what we are up against. Like railroad routes, factory locations, etcetera."

"No, I will not give you any such details. I am not a spy. But I can give you insight into how the Governor and officials of Georgia think. Consider me a devil's advocate wanting to help anyone in the government trying to negotiate an end to the conflict."

"Would you swear your allegiance to the Union?"

"Yes," Jeremy replied quickly.

The official sat perplexed for several moments. Should we trust this guy? He seems bright and sincere. But he's from Georgia. "I will talk to the Secretary. We will be back in touch."

Jeremy had a follow-up meeting with the official, but they did not ask him to join the government staff. "Clearly, you have connections that got you this far. Please stay in town. We have your contact information if we need to reach you."

In October 1862, Eleanor Madstone received a letter from a soldier whose name she did not recognize. The soldier explained how he had served with Hawk Madstone in several battles over many months and was proud to fight alongside such a brave and fierce warrior. The letter gave a brief account of the savage fighting and deaths of thousands of soldiers at the Battle of Sharpsburg in September. Unfortunately, Hawk was one of those killed in action.

Eleanor and Willow were devastated. Eleanor wrote a letter to President Davis asking for details of where Hawk was interred and how they could bring his body home for a proper burial. She received no response.

WILLOW *and the boys*

Willow vowed to find out more about her brother. She was ready to travel to Richmond for answers, but Tim convinced her to wait until it was safe.

Chapter Twenty-Three

1863

Two years later...

The War raged on through 1862 and 1863. General Ulysses S. Grant gained control of the Mississippi River Valley after winning the Battle of Vicksburg in July 1863. General Robert E. Lee defeated the Union Army at Chancellorsville in May but was defeated at Gettysburg in July. Hundreds of thousands of men had already died. Only a third were killed in action; the others died of dysentery, malaria, and typhoid due to unsanitary conditions, poor diet, and crowded surroundings.

So far, Georgia had remained behind the front lines of the War. When the Confederate Army of Tennessee retreated from Chattanooga in the summer of 1863, Atlanta became a major center for treating sick and wounded soldiers. With the War getting dangerously close and the cry for help growing louder, Willow decided to serve. She would go to Atlanta to help the wounded.

Willow and Tim met in Copperhill to discuss her plans.

"I think Carrie can handle things at home," explained Willow. "Glory has become a ghost town with all the men gone and very little commerce. She insists that she and Adam will be safe."

Tim held his wife in his arms. "I hate to see you risk your health at a hospital, but I know you will make a big difference. Maybe this War will be over soon, and we will all be back together."

Willow arrived in Atlanta and was assigned to a Presbyterian church on Marietta Street near a railroad terminal. A civilian administrator ran the place like a drill sergeant, making it clear that their mission was to heal the men of their wounds or illnesses and get them back to the front as soon as possible. Willow was part of a detail that dispensed medicines, changed dressings, and monitored the condition of patients. If they had time, they wrote letters for the soldiers. Slaves were assigned to the hospital by their owners to handle the menial tasks of serving meals, bathing the men, and cleaning the facilities.

Treating soldiers who took weeks to recover at the hospital became fairly routine until the middle of September when hundreds of wounded soldiers began arriving by train from the field hospitals around Chickamauga Creek. This first battle fought on Georgia soil was a Confederate victory, but the over 18,000 Rebel casualties were second only to Gettysburg.

Willow worked sixteen-hour shifts for weeks. She became conditioned to the amputations, the screams of battled-hardened soldiers, and puddles of blood covering the floor. There was a constant flow of soldiers being carried from their beds to Oakland Cemetery or a new graveyard created on donated land in Marietta.

Willow kept her sanity by focusing on the men she helped to recover, the joy families might receive from her letters, and her prayers that the war would soon end. But the news from the front was not good. General William Tecumseh Sherman was at the doorstep of Georgia.

Tim and Noah were also about to see the storm skies roll over Copperhill. The owner of the copper mine was a German immigrant who had refused to swear his allegiance to the Confederacy, so the CSA sequestered the property and put Tim in charge of the mill and Noah in charge of the mine. After nearly three years of supplying thousands of copper rolls to Confederate munitions and bronze manufacturing plants in the Southeast, word reached the mill that Union forces were on their way.

In November 1863, 1,500 federal troops led by Colonel Eli Long marched into Cleveland, Tennessee. There was no battle because all Confederate soldiers had been ordered to Dalton, Georgia, after Union forces took nearby Chattanooga. Unchallenged, the Union forces began destroying the copper mill and railroad tracks, ransacking businesses and homes, and causing general havoc.

Tim advised his workers not to resist but to flee town or bunker down in their homes. He then decided to ride thirty-five miles east to the mine to warn Noah of the advancing enemy and then to Dalton to alert the Army of the attack in Cleveland. Four days later, Tim returned to the mill town with 500 Confederate cavalry led by General John Kelly. Colonel Long and his Union forces knew they were outmatched and retreated, but the damage had been done. The largest rolling mill in the South lay destroyed along with the train tracks and rail cars.

Tim returned to the mine in Copperhill to inform Noah of the Union retreat and the mill's destruction.

"What do we do now?" asked Noah. "The mine is still intact."

"You stay here and operate the mine until Richmond determines what to do next. I am returning to Dalton to find out what the Army is planning. If the Yankees can so easily waltz into Cleveland, I fear North Georgia may be at risk."

Tim met with some officers at the Confederate base camp in Dalton. Following the Rebel victory at Chickamauga, the CSA forces camped in an easily defended position at nearby Rocky Face to regroup. Tim offered his services, hoping to get a leadership position. But the only offer they made was as a foot soldier. He hadn't expected to take up arms, but his mill was in ruins, and his homeland threatened, so he accepted. He would never be able to live with himself if he had sat out the fight.

Tim served under General Joseph Johnston, commander of the Army of Tennessee. Johnston was a veteran commander with several victories but was notorious for getting outflanked and retreating. His primary directive from President Davis was to stop Sherman from moving south. The good news from Tim's perspective was that it was clear that Sherman was following the railroad route south from Chattanooga to Atlanta. Union forces would be on the far side of the Cohutta Mountains from Glory and the rest of central North Georgia.

In May of 1864, Sherman slipped past Johnston's Army at Dalton, then Resaca, and again at Adairsville, moving ever closer to Atlanta. Finally, the two forces, each seventeen thousand men strong, met head-on at Kennesaw Mountain.

By June, Tim's company was dug in on Cheatham Hill near Kennesaw Mountain as part of Johnston's seven-mile-long defense line to protect the railroad tracks to their rear. Sherman, best known for his flanking maneuvers, ordered an out-of-character frontal attack aimed directly at Tim's company. It was by far the fiercest fighting Tim had ever seen or imagined.

Waves of Union troops struggled to attack the hill defended by Confederates who had spent days digging in at the hill's crest. The Rebels had built walls and fences and planted thousands of pointed sticks on the hill to slow the advance. Once within range, the Rebs mowed them down with gunfire. But the Yanks kept coming and eventually broke through the Confederate lines, and soldiers began killing each other with bayonets, rifle butts, pistols, and knives.

Four hours later, the Union forces at Cheatham Hill retreated. But Tim lay on a blanket on the ground with a bayonet wound to his right shoulder. The doctor stopped the bleeding, but Tim couldn't feel or move his right arm. He was loaded onto a wagon and then onto a train that would take him to a hospital sixteen miles away in Atlanta.

The South suffered one thousand casualties at Kennesaw; the North suffered three thousand. The battle was a Rebel victory on the field but did not stop Sherman's advance. With Union troops on the doorstep of Atlanta, Johnston moved his troops inside the city perimeter defended by Georgia militia. A few weeks later, President Davis replaced Johnston with General John Bell Hood in command of CSA forces.

Jeremy was surprised to find more people than he expected in Washington who were frustrated and weary after four years of war and wanted to reconcile with the South. He also found many hard-core Republicans who doubted Lincoln's ability to defeat the South. Lincoln understood that his 1864 re-election was in doubt. The South hoped that, if they could further bog down the Union advances, the Democrats would defeat Lincoln, the War might end, and the Confederate States of America would find a pathway to coexist with the United States of America.

General George McClellan disliked Lincoln ever since the president had removed him from command of all Union forces. He decided to oppose Lincoln and run for president as a Democrat in the 1864 election. Jeremy believed McClellan was the best hope for peace and volunteered to work in his campaign.

As Jeremy wrote to Buck in Macon, McClellan might publicly campaign as a fiercer war hawk than Lincoln, but if the General won the election, he would likely follow the majority of his Democrat constituents in negotiating peace with the South.

The November election hung on what happened in Atlanta.

Tim hoped to go to the same hospital where he sent letters to Willow.

But there were at least five hospitals in Atlanta, and he was taken to one on the north side of town. The stitched-up, two-inch gash in his shoulder was healing well, but the doctor gave little hope that he would ever regain use of his right arm. He asked the nurse caring for him to write a letter to Willow, letting her know of his situation.

The influx of wounded soldiers from Kennesaw overwhelmed the staff at Willow's hospital. The exhausted volunteers could not attend to all the suffering and dying soldiers. To make matters worse, many medical staff joined the hundreds of citizens fleeing Atlanta. The Confederate soldiers defending the hospital began deserting as the Yankees started to surround the city. And then, in July 1864, the Union Army began shelling the downtown area.

Tim's letters to Willow never reached her. But after two weeks, Tim's shoulder had healed sufficiently for him to walk. He followed the rail tracks south to Willow's address. She wasn't at the hospital, but Tim got directions to the school where she was staying.

Tim found Willow's location but was asked to wait in the school lobby because Willow was sleeping in a classroom with fourteen other women. After an hour, Willow came to the lobby to discover Tim slumped on the floor, exhausted.

"Thank God, you're alive!" exclaimed Willow on seeing her husband. The sling and bandages kept her from embracing him. He was unshaven, his hair was long, and his clothes were torn and filthy.

Tim drew on all the energy he could muster. "I am so glad to see you, Willow. You look like an angel. I hurt, but I am going to be okay." Tim explained his injury as Willow checked the bandages.

"I can put new dressings on your shoulder. Let's get you to my hospital, or what's left of it."

"I think we should get out of the city as fast as possible," Tim suggested.

"But where? The Yankees have surrounded Atlanta!"

"We need to get to Macon," said Tim. "The train is still running, last I heard."

"But Sherman will follow the railroad," exclaimed Willow. "Macon will be his next target!"

"At least we can be with Buck. He'll know what to do."

"What if he has already left Macon?"

"I think we need to take that chance. We can't go to the north, east, or west. Those trains have stopped running, and the tracks are destroyed."

"We could stay in the city and take our chances," said Willow.

"I'd shoot the first Bluebelly I see, which would only get us both killed."

Willow felt terrible about abandoning her position at the hospital, but her husband needed her more. She collected her few personal belongings in a sack, and they went to her hospital. The doctor looked at Tim's wound, cleared him for traveling, and advised them on the railroad escape route. As far as he knew, the train was still running to bring provisions from Macon to Atlanta.

Tim and Willow boarded the train at the depot just outside the hospital. The train crept along for an hour and then stopped abruptly. The passengers looked at each other, wondering why they were not moving. Suddenly, a Union soldier boarded the train.

"Everybody off!" he bellowed. "Now!" The soldier looked to be no older than fifteen.

It was clear that the people on the train were a rag-tag lot of unarmed refugees and no threat to the soldiers. They were allowed to disembark peacefully and followed the soldier's orders to walk south along the tracks. As they walked in front of the train, they saw Union men using picks and steel bars to remove the rails from the track. Other soldiers were heating the rails in fires and bending the steel in what would come to be known as "Sherman's neckties," never to be used again. Hundreds of feet of rail track lay destroyed.

The group of about sixty passengers walked together until they reached a depot marked Lovejoy Station. Once inside the station, the passengers considered what to do next. Except for the soldiers destroying the tracks, they had not seen anyone else around. Someone familiar with the area said they were about thirty miles from Atlanta and fifty miles north of Macon.

It was dark by now, and the passengers decided to stay together and spend the night in a nearby warehouse partially damaged in a battle between Sherman's troops and a brigade of infantry from Arkansas.

In the morning, a few passengers volunteered to search the nearby village for food and gather information. There was little food to be found, but one resident who had worked at the depot suggested that the passengers continue toward Macon on foot. There was a possibility that a train from Macon might be running as far as Griffin, a town fifteen miles south.

As the group headed south, they passed a crossroad where scores of dead Confederate soldiers lay stacked like firewood along the road. Some bodies were dismembered from battle, and the flies and stench made the group scurry past the horrific scene.

The group spread out as they walked along the track. Tim and Willow fell behind because of his injuries. Every step he took sent sharp pains through his shoulder. He was exhausted but determined not to quit.

They reached Griffin before sunset. The town was partially deserted, but there were no signs of Union soldiers. Willow and Tim found a hotel and enjoyed a hearty dinner. That night, Willow bathed Tim, and they slept together in the same bed for the first time in months. In the morning, refreshed and given bread and water for their journey, Willow and Tim continued their trek south along the tracks.

"I recognize this area," exclaimed Tim after a couple of hours of walking. "This is the route my father and I took when we left Macon and headed north. Lord, that was thirty-odd years ago."

"You were on your way to meet me!" declared Willow.

"At the time, I thought I was on my way to find gold, but things turned out a little differently than I expected." He pulled a strand of Willow's hair from her eyes and tucked it behind her ear. "I discovered a different kind of gold than you find in a creek."

Willow rubbed his back tenderly. "And now you've got two wonderful children who will be jumping for joy to see you," she reflected.

"Not as glad as I will be to see them! And I will tell them how I met the prettiest girl I had ever seen up in those mountain woods. She was tall and lean and could almost outrun me. She was tough and adventurous enough to put up with me." Tim hurried to the right side of Willow and put his good arm around her. "I love that woman more than anything."

Willow reached over and kissed his cheek as they continued walking.

Tim needed to rest every three or four miles and could only travel about twelve miles a day. They slept each of three nights in whatever shelter they could find and scavenged for food in the towns they passed through – Milner, Barnesville, Forsyth, Smarr, and Bolingbroke. On the fourth day, they reached the outskirts of Macon and headed for Buck's house.

"I can't believe Carrie ever left this beautiful place with all the brick houses and tree-lined streets!" remarked Willow. "The homes seem untouched by war."

"It wasn't quite this grand when I was growing up," Tim stated. "Things have improved a lot."

"Maybe Glory will look like this someday," exclaimed Willow.

They reached the Bowers' house, and Abigail answered the door. It took her a moment to recognize Tim, but when she did, she sprang forward, hugged him, and invited them inside. Abigail and Willow had met only once, years ago, at Jeremy's wedding in Milledgeville, but Abigail greeted her like a long-lost sister. "I am so glad to see you! Everyone in town is in an absolute panic, and it's so wonderful to have all the family together. Lord knows what's going to happen."

Abigail studied Tim's sling, bandages, ripped trousers, worn-out shoes, and gaunt face. "Are you okay? What's happened to you?"

"I think I will be fine once I recover from that hug!"

Abigail winced, and Willow explained Tim's condition and what they had been through since leaving Atlanta.

"Oh, I can't wait," exclaimed Abigail. "Buck is going to be so glad to see you! He's working at the mill and should be home by dinner. We hadn't heard from you for so long!"

"We are happy to be here, believe me," said Tim. "How are things in Macon?"

"Not a lot has changed so far, but most people are bracing for disaster to come our way. Most of the men in town are gone. Many have died in battle." Abigail shook her head and looked down. "People are escaping to the countryside, but Buck insists on staying."

Tim wanted to calm her fears, but he couldn't think of anything positive to say.

Abigail continued, "We have enough to eat, but many people think this winter will be bad. All of our house servants are gone, working at the mill."

"And the children? How are they?"

"Buck Jr. is in the Army in Savannah. I pray for him every day. The girls are working with Buck at the lumber mill. Melissa's husband was killed back in August in Tennessee." Abigail's voice began to quiver. "We just got word a couple of weeks ago. It was so tragic."

Abigail was doing her best to keep it together, and having guests was a great diversion from her fears. She made Tim and Willow comfortable in a guest bedroom. They bathed and napped until Buck got home with his three daughters. Buck was shocked to see Tim come down the stairs. Abigail warned her husband, "Now don't you go tackling your little brother in celebration! His shoulder is injured, and he's worn out."

Over dinner, they discussed Tim and Willow's stories of Kennesaw, Atlanta, Lovejoy, and their trek to Macon. "I fear that Sherman is following the railroad south, which leads him straight to Macon," observed Tim.

"The Yanks have already conducted raids on the east side of the Ocmulgee River. They want to destroy our factories and free the hundreds of Yankee officers we hold in Camp Oglethorpe prison at the old fairgrounds. They lobbed some cannon shells into town, but the damage was minimal. The Governor sent reinforcements, and the Yankees retreated. Some think Sherman will bypass Macon and instead go east toward Milledgeville."

"When we left Atlanta, it was in shambles but still in Confederate control," said Tim. "The perimeter defenses were holding, but the Yanks were bombing the daylights out of downtown, and hundreds of people were fleeing the city. Us included."

"We hear that Sherman has surrounded the city and cut off all of the railroads," said Buck. "Maybe he doesn't need to lose more men by attacking a crippled town, but so far, General Hood has had no success stopping Sherman."

"What do you plan to do if Sherman approaches Macon?" asked Willow.

"We'll go out to the farm until things settle down," responded Buck. "We've stored provisions there, and I hope they would take mercy on a family on a small farm. Besides, where else could we go?"

"Sherman is showing no mercy," expressed Tim. "He's a barbarian. You may want to flee to the west."

"Will you stay with us as we try to figure things out?" asked Abigail.

"I wish we could, but we need to get back to Glory," said Tim. "Looks like the Yankees bypassed that area, but we need to get back to Carrie and Adam. They're old enough to care for themselves, but they've been on their own for many months. You are certainly welcome to come with us."

Buck sighed. "Even if the Yankees come through here, things will eventually have to settle down. Macon is home for us, and when this crazy war is over, I believe people will rebuild. I want to be part of that."

"Have you heard from Jeremy?" asked Willow.

"We got a letter a few weeks ago. He's still in Washington and thinks he can do more for Georgia up there than shooting at Yankees down here."

"I wish he would come home to Macon or Glory," said Tim. "It just seems wrong him being up there."

"At least I have one brother who wore the uniform and took up arms. I'm sorry you got injured, but maybe that kept something worse from happening." Buck walked around the table and extended his left hand to shake. "I'm proud of you, brother!" He patted Willow on the shoulder. "And you, too, Willow. We wouldn't be together right now if it weren't for you."

General Hood abandoned Atlanta in August 1864. But before leaving, his Confederate troops destroyed their munitions and everything else of military value. Sherman took control and had his troops burn hundreds of residences and businesses and destroy the railroad hub that had put the city on the map. Typical of his brutality, Sherman had his troops arrest hundreds of women who had dared to continue working at a cotton mill in Roswell. He loaded the women and their children in boxcars and abandoned them in Kentucky and Indiana to fend for themselves. If they survived, they didn't return to Georgia.

Sherman had no intention of keeping his sixty-some thousand men around the ruins of Atlanta. There was no reason for him to defend his prize or for the Confederates to want to reoccupy the scorched remains. Confederate forces were already retaking sections of the railroad north of Atlanta to disrupt Union supply lines. Instead of following the railroad south, he would order his men to loot and plunder all the supplies they needed on their way to his next target, Savannah.

Sherman would not only confiscate livestock and grain to feed his troops. He intended to break the spirit of Georgians and the South by ransacking and burning buildings, forcing the women and children to scatter, and freeing every slave in his path. Nothing of value would be left behind. His March to the Sea would be a war of terror to bring the South to its knees and end this conflict once and for all.

Meanwhile, Jeremy was hard at work in Washington on McClellan's presidential campaign. He was part of the inner circle that brainstormed strategies and accompanied the General on campaign stops in Philadelphia, New York, and Boston. Jeremy's best hope to save his homeland was a McClellan victory, and he believed their chances of winning the election were good. If Lincoln won reelection, there would be more killing and destruction until the South surrendered. And Southerners were not quitters.

But when Sherman took Atlanta, all hope faded. Everyone in the North was jubilant that they finally had two generals who could win the war. Sherman was splitting the Confederacy in half in Georgia, while Grant was maintaining control of the Mississippi Valley and moving east to close in on the Confederate capital of Richmond.

Jeremy was devastated by the news from Georgia and considered his next move in the now likely event that McClellan would lose to Lincoln. Should he stay in Washington and try to find some sort of soft landing for the South or return to Georgia? But what would be left of Glory or his hometown in Macon?

Chapter Twenty-Four

1864

Buck provided Tim and Willow with two horses, and Abigail packed bags full of rations and clothing for their long trip to Glory. It was October when the temperature in Georgia could range anywhere between the eighties and the twenties. Abigail provided them with jackets, plenty of salted meat, and fire matches.

"We're going to miss you!" said Abigail with tears in her eyes. "It was so nice having you here. I wish you would stay!"

"We've got to get back," said Tim, "and make sure Carrie and Adam are all right."

"Thank you so much for everything!" added Willow.

Buck handed Tim a revolver and a sack of cartridges. "Be safe. Don't take too many risks."

Tim handed the gun to Willow, who stuffed it in her waistband. "I haven't yet practiced shooting with my left hand," said Tim.

"She's probably a better shot than you anyway," quipped Buck.

Tim laughed. "Y'all need to come up to Glory when things settle down to give us a chance to return the favor for all you've done for us."

Abigail cried in Buck's arms at the sight of the pair riding off. "God's speed!" she hollered.

While riding to Glory was faster than walking, they planned to take a longer route east toward Athens to avoid the embattled Atlanta area. They practiced what to say if confronted by Union soldiers: Tim was disabled, they had no money, and they were headed north to reunite with their children. All of which was true.

Yankee scouts roamed the land south and east of Atlanta ahead of Sherman's advance. Tim and Willow were able to avoid two soldiers on horseback that they spotted just south of Monticello, Georgia. The next day, they were riding toward Madison when two soldiers on horseback confronted them. Two more soldiers with rifles drawn rode up from behind to surround them.

"Stop and dismount!" yelled the soldier in charge. Once Tim and Willow had complied, the officer dismounted, walked toward them, and began slowly circling them. The Yank asked them who they were and where they were going, and Willow replied.

The soldier riding with the leader dismounted and led the Bowers' horses a few feet away. He removed the rifle from the saddle scabbard and started throwing the clothes and food in the saddlebags onto the ground.

"Do you have any more weapons?"

"I lost the use of my right arm and can't shoot," muttered Tim. "My wife has a pistol on her side."

Willow went to pull her vest away from her waistband to expose the pistol.

"Don't move!" the Yank yelled at Willow. "Touch that gun, and we'll shoot you where you stand!"

The officer stood directly in front of Willow. He put his hand on her chin and started to tilt her head left, right, up, and down. "You are a pretty thing! Part Indian, I'd say, from the tan skin." The Yank's other hand began patting her down from the shoulders to both breasts and then to the pistol on her side. He removed the gun and handed it to the other Yank. "But how do I know that's the only one?" He grabbed her breast with one hand while his other rubbed her sides and between her thighs.

Willow struggled to keep her balance, terrified but saying nothing.

"Stop!" yelled Tim. "Please leave her alone. She is no threat to you. Where is your honor, soldier?"

The officer did stop and slowly walked back to confront Tim. He stood right in Tim's face, studying him. He pulled a knife out of his belt and sliced the sling off Tim. Then he slapped his dangling arm hard. Tim yelped as his arm swayed like a pendulum. "So, how did you lose use of your arm?"

Tim didn't say anything for a moment and then lied. "A mining accident. I worked in a rock mine north of here."

The sergeant took his knife, slit Tim's shirt down the middle, and yanked half the shirt over his right shoulder. He studied the wound and poked hard at the scar. Tim groaned and winced. "That doesn't look like any mining accident," he said, jabbing the skin with his knife. "I'd say that looks like a knife wound and a pretty recent one."

Tim replied in a calm, conciliatory tone, "Look, Sergeant, we mean you no harm. Just let us be on our way."

"Oh, you recognize rank, eh? You must be one of those Johnny Rebs we hear about. We don't get to see many because they all ran off." He pushed Tim hard on his bad shoulder. Tim lost his balance and fell onto his hands and knees. The officer kicked him hard in the chest with his boot. Willow screamed, "No!" and went to help her husband. The sergeant grabbed her forcefully by the arm and flung her away.

"What are we going to do with this old Reb and his Injun?" the officer bellowed to his men.

One of the soldiers still mounted was not amused by his leader's conduct. "I think you've humiliated them enough. I say we take the guns and horses and let them fend for themselves."

The sergeant snickered at the response. "No, Jonesy, I think you ought to shoot them. Drag them into the woods and put a bullet in their heads. If we let the Rebs and Indians go, we'll be facing them again on a battlefield. Get down here and do your job."

The other soldier spoke up. "We can't just murder them here. We got what we need. And killing a woman and a one-armed man ain't right. Let 'em go."

The officer turned to the soldier holding the horses. "And you?"

"I think we ought to show the pretty one a little love."

That was all the encouragement the sergeant needed. He kicked Tim again in the side as he lay on the ground. Then he grabbed Willow, manhandled her into the brush on the side of the road to lie on her back, and began ripping at her blouse and trousers until she was naked from her neck to her ankles. "Make this easy, or I'll shoot your man and take you anyway." He stood above her to throw his gun belt on the road out of reach, undid his pants, got on his knees, and spread her legs.

Willow lay motionless, crying quietly in agony.

When the sergeant was done, the other Yank had his way with Willow.

The officer got dressed and retrieved his belt. He yelled to the two other soldiers sitting idly on their horses, "You boys are welcome to a turn."

They said nothing, slowly shaking their heads in disgust.

The second soldier got dressed, put Willow's rifle back in the scabbard, grabbed the reins of their horses, and mounted his horse.

The leader yelled, "Those two shouldn't cause any more trouble. Let's get out of here."

The soldiers rode off with the horses and guns.

Willow lay in the brush for a few minutes to settle down. She wrapped her torn clothes around her as best she could and went to Tim, still lying helplessly on the road. "Are you okay?" she asked.

Tim groaned and slowly regained his senses. He dabbed at some blood trickling from his wound with the end of his torn shirt. "I don't think anything's broken. I'll be all right." He took one look at Willow's torn clothes and howled in anguish. "Oh, no, sweetheart," he moaned, "I am so sorry." Tim reached up and tenderly caressed her cheek. "Are you okay?"

"I will be all right, but we've got to get you on your feet."

After several minutes of resting on the side of the road, they moved about to test their strength. Willow grabbed some clothes the soldier had thrown on the ground. She handed Tim a clean shirt and changed from her torn rags. Tim helped her gather the remaining clothes and food into a jacket, which Willow tied up and slung over her shoulder. "I guess we're hoofing it from here," Willow said, trying to smile.

Tim sighed, still feeling terrible that he was unable to protect Willow. "God, that was awful, but we still have each other."

It took several days for Tim and Willow to travel to Glory. They were fortunate to hitch occasional short rides on wagons going in their direction. During that time, they had a chance to heal physically and begin to recover emotionally. They vowed never to mention what happened to Willow to another soul. And Tim would never forget the face of that Bluebelly sergeant.

WILLOW *and the boys*

Their reunion with Carrie and Adam in Glory was full of joy and tears. The kids looked healthy and fit. Their house in town was in good condition, and there was food in the pantry. For the next two days, they shared each other's stories from the War and how the children and town had faired for the past many months. The worst impact on Glory was the absence of nearly all the men, the flight of a few families to safer places, and the suspension of almost all commerce. Carrie and Adam's meals had come from hunting, fishing, and whatever produce the Morgans and other families could share.

Willow and Tim went to her family farm. The place had been abandoned for years following her mother's move to join her sister in Tennessee after Hawk was killed at Sharpsburg. The house needed painting, the fences required repairing, and the livestock was gone. The house was still full of furniture, plus a lot of spider webs, a couple of birds, and a snake. It hadn't been raided, just neglected.

"Look!" exclaimed Tim as they exited the house. "There's smoke coming out of the still!"

They walked over to the outbuilding housing the distillery. The boiler was burning, but no one was around.

They crossed the river and stopped at Roy's old cabin. Tim saw movement in the distance. "Oh my God!" yelled Tim. He hobbled as best he could toward a figure standing near the sawmill building.

"Kitch!" yelled Tim. "You're here!" Willow came running behind him.

Kitch stood bewildered for a moment until he made the connection. Then he went running toward Tim.

"Tim! And Willow!" The three embraced in a big bear hug.

"How did you end up back here?" asked Tim. "I thought you moved up north!"

"I came back to my roots!" Kitch began walking toward the cabin, and the Bowers followed. "C'mon, I want to introduce you to a couple of people." They entered the front door to find a woman sitting at the table holding a baby. "This is my wife, Nora, and our baby boy, Samuel." Kitch provided some background to Nora as Willow fussed over the baby.

"I hope you don't mind us staying here at the cabin," said Kitch. "The family I sold my house to in town still lives there."

"Hell, no!" replied Tim. "I'm glad you're taking care of the place!"

"I love that fancy shower off the bedroom!" said Nora.

"And we're close to the mill and . . ." Kitch paused momentarily. "Willow, I hope you don't mind my keeping up your daddy's old whiskey still."

"Of course not!" replied Willow. "But where do you get the corn?"

"I grow a patch of corn in the field," said Nora.

"Wow!" said Willow. "You two are working hard!"

"Sales of lumber are slow," continued Kitch. "About the only customer buying lumber was the Army. They stopped needing wood, but they sure do buy all the whiskey I can make! We're saving up what we make to buy a place of our own."

"I thought we lost you to the North," said Tim. "What made you come back?"

"Them Yankees may talk about emancipation, but they just ignore Black folks. I joined the Army to fight, but all I did for three years was clean latrines and work in the mess tents. We were always behind the front lines. The pay was lousy, and all the barracks and dining were colored-only. I don't think I ever had a conversation with a white woman. But here, I just got a hug from the mayor's wife! The best thing that ever happened to me was meeting Nora in Fredericksburg and her agreeing to come back here with me!"

"He made it sound like heaven," added Nora. "I had my doubts, but Glory really is wonderful! It's so peaceful here on the river. We may be the only colored folks in town, but everyone I meet is kind."

"Well, we are so glad you are back and making a good life here," replied Tim. "And you're welcome to stay at the cabin as long as you need." Tim looked out through the window. "And the few horses that were here, are they all gone?"

"They were gone when we got here. I think a fellow on the other side of the road from town is raising some horses."

"Good!" replied Tim. "I'll have to go see him. And how about Noah? Is he back at the mine?"

"Should be. I don't think the mine is operating much, but Noah and a few Welshmen spend a good bit of their time there."

Tim and Willow said their goodbyes and headed toward the mine.

"What a miracle to see you!" exclaimed Noah on seeing Tim. "You left for Dalton and disappeared! I didn't know if I'd ever see you again."

Tim explained the highlights of what he and Willow had been through. "I'm glad to see you back here! Is the copper mine closed?"

"Just about. They're still digging some ore, but the smelters are down," replied Noah. "The old German took over again. After you left, the little bit we mined had to be transported by wagon over the mountains to North Carolina, which was not worth the effort. And I guess the fighting is mostly in Virginia now, so the need is dwindling."

"And how are things here?"

"The place is in good shape, but it's hard to get much done with four men. We don't have paying customers, so we're just building a big inventory."

"Things may stay depressed for some time," said Tim regretfully. "But I have faith that business will return. Plus, I will need time to learn to do what needs to get done with one good arm."

"Does that sling mean that your arm is on the mend?"

"It's as good as it's gonna get. I wear the sling to keep my arm from getting in trouble. But it doesn't look like I'll ever have use of my arm again."

"But you're back here in Glory. That's all that counts. We'll just have to start calling you Lefty."

Over the following weeks, Sherman abandoned what was left of Atlanta and moved his forces in two wings, about twenty miles apart, toward the agricultural center of the state. He would no longer rely on the rail lines to supply his troops but instead live off the land. The harvests were in, and the livestock on farms was plentiful since the interior of Georgia had not been impacted by any battles of the war.

The main columns of the Union Army met little resistance in their path. However, the small groups of Union cavalry that broke off to raid towns such as Athens and Macon were met with fierce resistance and repulsed.

Jeremy Bowers had decided to return to the state capital in Milledgeville. There was no point in his staying in Washington among the uncompromising Republicans. And there was now no chance of peace without a military victory by the North.

Sherman's force of sixty thousand soldiers continued marching toward central Georgia unopposed. One wing moved south as if they intended to attack Macon and then camped east of the city in Clinton, Georgia. The other half of the Union troops marched east to feign an attack on Augusta, then headed directly for the capital in Milledgeville.

When Jeremy arrived in Milledgeville, news that Sherman's troops were quickly approaching created panic throughout the once-proud town. The Governor fled to Macon with wagons full of furnishings and records. The legislators were long gone, and most government staff had taken flight. Jeremy decided to stay. He was a scalawag tired of skedaddling.

Jeremy watched as thirty thousand Union forces marched into town. No shots were fired. Instead of fighting, the soldiers ransacked the statehouse, destroyed the state arsenal and train depot, burned the penitentiary and Lunatic Asylum, and destroyed most of what was left in the town and surrounding countryside. They even poured molasses into the pipes of the organ at the big church. The citizens were left destitute to face winter.

The soldiers marched east through town to camp near the Oconee River. Hundreds of supply and ambulance wagons followed the troops. Multitudes of slaves, now free of their bondage, celebrated the arrival of the soldiers along the streets. They followed the troops to camp, for they were now homeless and hungry.

Jeremy was not sure how to receive the onslaught. He didn't know whether to hide somewhere or greet the men like an ambassador. He decided to observe things quietly and not make any fuss. He was dressed modestly in civilian clothes and unarmed, and the soldiers ignored him.

General Sherman arrived with his entourage in the middle of the wave of forces, and Jeremy watched him ride up and down Hancock Street to observe his troops before stopping at the Governor's Mansion on Clarke Street. The mansion was abandoned, and Sherman walked in as if he owned the place. Jeremy waited a few minutes and then walked in that direction.

"What's your business?" asked the soldier guarding the mansion's door.

"I want to talk to General Sherman or one of his top officers," replied Jeremy.

The soldier snickered. "The officers are in the field, and the General is not taking visitors. Who are you?"

"My name is Jeremy Bowers, and I worked with General McClellan in Washington. I just wanted to see if the General needs any local assistance."

"You're local?"

"I no longer live here but know the town from being a member of the legislature before the War. When Georgia seceded, I went to Washington and have just recently returned."

The soldier cocked his head as though he didn't know whether to believe Jeremy or shoot him. "I'll inform the General of your visit. Come back tomorrow morning, and we'll see what he says."

Jeremy returned to the mansion in the morning and was greeted by Major General Henry Slocum, commander of Sherman's left column wing.

"The sentry told me that you worked with George McClellan in Washington," said Slocum.

"Yes, sir, on his campaign."

"I met him once at West Point. He's a bit older than me but seemed like a good guy." The general spoke softly, "Don't tell anyone, but I voted for him."

Jeremy smiled but didn't respond immediately. "Sir, I served in the legislature here but resigned when they voted to secede. Then, I moved to Washington. I hope to serve here again once the War has ended. I wanted to beg you and your men not to cause any further damage to the town. I think you've neutralized everything of military value, and I hope you will spare the rest of the houses, businesses, and state buildings."

"Well, that's a tall request, Bowers. We have depleted the supplies we brought with us from Atlanta. How do you expect us to feed this Army?"

"I can understand destroying the arsenal and train depot, and I know you need cattle and grain, but why burn all the cotton and destroy the prison and asylum? What military value do they have?"

"They have no value!" Slocum nearly yelled and continued in an agitated tone. "And that is what you need to understand. Our goal here is not to win battles; we won this war when we took Atlanta. We are here to settle a score. There must be consequences for starting all of this fighting and death. Your aristocratic leaders may think they can still win, but the people of Georgia will pay a steep price for their arrogance." Slocum's expression soured, and his tone became even angrier. "By the time we are through with Georgia, your governor and his plantation barons will be begging for their lives in front of a firing squad of colored soldiers!"

Jeremy sat quietly for a moment to let the General calm down. "I did not come here to upset you, General. I will take my leave. Good day." Jeremy left the mansion at a quick walking pace, though he felt like running and screaming.

Jeremy ducked into an abandoned store to gather himself. The door was wide open, and he sat on one of the overturned shelves away from the shattered storefront window. What was he to do next? There was nothing for him in Milledgeville. Macon was probably also under attack.

Jeremy went to the town stables where he had boarded his horse. All the horses were gone, and the man who managed the place sat on a stool as he told Jeremy how the soldiers had been there earlier and stolen all the horses. "I'm gonna get those horses back from them soldiers!" declared the old man angrily, spitting out his words. "You gonna help me?"

"That's not a good idea," replied Jeremy. "Sherman's troops won't be here much longer, and maybe they'll leave some horses or other things of value when they break camp. I'm not going to help you get killed."

"What are you going to do without a horse?"

"I'll hoof it or find another. I got that horse weeks ago in Augusta, and we never really got along anyway."

"Where you headed, that you came here for your horse?"

"I'm headed to Athens. I hear the town's still there."

"Want some company? I got nothing left here."

Jeremy didn't like the idea, but he couldn't say no. "You any good with that pistol?"

"All those years in the Army taught me a few things. I was part of General Winfield Scott's force that took Mexico City in '47. Then I went to California in search of gold, got cheated there, and came back to where things were quiet and peaceful. And now the Army I fought with against the Mexicans has destroyed my hometown."

Jeremy cut the guy off. There would be plenty of time for war stories on their hike to Athens. "Let's meet here at dawn with some supplies for a three or four-day trip."

That morning's weather was cold for November, but the older man kept pace with Jeremy as they began their trek.

"I never did catch your name," said Jeremy.

"Theo."

"You have a family?"

"My wife took off for North Carolina with our five children when I enlisted in the Army, and I haven't seen them since."

"What rank were you in the Mexican War?"

"I was in the Army for nearly fifteen years and killed a lot of Mexicans, but never got past the rank of corporal. I guess it had something to do with my affection for tequila and senoritas."

"And what did you do before the Army?"

"I worked on a railroad surveying team based out of Savannah in the 1830s."

Jeremy was tired of talking but stored that little bit of information away.

They arrived in Athens and decided to split up. Jeremy was delighted that the town was mostly spared by the War, having repelled raids by some of Sherman's forces more intent on heading for the capital. Instead of fighting in faraway Virginia, many local men worked in factories that produced rifles, cannons, and uniforms for the Confederacy. Jeremy called on a friend from his old law firm and found he was now working for Cook Brothers, a firearms manufacturer working on an experimental double-barreled cannon that would never see action.

Jeremy stayed with his former coworker and asked several people in town if they knew how the War was impacting North Georgia. Reports were that little was happening in the region around Glory. So, after a few days, he purchased a horse, tent, and provisions and was ready to move on. As he was about to leave, he thought about his former hiking companion. Jeremy went to the boarding house where Theo said he would stay to find that he had left to join a team working to repair the railroad tracks leading to Augusta. Jeremy rode east and soon found the crew.

"Where you headed now?" Theo asked Jeremy.

"I'm headed home to a small mountain town about a hundred miles north. My family has a ranch and a mine that probably need attention."

"You want company?"

"You got a horse?"

"No, but I can keep pace walking," answered Theo.

"Over mountains?" asked Jeremy.

"And rivers and deserts."

Jeremy smiled. "Well then, let's go!"

Theo walked alongside as Jeremy rode his horse. He talked non-stop about the war in Mexico.

"Why didn't you join the Confederate Army?" asked Jeremy.

"I had enough of killing, I don't care anything about protecting slavery, and the Governor asked me to run the stables. He gave me a deferment. I guess it didn't hurt that he's my cousin."

"You're related to Governor Brown?"

"He's my mother's brother's son."

WILLOW *and the boys*

Jeremy thought the connection was interesting, especially given Theo's ragged appearance and plain-spoken ways. But Brown was in exile in Macon, and if Sherman were successful in Georgia, he would no longer be Governor. "I'm surprised you left Milledgeville, given your royal bloodlines."

"You seemed like a good fellow, and I was ready for an adventure. And I don't want to get blamed for losing all those horses."

Jeremy told Theo about the history of his family's land grant and the slate mine. "I must confess, Theo, when you told me you worked for the railroad, it got my attention. The mine will never amount to much shipping slate on flatboats and wagons. The real opportunity depends on getting the railroad to Glory from Atlanta. That is if Atlanta ever recovers from this War. And you might be a very valuable resource."

"I ain't ever been called a resource, but I'll be glad to help if I can."

Chapter Twenty-Five

1865

It took Sherman's force only twenty days to march from Atlanta to Savannah. On December 22, 1864, Sherman wired a message to President Lincoln: *"I beg to present you, as a Christmas gift, the city of Savannah . . ."* The last major Confederate port city was now under Union control. Sherman had accomplished his goal. Georgia was brought to its knees.

Sherman spared Savannah because the city had quickly surrendered and represented an essential port for supplying his troops to secure the Georgia coast. The Union Army crossed the Savannah River and marched through South Carolina, continuing to confiscate or destroy everything in its path. They destroyed the city of Columbia, the capital of the state that had started the war. Sherman spared Raleigh, the capital of North Carolina, and eventually joined Grant's Army of the Potomac. General Lee's Army in Virginia was the only serious threat remaining for the North.

Soon after Lee's forces were repelled at Petersburg, Richmond fell. The War ended at nearby Appomattox, with Lee surrendering to Grant on April 9, 1865. Six hundred and twenty thousand Americans died in the War between 1861 and 1865.

During that same period, the population of Georgia decreased significantly due to battle casualties and the flight of Blacks and whites to other states. Some even fled to South America and Europe. Georgia was no longer a state but an occupied territory under U.S. military command. The new military government relocated the capital to Atlanta and provided civil control and food rations where needed.

Vice President Andrew Johnson, a Democrat from Tennessee, became president after Lincoln was assassinated in April 1865. Johnson appointed a pre-war state official as the new governor of Georgia and took the generous position of allowing each Southern state to elect its own leaders to begin rebuilding. He believed he was dealing with the South as Lincoln intended, but his actions infuriated Republicans in Washington.

The new Georgia General Assembly abolished slavery as required, but the mostly ex-Confederate legislators who were elected did little to help former slaves transition to freedom. The federal government provided education and passed new regulations, such as recognizing Black marriages. Churches soon became the center of community and education for former slaves.

Jeremy was easily elected to represent his district around Glory in November 1865. While his opposition to secession was well known, he was no longer a pariah in the Senate as many of his new colleagues shared his moderate positions. While some states, such as Mississippi and Alabama, passed Black Code laws limiting Blacks from conducting business and moving freely in public places, Jeremy helped defeat such measures in Georgia.

In a letter to Buck in Macon, Jeremy wrote, *"What a surprise that President Johnson is allowing ex-Confederates to serve as our U.S. Senators and state representatives to the General Assembly. It is as if the South never lost the war!"*

Buck replied, *"Perhaps you should come to Macon to see the chaos and unrest we are witnessing in our area. Half of our population are former slaves, and many of them are homeless and dying of disease. If I had the work, I would employ them, but our economy has collapsed. Most of the cotton goes unpicked, rotting in the fields."*

Jeremy replied, *"I am aware of the turmoil in towns like Macon and Savannah. I believe that Washington will eventually help rebuild*

Georgia, but we must show some humility and stop fighting the war all over again."

The outraged Republicans in Congress began drafting amendments to the Constitution that would recognize freed Blacks as citizens with the right to vote and regulations to prevent ex-Confederates from setting policies. Congress denied representation to the old Confederate states until they endorsed the 14th and 15th Amendments, which granted citizenship, equal protection, and the right to vote for all former slaves.

In effect, there were two reconstruction periods, one led by Andrew Johnson and the next, which was more punitive to the South, as demanded by Republican lawmakers. President Johnson would be impeached by the House but acquitted by the Senate. And separate but equal became the new standard for how freed men and women would now be treated in the South.

Mayor Tim Bowers was having nothing to do with the Jim Crow laws adopted by many other Southern towns. The only Black people in town were Kitch and his family, and they were welcome everywhere, including church and town meetings. Not only were they a very kind and educated family, but Kitch ran two of the most successful businesses in Glory, the lumber mill and distillery.

Glory's economy was struggling, but the townspeople were resolute in returning to normal. Noah was preparing to ramp up production at the slate mine. The Morgan family resumed selling town lots and running the tavern. Jeremy helped Noah at the mine when he wasn't lobbying the government to provide funds to expand Glory's school and infirmary or making proposals to bring the railroad to town. Tim and Willow were buying horses to breed and sell at the ranch and planned to build a livery stable on the south side of the main road. Carrie was expanding the plantings on her grandfather's farm. While the rebuilding was robust, Glory had a long road to reach the level of growth of the pre-war years.

Tim held quarterly town halls, which nearly every citizen attended to take advantage of the free pig roast that followed each meeting. Following the prayer, introduction of new landowners, and discussion of open action items, Tim opened the meeting to new business.

Miriam Morgan, who had become a bit less outspoken in her old age, asked to take the floor. "About thirty years ago, I was the one who recommended that we name our town Glory. Roy Bowers was the one who founded this town, but he let me do most of the talking in meetings like this back then." She took a moment to wipe her mouth and straighten her blouse. "Well, I don't like the name Glory anymore, and I know a lot of you feel the same way."

"It sounds Yankee!" yelled one man. "Glory, alleluia, my arse!"

"These times are not Glory!" hollered a woman. "They're more like hell!"

The crowd erupted in dozens of side conversations, and Tim asked Willow to regain order with one of her thumb-and-finger whistles. "I have heard your objections, and I don't disagree," said Tim. "But back when we chose the name Glory, it was mostly because we couldn't agree on anything else. Does anyone want to make a motion to change our town's name?"

Jeremy stood and raised his arms. "Changing our name is no small matter. The state must approve new articles of incorporation and various other costly actions. Whatever we decide, we must be serious and committed."

Miriam Morgan rose again. "You didn't expect me to complain without offering a solution, did you?"

"Let's hear it, Miriam!" replied Tim.

Miriam walked to the front of the room and stood between Tim and Jeremy. She put one hand on each of their shoulders. "The two men who run most matters in Glory are both named Bowers. As I said, their papa who had the vision and organized this town, well, his name was Bowers, too. I say we rename our town Bowerton!"

Tim and Jeremy were a bit taken aback, and the audience fell into another outburst of side conversations. Miriam raised her voice above all others, "Well, what do you say? Clap if you agree!"

The meeting erupted into loud applause. Soon, everyone was standing.

After a few moments, Tim waved to Willow to come stand by his side. His eyes glistened. "I know I speak for Jeremy and Willow in saying how flattered we are. Of course, we owe all the glory to our father. He wouldn't like getting this kind of attention, but he'd be busting with pride that y'all are thinking this way. We are deeply grateful." Tim turned to his brother and put his hand on Jeremy's shoulder. "Jeremy, do you think the state will accept you making such a self-serving request?"

Jeremy smiled brightly and chuckled. "I'll see what I can do."

Tim closed the meeting and invited everyone to supper. All during the meal, he kept going over the new name. Bowerton. It had a good ring to it.

The new Amendments and Second Reconstruction policies from Congress changed the entire political landscape in Georgia. Nearly half of all voters were now Black. Thirty-two members of the General Assembly were Black. Carpetbaggers from the North served in state and federal offices. Republicans ruled the state. In response, the rise of the Ku Klux Klan led to several murders, and Washington sent federal troops to Georgia.

WILLOW *and the boys*

Macon was once again becoming a hub for rail service in all directions, and the development of sharecropping increased yields in the cotton fields. Bowers Builders began receiving new construction orders thanks to rebuilding the rail system and rebounding cotton production. Buck made it a point to hire Black employees, many of whom quickly learned carpentry skills and how to read drawings. After several skirmishes, however, he was forced to separate the men into mostly segregated crews.

The slate mine was back in production in Bowerton. Jeremy had convinced Noah and Tim to invest in a marketing campaign to highlight the fire safety advantage of slate roofing tiles, especially for the rebuilding frenzy in Atlanta. Traditional wood shingles were a fire hazard. Clay roof tiles were too brittle and difficult to install. Slate tiles lasted a lifetime and were manufactured in Georgia!

Jeremy kept calling on several railroad companies to expand their rail service to Bowerton. The tracks from Atlanta to Chattanooga, which ran well west of Fannin County, were the established route. But Jeremy showed railroad executives and engineers his maps demonstrating how they could find plenty of new passenger and freight business by connecting rails to the mines in Bowerton, Copperhill, and Knoxville.

After months of getting nowhere with the railroads, Jeremy met with the Governor for help. The state didn't have the funds to subsidize the project, but they did develop a clever new scheme. Georgia would offer the railroad companies state prisoners to perform manual labor for a low leasing fee. The initiative cleared the General Assembly thanks to Jeremy's experience and connections. The Marietta and North Georgia Railroad Co. signed on immediately. It would take a few years to complete the new rail line, but construction began that spring.

Willow and Carrie Bowers found that rebuilding the Madstone farm to raise more three-sister crops was too labor-intensive. With all the slaves gone to find work elsewhere, not enough workers were available to plant, maintain, and harvest the crops. Willow downsized the growing fields to match the few workers she could find while Carrie continued to expand her chicken ranch and maintain her small apple orchard.

Of the six seeds Carrie had received from the farmer in Ellijay twelve years earlier, four trees were now producing a bounty of Stayman apples she shared with family and sold to Galloway's store. In follow-up trips to Ellijay, Carrie learned how to germinate the seeds from her trees. The farmer warned her that the new crop might not be Stayman apples, but any variety would be good enough to make cider. The farmer also showed her how to graft cuttings from her mature trees to produce Stayman apples.

Willow became interested in her daughter's apple business, and they began experimenting with producing different ciders. Hard cider was very popular because the alcohol killed the harmful bacteria often present in surface and well water. Willow ordered a press to crush apples and brewer's yeast to turn the juice into alcohol. Soon, they were bottling their homemade sweet cider, hard cider, apple brandy, and apple cider vinegar and ordering casks to produce more cider to sell.

Tim and Jeremy often complimented Carrie on her initiative and persistence. As Willow observed, "The girl has a lot of Roy in her."

Chapter Twenty-Six

1869

Four years later...

Mateo was a teenage boy who lost his parents to a tragic epidemic that ravaged his hometown in Cuba. He felt fine, having suffered none of the fever, chills, and jaundice that killed his mother and then his father. Deciding to leave the island and join his uncle living in Georgia, Mateo arrived by boat in Savannah and took the train to Atlanta. He learned that his uncle worked for the railroad, and his crew was laying new tracks northeast of Ellijay.

Mateo was immediately hired for the same crew and took the train carrying men and supplies to the end of the existing rail line. His uncle was happy to see his nephew but shocked to hear of the death of his brother. They talked as they worked shoulder-to-shoulder with pickaxes to level a path for the tracks to run through the hilly terrain.

"How much further will the tracks go?" asked Mateo.

"In a day or two, we will be near a town called Bowerton. I believe this is the last hill we must cut before coming to a river near the town."

"These men complain of the heat and humidity!" Mateo told his uncle in Spanish as they worked. "This is winter weather in Cuba!"

"These men complain about everything," replied the uncle. "Many of them are convicts, so keep your distance. Stay with me."

"Not a problem. You are the only other person who speaks Spanish."

The crew worked until twilight, then walked to camp for a dinner of beef, bread, and black coffee. Mateo and his uncle sat talking beneath the lantern light outside their tent before turning in for the night.

A female mosquito was in flight searching for a blood meal when she sensed a nearby source of carbon dioxide and landed on the back of Mateo's neck. She pierced the skin with a saliva coating to numb the injection point and began sucking the blood out with her spear-like mouthpiece. But her prey was not entirely defenseless, and the mosquito flew off just before a hand slapped the point of skin she had pierced a split second earlier.

The mosquito had not ingested enough blood to produce her eggs, so she went on to bite two more victims. Without any awareness or intention by the mosquito or her prey, she had successfully transmitted the yellow fever virus from Mateo to two more humans. Other mosquitos would bite Mateo and other humans, and the virus would spread geometrically.

It would take three to six days for the infected victims to feel the symptoms of yellow fever, which included fever, chills, back pain, yellow skin, and black vomit. This gave the mosquitos a few more days to infect more unaware people. While only one in eight would get seriously ill, half of those who became sick were likely to die of liver or kidney failure.

Mateo's uncle was one of the unfortunate souls. By the time the crew reached the river near Bowerton, he was bleeding from the mouth, nose, and eyes and eventually stopped breathing. The town doctor immediately recognized the symptoms from reading stories of how past yellow fever outbreaks in Boston and New York had killed thousands. The cause and cure were both unknown. All the doctor could do was make the patient comfortable until he died.

Panic ensued as word of the deaths of other rail workers spread throughout Bowerton. No one understood how the disease was transmitted, but people started avoiding contact with others. Some concocted homemade tonics and other useless remedies. The one thing that people did understand was that there was no disease before the rail workers arrived. Mateo and the other rail workers were ordered to leave town.

Just as Bowerton was recovering from the War, this tragic sickness crippled the town again. Many people were soon showing some signs of fever. Tim immediately sent telegrams to his brothers in Macon and Atlanta to report the terror that had struck Bowerton. Buck replied that, as far as he knew, no one in Macon was sick. Jeremy had the same news from the capital. Tim warned them to be on the lookout for signs of the fever and not to come to Bowerton. He would leave town if he weren't the mayor.

Tim and Willow decided to move from their home in town to her family's abandoned mansion to put some distance between them and those who were ill in town. But it did no good. Soon, Tim was getting a fever and chills; he felt so exhausted that he could hardly get out of bed. Willow asked Adam to get help, but the doctor was also sick in bed. She felt helpless but tried everything she could to make Tim comfortable.

A couple of days after Tim got sick, Carrie came down with the same fever, chills, and fatigue. They both started vomiting, though Tim's was a putrid dark color. Willow wondered if it was dried blood and began worrying that she might lose her husband. Fortunately, she and Adam felt fine and could care for the others.

After four days, both Tim and Carrie started feeling better. Carrie was anxious to return to her chickens, which were barely getting by under her brother's care. Tim was still achy all over but managed to sit in a chair and make trips to the outhouse. However, after a few hours, he returned to bed exhausted.

That night, Willow looked in on Tim and shrieked when she saw blood spots on his pillow. His skin had turned a pale yellow. She changed the pillowcase and called for the children to come to the bedroom.

"I'm afraid your father might be failing," she said, trying to hold back the sobs. "I don't want to scare you, but you may want to spend some time with him, pray he recovers, and maybe say your goodbyes."

Adam looked dazed. Carrie began crying. Willow left the room, and Adam followed.

"Daddy, I hope you can hear me," said Carrie as she sat on the side of the bed and held his hand. She thought she felt a slight tug of his hand. "You've got to get better! What would we do without you? Who's going to haggle with the horse sellers? Who's going to manage the mine and run the town? And who is going to give me those big bear hugs? Please, Daddy, please get better. I love you so much." At that, Carrie began crying and could not go on. She stood and looked down on the pale, sick man who was once her strong, rugged hero. She slowly slipped her hand from his and quietly left the room.

A few well-wishers came to the house, but Willow had them come no closer than the bottom porch step. Mr. Morgan came to wish Tim well and report that Miriam had passed. Noah checked on the family and explained that the gruff old Welshman Owen had died. Kitch came by every afternoon; his family was still okay. The courier delivered telegrams from Jeremy and Buck checking on the family. Willow read the messages and left her replies on the porch for the courier to send.

Two more days passed, and Willow's prayers were answered. Tim began sitting up to drink water and could keep down small amounts of food. Soon, he was able to walk and eat with the family. He was weak but slowly recovering.

One night, Tim asked Carrie to join him in the parlor.

"I sat in this chair when I asked your grandfather for your Mama's hand," Tim began. "You're sitting where rough old Waya Madstone sat. I don't think I left a stain, but I've never been so relieved as when he finally gave his consent!"

Willow came to the doorway when she heard the two laughing. They were unaware of her presence.

"Honey, I heard parts of what you said when I was so sick in bed." He reached over and took her hand in his. "I appreciate what you said, but I want you to know that it's your mama who is the real strength of this family. Fortunately, she'll be around much longer than me. But the remarkable thing is that you're just like her, brave and confident. You make things happen and finish strong. Hell, you could get elected mayor, but I think more important things deserve your time and energy. You are a wonderful young woman, and I am so very proud of you!"

"Thank you, Daddy. I love you so much, and I'm so glad you're feeling better. I won't let you down, just like you carried on when Grandpa Roy passed away. We Bowers persevere!" Carrie stood up and extended her arm toward the ceiling.

Tim got up slowly and gave his daughter the biggest bear hug he could muster. "I love you, honey."

Willow slipped from the doorway, wiping the tears from her cheeks as she returned to the kitchen.

The weeks passed, and the spread of yellow fever ended as mysteriously as it began. The town of about five hundred people lost thirty-one good souls to the fever. When it was clear that the danger had passed, the Methodist church in Bowerton held a special service remembering those who had died and offering comfort to the loved ones who mourned their passing.

As autumn arrived and the trees exploded in a kaleidoscope of amber, crimson, and purple foliage, the citizens of Bowerton realized how fortunate they were that the epidemic had not been worse. They immediately got back to rebuilding despite the fear that the fever might strike again. Some lamented that the weather was getting cooler. Little did they know that the first morning of frost ended the pestilence by killing the mosquitos.

The epidemic seriously disrupted one major initiative in Bowerton—the completion of the final leg of the railroad to town. When some of the crew died from yellow fever, the other workers building the wood trestle over the river ran off, and it was hard to find other rail workers willing to come anywhere near Bowerton. Meanwhile, the Marietta and North Georgia Railway paid Bowerton citizens to build a fine passenger and freight train depot in town, in just the spot where Roy had envisioned.

As winter passed, the trestle was completed, work on the tracks resumed, and the train made its inaugural stop at Bowerton Station. The whole town turned out to welcome the train as it chugged along, bellowing clouds of white steam high into the air. It might be years before the tracks continued north, but the four-hour trip to Atlanta provided connections to just about anywhere in the country.

For years, Willow had thought about her brother Hawk and how he died in the Battle of Sharpsburg, or Antietam as the Yankees called it, without any acknowledgment of his sacrifice. She decided it was her duty to honor his final resting place. Now that Bowerton had a station, the train could take her to the closest depot near Sharpsburg in Frederick, Maryland. From there, she needed to find transportation to the village and cemetery. Tim saw her off at the station with a half-kidding warning about the robberies and hobos now plaguing the railroads.

The train ride along the beautiful mountains of North Carolina and

Virginia took her mind off her sad mission. But entering the Union state of Maryland triggered the horrible memories of her rape by those two Yankee soldiers. Willow was a resilient person and knew she had done nothing wrong. She was simply a woman overpowered by animals who were sure to burn in hell. Thank goodness that Tim had been tender and patient, making her feel safe and giving her time to rebuild her trust in men.

She had no idea what state those men had come from, but if she happened to see them again, she would casually pull the small pistol out of her handbag and shoot them between the eyes.

She arrived in Frederick and found a carriage driver who knew his way to Sharpsburg, twenty-five miles west of town. Near the battlefield, the U.S. government created a stately cemetery for the fallen soldiers. But as Willow walked the grounds, she could find no Confederate graves. She returned to the inn in Sharpsburg, where she and her driver were staying, and asked to find someone to help her find her brother's grave.

"You didn't expect to find Graybacks buried alongside our boys, did you?" expressed the inn owner.

Willow held back her fury. "So where are the Southern boys buried?" asked Willow.

"Those Union soldiers that died in battle were quickly buried where they fell out in the fields by other soldiers. The Rebs had retreated, so they didn't bury their dead. Those of us living in Sharpsburg couldn't just let the bodies rot on the ground, so we dug trenches and buried the Graybacks in common graves.

"After the War, the military dug up those thousands of shallow graves, both blue and gray, and tried to identify the bodies. They buried the Union soldiers in the National Cemetery, and the remains of the Confederate soldiers were hauled away in wagons and buried elsewhere, mostly in Hagerstown."

Willow was heartbroken at the man's horrifying description of the aftermath of the battle, but she needed to keep going. "Hagerstown? Where is that?"

"Hagerstown is northwest of here, about fifteen miles. The town is bigger than Frederick and has a train station."

Willow had her driver make the trip to Hagerstown. After asking around, she was directed to Washington Confederate Cemetery, where a section of the graveyard contained the remains of Confederate dead. But there were no gravestones, just a single monument. Over twenty-four hundred brave Confederate soldiers were buried in one mass grave.

Willow stood at the site and wept.

Jeremy was also on a mission to find his son Billy. He would be thirty-four years old now, and the only way Jeremy knew to track him down was to find his mother, Hannah. There was no telling what crazy falsehoods Hannah told Billy, but he had to believe that her lies kept him from trying to find his birth father. Jeremy braced himself for a challenging encounter.

Jeremy took the train to Macon and stayed with Buck and his family at the old homestead. Abigail was a gracious hostess, and Buck gave Jeremy a tour of post-War Macon. As planned, they ended their ride at the Kendall plantation, where Jeremy had previously visited but failed to see Billy.

The once grand plantation was now in shambles. The fields needed plowing, the house needed repairs, and no one was in sight. Jeremy knocked at the front door. After several moments, a young man in his thirties opened the door.

"Billy?" asked Jeremy, unsure he would recognize his son after all these years.

"No, I'm Stephen. Who are you?"

Jeremy made the introductions and explained that they were trying to find Billy Bowers.

"My stepbrother was Billy Kendall, not Bowers."

"Was?" asked Jeremy.

"Yes. Billy died at Chickamauga."

Jeremy covered his mouth with his hand and turned away from the house. The thought that Billy was involved in the War had often crossed his mind, but he hoped things had somehow turned out for the better.

"Are Mr. Kendall or Hannah here?" asked Buck.

"Why are you looking for Billy and asking all these questions?" asked Stephen.

Buck wasn't sure this was the right time or place, but the opportunity to find out more might not come again. "My brother was Billy's father," said Buck, gesturing toward Jeremy. "He and Hannah were once married, and Billy was their son."

Stephen seemed doubtful, so Buck provided more information. "They met in Athens and married. Billy was born after they moved to Macon on Magnolia Street. Then they separated when Billy was about six, and my brother moved away."

Stephen listened intently and paused. Finally, he nodded. "I'm sorry, but things have been really rough here. My father died of injuries after getting wounded at the Battle of Griswoldville. My mother is here, but she isn't well. She doesn't want to see anyone."

Buck reached into his pocket and handed Stephen his business card. "I hope you'll tell your mother that we came to visit. If either of you want to talk or need any help at all, please come see me at my office."

After saying farewell, Buck put his arm around his brother as they walked to their horses for the ride back home.

Willow had returned from her long trip to Maryland by the time Jeremy arrived home in Glory. They shared their frustration and grief at the brutality of the War. Everyone in the South felt the impact in some way, but those who lost young loved ones on the battlefield carried the wounds in their hearts for the rest of their lives.

Chapter Twenty-Seven
1872

Three years later...

After years of rebuilding from the Civil War, the nation began to experience rapid growth. Ulysses Grant was reelected president, and the ugly era of Reconstruction was ending in the South. J.P. Morgan was building his banking empire. Cornelius Vanderbilt was expanding his railroad network across the country. John Rockefeller refined and piped vast new supplies of oil to the East. Andrew Carnegie was providing the steel for a new industrial revolution. Women began fighting for suffrage. Immigrants once again streamed into the country.

Bowerton shared in the economic boom led by expanded production at the mine. The latest steam engines brought more ore out of the pit and powered the machinery inside the plant building. A railroad spur next to the plant allowed finished products to be loaded onto train cars and transported to Atlanta and beyond. Noah, Jeremy, and Tim hired dozens of new employees for the operations.

The post-war boom saw a surge in people wanting to belong. Union and Confederate veteran organizations attracted hundreds of thousands of members in local clubs and national reunions. Social and civic clubs like the Freemasons and Odd Fellows flourished. People had money, trains to ride, and a new drive to socialize with like-minded people. The boom also spurred a golden age of grand hotels in cities and resorts in getaway locations.

Given this new Age of Fraternalism, the Bowers wanted to do something special with the money they had accumulated from the mine. Something that would put Bowerton on the map. Jeremy, Tim, and Willow sat in Tim's parlor sipping Kitch's special reserve whiskey.

"We could erect statutes honoring our heroes," offered Tim.

"We can do that, but I was thinking of something bigger," replied Jeremy.

"Sounds like you already have something in mind," offered Willow.

"I think we should build a grand lodge," announced Jeremy. "We have land not producing anything and can acquire more if needed at a good price."

"Where did you come up with that idea?" asked Tim.

"Grand hotels are being built in cities all over. We saw the Lanier House under construction in Macon. Atlanta has the Trout House, and other big projects are being planned. Most are brick buildings several stories tall, with grand lobbies, restaurants, and well-appointed rooms. There is nothing like that in North Georgia, and we have such great scenery and weather."

Tim was immediately excited about the idea. "I see a lodge built of rock with flagstone floors and a slate tile roof. How many stories?"

"I think three stories would be right. Plus, a basement for utilities and storage. Nothing too extravagant to start."

"Do we know any contractors who could manage such an undertaking?" asked Tim rhetorically, referring to Buck.

"It would be so great for us all to work on this together!" replied Willow excitedly.

"The train can deliver building materials and transport guests," added Jeremy. "Buck and Abigail can visit more often traveling by train."

Tim was getting more enthused about the idea by the minute. "With Buck Jr. running the company, they can spend more time away from Macon."

"I love it!" exclaimed Willow. "Where are you thinking of putting the lodge?"

"On your family's old farm," explained Jeremy. "Together with the ranch, we would have hundreds of acres with a river running right through the property. If we need more land, we could buy one of those adjacent lots to the west."

"And what happens to my parent's house?" asked Willow.

Neither brother had a quick answer. "We need to find a good architect to create elevations that fit the landscape," said Jeremy. "I see the hotel sitting on a hill overlooking the river with the mountains in the background. I don't know how the house fits into the plan."

Willow's excitement faded a bit. "I was hoping Carrie or Adam might want to live in the old house eventually. I'd hate to see anything happen to Carrie's chickens, apple trees, or the distillery and sawmill."

Jeremy recognized this as their first challenge. "Let's walk the property with an expert and see if we can make everybody happy. Carrie and Adam will be the ones to inherit this castle, so we'll bring them into the planning process as well."

Jeremy had heard and read good reviews for the Greenbrier Inn in White Sulphur Springs, West Virginia, and decided to check it out. The Chesapeake and Ohio Railway took him directly to the front gate. The rooms were spacious and well-furnished, and the dining was excellent. The prices were high, which was of no consequence to the powerful and wealthy families who made "The Old White" their favorite place to visit.

The Greenbrier resort, founded in 1778, was nestled in the mountains with an elevation of about two thousand feet. A village with shops and residences for staff was within walking distance, which was good because the Inn was distant from any large population. The mountain vistas reminded Jeremy of their planned location, but the Greenbrier had three unique features. The spring water used in the indoor pool wasn't available on their property. The game room for gambling was not something he cared to duplicate. Jeremy was unfamiliar with the outdoor courts built for some new sport called tennis, but adding similar grass courts would not be difficult. Jeremy's current vision of their lodge featuring stables, a distillery, chicken ranch, and apple orchard would distinguish their inn as more Deep South chic.

Jeremy spent two days at the inn to get some background information on the owner, architect, and builder. As it turned out, the architect was on staff and living at the inn as he worked on plans for a major expansion. He was not interested in taking on a project in Georgia but gave Jeremy the name of a well-respected hotel architect in Charlotte.

The Charlotte architect came to Bowerton and walked the grounds. Tim had purchased one of the lots west of the original Madstone property, so there were now over six hundred acres for him to work with. They held a meeting the next day in the old Madstone home and invited Carrie, Adam, and Kitch to join them.

"Can this house be preserved as part of the resort?" Willow asked the architect.

"I like this house, and we can work around it if you insist, but I thought this location would be ideal for a row of cabins close enough to hear the water burbling over the rocks in the river." The architect presented a large plat he had prepared after surveying the property, showing his recommended locations for the hotel, cabins, entrance road, several outbuildings, and a maintenance shed hidden in the woods.

"What about the barn on this property?" asked Carrie, referring to the

Madstone barn.

"We already have a horse barn and pastures on the east side of the river," replied the architect. "I don't think two barns are needed."

Tim glanced at Kitch and then asked, "Would expanding the horse barn displace a family already living in that old cabin?"

Kitch spoke up. "I love the idea of this project. It's high time I left the cabin to build a home for my family in town."

"What about my chicken farm?" asked Carrie half seriously. "And apple orchard?"

"Can we build you some new, fancier chicken pens? And maybe add some cows and pigs near the stables? The apple orchard is fine where it is. And I think a big garden in the field between the lodge and the row of cabins would be a nice feature. The garden could supply the dining room with fresh produce."

"What about the mine on the other side of the ranch?" asked Tim. "There are loud explosions every day. Would that be a problem for the guests?"

"I think it will be fine. We can explain to the guests that the stone used in the hotel came from that mine. I didn't think you would close the mine when the lodge opens, would you?"

"No," replied Tim. "It's a major source of employment for families in Bowerton."

"Good! I think it only adds to the unique personality of the place, as long as you schedule the explosions during daylight hours."

The architect looked out over the seemingly satisfied, smiling faces of everyone. "When this is completed, I believe you will have a destination that ranks up there with what they are developing in the Adirondacks, Poconos, and Hudson River Valley. They may have steeper mountains or mineral springs, and there may be fancier hotels in big cities like Memphis, Baltimore, and New York, but you have wonderful vistas, pastures, and a rocky river. I am excited for you and the community."

Tim asked, "Do you happen to know a good architect we could hire to develop the detailed plans?"

"I would be honored to commit my firm," replied the architect.

Tim looked at Willow and then Jeremy, who both gave him a nod. "You're hired! Let's get started!"

"It will be several weeks before we can complete the drawings. In the meantime, we need to research the names of potential contractors. Working with stone will take a large crew of skilled masons."

"We were hoping to employ our brother, Buck, in Macon," said Tim.

"Builders in Macon are respected for their wood and brick construction. But you want stone, so I was thinking of a contractor with access to stonemasons from Europe."

"We'll have to work on that," responded Jeremy. "We just wanted our brother to be part of the team."

"There can be plenty of work for Buck's company," said the architect. "We'll incorporate lots of timber features in the design." He began to roll up his drawings. "In time, you'll have to come up with a special name for your lodge."

"We can work on that, too," added Tim.

The family became consumed with planning for the lodge, especially

Kitch. The cabin where he and Nora lived would be in the middle of construction if it survived at all, so he began planning where to build a new home in town, one large enough for his family. He didn't need to borrow funds because the distillery, lumber mill, and living rent-free in the cabin for years had allowed him to build a sizable nest egg.

Willow began thinking of ways to convert the horse barn to riding stables and adding new pasture fencing for the horses and other livestock. Jeremy was shopping for financing with banks around the state. Carrie was planning to relocate and expand her chicken pens.

Tim was exchanging letters with Buck, asking him to visit Bowerton for an extended stay to get in on the ground floor of their planning. Buck was initially reluctant to get involved in something so large and far away but, like his father, was ready for a new adventure. And he was now comfortable leaving the building company in the hands of Buck Jr., now in his forties.

Tim also decided to retire from his service as mayor. He tried to convince Willow to announce her candidacy at the same time he announced his departure. But she said she wanted no part of serving if she wasn't allowed to vote. Carrie was too young, and Bowerton would be better off if Jeremy continued to serve as their State Senator in the capital. Tim hoped they could find someone in town with leadership experience to take the position.

Once Tim announced his retirement, a relatively new resident of Bowerton began campaigning to be the next mayor. Charles Lambert was from Pittsburgh and transferred to town by the railroad to manage the Bowerton Station operations. He was in his late twenties, educated, and married with five children. Tim met with Lambert at the tavern and, on first impression, thought he seemed responsible enough to handle the job. Two other people offered to run, but Tim knew them and thought Lambert was a better candidate.

With Tim's endorsement, Lambert won the election. But within days of taking office, Tim could see trouble brewing. Lambert was full of big ideas, such as hiring a city manager for day-to-day operations and adding staff to collect unpaid taxes and fees. He wanted to attend conventions in New Orleans and Memphis to hobnob with other mayors, and he failed to continue holding quarterly town meetings.

After a few weeks, Tim requested a meeting with the new mayor. Lambert put him off for several days but finally arranged to meet.

"Have you circulated your plans and a budget to the town council?" asked Tim.

"I will present them at our next meeting," replied Lambert.

"And when will that be?"

"I don't know. Council has not informed me of a date."

"But you know they need to approve the budget, right?"

"Right."

"And how will you balance the budget and fund the costs of your new initiatives?"

"I intend to raise the money by creating a business license fee based on the number of employees."

"So you're going to increase taxes on the businesses that employ the most people?"

"It's an annual fee, not a tax."

"But our larger merchants will pay more to the town than they do now, right?"

"They require more support from the town, so they need to pay more of the common costs."

"I think they will rebel," offered Tim. "You said nothing about higher taxes during your campaign."

"Of course not. What candidate would?"

"An honest one," replied Tim.

Lambert huffed and raised his hands in protest. "Mr. Bowers, I know you own the slate mine with more employees than any other business. But the town needs to support all citizens, and you and the other businessmen have the means to contribute more."

"It's the businesses that create jobs that give more people a reason to live here and raise a family. If you increase taxes, businesses will have less money for raises and hiring new employees. I know you work for the railroad, but if you had your own business, you would better understand how things work."

Lambert grinned, shaking his head slowly. "I appreciate your time this morning, Mr. Bowers, but I must attend another meeting." He stood and offered his hand.

Tim slowly rose from his chair to shake his hand. He left deeply concerned for the future of Bowerton. Lambert was about to learn the economic realities of running the town that years of experience had taught Tim.

None of the five Councilmen had been informed of a date for their next meeting with the mayor. They were all concerned about the communication level, or lack thereof. Tim informed them of the concerns he had after meeting with Lambert.

There was a loud outcry when the merchants in town received their assessment for business fees based on the number of their employees.

The bill for the Bowers Slate Mine was almost as much as the property taxes they already paid annually. Several merchants requested a meeting with the mayor, but Lambert apparently didn't think it necessary to reply.

Tim checked with Jeremy for advice. Jeremy agreed that the bylaws were incomplete in differentiating fees and taxes or laying out what actions could be taken if a mayor went rogue. Unbeknownst to Tim or Jeremy at the time, the railroad had sent a formal letter to the mayor challenging the assessment and threatening to close Bowerton Station if the town did not void the bill for business fees.

Jeremy was preparing to sue the mayor in the Superior Court Circuit when he received a visit from Charles Lambert.

"Would you consider advising me of my options?" Lambert asked Jeremy.

"I'd be glad to," replied Jeremy. "What advice do you need?"

"I'd like you to reply to the railroad and any other business that objects to paying their business fees."

Jeremy looked over his reading glasses and shook his head to reign in his emotions. "Mr. Mayor, I cannot represent you. Not only do I thoroughly disagree with the way you went about this, but I have a conflict of interest. I am one of the businesses that object to your charging fees for my five employees. I am preparing to sue you myself."

Lambert looked at Jeremy with surprise and then disdain. He took a moment to speak, but before he could, Jeremy continued, "And I was considering writing to the railroad to inform them that the mayor who sent them that bill happens to be one of their employees."

Lambert took a deep breath. "You don't want the improvements I'm proposing for the town?"

"Some of them, sure. But there's a right way to do this. First, taxes and fees are the same; they are both public revenues. Next, you need to put together a budget by working with the council. I'm pretty sure that when you do, you'll reverse course. You should postpone any new spending initiatives until you convince the council and the town that the benefits of your plans are worth the costs."

Lambert was listening, and Jeremy continued. "You need to understand that the town's revenues will increase by attracting new businesses and growing the ones we already have, not by raising more taxes. And a business like mine can simply move outside the town limits to avoid the tax entirely."

Jeremy didn't expect Lambert to accept what he was saying immediately. The guy wasn't a bad person, just inexperienced and uninformed. He gave the mayor a minute to respond.

"You've given me some things to think about, Mr. Bowers. I will take what you've said into consideration."

Within three weeks, each business charged the new fee received notice that their bill was canceled; something about a misunderstanding. The mayor announced a date for the next council meeting and invited the public to attend.

Tim saw Jeremy that afternoon. "Brother, I don't know what you said to Lambert, but he has seen the light. I spoke with some councilmen, and things seem to be back on track."

Buck arrived in Bowerton. Abigail had stayed behind but promised to join him if he needed to extend his stay to work on the plans for the lodge. Buck stayed at the Madstone mansion, and Willow invited him and Jeremy to her house for dinner.

After the meal, Willow reflected on Buck's visit. "You have no idea how nice it is to see you three brothers together again. I guess the last time we were together was Roy's memorial service. We've all gotten a bit grayer and stiffer . . ."

"She'll be fifty-seven next week!" injected Tim, pointing his good arm toward his wife. "Y'all believe it?"

"People probably think she's your daughter!" added Jeremy.

"Hell, I'll be seventy-three this year!" added Buck.

"You don't look a day over seventy-two," chided Tim.

Willow gave them one of her 120-decibel finger whistles and then patted the air above her head with both hands. "Excuse me! I'm trying to make a speech here!" Everyone quieted down. "I just wanted to say that I hope y'all appreciate what you have! Men never take the time to express these things, so I will! Not only do you three brothers get along well, but y'all have done so much for your families and communities!" Willow looked at them each. "What a picture! Three handsome old lions, sitting there laughing and scheming and enjoying each other's company! I love y'all!"

Jeremy took a moment to end the silence that followed. "Thank you, Willow. You're the best sister-in-law anyone could have!"

"Don't let Abigail hear you say that!" said Tim, "Or Hannah!"

Jeremy threw his hand in the air toward his brother. "Go to hell!"

Buck continued, "You called us lions, but I guess you know the lionesses are the ones who raise the cubs and do all the hunting. It would be more accurate to call us Willow and the boys."

"But the lions do the fighting and protecting," Willow responded. "You boys have been great keeping us safe, yet I've never seen you fight."

"That's because Buck and I would never dare challenge a disabled veteran," replied Jeremy.

"I can still lick you both one-handed," said Tim.

"I'd whip your ass," said Buck, "but I'm afraid my . . ."

They waited for Buck to finish, but when he couldn't remember what he was going to say, they erupted in laughter. Beneath the frivolity, the reality was that the handsome old lions were entering their twilight years.

The dining room of the Madstone house became the war room for planning the design and construction of the lodge. Buck joined the group meeting with the Charlotte architect, who had brought preliminary drawings and cost estimates. The family had agreed that ownership of the enterprise would be based on how much of their savings each pledged, taking into account the land contributed by Willow and Tim. Once they agreed on a total project budget, Jeremy arranged to borrow the remainder from a bank.

The architect started with some bad news. "Based on my estimates, the total costs with contingencies and soft costs exceed the budget figure you gave me. If you are firm with how much you want to invest, we must pare back some parts of the project."

Jeremy spoke first. "I believe we need to stick to our original budget. I am not comfortable investing more personally, and I don't think the bank will increase our credit line."

Everyone agreed. "And you have some ideas for reducing the scope of the project?" Buck asked.

"I do," replied the architect. "I think we could postpone building the row of cabins, and instead of rebuilding the horse barn and distillery in stone, we could go with wood construction."

"We can build the cabins later, and I like the idea of wood outbuildings more, anyway," remarked Tim. "Wood is more mountain-style and would detract less from the big stone lodge on the hill. And besides, we could manage the construction of the barn and outbuildings ourselves, right Buck?"

"I'll have to look at the plans more closely, but you're probably right."

"You boys are too old to be hauling logs and climbing barn roofs," remarked Willow.

"I haven't climbed a ladder in ten years," exclaimed Buck.

"And I haven't hauled anything heavy since Kennesaw," added Tim, letting his bad arm dangle at his side. "Hell, Jeremy never built anything with his hands in his life."

Jeremy just looked up and smiled. "But we do know how to hire men who follow directions," he added.

"One thing I don't want to compromise on is the new bridge," suggested Tim. "It needs to be built of stone, wide enough for wagons, and high enough for flatboats to pass under."

The architect made notes of the owners' feedback and then rolled out a detailed map of the site to point out different features. "Here's the primary lodge, with a nice deck looking out over the river and mountains. This first phase includes seventy rooms, plus a grand lobby, dining, lounge, and meeting spaces. The building can be expanded later with wings on either side, and the ten suites on the main level could be repurposed to enlarge the dining, lounge, or meeting spaces when needed."

"What do you think, Buck?" Tim asked.

"I like the forward-thinking!" Buck replied.

"How long do you think it will take to complete this first phase?" asked Tim.

"If we find the right stonemasons, I'd say about two years once we finalize our drawings and get contractors lined up," replied the architect. "I added a few extra weeks because our location here is pretty remote."

Tim looked at Buck again. "That sounds about right," replied Buck. "But I've never worked with a crew of stonemasons. Where do you find them?"

"The best come from Italy, France, and Spain," replied the architect. "They've been building cathedrals and huge stone buildings there for centuries. There are immigrant stonemasons here in the U.S., but they're mostly up north working on projects in the big cities."

"Hell, if Roy could find slate cutters from Wales," exclaimed Tim, "we can find some Frenchmen to build our lodge!"

"I'm worried about finding the staff we'll need for cooking and cleaning once we open," said Willow.

"That will be your job as general manager," said Tim.

"Then I delegate the recruiting to Carrie," replied Willow. She looked at her daughter, who smiled and nodded.

The meeting ended, and the three brothers walked from the mansion to the ranch across the river to get a better sense of what the architect planned for the stables. As they passed by the old cabin, Jeremy stopped to reflect. "I remember the first time I came here. There was nothing but a collection of tents in the woods."

"That's the original fire pit I built," said Tim, pointing to the circle of rocks. "It's about the only thing that hasn't changed." Tim looked toward the river. "No. I'm wrong. There's one more thing that's still the same." Tim motioned to Jeremy and Buck to follow as he led them to a tall stack of river rocks. "Here lies the best dog we ever had."

"Jax?" asked Buck. "Right here?"

Tim nodded. "He died fighting a six-foot-long copperhead," he exaggerated.

The three men stood reverently over the stones, telling stories about Jax and the good times four decades ago.

After a few moments, Jeremy raised his arm and exclaimed, "To a damn good dog!"

They looked at each other and nodded.

"C'mon, let's get a drink in Jax's honor," bellowed Tim, and the three brothers turned to walk back toward the mansion together.

Chapter Twenty-Eight
1873

A few months later...

Cooke & Company became one of the largest banks in the country during the Civil War by selling hundreds of millions of dollars of Union war bonds. When the War ended, they switched to financing the railroads. When the boom in railroad expansion began to sputter, the bank had trouble selling its bonds. The banks became owners of the rail operations, which they had no business running. Depositors made a run on the bank, its stock value plummeted, and Cooke & Company was soon bankrupt.

The failure of Cooke started a chain reaction. Many other banks were soon closing, the stock market crashed, and the U.S. entered its longest and deepest depression to date—the Panic of 1873.

Within weeks, the bank that had agreed to finance a portion of the lodge project reneged on its line of credit. Roy had taught his sons to favor holding gold and silver over investing in banks or stocks, but the Bowers still lost a significant portion of their savings. After spending months finalizing the design and budget, they found the lodge project was suddenly in jeopardy.

Buck felt the deepest impact of the downturn from a sudden decline in building projects in the Macon area. He informed his brothers that he had to withdraw from the lodge project to spend more time with the business and protect his family's remaining reserves.

Jeremy and Tim met to consider their options.

"We've had banks go bust and the stock market crash before," said Tim. "Maybe this will all soon pass."

"I'm afraid this is a serious one," Jeremy replied. "Europe is in a panic, and so is New York. Everyone is blaming the other in Washington. Cotton and grain prices are crashing, and people are getting laid off everywhere."

"Are you saying that we should quit the project?" asked Tim. "We still have a pile of money from the mine to invest."

"I don't want to quit, but we have to rethink this," replied Jeremy. "We need to find those things that won't cost a lot but still move us forward. Take the quarry, for example. Instead of shutting down, we could keep producing rock for the lodge and use our savings to save the jobs of some of the crew. But one thing is certain; we are no longer on a two-year timeline."

Tim took a few moments to think. "I believe we should keep the architect on board to supervise whatever we do. I like him, especially with Buck cutting back. And let's start the grading; it's not that complicated. If the economy does stay in the ditch, we could keep men in town employed with site work."

"I agree," replied Jeremy. "And we could begin renovating the distillery, bridge, and stables. We can do that locally, and maybe Buck will still help us some. I don't think he wants to back out of the project entirely. He was just hesitant about building with stone."

"Sounds like we agree," said Tim. "Let's meet with the architect and see if we can convince Buck to get back up here for a new strategy meeting."

Buck agreed to make another trip to Bowerton, and this time, Abigail came along on the train. He was not surprised that his brothers were still determined to continue the project. Buck offered his advice on grading the site for the foundation of the lodge structure and renovations to the outbuildings.

Excavation began on a hill once covered by Madstone's cornfields. They soon hit rock, and Noah provided the explosives and expertise for blasting. Noah also installed tram cars on rails once used at the mine to move the excavated rock and soil to areas that needed more fill. The architect kept remarking on how resourceful this team could be.

Meanwhile, Tim hired a local crew to rebuild a larger, more elaborate distillery. The highly flammable ethanol gas produced in the distilling process could cause an explosion, so the boiler, thump keg, and pipe hardware would be located in an open pole barn. The adjacent warehouse would provide space for barrel aging and material storage.

The architect designed a wide stone bridge to connect the properties. Buck oversaw a crew to build the foundation in the riverbed as the mine delivered rock. Steel girders were on the way.

Willow supervised the expansion of the barn on the Bowers side of the river to include thirty stalls and an oversized saddle room. All of the lumber came from local trees milled by Kitch. Willow wished she had more time to spend with Abigail, but her sister-in-law seemed perfectly happy to explore the town, plan the meals, and visit all the busy Bowers with cider and homemade biscuits.

Carrie worked on installing new fencing around the pastures and building a new chicken house near the stables. The architect thought the lumber mill was okay to stay as it was, and Roy's old cabin would serve as an office, meeting space, and supply room for the stables.

It wouldn't be ready in two years, but the lodge was taking shape despite the terrible economic times in faraway cities.

As construction continued, the conversation at meals turned to finding an appropriate name for the resort.

"How about Toccoa Lodge, after the river?" offered Carrie.

"That name might get mixed up with a town east of here that just got its charter approved by the General Assembly," responded Jeremy.

Willow thought for a moment. "Well then, how about Greystone?"

"Sounds a bit dreary," quipped Jeremy. "And I've been through a village north of Atlanta called Greystone."

"How about Eagle House?" added Carrie. "Or Eagle Manor?"

"Do you see any eagles around here?" questioned Tim.

Carrie offered, "How about Turkey House? Or Chicken Pen? Or Equine Manor?"

"I kind of like turkey in the name!" exclaimed Tim. "There are plenty around, and they are good to eat."

"Then how about Turkey Pen?" Carrie followed up.

Heads nodded, and no one offered any new suggestions. "Turkey Pen is unique!" said Abigail. "It has a kind of down-home ring to it. I like it!"

"I like it, too," said Willow, "but how about Turkey Hollow? You know, hollow like what we call a valley surrounded by mountains on three sides with a creek running through it."

"Did you say holler, as in yelling?" asked Abigail.

"Yes. It's spelled hollow but pronounced holler," replied Willow.

"I like it!" declared Tim. "Can we all agree on Turkey Hollow?"

They all yelled yes, and the matter was finally settled.

WILLOW and the boys

Buck and Abigail returned to Macon, and Tim and Noah went on a field trip to find stonemasons to build the lodge. Noah had heard about a mining operation at Stone Mountain, east of Atlanta. The massive dome of granite that rose over eight hundred feet above the surrounding terrain was not difficult to find.

"We're in the market for some stonemasons," Tim announced to the mining operation manager. "We were hoping that you might know of some for hire or tell us about a customer that is winding down their project."

The manager shook his head and pursed his lips. "I don't know any masons available right now, and I'm not going to tell you about my customers' crews so you can steal them away. I sell stone; I don't build anything."

As Tim tried to loosen up the manager, Noah looked around at the operations and was impressed with what he could see. "You have a full-gauge rail spur?"

"We do. Goes right to the Central lines."

"And I see you're using the new Ingersoll steam-powered rock drills. Are they worth it?"

"The men love them. Beats doing it by hand."

Noah and the manager continued their shop talk until Tim gave Noah a nod to wrap it up.

The manager shook Noah's hand. "I've enjoyed talking to you. If I'm ever in the mountains, I might stop by and see your operation." He hesitated a moment. "You know, there are a couple of people you might talk to about masons. One is the contractor building the Harris place in Atlanta. They call it Wren's Nest or some strange name. He's some writer who insisted on French masons. And the state engineer in Atlanta is getting bids to build a new capitol building. The bugger is giving the contract to an outfit in Indiana for limestone block, so feel free to poach his people."

Tim and Noah rode into Atlanta looking for stone-built projects and the craftsmen building them. According to the architect, five or six experienced masons could probably accomplish the work if supported by a larger team of laborers to mix mortar and haul rocks. As they rode through the city streets, they found that almost every structure was built with brick and lumber.

They visited the Harris home project on the west side of downtown, but construction had not started. They went to the state capital offices, temporarily housed in the Kimball Opera House, and called on the state engineer. He had not yet begun hiring a masonry contractor and suggested they try the Freemasons lodge, which turned out to be a fraternal organization, not a guild of stonemasons. They went home frustrated.

The architect, however, was successful in finding a source for Italian masons by inquiring with other architects in the Southeast. A mason subcontractor was available, but the crew would be coming from Trenton. Tim hoped they spoke English because he knew no one in North Georgia who spoke Italian.

The rest of the construction workers could be found in Bowerton. The prolonged depression may have forced the Bowers' budget to decrease and the timeline to extend, but men were anxious to find work to support their families, even if it meant backbreaking construction tasks.

Weeks later, Tim took on the task of welcoming the five Italian stonemasons who arrived from New Jersey.

"Do y'all speak English?" Tim asked them at lunch after he picked them up at the train station. They continued eating without responding. "Do . . . any . . . of . . . you . . . speak . . . English?"

Finally, one of the men replied. "I speak English, but not so good."

Tim just shook his head. How were these men going to take direction? Hopefully, the architect had dealt with a language problem before and knew how to communicate his message.

After lunch, Tim rode the men in the wagon to their new housing assignments. After dropping off their luggage, he drove them to the mansion war room to meet the architect.

The architect barely understood the lead mason but didn't seem upset. The key was that the men could read plans, which spelled out on paper all they needed to know.

The architect led the masons on a tour of the job site. The Italians started inspecting the masonry work completed at the basement level and began yelling in Italian at one another. One would point to an area in the wall, the others would come to look, and they would all start fussing and laughing.

The architect went to the leader. "What's funny?" he asked.

"Need to start over. Bad work."

"The work is fine," replied the architect. "It's plumb and strong and will be covered by dirt. I'm not concerned. Your work begins on the next floor."

"Look!" said the mason, pointing to a spot on one of the walls. "Bad work. Too many cements."

"It's fine," stated the architect. "You build from here up."

After their site visit, Tim took the men through town to show them where to buy food and dry goods, get a haircut, and go to church.

"Where's Catholic church?" asked the spokesman.

"We don't have a Catholic church. There are few Catholics in town. You can choose between Methodist and Baptist. You ought to choose Baptist because they serve better food more often."

Tim's attempt at humor went nowhere.

"And where is liquor store? We need vino."

Tim exhaled loudly. "They serve drinks at the tavern, but you can't buy alcohol in Bowerton."

"No one drinks vino? With dinner?"

Tim knew Willow would probably serve wine with dinner, which she routinely bought by the case from Zeke. "I'll tell you what. I will provide you with two jugs of wine every Saturday after work, but only if there are no complaints from anyone in town about you. Think of it as a bonus for staying out of trouble."

"Free vino?"

"Yes, but only for good behavior."

Tim's next step was taking the men to his house, where Willow had agreed to serve dinner to their new international guests. But during the meal, the Bowers became uncomfortable with how much attention the men were directing at Willow and Carrie. They would gawk and say things in Italian that amused the others.

Finally, Tim had had enough. "Listen up! I have no idea what y'all are saying, but we can't have this. Here's your first rule. Gazing, flirting, and touching women in town, especially these two, are strictly off limits."

Tim gave the spokesman time to translate. There was no way to know if the man could understand or communicate the message, but the mood of the men went from jovial to confused and agitated. "If I see or hear about any of you carrying on with any women, there will be no jugs of wine that week. And if it's bad, I'll put you right back on the train you rode in on. Am I understood?" Tim gave the spokesman time to translate.

"No fornicate?" asked the spokesman.

"Fornicate?" echoed Tim, exasperated. "No fornicating, no touching, no jeering, or even flirting! Period!"

"Flirting? Whata you mean, flirting?"

"Staring at a woman for more than three seconds."

The spokesman explained this to the men and then made an announcement. "Okay, boss, we do as you say."

Willow and Carrie couldn't hold back and busted out laughing. The men all started laughing with them.

Tim sat back in his chair and just smiled. Dealing with this group was going to be a challenge.

The mine began delivering a steady supply of rock by wagon, and the Italians exceeded everyone's expectations for their non-stop effort and attention to detail. The stone used for the exterior walls was sandstone, found in abundance at the mine adjacent to the vein of slate to be used for the floors and roof. The lodge was starting to take shape.

Jeremy stayed in close touch with his brother Buck in Macon. Buck had not made the trip to Bowerton for some time because his legs ached constantly, limiting his mobility. But Buck did monitor the progress from a distance and agreed to send two of his experienced men to Bowerton, a carpenter and a bricklayer who had done some stonework. Buck sent his best craftsmen in an effort to help the lodge and to keep as many men as possible on his payroll during the continuing economic depression.

Tim met the men from Macon at the train station to show them around the town and job site. Both men spoke Southern English, making his job much easier, but he was surprised that both men Buck had sent were Black. Tim added a stop on his orientation tour to visit the sawmill to consult with Kitch on how to avoid any issues this might present.

Bowerton did not experience the racial tension found in many Georgia towns. There was only one Black family among the hundreds of people in the area, and Kitch was a successful, well-respected business leader. There had been no slaves at Madstone's since the War. There were no "colored only" facilities; the town's bylaws banned segregation.

As it turned out, Bowerton's newest guests created a new music scene in town. One of the Italian masons played the violin, which he turned into a fiddle. The Black carpenter from Macon played the banjo, which he began bringing to the job site to play during breaks. Once they discovered each other's talents, they began meeting after work to arrange songs, playing music from their own cultures and their version of local mountain favorites. They found a singer, a teenage girl from town, to add local flavor to their group.

Word spread within weeks that the group was exceptionally talented and entertaining. People wanted to see them perform, so Tim arranged casual concerts in the downtown park on Saturday evenings. Scores of people, young and old, came to dance and sing along, filling the tip bucket at each performance. While the crowd often requested that they play songs like *Bonnie Blue Flag* and *Dixie's Land*, the banjo player insisted they stick to music with a broader appeal.

Chapter Twenty-Nine
1874

The next year...

The lodge was now about a story tall, and the architect was pleased with their progress. He estimated it might take another two years to complete Turkey Hollow at the current pace, but that was okay. The cool weather kept the workers moving, but the frequent spring rains limited progress in a muddy work site.

The steel for the floor beams came from a mill in Macon. The limestone mortar mix came in sacks from Atlanta. Kitch's mill produced oak, maple, and hickory lumber cut from local trees. The exterior sandstone and flagstone flooring came from less than a mile away.

The outbuilding projects were mostly completed. The updated distillery was operational. Horses now split their day between the expanded stable and the green pastures surrounded by new wood fencing. A maintenance shed for carriages and equipment storage stood behind the distillery in the nearby woods. The bridge over the river was now wide enough for a carriage, tall enough for boats to pass under, and sturdy enough to withstand high water.

Turkey Hollow was built to stand the test of time.

Willow was dismayed that the Madstone farm fields around the construction area remained fallow. She encouraged the workers on the construction team to plant their own gardens with seeds and tools she would provide, but scores of acres outside the construction area remained unproductive.

Tim met with Mayor Lambert to check on how the town was coping with the economic depression. "How are the town's finances?" Tim asked.

"Poor, I'm afraid," replied Lambert. "Tax collections are down, and spending is rising. We may have to make some deep cuts soon."

"I heard that you started providing food and rent to people."

"We do, to families in need. Times are really tough, and the church is running out of funds, so I'm filling the gap as necessary."

"I know this sounds harsh, but like the church, there's only so much the town can do. Have you considered requiring those who want assistance to work if they are able?" asked Tim.

"Most would work if there were jobs available."

"I have an idea for creating more jobs, but it may not be the kind of work they want."

"And what would it involve?"

"We have acres of land at the old Madstone farm that can be planted this spring. I can provide the tools and seeds. Whatever is harvested can be shared between those who do the work and those in need."

"That is a great idea!" replied the mayor. "And quite generous."

"After the harvest, we expect to need more workers for the lodge construction. If they qualify, we can keep them employed there."

"Thank you, Mr. Bowers. I'll start working on getting things organized."

Carrie was excited about the progress of the lodge and wondered what role she would play in its operations once it opened. They could hire a manager, but no one cared about a business like an owner. And one day, she would be an owner. Her brother Adam might own half, but Adam cared more about hunting turkeys than making sure the staff was attentive, and the food was worth a return visit.

And what did she know about running a lodge? Not much. Should she go back to school? The right school might teach culinary skills or mechanical engineering, but she had never heard of courses in lodge management.

"Daddy, I want to talk to you about how we're going to manage the hotel," said Carrie.

"We'll hire an experienced manager when we're ready," Tim responded. "That decision is a good year or eighteen months off."

"I want to be the manager," replied Carrie. "But I have no experience."

Tim thought the prerequisite for the position would be a man, but he knew better than to say that to his daughter. It would only strengthen her determination. "So what are you thinking?"

"While construction continues, I want to go work at a big hotel or lodge to get first-hand experience. Maybe I can find a mentor."

"You mean move away somewhere to find a job? Where would you go?"

"I thought about Atlanta or Macon. But Savannah might be the best place."

"Your Uncle Buck raves about Savannah. Have you written to him about this?"

"I wanted to talk to you first."

"But what about your chickens?"

"They can survive without me. Just don't eat all the good layers. And tell them every day that I will return soon."

Carrie received a reply from Uncle Buck suggesting that, while Atlanta and Macon had fine hotels for business travelers, Savannah was more of a resort destination like Turkey Hollow. Buck wrote that he always enjoyed his trips to Savannah when they stayed at the Marshall House. He had met the owner and was impressed by her grace and success in business.

Buck sent letters of introduction, and within two weeks, Carrie was on her way to Savannah to interview for a position at the Marshall House. She met with the hotel's general manager, who explained that the best opportunity for a young woman was to start at the front desk. Carrie felt a little guilty that she only intended to stay for a few months, but she was determined to learn as much as possible while giving them her full effort in that limited time.

Carrie spent the night at the hotel and learned of its rich history. Born in 1783, Mary Marshall had expanded two small properties inherited from her father into a cluster of first-class properties in the heart of the city. She built Savannah's finest hotel, the Marshall House, in 1851. Three years after being completed, the hotel served as a hospital for yellow fever, and in 1864, it was occupied by Sherman's Army officers. Following the War, Mary restored the hotel to its former glory.

The manager offered the position, and Carrie agreed to start work the following week. She rode the train back to Bowerton to make preparations and start packing.

On a clear, cool morning, the Bowers clan was at the train depot to see Carrie off. She would visit Uncle Buck's family in Macon and then travel to Savannah to start her new job at the Marshall House.

Aunt Abigail was at the Macon train terminal to greet Carrie and transport her by carriage to the house.

"I have to warn you that your Uncle Buck is getting up in age," said Abigail. "He's pretty much confined to bed and a chair. His legs have just about given out, and he's often in a good deal of pain."

Carrie was taken aback at the first sight of her uncle. He was gaunt, slumped over, and occasionally winced in pain. Nonetheless, she gave him a big hug and a kiss and said how all the Bowerton Bowers sent their best regards. Not only was he confined to a deeply cushioned chair, his hair had thinned, his beard was solid gray, and his wrinkles were deep.

"How are things at Turkey Hollow progressing?" Buck asked.

"A lot better since you sent those two men! The first floor is well underway, and the whole team is happy and productive. They even sing and play music together after work!"

"I figured that Andy would insist on taking his banjo to the job," replied Buck, hacking some and wiping his mouth with a handkerchief. "I'm glad things are going well!"

"And thank you for making an introduction for me at the Marshall House!"

"We love that place!" added Abigail. "They make you feel so at home! And it's right in the middle of downtown where you can walk to the shops and parks and go to the river to see the ships go by. I think you're going to love it there."

Carrie was about to say something to her uncle, but he had dozed off. She turned to Aunt Abigail. "How many grandchildren do you have now?"

Abigail counted on her fingers. "Seven! But only five live here in Macon. I wish all my grandbabies were here in town."

The conversation continued through dinner and the evening. Before retiring, Carrie asked her aunt for paper and a pen. "I promised my family I would keep them updated on my travels," she told her aunt. However, the content of her letter was all about her uncle's condition. "*He looks very unwell and is confined to a chair. He had trouble making conversation and had to excuse himself during dinner. I didn't see him for the rest of the evening. I think you should consider a visit to Macon.*"

The manager at the Marshall House had recommended a boarding house where many of the hotel staff resided. Carrie found the accommodations Spartan but adequate and an easy walk to the hotel. Her coworkers at the front desk were welcoming and quick to help her learn the ropes, as the sailors in port would say. She delighted in strolling the streets of Savannah after work, past grand townhouses and park squares with lots of benches under magnificent oak trees dripping with moss.

Within weeks, Carrie understood the various rates and fees charged to guests, the wage scale of workers, productivity standards for cleaning rooms, how the kitchen stored food, the structure of the hotel organization, and proven marketing practices for attracting patrons. She also took note of the furnishings and equipment, from the guest rooms and dining room to the loading dock.

Marshall House produced as much revenue from the dining room and meeting spaces as from lodging fees. Perhaps Turkey Hollow could do the same by attracting reunions, business conferences, and weddings. Bowerton was no Savannah, but the Marshall House didn't have mountain views, an equestrian center, and farm-to-table dining for produce, trout, apples, and chicken.

One highlight of Carrie's work was a chance to meet Mary Marshall, owner of the hotel. She was ninety-one years old and very much a Southern lady of means. Everyone in the hotel treated her like royalty because she was all business, yet treated her staff with respect and rewarded those who delivered results.

The front desk team leader was a handsome young man who took an immediate liking to Carrie. He made little effort to mask his attraction, and Carrie made every effort to repel his advances without upsetting her boss. Finally, she told him she was married.

"I don't see any man around," replied the boss man. "And I don't see any ring."

"None of that is your business. And bosses should not be hounding their employees while they're trying to work."

"But I like you! I told the manager he should make you the boss when I get promoted."

"You're getting a promotion?" asked Carrie incredulously.

"My father is the night manager. He's planning to retire and has recommended me to replace him."

"Then I guess I'll get more done during the day," replied Carrie as she walked away. Later, she made another entry to her list of policy recommendations for Turkey Hollow: no fraternizing amongst the staff and no working for relatives.

Months later, it was time for Carrie to return home with the book of notes she had gathered from her experience.

"Where are you going?" asked her badgering boss, watching her pack her things.

"I got promoted to night manager," replied Carrie.

"Yeah, sure," the man said smugly. He had not gotten the promotion he expected and didn't think her comment was funny. "You are a very mysterious woman. You come out of nowhere, and then you vanish. Where will you land next?"

"After working with you, I'm going to check into a convent," Carrie replied.

The guy stood closer. "Do I at least get a goodbye kiss?"

Carrie rolled her eyes, slowly shook her head, spun around him, and left the hotel to catch the train back to Bowerton.

Chapter Thirty

1875

Just days after Carrie had returned to Bowerton, a telegram came to Jeremy from Abigail saying that Buck had passed away. All of the Bowers packed their bags and caught a train to Macon the next day.

Abigail welcomed the family to her home. It was the first time all the cousins had been together, and the joy of getting to know each other better dulled some of the sting of losing their father and uncle.

Buck lay in repose in the same parlor as his mother four decades before. The same Mr. Thompson who had made the casket for Helen handled the funeral arrangements for Abigail. He now called himself an undertaker.

The service was held at the Mulberry Street Methodist Church, a grand structure built by Bowers Builders in the late 1840s. The centerpiece of the sanctuary was the organ with its complex system of turbines, wind chests, and a labyrinth of straps connecting the console and pipes. Buck Bowers had supervised the organ's installation, and each of the hymns that roared from the thousands of pipes in the walls surrounding the chancel was selected by Buck Bowers: *Amazing Grace, Rock of Ages, Oh God our Help in Ages Past.*

Jeremy gave the eulogy, highlighting Buck's commitment to his family, company, and the Macon community. The mayor read an ordinance recognizing Buck's contributions and proclaiming the day in honor of Buck. Tim read two scriptures that his brother had chosen.

The family walked behind the wagon carrying Buck's casket from the church to Rose Hill Cemetery, where he was buried in a new family plot on the hill next to his mother. Years earlier, Buck had Helen moved from City Cemetery to Rose Hill to keep past and future generations together. A big luncheon was held at the house following the funeral, and lurking in the background, Willow spotted a familiar face. She rushed over to greet Zeke Walker.

"How did you ever hear about the funeral?" asked Willow.

"You probably think I'm stalking you, but I saw the obituary in *The Macon Telegraph* and wanted to add my condolences. I'll use any reason to catch up with you Bowers."

Tim saw the two talking and came over to greet Zeke. "Hear anything from my boy, John Roberts Sawyer?"

"Never did."

"Good riddance," replied Tim. "Jeremy got the judge to annul the marriage, so that chapter is closed."

"Where is Carrie?" asked Zeke. "I thought she'd be here."

"She's in the kitchen helping her aunt," said Willow, pointing the way.

Zeke excused himself and walked to the kitchen.

"Why's Zeke always so interested in Carrie?" asked Tim. "He comes for her wedding, rescues her from a bad marriage, and now he's here."

Willow wanted to explain, but now was not the place. "I don't know," she said as convincingly as she could.

Four minutes later, there was a commotion in the kitchen. Willow ran in to find Tim pinned up against the wall by Zeke. Abigail and Carrie stood feet away, horrified. "Please go and let the guests know that everything is okay," Willow said to Carrie and Abigail. "I'll take care of this."

"I'm afraid to let him go," said Zeke. "He's crazy."

Tim struggled to get free with his one good arm. "He said you two had relations before we got married!" said Tim breathlessly. "What's he talking about?"

Willow decided to get defiant. "This is no time to be fighting! We'll go outside and talk! Tim, calm down!" Zeke let go of Tim, and Willow grabbed Tim's arm. "Both of you, follow me!"

Willow led them outside to chairs on the patio. "Sit down, both of you. Zeke, what did you say?"

"Tim asked me if I thought I was Carrie's real father," said Zeke.

"In front of her?" asked Willow.

"No, she was on the other side of the room," Tim replied.

"I couldn't deny it because I've had my suspicions all along," continued Zeke.

Willow winced and clenched her fists. "Zeke, I've told you before that Tim is Carrie's father."

"When did you say that?" asked Tim. "Why would you say something like that?"

Willow hesitated to say more for fear of making matters worse. "It came up before, years ago," she said and then tried to regain control of the situation. "But we shouldn't worry about the past. All that matters is Carrie. She loves her father. And Zeke, she is very grateful for your help. Can't we let this rest?"

Zeke stood. "I'm leaving. I came here to pay my respects to the family, not to disrupt a funeral." He marched around the house to catch a train back to Atlanta.

"You didn't answer the question, Willow," said Tim. "You could have settled this. But you didn't."

Tim got up and walked back into the house. Willow sat crying in her chair.

Abigail was comforted by having the Bowerton clan at the house for two more days. She didn't want them to leave. Tim and Jeremy spoke to Buck Jr. and were confident he would take good care of his mother. Tim and Willow barely talked to each other.

When it was time to leave, Abigail accompanied the Bowers to the Macon train terminal. She hugged them all and thanked them for coming. "Y'all need to come back soon!" She waved as the train left the station, dabbing her eyes with one of Buck's handkerchiefs.

The family spent hours on the train. Tim was sleeping while Willow read a book. Carrie took a seat next to Jeremy to talk about the lodge. They discussed hiring staff, greeting guests at the train station, and making the dining experience extra special.

Jeremy thought for a few seconds. "I don't have much experience with those things, but I'll tell you one thing. I love the way you are taking ownership in the lodge. Your parents and I are getting up there in age, and we've been so caught up in construction that we haven't given enough thought to how to run the place. What a blessing that you are giving attention to the operations. Those months in Savannah were a very wise investment! You learned more about the hotel business in a few months than you would have at a university in four years!"

Chapter Thirty-One
1877

Two years later...

The Long Depression that began with the Panic of 1873 was starting to ebb. Rutherford B. Hayes was president of thirty-eight states. Crazy Horse fought his last battle in Montana. Edison invented the phonograph, and the first telephone line was installed in Boston. Labor unions grew stronger following the first national railroad strike, and Billy the Kid began his career as a wanted gunslinger in New Mexico.

Conditions in Bowerton, Georgia, were more settled. The death of Noah Lewis, the geology professor from Athens who helped Roy develop the slate mine, caused Tim and Jeremy to search for a buyer. After months without any serious offers, they decided to shut it down. The brothers were too old to manage the place, there was no obvious successor to Noah, and the primary customer, Turkey Hollow Lodge, would no longer be placing new orders for stone. The lodge was complete!

The Bowers held the ribbon-cutting ceremony on the Saturday before Confederate Memorial Day, the fourth Monday in April. Jeremy had arranged for Governor Colquitt to attend, and everyone in town was welcome. Following the ceremony and some speeches from the front steps, Jeremy, the Governor, Willow, and Carrie greeted each visitor at the front door. Tim would have talked too long to his friends, so he was stationed in the lobby. The staff gave everyone a guided tour of the facility that ended in a hosted meal on the back patio featuring fried chicken, green beans, coleslaw, and cornbread.

Most everyone in town had contributed to the construction or had visited the site over the past four years, so the event was more of an opportunity to thank those involved and invite workers to apply for the remaining open staff positions.

Tim, Willow, and Jeremy appointed themselves trustees of the corporation that owned the property. Carrie was named president, and they hired Henry Keller from Markham House, one of Atlanta's most prestigious hotels, as the general manager.

The grand opening for lodging and dining was scheduled for mid-May. Advertisements in the Chattanooga, Atlanta, and Macon newspapers quickly reserved all seventy rooms for that weekend and various times throughout the summer. Carrie would ensure the guests had a wonderful experience and count on them to spread the word to their friends throughout the Southeast.

The guests who arrived by carriage were welcomed at the front door by a bellman who took their bags as a valet took their carriage to the stables. Most guests were picked up at the train station in a lodge coach for a ride-by tour of the stables, chicken farm, distillery, and gardens before checking in at the lobby. The drivers were trained to inform the guests of the town's history and point out activities they could enjoy during their stay.

The most popular coach driver was Theo, Jeremy's buddy from Milledgeville. He had worked at the mine until the lodge opened and then took a job where he could earn more just in tips. Carrie noticed that every guest Theo transported entered the lobby laughing and smiling. When Carrie rode his carriage, he explained things by the book; nothing was particularly funny. There was no telling what stories he told the guests, but Carrie was okay with not knowing.

Carrie insisted on living in the restored Madstone mansion. Living on the grounds made her available for urgent lodge matters during off hours. She dedicated half of the downstairs to childcare and hired a woman to watch the children of several mothers who worked in the kitchen, custodial staff, or office.

President Carrie and general manager Henry quickly worked out their distribution of responsibilities. He ran the dining, meeting, and lodging operations while she took care of the stables, gardens, fishing, and overall operations. When the weather allowed and she had time, Carrie worked on adding new varieties of apples to her orchard. She made a deal with the apple farmer from Ellijay to stay free at the lodge in exchange for his grafting some of his new Winesap cuttings to her trees.

Carrie considered adding bee hives near the orchard. Beekeeping could add another point of interest for guests, supply the kitchen with honey, and help pollinate the apple trees. She wanted a project she could share with her dad, but his energy level was waning.

Henry was twelve years older than Carrie, and while he was not married, there was no attraction or paternalism to tamp down. Outside of running the lodge, Henry was interested in working with Kitch at the distillery. He understood that part of the image and quality of fine whiskies was in the aging process and the different types of wood used to make casks, things Kitch considered secondary to the distilling process. Carrie was concerned that Henry could be sampling too much of the product, but there was no evidence of tipsy behavior or oral scent.

Carrie was also keeping an eye on her brother, Adam, who was now the father of three. He had matured significantly after having children, and Carrie considered giving him more responsibility at the stables.

One day, Carrie was leaning up against the corral fence watching her brother work with a three-year-old colt when a man came and stood at her side.

"He seems to know what he's doing," observed the man.

Carrie turned to face the handsome, well-dressed gentleman. He was about her age, maybe a little younger. "You know about horses?"

"I grew up on a horse farm, but now I spend my time buying and selling racehorses."

Carrie thought the response was a bit pretentious, but she was glad he was a patron of Turkey Hollow. "Are you enjoying your stay here?"

"Very much! It's nice to get away from the bustle of city hotels."

"You're here with your family?"

"No, I'm by myself. I am unmarried and live in Aiken, South Carolina." He smiled brightly. "That's me; how about you? Are you enjoying your stay, where are you from, and are you married?"

Carrie couldn't help but laugh. "I didn't intend to get personal. I work here and just wanted to make sure you were having a pleasant stay."

"Oh? And your job is watching horses being trained?"

"No, I'm making my rounds and came to see my brother. That's him," she replied, pointing toward Adam with her thumb.

"Does he appreciate his little sister watching him?"

"Probably not," she replied whimsically. "But as the older sister, I must set the example and return to my work. It was nice chatting with you, mister . . ."

"McGrath, Gordon McGrath. And you are?"

Carrie extended her hand. "Carrie Bowers."

"Carrie, would you do me the honor of joining me for dinner tonight?"

"I appreciate your offer, but we have rules about staff dining with guests."

"Then, how about a cocktail after dinner? A glass of wine or sherry on the veranda at dusk?"

"Thank you, but I have things to take care of." Carrie smiled to relieve the awkwardness of the moment. "But it was nice to meet you, Mr. McGrath." Carrie turned to return to the hotel.

"I hope I see you again, Carrie!" said Gordon, loud enough for Adam to turn and wonder why his sister was fraternizing with a guest.

For years, Willow had been concerned that Carrie was spending too much time on lodge business and not enough time making the social connections necessary to meet a new mate. That all changed when the gentleman from Aiken arrived. And he kept extending his stay at Turkey Hollow to five days and counting.

Willow met up with Carrie in her office at the lodge. "You're getting pretty serious about this fellow."

"I like him," said Carrie, "but he's leaving tomorrow."

"And will you stay in touch?"

"He promises to return and tell all his friends about Turkey Hollow."

The finances for the lodge in its first months of operation were positive but not sufficient to build the reserves needed for the lean months between January and May. Carrie planned to close in January for deep cleaning and to give the staff some rest. At their next meeting, the trustees brainstormed ideas for attracting more guests in the summer or extending the season.

"I think we should consider a horse race in the fall or spring," suggested Carrie.

"Who gave you that idea, your horse racer friend?" replied Tim.

"I think it's a great idea," continued Carrie. "We could map out a route from the lodge into downtown, through the woods, and back across the river."

"Horseracing is getting very popular," observed Jeremy. "That raceway in Louisville has attracted lots of attention after they built a mile-long track and stands for spectators."

"I'm not talking about anything like that," responded Carrie. "I'm thinking more of a steeplechase-style race with obstacles throughout the fields and woods, as well as a run through the streets of Bowerton. People could line up all along the route, but the start and finish would be here at Turkey Hollow."

"It's not a bad idea," mused Willow. "Something worth considering. But how does it increase lodging and dining?"

"For one, the horse owners who compete would be here for days. And once everyone sees how exciting we make the race, we will draw guests from all over."

"This horse race does sound interesting," said Tim, "but what do we know about putting on such an event?"

"Like the Bowers have always done, Daddy. Hire someone with the expertise."

There was a loud, collective sigh. "So, this is where that Gordon fellow comes in?" asked Tim. "Am I right?"

"They have similar races in Aiken that have become very popular."

"Never heard of 'em," said Tim.

"Gordon said Aiken is flat and sandy. Our hills and terrain would make this race event unique."

"So tell us more about this Gordon fellow," said Jeremy. "What is his background?"

"He's originally from Pennsylvania, but after the War, his family bought hundreds of acres of farmland in Aiken to raise racehorses. He likes the weather around here, and so do his horses."

"Sounds like a dang carpetbagger to me," said Tim.

"I think he moved here for all the right reasons," replied Carrie. "The whole town of Aiken has gotten behind his efforts to promote horse racing."

"You are such a fan!" said Tim. "Sure you're not just falling for his dandy outfits and smooth talk?"

Carrie threw up her hands in frustration and looked skyward.

"Stop it, Tim!" scolded Willow. "Maybe this idea does seem a bit wild, but I think it's worth pursuing. Maybe we could invite Gordon to present his ideas to us on his next visit."

"As long as it doesn't turn into one of Daddy's interrogations," replied Carrie. "Maybe we could ask Henry to stand in for him. And invite the stable manager, too."

"Go ahead and invite your boyfriend to talk to us," Tim yielded. "I promise not to embarrass you."

Carrie realized that she was at another crossroads in her life. She liked Gordon but didn't want a relationship to interfere with her career or risk more grief at the hands of a man. She wasn't sure if Gordon was entirely serious about her or his offer to help organize a race at Turkey

Hollow. Inviting him back to the lodge would test the waters.

If the relationship heated up, where would things go from there? There was no way she was moving to Aiken, and he probably wouldn't want to move to Bowerton. A long-distance relationship involving two days of travel wasn't practical. She would let destiny decide.

Gordon immediately accepted the invitation to come and discuss the prospects of starting a race at Turkey Hollow. Carrie insisted on hosting his food and lodging to balance the obligation scorecard. She greeted him at the train station, and he kissed her hand. A long embrace and passionate kiss would have been more consistent with how they left things when they were last together, but lodge employees might be watching.

The Bowers group got together in one of the lodge meeting rooms. Willow was intent on finding out more about this Mr. McGrath. Tim was negative, more on Gordon than the idea of a race, but had promised to be kind. Jeremy, GM Henry, and stable manager Colton were simply anxious to explore the details of this intriguing concept.

"Please tell us about your family," Willow opened with the first question following Gordon's presentation.

"My parents came from Ireland in the '50s and settled in Hershey, Pennsylvania. My father worked in a stable that had hosted steeplechase races, and when he came here . . ."

"Steeplechase?" asked Jeremy, "What is that exactly?"

"The term came from the original Irish races that went from a church steeple in one town to the steeple in the next. The racecourses differ widely but involve jumping fences and ditches through the countryside over a two- or three-mile distance." Jeremy seemed satisfied, and Gordon continued. "So, my father bred and trained steeplechase horses, and I grew up on the ranch."

"Did you serve in the War?" asked Tim.

"Yes, sir. I served in Sherman's Army."

Tim let out a deep, complaining groan.

"I was late getting drafted and assigned to the veterinary corps as a farrier because of my experience. I never shot a rifle. I just took care of horses. I was impressed with the warm weather and great conditions for raising horses in the South, and when the War ended, I convinced my father to move to South Carolina."

"Carrie says that you are well-known in Aiken," said Willow. "How do you gauge that?"

"We got such a great deal for the land in Aiken that we were able to sponsor races and help revitalize the town. I'd say my family has been very well received despite being Yankees."

That got some chuckles from the group.

"If you help us, won't that take away from your efforts in Aiken?" asked Henry.

"I've given that much thought, and I believe there will be time for both. Aiken has hot, humid summers, and there is no grand hotel or lodge in the area to attract visitors from distant cities. It's a wonderful town, but it's flat and buggy. Here, it is hilly, cool, and full of nature. This race would be quite a different kind of event for the horses and riders."

"What kind of horses do you race?" asked Colton.

"Almost all Arabians. I see that you have Quarter Horses here, and they may turn out to be just as competitive on this hilly terrain."

WILLOW *and the boys*

"And you think we could successfully hold such an event?" asked Jeremy.

"I believe so, but it may take more than one season to catch on. The two main challenges are attracting racers and attracting a crowd. I can't promise big crowds, but I can almost guarantee a good field of racers from Florida to Tennessee with the connections I've developed."

"What brought you to Bowerton in the first place?" asked Willow.

"I was in Atlanta looking at horses and was headed to Knoxville when I heard good things about this new lodge in North Georgia. I wanted to check it out, and I must say, I have been impressed."

"Gambling is a big part of horseracing, wouldn't you say?" asked Tim.

"Yes, sir. Betting certainly increases the excitement of the crowd," answered Gordon. "Are you okay with that?"

"Hell yeah," replied Tim. "This family has been taking chances for decades!" Tim looked at Jeremy. "There aren't any laws against betting on horses, are there?"

"No, but the preacher may request a word with you," replied Jeremy.

Everyone laughed, and Gordon continued, "I hope you don't mind my asking, but has the lodge generated the funds for what it will take to promote and put on a good race?"

Tim liked the bold attitude of the question. "We do have the resources, but they didn't come from the lodge. Have you seen the slate mine?"

"Yes, sir, Carrie and I rode over there one time. Looks like it was once a major operation."

Tim slowly nodded as he looked around the room to gauge everyone's interest. Having seen plenty of enthusiasm, he stood up to speak. "Young man, I like you, and I like the idea. Can you give us a few minutes to discuss what you've presented?"

Gordon went into the hallway and began admiring the photos of the lodge during its construction hanging in the hallway. Ninety seconds later, Jeremy asked him to rejoin the meeting.

"Gordon, if you are willing to help us put on a race in the spring, we would like to hire you as a consultant," announced Jeremy.

"I'm excited to accept your offer," beamed Gordon. "We could make this race as popular as Churchill Downs or Pimlico. You just come up with a clever name for the event, and I'll take care of the rest."

While everyone surrounded Gordon with handshakes and thanks, Carrie stood back, beaming with relief, pride, and hope. Her mother seemed to be warming up to Gordon from both a business and personal perspective. And she never expected such a positive response, especially from her father.

Gordon spent two nights at the lodge before he needed to return home. He was now a business consultant to Turkey Hollow, neither employed nor a guest, so Carrie's conscience was clear to have meals with him. She spent the night in Gordon's room, having booked him in a ground-floor suite to facilitate a clandestine predawn exit.

"So when can you come back?" Carrie asked Gordon when they met for breakfast.

"It will be a few weeks. We have a steeplechase event coming up in Aiken, and then I need to go to North Carolina for a race up there. Would you like to come with me?"
"I would love to, but I can't leave the lodge during our busy season." Carrie hesitated and squirmed a bit. "Let me ask you a question. Would you consider making Bowerton your home base if we got

more serious?"

"Miss Bowers, do you not think we are serious? I am well past serious when it comes to you. Enchanted, you might say."

"But we haven't spent that much time together. And I've never asked you if you have a girlfriend somewhere."

Gordon grinned. "I am completely unattached. But let's agree that we've both had a past, and there's no need to bare our souls about previous relationships." He read the inquisitive expression on Carrie's face. "And no, I've never been married, nor do I have any children."

"I do hope our relationship grows, but it's so hard when we're apart so much."

"I agree. And to answer your original question, yes, I would consider making Bowerton my home. It's just that my parents are getting older, and we'd have to do a lot of downsizing of the ranch operations before I would be comfortable moving away."

"Would your parents consider moving here?"

"No. My sisters are there, and they both have families."

"Could one of your brothers-in-law take over?"

"One, maybe. The other is useless. It wouldn't be hard to downsize our herd; it will just take some time."

"I hope you can see that you've made quite a good impression on my family."

"I like them, too. Your father started calling me Gordo, which I take as a positive sign. I like your history, I like you, and I like what you've done with the place!" Gordon extended his arms, palms up, and glanced left and right.

"I like you, too," replied Carrie. "And I hope we can spend more time together."

⸻

The family held a monthly board meeting to review operations and address any new concerns.

"The bank notified me that they are now willing to loan money to the lodge," reported Jeremy.

"Yeah, they're always willing to lend to those who don't need it," Tim responded.

"They were addressing the possibility of expanding the hotel. Personally, I don't think we're ready, but I just wanted to let y'all know that things have loosened up a bit."

The group agreed not to expand or borrow.

"July has been a good month!" reported Carrie. "The Fourth of July celebration was a big hit!"

"More people from South Georgia and Florida are coming up here to escape the heat," observed Tim.

"And I remind them that, in winter, we are the closest place to have fun in the snow," added Carrie.

"When is Gordon coming back?" asked Willow.

"Not for two or three weeks," replied Carrie.

"Maybe he was kidding," said Willow, "but he said we need to come up with a good name for the race. I've been thinking about that and believe we should call the race the Turkey Chase."

"That's good," replied Tim, "but it sounds too much like a hunt. How about Turkey Quest?"

"I like that better!" responded Willow. Everyone else nodded approval.

"And not to be outdone by the mint julep," exclaimed Henry, "we need to come up with a name for a special cocktail to serve on race day. I have the recipe but no name. It's our best whiskey, bitters, a sugar cube, and an apple peel."

"Sounds like your version of an old fashion!" responded Jeremy. "I like the recipe, but it's best served over ice, which requires refrigeration, which requires electricity. And that reminds me of something we need to talk about. Atlanta is building a power plant to provide electric streetlights and eventually power factories and homes. Should we consider this for Bowerton?"

"I've read about those new plants!" added Carrie. "Some burn coal, but if you have a river, you can use the current to turn a wheel to generate electricity. I don't understand the details, but towns up north are building power plants that work."

"Is it safe? Does it cost a lot?" asked Tim.

"I don't know exactly how they work," responded Jeremy. "We'd have to hire an engineer to study it."

Tim added, "It certainly sounds like something we should look into. Wouldn't it be something if Bowerton was the first town in North Georgia to have streetlights?"

"And it would draw more guests to the lodge!" exclaimed Carrie.

"Maybe we could poach one of the experts working on the plans for the plant in Atlanta," added Jeremy.

"Just what Roy would do!" yelled Tim. "Let's go for it!"

Henry waited for the group to quiet down. "And I thought of a name for our cocktail. How about the Turkey Hoof!"

Carrie held up her arm, pretending to hold a drink for a toast. "We will serve the Turkey Hoof cocktail at the Turkey Quest steeplechase race at Turkey Hollow Lodge! I love it!"

Something said at the meeting caught Carrie's attention, and she followed up with her Uncle Jeremy.

"You mentioned that we need ice for our cocktail," said Carrie. "We had ice at the Marshall House years ago. How can we get ice for the lodge?"

Jeremy replied, "Up north, they cut blocks of ice out of frozen ponds or lakes in the winter, insulate it with straw and sawdust, and ship it to customers. Savannah probably got it off a ship, but we are not near a port, and our lakes don't freeze. A few years ago, they invented machines that make and refrigerate ice, but they require electricity, which is years away for Bowerton."

"Couldn't we get one of the ice-making machines and power it with a generator?"

Jeremy hesitated. "That's an interesting idea," he said, nodding. "It probably could be done."

"I'm going to look into that!" replied Carrie.

Jeremy smiled and patted Carrie on the back. "You're a smart one, Carrie Bowers!"

Gordon returned to Bowerton Station and into the arms of Carrie. "I've started the conversation with my family about spending more time here," he reported as they rode the buggy to the lodge.

"And what did they say?" asked Carrie.

"They asked, who is she?" he laughed. But Carrie didn't. "What's wrong? That wasn't funny?"

"No, it's not funny. It sounds like your family thinks of you as a woman chaser."

"That's not what they think! They just sensed that I had a little extra spring in my step!" Carrie was still unhappy, and Gordon put his hand on her shoulder. "Okay. After you're done work, how about you and I take a ride and explore a good route for the race."

Carrie broke into a smile. "That sounds fun! And we have dinner tonight at my parents' house."

"Perfect!"

Carrie and Gordon discussed the different routes the racecourse could take at dinner. Gordon wanted to eliminate possible shortcuts, and Tim suggested blazing a trail through the bush around the far side of the quarry. Gordon agreed to check that out. The conversation then turned to electric power plants. It happened that Gordon was well-read on the subject.

"Is there a waterfall nearby on the river?" asked Gordon.

"There is a small one south of here," replied Tim.

"That might be a good place for the plant. There's a fellow out in California named Allan Pelton who developed this fancy water turbine. It's supposed to be much more efficient than the old water wheels."

"Maybe if he travels east, we could host him at the lodge," offered Willow. "I could write him a letter if you can get me his address."

"I'll do that," said Gordon.

Carrie and Gordon walked to the lodge after dinner.

"You're rapidly endearing yourself to my father with all that talk about turbines and electricity," exclaimed Carrie as she snuggled under his arm.

"I like your daddy," replied Gordon. "He's no-nonsense."

"No, he's a lot of nonsense," chuckled Carrie, "and not easy to win over. But you seem to be doing it, Gordo!"

Chapter Thirty-Two

1878

Several months later...

"Miss Carrie!" yelled Colton, the stable manager, from across the lodge lobby. "Come quick! It's Mister Tim!"

Colton turned and began running down the hill toward the stables with Carrie close behind. "What's wrong?"

"I don't know," replied Colton. "He was about to mount Diamond, and he collapsed. He just fell to the ground."

"Is he talking? Is he conscious?" asked Carrie, beginning to lose her breath in their long jog to the barn.

"No, I couldn't wake him. So I ran to get help."

They arrived at Tim's side near the entrance to the barn. He was sprawled on the ground with his arms and legs flailed in unnatural positions. Carrie rolled him onto his back. "Daddy! Daddy! Tell me what's wrong!"

Tim was unresponsive. His breathing was uneven. Carrie found a pulse in his wrist, but it was beating far too rapidly. One side of his face was drooping, and he winced in pain sporadically.

"Ride for a doctor!" Carrie yelled excitedly to Colton. "And then go fetch my mother and bring her out here. Hurry, Colton, please!"

Colton jumped on Tim's horse, Diamond, and took off in a cloud of dust.

Carrie didn't know what to do except try to make her father comfortable and get him to respond. She loosened his shirt collar and asked a stable hand to bring her a blanket from the barn to roll up as a pillow. "C'mon, Daddy, tell me what's wrong. The doctor is on his way."

She felt the back of his head. There was no bleeding or lumps. All of a sudden, he vomited. Carrie pulled his upper body away from the mess and turned him on his side.

In the fifteen minutes it took the doctor to arrive, Carrie never stopped pleading with her father to speak, squeeze her hand, blink, or respond in some way. She said a short prayer as the doctor did his examination, still holding her father's hand and gently combing through his hair with her fingers. The stable hand provided wet compresses for his forehead. A couple from the lodge who came to ride horses kneeled near Tim with their hands clasped in prayer.

"I'm afraid he has had a stroke," concluded the doctor. "Apoplexy."

"What can we do?" pleaded Carrie.

"There is internal bleeding in his brain. There's no good treatment except to make him comfortable and pray for the best."

The doctor asked the nearby men who had gathered to help him load Tim into the bed of his wagon. Carrie jumped into the wagon to her father's side, and the doctor rode off toward town. On their way, Willow appeared riding on the back of Colton's horse. She dismounted and rode in the wagon next to Carrie. Staff at the town's medical office loaded Tim onto a stretcher and carried him to a private room, where they transferred him to a bed.

"What can you do for him?" Willow asked the doctor.

"There's not much I can recommend. I don't believe in bloodletting, and I'm not trained to operate on the brain where the bleeding has occurred. Sometimes, stroke victims recover completely, some have disabilities, and some don't make it. He's only sixty-one and in decent health, which works in his favor. I will give him a little morphine to ease any pain and help him rest. You can stay here by his side, but I don't want more than two people in this room at a time." The doctor reached for Willow's hand. "Pray. Pray hard."

Over the next several hours, dozens of people gathered in front of the medical office to check on their friend. Jeremy arrived to sit with his little brother and talk to the doctor. He took breaks to inform people waiting outside of any change in Tim's condition.

Jeremy spent the night switching between Willow and Carrie to sit with Tim. He kept thinking how Tim had sprung back from getting injured at Kennesaw and battling yellow fever. He was a fighter.

Later that night, Jeremy dozed off in a chair in the office lobby and woke just before dawn. He re-entered Tim's room to find Carrie slumped in a chair asleep. Willow was slouched over the side of the bed, holding her husband's hand and weeping quietly. Tim was no longer breathing.

Jeremy slowly walked to Willow's side, knelt down, and put his arm around her.

"He's gone, Jeremy. He is with God in heaven."

The commotion woke Carrie, who took one look at her mother and immediately collapsed onto the side of the bed. "No, Daddy, please, no. You can't leave us."

Jeremy spent several minutes grieving with his family, then went to the lobby to get a nurse. He went outside, where people were still gathered. "I'm sorry, but . . ." Jeremy had trouble getting the words out, ". . . my brother, Tim, passed away. He never regained consciousness." Jeremy saw the preacher among the well-wishers and asked him to come inside to be with the family.

A solemn hush blanketed the town as word spread that Tim Bowers had died. The bells in the Methodist church slowly rang three times each hour that day. A black cloth was draped over the church entrance, and many citizens began wearing black ribbons on their arms. The lodge staff announced the death of one of the lodge's founders and informed the guests that service would be suspended for the funeral in two days.

There was sobbing and lots of wet eyes at the funeral service. Jeremy gave a heartfelt eulogy for his brother, covering how the young teenager came north hoping to strike gold but instead found rock even more valuable, how he volunteered and was injured in the War, and how Tim grew into an outstanding leader and advocate for the community he loved.

Willow insisted on speaking despite the pleas of her family. She slowly walked to the lectern, dressed in black, with a piece of paper in one hand and a hanky in the other.

She took a moment to look out over the crowded sanctuary. "Thank you all for being here."

Willow shuffled quietly before continuing. "When I was a teenager and lived on my family's farm, I met this young man who had come with his father to claim their new land. He was confident and brass, and he wouldn't stop trying to get my attention even though I already had a boyfriend. We fell in love, got married, and have two wonderful children. And now that man lies before God and all of his family and friends here today." Willow took a deep breath and continued in a shivering voice, "I love you, Tim Bowers. Thank you for a beautiful, joy-filled life. You are with your Savior, now."

Willow hesitated as she folded the paper in her hand. That was all she had prepared to say, but there was more she wanted to express. "There were two things that made Tim especially proud. One was his family, and the other was watching this town grow from a backwoods to a

WILLOW and the boys

thriving community. Jeremy gave Tim credit for growing Bowerton, but it was a team effort. Oh, how I loved to see those three Bowers boys together. Tim's father, Roy, was quiet and humble, but he was the one with the vision. Tim was by his side the whole way. Jeremy was the brains of the family. The oldest brother, Buck, didn't come here often, but he ran his father's business down in Macon that provided the resources to open the mine, which allowed the town and, eventually, the lodge to grow. I wish everyone could have a family like that. I was blessed to be part of it.

"And it wasn't just their hard work and money. My father was a full-blooded Cherokee. Some called me a half-breed and treated my family cruelly. But not the Bowers family. They opened their arms and hearts to me and my family. They could care less about skin color. They were good people, and they made sure that this town had a good heart. And that it was an open community. I know one family sitting right there," Willow pointed to Kitch and his family, "who might not have had the opportunity to become so successful if the Bowers hadn't made sure that this town welcomed everyone."

Willow took another deep breath. "And now Roy is gone, Buck is gone, and Tim is gone. Thank goodness we still have Jeremy. But this town lives on because of the values and traditions they built. Roy always talked about getting the railroad to town. Now we have it. Tim and Noah built the mine into a thriving operation. The brothers had a vision for a resort-style hotel, and now Turkey Hollow brings visitors here from all over. Tim had been obsessing about building an electric generation plant in the last few months. I'll bet that happens as well, and soon.

"Tim is gone, and I will miss him with all my heart." Willow started to cry and took a moment to collect herself. "But when I walk through the streets of Bowerton, or greet visitors at Turkey Hollow, or stroll on our flagstone walkways . . . and when I hug my two precious children, I think of Tim. Thank you, sweetheart."

Sobs could be heard throughout the sanctuary as Willow quietly returned to her pew. There was not a dry eye in the church.

When the service was over, everyone in the church walked behind the wagon carrying Tim to the cemetery, where he was laid to rest next to his father.

Perhaps the person most moved by the funeral service and burial was Gordon. He knew the Bowers were the town's founders and a successful family. But never had he seen so many people stand in a long line waiting to express their sincere condolences and thanks to Willow, Jeremy, and Carrie. Everyone seemed to have a personal story about how Tim Bowers had helped his neighbors.

"I feel honored to have been at that service," said Gordon to Carrie as he walked her home.

"It made me proud. I loved my father, but he could be tough and ornery. I guess you get that way when people don't give you their best. And I guess I'm like that a bit, too."

"You, ornery? I'd say you're more like your mother. She was so brave and inspiring!"

Carrie snuggled under Gordon's arm. "Thank you for being there with me today. It meant a lot."

Gordon stopped and took Carrie in his arms. They were nose to nose under the canopy of trees shading the moonlight. "Thank you for letting me see a whole other side of your family. I love you more every day that I spend with you."

Carrie kissed him, and they smothered each other in a long embrace.

"You've had an exhausting day," said Gordon, gently disengaging from her arms.

"It was exhausting, but I feel energized to keep the town and lodge going to honor my father and mother. Does that make any sense?"

"Yes, I understand. I'm with you. And I'd like to be your partner in the journey."

Carrie stopped and gazed into his eyes. Did he just propose? "Well, I accept you as a partner, Gordo!" she replied brightly.

Gordon stared back at Carrie. Did I just ask her to marry me? But this is not the time or place. He smiled back at her. He shook his head and extended his arm. "Come on, let's get you home."

Days later, the family met to talk business. Willow now owned most of the stock in Turkey Hollow. She and Jeremy were not getting any younger, and the death of Tim, who was younger than them both, prodded them to spend some time thinking about the future and the need for more formal governance.

"Here are the changes we propose," began Willow, referring to her notes, "to formalize the way decisions are made around here. Both Jeremy and I are in our sixties, and while we plan to stay involved with the lodge for some time, we must think about the future.

"We will form a new holding company called Bowerstone, Incorporated, that will own all of the land and improvements formerly owned by the Waya Madstone and Roy Bowers families, except my and Jeremy's residences. My newly revised Last Will states that, upon my death, Carrie will receive sixty percent of my stock in the corporation, and Adam will receive forty percent. Did I say all of that right, Jeremy?"

Jeremy nodded in agreement, and Willow continued.

"The corporation will have a board of directors elected by the shareholders. Jeremy, Carrie, Adam, and I will be the initial members of the board, and we will expand the number of directors to include the mayor and two independent local business leaders. We will hear reports from lodge officers at each quarterly board meeting. Carrie, you will be the first president of the corporation. You have most certainly earned the position. This will all be explained in more detail in a set of bylaws that Jeremy is drafting."

"Getting a little fancy, wouldn't you say?" Adam smirked.

"Maybe, but it's important," replied Jeremy. "How would things work if something happened to your mother tomorrow?"

"Carrie would continue bossing me around like she does every day," Adam replied.

Carrie just rolled her eyes and shook her head.

Gordon spent more time in Bowerton than at his family's Aiken ranch, which he visited twice a month. When in town, he spent every evening with Carrie, alone or visiting with Willow or Jeremy.

During the day, Gordon worked on laying out the racecourse. His idea was for the racers to stage at the stables and then walk in parade fashion to the starting point behind the lodge. Spectators would watch from chairs and blankets on the hill. From there, the course would go west around the orchard, south to a grass shoulder along the main road, over the bridge, and into town. From the end of town, the route continued north through the woods, around the quarry, and back to the lodge across a wide but navigable section of the river.

When Gordon pitched the event to other owners, he bragged about the excellent accommodations for horses and owners, the cool weather, and the beautiful mountain scenery. The purse would be competitive, and the Turkey Quest would be scheduled around other steeplechase races to give the participants a steady but comfortable pace of spring events.

Working alongside some helpers to clear brush and remove stumps along the race path was exhausting, but Gordon found himself randomly grinning about his future with Carrie. He had had relationships with other women over the years, but not anyone like Carrie. She was independent but affectionate, intelligent but anxious to learn. She was beautiful without obsessing over fashion, makeup, or jewelry. She was perfect.

A proper amount of time since Tim's death had passed. It was time to propose, and Gordon worked on how to make the event memorable.

One night, after dinner, he and Carrie went for a ride and then went to the lodge for an evening cocktail. As they were walking through the lobby, bustling with guests, Gordon lagged behind Carrie. When she looked back to see why he was no longer by her side, Gordon had stooped on one knee with his hands clasped. She walked back to see if he was okay, and he announced in a booming voice, "Carrie Bowers, I love you. Will you marry me?"

Carrie stood before Gordon, stunned and a bit embarrassed by the commotion he had stirred. She covered her open mouth with her hand and stood frozen for a long moment. "Yes! Yes, I would love to marry you!" Gordon put a gold band on her finger and quickly stood. Carrie jumped into his arms for a long embrace.

The guests in the lobby and several employees at the front desk had been fully engaged in the exchange, and when Carrie said yes, everyone began clapping and cheering. Gordon had told Willow and Jeremy of his plans, and they came from the lounge to congratulate the jubilant couple. After a few minutes, they all returned to Willow's table for a celebratory toast and conversation about wedding plans. It was a night Carrie would never forget.

Carrie insisted on a small wedding for her second time down the aisle, though it could not have been a more beautiful scene. A hundred chairs had been set up near the stone bridge facing the river, with Willow seated in the front row. Dozens of lodge staff snuck out to the terrace to view the event in shifts. Gordon, Adam, and two of Gordon's best friends rode up from behind the crowd on horseback to the foot of the bridge, dismounted, and stood waiting for the bride. The bridesmaids processed from Roy's old cabin over the bridge, followed by Carrie on the arm of her Uncle Jeremy. They stood before the preacher and recited vows they had written to each other.

Most of Gordon's family from Aiken were in attendance, and Zeke and his wife from Atlanta made the trip. Carrie wanted to invite Zeke to the wedding; Willow decided not to explain why that might not be the best idea. After the ceremony, all the guests strolled to a tent outside the Madstone mansion for a feast of steak and shrimp prepared by the head chef from the lodge. A violin played during the meal, and then the town band played songs that encouraged everyone to sing along and dance.

Willow spent time with Zeke and his wife, Clara, but couldn't get Zeke alone to apologize for the scene at Buck's funeral in Macon. Tim was now gone, and Zeke lived a hundred miles away. Zeke could think what he wanted, thought Willow.

"Elegant but casual!" remarked Gordon to Carrie at the end of the evening. "Just like you." He hugged his new wife and kissed her cheek. "You and your mom made quite an impression on my family!"

"I love them! Your father is a real hoot, getting up there and performing a jig!"

"Give him a couple drinks, and he hams it up."

"I look forward to spending more time with them."

"That will have to wait. We leave in the morning."

"Leave? What do you mean?" asked Carrie.

"You and I are spending three nights at the Finney home on Jekyll Island. They are forming a club with some influential members from around the country and invited us to see what they have planned."

"But I can't leave here. I want to spend time with your family, and there's work to do."

"We can visit my family later. And your mother and Henry will take care of everything at the lodge. It's all been arranged."

Carrie thought for a moment and realized how much work Gordon had put into planning the trip. She got excited. "Just the two of us? You're taking me on a honeymoon?"

"Yes, indeed."

"And they consider us influential people?"

"It helped to know Finney's son. Plus, old man Finney has heard good things about Turkey Hollow and probably wants to pick your brain."

"We better get packing!"

"Your mother has already packed a trunk for you." He gathered her in his arms, nose to nose. "Tonight, it's just you and me."

The wedding had worn Jeremy out. He was beginning to feel old. His mind was still sharp, but he could no longer walk far before he had to sit and catch his breath. The sixty-two-year-old took an hour to get moving in the morning and couldn't get through the day without an afternoon nap. His law practice was still going strong because he could delegate most cases to his young assistant with some coaching. He remained a state senator with the second-highest tenure but no longer sat on any committees.

Jeremy still had big projects he wanted to get done. One was building a hydroelectric plant to electrify the town and lodge. The second was building an opera house in downtown Bowerton. The churches had fellowship halls that could hold hundreds of people for funerals, weddings, and town hall meetings, but the town deserved a performance space.

The townspeople probably wouldn't pay to attend an actual opera, but musical performances and traveling theater groups were becoming quite popular everywhere. Entertainment was becoming an industry, and Bowerton deserved to share in the good times. The cost to build a stately structure with seating, a stage, an orchestra pit, and space for dressing rooms and set construction was not cheap. Ticket prices might cover operating expenses but wouldn't pay the mortgage.

Jeremy and Willow had agreed to build the reserves of Bowers, Inc. in anticipation of expanding the lodge, so their contribution to the opera house would be limited. They needed other sources for the funds. The newspapers were full of stories of so-called robber barons who contributed generously to cultural projects. Names like Mellon, Rockefeller, Aster, Vanderbilt, and Carnegie topped the list.

Jeremy wrote to them each, hoping they would consider a contribution to a town cultural center to be named in their honor. He did not hear back from any of them. They made their fortunes from enterprises throughout the country, but their philanthropic efforts appeared to be focused on New York, Pittsburgh, and Boston.

Jeremy then met with the town council to present his idea. There was plenty of support but no money. He met with the mayor to come up with an alternate plan. The Morgan family would donate a lot near the town center. Volunteers would cut down trees and haul them to the mill. Kitch would mill the lumber. Volunteers would construct the building under the supervision of the town's leading contractor. Small contributions from scores of local merchants and families would fund the furnishings. All contributors would be recognized on a large brass plaque in the lobby.

The Bowerton Opera House might not match the grand scale that Jeremy first envisioned, and it might take years instead of months to complete. But Bowerton would have a place for the community to enjoy culture and entertainment.

It took Gordon and Carrie a whole day to reach Jekyll Island, traveling by train to Brunswick and by boat to the pier on the island. Carrie felt guilty about not visiting Aunt Abigail when the train stopped in Macon, but there was no time. Abigail had written a thoughtful letter to Carrie apologizing for not coming to the wedding, but she didn't have the strength at eighty years old.

Newton Finney and his wife greeted the McGraths warmly at their island home. "I know you two are on your honeymoon," said their host, "and you will have all day today and tomorrow to enjoy the island by yourselves, but I did want to show you our plans for a private resort here on Jekyll." He led them to a table in the study covered with maps and drawings.

"You do know that we have a hotel in North Georgia, right?" asked Carrie after seeing some of the plans. "I hope we are not competing for the same clientele."

"I am well aware of your fine lodge in the mountains," responded Finney.

"However, I see our project here as a compliment, not a competitor for guests. First, there are differences in latitude and altitude. Second, we will focus on hunting versus your equestrian activities. And most importantly, ours will be a very selective club of invited owners, whereas Turkey Hollow is open to the public."

Carrie and Gordon nodded with understanding and agreement, and Finney continued. "We are talking to the Vanderbilt, Morgan, Pulitzer, Macy, and other families. The Jekyll Island Club will be the most exclusive and least accessible resort in America, and we invite you to consider joining us."

"We are honored by your invitation!" exclaimed Gordon. "There is a contract, I assume?"

Finney reached for a document on the side of the table. "Please look this over at your convenience." Then he gestured to the front door of the cottage. "Right now, there's a carriage outside to take you over to the beach."

Gordon scanned the contract on their brief ride across the island. There was not only a considerable fee to join the club but also a commitment to build their own grand cottage within ten years. Gordon pointed to some figures and clauses for Carrie to see. Her jaw dropped. She almost burst out laughing but was careful not to let the driver see her reaction.

"Oh, my lord!" she mouthed to Gordon, who sat shaking his head in amusement.

They arrived at the beach and waded in the ocean surf, watching pelicans dive for their dinner and dolphins jump playfully in the waters close to shore. There was not another person in sight. They returned to a blanket the driver laid out for them on the sand.

"I can't speak for your family," remarked Gordon, "but Mr. Finney obviously didn't do his homework on my family's net worth. Their plans for this place are extraordinary!"

"I agree," said Carrie, sitting with her arms over her knees as she stared out at the sea. "But this is heaven on earth, and I'm so glad we came."

"I wish we had another blanket to cover what I'd like to do with you right now."

Carrie slapped him playfully. "There'll be time for that later, Gordo."

Gordon snuggled up to his new wife. "I'm just happy to be by your side, Mrs. McGrath."

Carrie looked at Gordon pensively and then turned back toward the ocean. "Can we talk about something that's been on my mind? It's kind of random and philosophical."

"Of course!"

"I look out and imagine all the fish living in that ocean. And then I look up at the sky that goes on forever in every direction. Only God could have created all of this. I know He exists, but I feel empty inside because I don't have a connection with Him." Carrie looked back to Gordon. "What do you think? Do you believe in God?"

"I do, of course! But I'm not religious in the sense of going to church regularly."

Carrie continued, "My parents had me baptized, and we went to a service every Sunday. Once Adam and I were about twelve, they let us decide whether to go or not. I always found something else to do on Sunday mornings. Now, for years, I've been working at the lodge on Sundays. And we weren't even married in a church. What about you? Were you raised in a church?"

"My parents were Catholic, like most immigrants from Ireland. But when they came to America and met people who thought all Irish Catholics were a bunch of uncivilized drunks, we started going to the local Presbyterian church. We never were a very religious family."

"My parents always went to Sunday service, but I never saw them pray or read the Bible at home." Carrie gazed out at the waves lapping the shore in a steady rhythm. "Sometimes I think I'm missing something by not being active in the church."

"I feel that way, too. I don't think we're any smarter than all the millions of people over the centuries who were led by their faith to build cathedrals, write hymns, and dedicate their lives to their faith. If it weren't for Christianity, the world would live in bondage. And in this country, the church is a perfect balance to all the freedoms we enjoy. Freedom without a moral compass leads to greed and injustice. So yeah, church should be an important part of anyone's life."

"Very profound!" exclaimed Carrie as she turned to Gordon. "So, can we make a pact? Let's start each Sunday by going to church and spending the day together."

"I'd like that!" said Gordon as he reached out his hand. Carrie accepted the promise of his handshake.

Chapter Thirty-Three
1879

Months later...

The inaugural running of the Turkey Quest race was held in the spring. Gordon had met with the ten racers to familiarize them with the course and rules of the race. Most of the riders knew each other from other chases around the Southeast. They were a competitive lot, full of jabs and sarcasm aimed jokingly at one another.

The temperature was chilly, but the bright sun promised to warm things up by the start of the race. The lodge was full of guests who gladly paid extra fees to view the start and finish of the race and enjoy a lavish assortment of food and drink. Carrie was proud to provide her homegrown sweet and hard cider. The Turkey Hoof cocktails were such a hit that the bartender asked guests to please limit their requests to two glasses.

In addition to guests viewing the race at the lodge, most of Bowerton was lined up throughout the course to see the horses run through the streets or jump over fences and ditches in the fields.

"I wish Daddy were here to see this," remarked Carrie to Willow, sitting beside her, wrapped in a horsehair blanket.

"He would rave at what a remarkable job you and Gordon have done organizing this event!" replied Willow, looking out over the cheery crowd.

"How disappointing Uncle Jeremy couldn't be here," Carrie expressed.

"I saw him this morning, and he said to give you his best. He could barely manage to get out of bed. You know he would love to be here."

Gordon had taught Henry and the lodge accountant how to manage the betting table. For an hour before the race started, they tallied the wagers and posted the odds on a board based on how much was bet on each horse. There were cheers as well as groans from the betting crowd as Henry kept changing the payout amounts.

As the horses exited the barn and crossed the bridge one by one, the crowd scrambled to get closer to the ropes to watch the start. The starting cannon blasted, and the racers took off to a roar from the crowd.

A few minutes later, the horses came back into view as they struggled to cross the river swollen from recent rains. A couple of the lead horses quit midstream and then recovered, tightening the field as they entered the final uphill sprint. The crowd cheered and hollered loudly as the horses crossed the finish line.

Some of the racers later groaned about the conditions, especially the steep hills and river crossing, but vowed to do better next time. Many guests expressed how much they had enjoyed themselves. And the lodge now had its signature event to be held every spring and fall. One adjustment they would make would be adding some water to the Turkey Hoof cocktail to reduce the number of guests who got a bit too excited.

Jeremy only lived a few more weeks. He died peacefully in his sleep. Willow found him on her morning rounds and called the town undertaker. The third Bowers brother was down.

Willow spoke again at the funeral service. "It has been less than a year since my Tim passed away. Now, the last of a generation of Bowers is gone. Their legacy was long and deep, but a new generation is ready to lead our family with the values passed on by their father and uncles. Jeremy was the steady brother, always considering the consequences before acting. He was a lot like his father that way. And now the boys are together in heaven with their Ma and Pa."

WILLOW *and the boys*

Carrie went up to help her mother return to her seat, then walked to the lectern.

"My Uncle Jeremy was my rock. Daddy taught me many, many things, but attention to detail and patience were not among them." There were some chuckles and lots of grins from those attending. "Uncle Jeremy was the one who went to college. He was the one who developed contacts with people outside of town. He found the right men to develop the mine and design the lodge. He sorted out the sticky challenges that our family faced over the years. He served honorably as a State Senator for decades, and we're proud that Governor Colquitt is here with us today. Uncle Jeremy loved this country, he loved this state, and he loved his family. We will miss him dearly."

Jeremy was laid to rest at the town cemetery next to Roy and Tim.

Days after the funeral, Carrie invited her mother to dinner. After clearing the table, they sat together in the parlor as Gordon went to the stables to check on a sick horse.

"That was nice what you said about Uncle Jeremy," observed Willow.

"Thanks. And you were great, too," said Carrie.

"Unfortunately, we're getting good at eulogies."

"Will you promise to give a eulogy for me?" asked Carrie.

Willow laughed. "Sure, when I'm a hundred and thirty years old!"

"It's just that I don't have any children, and I don't want Adam making stuff up about me."

Willow smiled. "You've had quite a full life, and now you have Gordon."

"I'm happy. And Adam's children are starting to warm up to me as they get older."

They sat quietly for a few seconds. "You always talk about the Bowers," Carrie said, "but you never say much about your family. Tell me more about the Madstones. You always said I favor your side with my dark hair and caramel skin. I'd like to hear more about them."

"You did get those blue eyes from my mother, but she never spoke about her past. I'll tell you what I know." Willow gathered her thoughts. "My father grew up just outside of what we call Ellijay today. He learned English to deal with the fur trappers and explorers who began coming through the area. Father believed adapting to their ways would be better than resisting their intrusion, so he enlisted in the Army during the War of 1812. His role was to fight the Creeks who sided with the British."

"This was before he met Grandma Eleanor?"

"Yes. Back before 1812, the Creeks occupied the land to our south, below the Chattahoochee River. When the settlers began invading their land, they retaliated and took white women as slaves. They killed my mother's family and took her hostage. When my father's Cherokee troops overran the Creeks, he rescued my mother, and they fell in love. And I came along!"

"Oh, my lord! Why haven't you or Grandma ever told me this?" exclaimed Carrie.

"I guess she didn't because it was just too horrible to talk about. My father told me."

"But how did they develop the farm and build the big house?" asked Carrie.

"After the Army, my father came to this area along the river and decided to grow vegetables in the fields. He was quite successful and kept expanding the acreage. White merchants from Ellijay and other villages started depending on his crops to sell in their markets.

"As the farm kept growing, my father tried to employ other Cherokees to work the fields, but the concept of working for others was not part of the Cherokee tradition, so he bought several slaves. When the government surveyors came through to carve the territory into parcels for the lottery, my parents appealed to the authorities to allow them to keep the land.

"The merchants who wanted my father to continue farming appeared in court to support him. They won the case partly because my mother was white, and my father was a war hero. He would never admit this, but the deed to the land was actually in my mother's name."

"The Madstones were the only people in this area, right?"

"For many years, we were quite isolated, just the four of us and our workers. And there were the Walkers. And then this man named Roy and his son showed up one day, and you know the rest."

"I am going to write this up. What an incredible life you have led! We need to preserve your story!"

"My life's not done yet!" exclaimed Willow.

"But think of the wonderful decisions you made and the good fortune you've had!"

"There were many times when I wondered if our luck was running out. There were difficult challenges, like when the militia harassed us during the Removal, the War Between the States, yellow fever, and risking everything we had to build the lodge during a depression."

Willow looked at Carrie and reached for her hands. "There were many wonderful times, too. Did I ever tell you about that time I overheard the conversation you and your father had in this very room?"

"I don't think so."

"He thanked you for what you said to him when we thought he was dying from yellow fever. He explained the many reasons why he was so proud of you. And then he said you were like your mother!"

"That was quite a compliment from someone usually short on praise!"

"And there was that day when your Daddy and I came back from the War and found you and Adam safe here at home." Willow began sobbing, and Carrie rushed to sit by her side. "Oh, I'll never forget that day!"

Carrie comforted her mother. But she could not know that Willow's tears were only partly from remembering the joy of reuniting after the War. The more significant trigger was the nightmare of being assaulted by the soldiers that day on the road. Willow wished the horror would fade. But it never did.

Chapter Thirty-Four
1887

Eight years later...

Gordon had brought Willow to the old Madstone house for dinner. After they ate, Gordon rose, went to the wall, and put his hand on a switch.

"Okay, Carrie, blow out the candle," announced Gordon.

The room went pitch black. Gordon flicked the switch, and a crude bulb hanging from the ceiling slowly lit up the room. Willow cheered, and Carrie rushed to hug her husband.

"It's a miracle!" exclaimed Carrie. "You're a genius!"

"All I did was flick the switch. I think Tesla and Edison deserve some credit."

"This is amazing!" declared Willow.

"Do you think we could light up the lodge?" asked Carrie.

"The architect is on it. There would be a lot of wiring throughout the building, so he's thinking of building chases that could also house indoor plumbing pipes in the future."

After a few minutes, there was a popping sound. The light flickered and slowly dimmed.

"Carrie, help Willow get outside! Now!" yelled Gordon.

Gordon quickly lit the candle as Carrie rushed Willow out the front door. He looked up to see that the rubberized cloth fabric insulating the wire to the light bulb was bubbling and melting. Soon, it ignited in flame. He flicked the switch off and then ran outside to where the wire entered the side of the house. He opened a metal box and turned the knife blade switch to the off position to break the circuit, just as the engineer had demonstrated.

"I'll go get help at the lodge," Willow told Carrie as they stood outside the house.

Carrie ran over to join Gordon. She saw the panic on his face. "How can I help?"

"I turned off the current. I hope that helped." Gordon ran back inside the house, and Carrie followed closely behind. Smoke was filling the dining room. The wire was still burning and had ignited the clapboard ceiling.

"Oh, no, hell no!" yelled Gordon angrily. He turned to Carrie in despair. "You need to go get help at the lodge!" He threw the water remaining in the glasses and pitcher on the table toward the fire, but it did little good.

Carrie ran up the hill toward the torches on the lodge terrace and soon passed her mother hobbling up the sidewalk. "Keep going, Mama!" yelled Carrie.

Carrie reached the lodge lobby and shouted to the receptionists and bellmen there. "The lodge is safe, but my house is on fire! Tell maintenance to get the fire wagon down there. Hurry!"

The staff knew what she needed; they had practiced fire drills often. The hotel's fire wagon was small enough to push through the hallways in case of fire. The wagon was equipped with a hand-operated pump, twenty-gallon reservoir, long hose, and a stack of metal buckets for refilling the reservoir.

Carrie ran to the front entrance and told the bellman on duty to ride to the Bowerton Fire Company, ring the bell outside the building, and lead them to her house. She ran to the rear terrace, where she could see the house. Bright flames now lit up the dining room. She hated to alarm the lodge guests, but they needed help desperately. Inside the lobby was a brass bell for use in case of an emergency. She began ringing the bell.

As guests came to the lobby, she explained the situation and asked for volunteers to form a bucket brigade between the house and the river. Then she ran down the hill to help Gordon, who was pumping water from the well into buckets to throw through the broken dining room window to fight the flames.

"Help is on the way!" she cried to her husband.

"Here, you do this," said Gordon, pulling her arm toward the well pump.

Gordon ran around the house and entered the back door. There was smoke, but the fire had not yet spread to the back of the house. He ran into the room they used as a library and study and began gathering things he could save. He threw them into a curtain he had pulled from the window and dragged it through the house to the backyard. He started to re-enter the house, but the heat and smoke had become too intense. Gordon ran around to the front yard.

Men were pushing the fire wagon down the hill toward the house. Other men with buckets were running toward the river to form a human chain to deliver water to the tank on the pump wagon. Everyone knew what to do because, unfortunately, fires like this were all too common.

Men began working the pump to spray water far deeper into the house than water heaved from buckets. But it was too late. The fire was spreading to the second floor and across the foyer into other rooms. By the time the Bowerton Fire Company arrived with their big, horse-drawn pump wagon, the roof was beginning to burn, and flames were shooting out the windows and exterior walls.

The house was beyond saving, and the firemen focused on protecting the nearby distillery and other outbuildings from flying embers. The volunteers from the hotel stood with the McGraths, watching the house slowly burn and collapse.

Carrie looked for her mother in the crowd. Not seeing her nearby, she looked up at the hill. Willow was halfway up the slope, sitting in the grass facing the house. The home where she grew up. Her hands covered her cheeks, and her face shimmered with tears flickering in the light from the flames.

By midnight, the flames were reduced to glowing red and blue embers. One of the bellmen drove Willow and the McGraths to Willow's home in town. Early the following morning, Gordon and Carrie returned to the house to see if anything of value remained. A fireman patrolled the ruins to ensure the fire did not reignite. Only parts of the four stone chimneys were left standing. The rest was ashes and charred wood. Men were hitching a horse team to the lodge's fire wagon to drag it back up the hill.

Gordon went over to help the men, and Carrie walked toward the fireman. "Thank you for spending the night here."

"I'm very sorry for your loss, Mrs. McGrath," he replied. "There are still plenty of hot embers, so please don't get too close."

Gordon returned to Carrie's side and reached for her hand. "Follow me," he said, leading her to the backyard and the curtain he had removed from the house. Gordon kneeled in the grass and began passing the contents to Carrie. "Here's your satchel full of work papers, your family Bible, a wooden box from your desk, and a few photographs I could see to grab. I'm sorry I couldn't save more."

"That was brave of you to save these. Thank you, honey," Carrie said as the tears began to flow. The shock of losing all of her other possessions was starting to overwhelm her. After a time, she took a deep breath and wiped her eyes. "Let's go clean up and get some breakfast."

Gordon packed the belongings back into the curtain and slung the sack over his shoulder as they walked to her mother's house. Willow was sitting at the kitchen table with a cup of coffee.

"It breaks my heart over the loss of the house," said Willow as she rose to pour coffee into two more cups, "but what a blessing that everyone was safe."

Carrie put her arm around her mother. "How terrible to lose the home you grew up in. So many memories."

Willow slowly nodded. "I remember the first plans for the lodge. The architect wanted to tear down the house and build a row of cabins. Now the house is gone. Maybe we can build those cabins." She tried to laugh, but it came out in a quiet sob.

Gordon spoke remorsefully. "I was the one that rushed to show off the electric light. I feel terrible, but the engineer who installed the wiring seemed to know what he was doing. He flicked that switch several times, and everything was fine."

"It was an accident," said Willow. "And it may be for the better. Maybe now you'll live here with me like I've been begging you to do for months."

Gordon looked at Carrie and said, "I like the idea. If we lived in town, Carrie would no longer be the first person the lodge staff calls on for help."

"We'll have to talk about it, Mama," Carrie added, "but it might just be time." Carrie raised her arms. "Now, do you have the fixin's for griddlecakes?"

"I do, and some blueberry preserves to go with them!"

One evening, Carrie sat getting ready for bed and picked up the small wooden box Gordon had rescued from the fire. Inside was her collection of picture postcards that had become all the rage for sending short messages by mail. There was one from Savannah, one promoting Ellijay as Georgia's apple capital, a drawing of the Greenbrier Hotel her Uncle Jeremy had sent her, and others. Also in the box were a printed brochure promoting Turkey Hollow, a woven bracelet that Adam's daughter had made her, and a few other trinkets. At the bottom of the box was the wooden band that John had given her when he proposed.

The following morning at breakfast, when she was alone with her mother, Carrie showed Willow the contents of the box.

"Maybe you could give that ring to one of your nieces without explaining where it came from," suggested Willow. "It's actually well done."

They reminisced a bit about John, where he might now be, and how Zeke happened to make the connection. "When are you going to tell me why Daddy and Zeke got into a fight that time in Macon?" asked Carrie.

"Some things are best forgotten," replied Willow.

"Come on! You know that only makes me more curious!"

"You might think less of us. Let it rest!"

"But I'd love you more if you didn't keep secrets from me!"

Willow considered making up a story about the fight but decided to go with the truth. She took a deep breath. "Okay." She folded her hands on her lap. "When I was young, Cherokee parents didn't control the

WILLOW *and the boys*

courting activities of their teenage daughters as much as people do today. Most young Cherokee girls were married by the time they were fourteen or fifteen, so getting in a family way before marriage wasn't a big risk. My mother would tell me never to be alone with boys, but that was about the extent of it."

Carrie sat spellbound. She had asked about the fight, not the sex practices of teenage girls.

"I was fifteen or maybe sixteen when I met Zeke. I would find him hunting in the woods, and we became friends. I had never met a white teenager who was so handsome and kind. Soon, we were kissing and holding each other. He kept wanting more, and I didn't know better than to go along. We fooled around in the woods a few times."

"Oh, my! Are you saying Zeke is my real father?"

"No. I had you when I was eighteen and married to your father."

"Were you pregnant when you got married?" Carrie had done the math before and suspected she was conceived out of wedlock but never mentioned it.

Willow hesitated and then let out a what-the-hell sigh. "Yes. Just by a few weeks."

"But Zeke thinks he is my father?"

"He does, but he is wrong because he doesn't know the details."

"What details?"

"When the Bowers arrived, I liked Tim as soon as I met him. Zeke picked up on that and soon started pressuring me to get married. I put him off because I wanted to see how things went with Tim, and it turned out that he liked me as much as I liked him. Zeke got mad and ran off to join the Army. But I had a monthly course after he left and before your father and I got serious, so I know the truth."

"Did Daddy know all of this?"

"Yes, I mean, they were both there to live it, but neither knew the exact timing of things. I can see how Zeke might think you are his, but I've told him that Tim was definitely your father. That day at Buck's funeral, your father got suspicious about why Zeke was always so concerned about you. The two of them had words, and that's when the fight started in the kitchen. I tried to have a talk with them, but Zeke left in a huff, and your father got upset. Tim never said another word about it."

"So, they each knew you had relations, but neither knew that you had relations with the other," said Carrie, summarizing for herself.

"I never told them the details that I just shared with you. I just couldn't. It made me sound too much like a hussy." Willow sighed. "I thought everything would work out after Zeke left for the Army, but then he appeared out of nowhere at your wedding." Willow rested her head in her hand. "I was a foolish teenager. And now my daughter thinks I'm a floozie."

"I don't think any such thing! I understand teenage urges."

"Oh? So now it's your turn to tell me about your early love life," teased Willow.

Carrie looked back at her mother with a feigned look of horror.

"I'm just kidding," replied Willow with a wave of her hand.

"What if I see Zeke again? How should I act toward him?"

"Think of him as your godfather, not your father."

WILLOW *and the boys*

After Carrie and Gordon agreed to stay in the house, Willow moved all her belongings to another bedroom to allow the McGraths to have the master bedroom. She hired a contractor to build an addition to the house, not only to give the McGraths more space but to eliminate the need for her to climb steps.

Carrie missed being a short walk from the lodge but liked being able to keep an eye on her mother, now seventy-one years old. But Willow was in good physical and mental shape and supervised a helper to handle the cooking, cleaning, and maintenance. For Carrie, it was like living in a hotel.

The fire had set them back, but the family was thriving. They had fun together, the family finances were quite comfortable, and everyone was healthy. But there was yet another dark cloud forming to the north.

One night at dinner, Carrie exclaimed, "I'm concerned with what I've been hearing about the copper mine up north in Copperhill. A guest at the lodge told me the other day how the plants and wildlife are dead or dying, the land is turning brown, and people are getting sick. All that destruction is only fifteen or twenty miles from here."

"It's not the mine causing the problem," added Gordon, who was well aware of the situation. "It's how they heat the ore in giant furnaces to extract the copper. The fumes from the smelter are toxic. The hundreds of men working there need those jobs but worry about their family's health."

"Good grief," moaned Willow, looking up to heaven. "After surviving war and epidemics, you might think I could enjoy old age without worrying about the air I breathe."

"Those fumes could threaten our water and land, too," exclaimed Carrie. "And publicity about the devastation will scare guests away from the lodge."

"We need an expert to assess the situation," added Gordon. "Maybe an official from Atlanta." He sat quietly for a few moments. "I wish your Uncle Jeremy were here; he'd know just what to do. But I'm going to see if there's any action we can take."

Gordon wrote to the governor and his representatives but received only words and no action. The attention was all on Atlanta these days, and the copper mine was far away in Tennessee. Gordon visited the mine and smelting plant but received a frosty welcome. "Maybe if my name were Bowers, they would have been more cooperative," he remarked to Carrie when he returned.

"You didn't remind them that your father-in-law saved the mine from Yankee attack back in 1864?" Carrie asked glibly.

"No, I don't think I've heard about that."

"Ask Mama about it sometime," replied Carrie. "It's a long story."

"When I asked what they were doing about it, they said we don't need to worry because we're upstream, miles away, and in a different air pattern from the smelter fumes. They told me to stop overreacting."

※

Gordon became an avid reader of the *Atlanta Constitution*, delivered daily by train to the lodge. He wrote letters about the copper mine pollution to Henry Grady, the editor. Grady would publish his letters in the paper and sometimes add a sympathetic comment. But the only reaction to his letter-writing campaign was a combative reply from the copper mine.

The newspaper was full of exciting new developments in Atlanta every week, which Grady called the New South movement. The old South was agricultural and dependent on slavery. The New South was about getting over the War and attracting more industries to create new jobs.

Grady was a champion for Black education and also instrumental in the founding of Georgia Tech. He traveled the country giving speeches to encourage companies to move to the New South and made a national name for himself with pithy responses to challenging issues.

Gordon invited Grady to stay at Turkey Hollow for a fall turkey hunt, and he accepted. Carrie found him entertaining and charming, but Gordon was upset that he was unwilling to take the short train ride to see the copper basin in Tennessee for himself. Gordon did get a good laugh when Grady told Carrie why he was a talker by inheritance. "My father was an Irishman, and my mother was a woman."

Gordon followed Grady's successes as the population of Atlanta doubled in the years he served as editor of the *Constitution*, and he didn't stop sending letters to the newspaper with pictures of the thousands of acres of scorched earth in Copperhill.

Chapter Thirty-Five
1893

Six years later...

Carrie crossed the breezeway to Willow's mother-in-law's suite and knocked on the door. "Momma, there's a man here to see you!"

Willow took a few moments to open the door. "Who is it?"

"He wouldn't say," fibbed Carrie.

"Oh my goodness," said Willow, flapping her hands in frustration. "Well, tell him I'll be there in a minute."

Willow fixed herself up and hurried to the living room. She shrieked when she saw her old friend Zeke and rushed over to hug him, fussing that he had not sent advance notice of his visit. Carrie arrived with a glass of cider for them each and took a seat to share their happy reunion.

"It's so good to see you!" exclaimed Willow. "You're looking handsome as ever. How has life been treating you?"

"Some good, some bad," replied Zeke. "I woke up again this morning, for which I am grateful, but I lost my Clara a few months ago."

"Oh, I am so sorry to hear that," said Willow. "Such a lovely woman." Willow shook off the sad news. "But if you're here to ask me to marry you, the answer is no."

Carrie yelled, "Mother!"

Zeke broke out in a hearty laugh. "No, I didn't come here with any romantic notions. I just came to see how you two were doing. Carrie looks as wonderful as ever! I love the new lodge addition, and Carrie told me about the horse race you sponsor."

"Yes, we are doing just fine. The old mansion burned down a while ago, but having Carrie and Gordon live here at the house has been a blessing. Or I should say, them letting me live here."

"There is another reason I came to see you," said Zeke. "My daughter and her husband are opening a butcher shop in Mobile and want me to help get things started. So this may be goodbye."

"There are trains that run between Mobile and Bowerton, you know," replied Willow. "I hope you will still come to visit."

"Yeah, but it's such a long trip. I barely survive getting here from Atlanta anymore."

"I hope you're not saying this is the last time we will ever see you again," exclaimed Carrie.

"You are welcome to come to Mobile," Zeke responded.

"I seldom leave this house anymore," returned Willow.

Zeke wanted to change the subject. "I've been cleaning out my attic and brought a few things your family might enjoy. They're out on the porch." Zeke got up slowly and used his cane to walk.

"Can you spend the night?" asked Willow.

Zeke stopped and turned as if he couldn't walk and talk at the same time. "Oh no, I've already checked in at Turkey Hollow."

"We have a guest room upstairs that you're welcome to any time," said Carrie.

"No, no. I like staying at the lodge." Zeke returned carrying a long deer hide case. He sat back in his chair and untied the laces. "I thought Gordon might appreciate this." He pulled out an old flintlock rifle.

"Golly!" exclaimed Willow. "Is that the rifle you used to hunt around these woods?"

"It is! Probably shot a rabbit or two right here where this house stands today." He reached into the case again. "And you might recognize this, too." He pulled out a coonskin cap.

"Oh my Lord!" Willow shrieked and rose to hold it in her hands. Then she thrust it toward him. "Put it on!"

Zeke held out his hands and shook his head.

"Come on! I used to think you were king of the wild frontier in that cap!"

Zeke dutifully put the cap on his head. "Now, will you consider a marriage proposal?" he laughed.

Zeke and Willow spent the afternoon talking about everything from the old days to great-grandchildren. He stayed for dinner, opening two bottles of good French Burgundy he had brought and entertaining Gordon with stories.

It was getting dark, and Zeke wanted to go check in at the lodge. Willow walked him to the door.

"Will you and Carrie have breakfast with me in the morning?" asked Zeke. "I catch the train back to Atlanta just after noon."

"I will see you in the dining room at nine A.M. Carrie's treat!" said Willow as she gave him a peck goodnight on the cheek.

Willow dressed in her Saturday best to meet Zeke at the lodge. Carrie was already at work and joined them in the dining room. They enjoyed a good breakfast and decided to take a stroll behind the lodge.

WILLOW *and the boys*

"You should be very proud of what you two have built here," said Zeke as he stopped along the hilly sidewalk and looked back to the lodge and the surrounding fields of flowers, vegetables, and apple trees.

"Most of the credit goes to Tim and Jeremy," replied Willow. "They had the vision and made it work."

"They were good men, but you were their compass. You were a great team."

"Yes, I miss them."

"I went by the town cemetery earlier. I saw the stones for Tim, his father, and brother, and it brought back so many memories."

Willow put her arm through Zeke's arm as they continued their stroll. "And now Carrie and Gordon are taking over and doing just great."

"And Adam?" asked Zeke.

Willow chuckled. "He's still a work in progress. He competes with his big sister for command, but he hasn't put in the work. There's still hope for that one, though. He is a good father and husband."

"I don't know if I can make it to your chicken ranch, Carrie," Zeke announced, "but I hear glowing reports about the chicken Marsala you serve in the dining room!"

"The chicken house is way across the river," responded Carrie. "We don't need to walk that far. Plus, it might upset my birds if a butcher gets too close."

They stopped near the spot where the Madstone mansion once stood. "I'll never forget the first time I knocked on the front door to see you, Willow," recalled Zeke. "My heart was beating out of my chest."

"We had some good times fishing and exploring," said Willow. "But to tell you the truth, my father didn't think too highly of you. I figured he resented how you tried to look like a Cherokee with your long hair and deerskin moccasins."

"So that's why you invited Tim to your house for dinner and not me?"

"Not really. Tim asked, and I responded. Besides, you ran away to the military, so that was the end of that," replied Willow.

There was a long pause as each recalled the past from their own perspectives.

Carrie broke the silence. "Zeke, how are your legs feeling? I don't want you wearing my mother out."

"Hey!" responded Willow. "I'm not the one leaning on a stick!"

"I've used a cane ever since I had a couple of falls. I don't climb trees anymore," Zeke laughed.

They walked past the distillery. "Kitch still making white lightning in there?"

"He helps, but his son has taken over," replied Carrie. "Kitch and Henry developed these new bottles with a fancy label, and now they sell Turkey Hollow whiskey all over."

"And the sawmill? Does it still operate?"

"Not much," answered Carrie. "We have a bigger mill that opened on the edge of town that does a good job."

They approached the stone bridge over the river. "This is a little nicer than the pine log bridge we built back in the day," said Zeke to Willow as he rubbed his hand over the sandstone sidewall capped with smooth flagstone. "Roy would be proud!"

WILLOW *and the boys*

Willow had had about enough sentimentality and remembrances for one morning. "Hey, I know what you need to get those legs limbered up again. Miracle waters!" She leaned against the side of the bridge and began removing her shoes and stockings. "Come on! Take off your shoes!"

"Mother!" declared Carrie. "What are you doing?"

Willow ignored her daughter. "Come on, Zeke!"

"I can't reach my feet without a chair!"

"Just do it. I'll help you."

Zeke went to the sidewall to steady himself. He seemed determined to join in, so Carrie helped him bare his feet and roll up his trouser legs. "You are crazy, woman!" he said to Willow as she approached him barefoot.

Willow handed him his cane, put her arm through his, and led him slowly but deliberately to the river's edge.

"Now my feet are all muddy," he complained. "I have a train to catch in a couple of hours!"

"Wash them off in the water. Come on." Willow stepped into the river, and Zeke followed. The water was cold and clear enough to see the rocks below. "Now, doesn't that feel great?"

Zeke put his hand on top of his head and laughed. "This is about the stupidest thing I've done in years. You are a terrible influence!"

A younger couple came from the stables across the bridge and stopped to watch. Carrie stood to the side, acting as if she didn't know her mother and Zeke, though she monitored their every move. "Everything okay down there?" asked the man.

"Oh, we're fine," replied Willow. "Just two old fools reliving our past."

"Well, have a good time," said the young woman from the bridge. "We'll ask someone from the lodge to bring you some towels."

"That would be very much appreciated," replied Zeke.

Willow and Zeke carefully walked back up the bank and stood on the bridge, looking over the rail to catch their breath. "Now that was fun!" declared Willow.

Zeke stood there staring at his old friend with a smile as they let their feet dry in the sun. Carrie stood at a distance, watching over their shoes and socks.

"Do you remember," asked Zeke, "when we had our little clubhouse over there in the woods? Tim and I would come over and compete for your affection."

"Oh yeah! We were Unalii! That was fun! We were so young and naive."

"Maybe it was fun for you, but your choice of Tim over me really hurt!" said Zeke.

"You have done quite well without me getting in your way."

"Yeah, I've had a good life, but I often wonder what it could have been. You made the right choice in marrying Tim, but I don't think he ever fully appreciated how you shaped his life. You made him successful."

"Well, I don't know about all that," said Willow. "He made a lot of great decisions on his own."

A bellman brought clean towels down to the bridge, and Carrie came over to help them clean up. "You two are both off your rockers!" she exclaimed.

They walked most of the way back to the lodge when Zeke stopped and stood before them both. "Before I leave to catch my train, I have a favor to ask. I'd like you both to stand right here. I'm going up to the terrace,

WILLOW *and the boys*

and when I look back, I want you to wave. I'd like to save that image in my mind of Willow Madstone and her lovely daughter Carrie standing at her daddy's farm by the river."

Willow hugged Zeke and kissed his cheek. Zeke hugged Carrie and kissed her cheek. "Goodbye, Zeke," Carrie exclaimed.

Zeke turned toward the lodge.

"God bless you, Unalii!" exclaimed Willow.

They stood still and watched Zeke walk to the terrace, turn around, pause, and wave. Carrie put her arm around her mother as they both waved back. Zeke turned and disappeared.

In another minute, Carrie turned toward Willow. "I'm going to go make sure he's okay," she said.

Willow stood there for some time as tears rolled down her cheeks. The last of her generation was gone. But, oh, what a journey!

THE END

Acknowledgments

I had a few advantages in writing this story. I am one of three brothers, love the history of frontier Georgia, and have been commuting for years between my home in Macon and a cabin near Blue Ridge, Georgia. I love both places for different reasons.

I am very grateful to two family members who are always willing to read very early drafts of my books and provide helpful feedback. Thank you, daughter Morgan Maier and brother Mike Maier. A very special thanks to my friend, Johanna Miklos. A writer herself (as well as a poet and painter), she encouraged and challenged me to improve my writing through many edits and changes in perspective. Another significant influence was Conie Mac Darnell, who knows Middle Georgia history. Discussions with Conie Mac and information from his book *Walking on Cotton* provided valuable historical detail and perspective for the story. Neighbor Mike Corrigan of Macon was a great help with my geology questions regarding the slate mine and stone lodge.

Anna Holloway (Annahollowaywrites.com) of Fort Valley, Georgia, performed the final edit. Thank you, Anna! Bridgett Joyce of Trinity Press in Norcross, Georgia, designed the cover and book interior. She and the team at Trinity were delightful to work with and indispensable in allowing me to turn a Word file into something I'm very proud to share. And special thanks to Charles de Andrade of Scribblers Press for his help in the final production!

Rick Maier

POSTSCRIPT

Nearly two hundred years have passed, but the Indian Removal (or Great Intrusion) and slavery remain raw events in America's past that evoke highly charged emotions. I wrote this book to entertain the reader. If parts of the story provoke political discussion, okay, but I hope the conversation remains respectful.

FOOTNOTES: FACTS AND FICTION

I made every effort to highlight—not change or invent—history in writing this book. My intent was to bring history alive through the fictional characters and their surroundings. The lines between fact and fiction may blur sometimes, so here are some notes to hopefully clarify the gray areas:

FACT: Early Macon, Georgia – Fort Hawkins operated between 1802-1828, the Creeks ceded land west of the Ocmulgee River in 1814, Macon was founded in 1823, City Cemetery began in 1825, Mulberry Street Methodist Church in 1828, Wesleyan College in 1836, and Rose Hill Cemetery opened in 1840.

FACT: Towns and landmarks – Except for Bowerton, the names and descriptions of towns are true. For example, Aiken SC has a rich steeplechase race history.

FACT: War of 1812 – General Andrew Jackson played a key role in ending the War in 1815. The Creeks sided with Britain and the Cherokees with the U.S.

FACT: President Jackson – "Old Hickory" served from 1829 to 1837. Famous as a champion of the common man, his legacy was stained by the Indian Removal.

FACT: Cherokee Territory – The corner of Georgia north and west of the Chattahoochee River was a sovereign territory until 1828, when Georgia effectively stripped the Cherokee of any rights to the land. The U.S. Congress passed the Indian Removal Act in 1830. President Jackson supported Georgia and ignored the Supreme Court decision (Worcester v. Georgia, 1832) that denied Georgia jurisdiction. The actual Cherokee removal occurred in 1838 as part of what is known as the Trail of Tears. Some Cherokee Natives owned Black slaves.

FICTION: Madstone – The name is fictional, but in early Native folklore, a madstone was a stony concretion thought to have medicinal value in treating an animal bite.

FACT: Land lottery – Georgia held eight lotteries between 1805 and 1833 to redistribute lands ceded by or annexed from the Creeks and Cherokees.

STRETCH: Madstone land claim – While unable to find documentation, I believe exceptions were made in allowing some Natives to own land after Georgia annexed the Cherokee Territory, especially if they were married to a white woman. The story of Waya and Eleanor Madstone securing a deed to their farm is fictional.

STRETCH: Treatment of slaves – There are innumerable accounts of brutal and inhumane treatment of slaves, and Georgia laws did prohibit the education and manumission of slaves. How Roy and Buck Bowers treated their slaves is fiction, supported by accounts of some owners treating their slaves kindly. Regardless of how they were treated, they were not free, and slavery is evil and morally indefensible.

FACT: Crops – The Native's success in growing the Three Sisters crop is true. Growing specific types of apples does indeed require skill. Apple cider was much more popular in the 1800s than today. The government did not regulate whiskey stills and distilleries until the 1862 Revenue

Act, and then enforcement was limited.

FACT: Georgia Gold Rush – The gold rush in Georgia, the largest for its time in the U.S., began in 1828 and spread throughout the Cherokee Territory. The richest deposits were found around Dahlonega. The rush faded in the 1840s as some Twenty-Niners in Georgia became Forty-Niners in California.

FALSE: Snakebite – The suggestion in the story of treating a snake bite by sucking out the venom or applying a tourniquet is bad medicine. Get to a doctor or vet immediately.

FACT: Trail Trees – still exist, though the trees would be well over 200 years old today.

FICTION: Glory/Bowerton – I imagined Bowerton being located on the Toccoa River at Old U.S. 76. That would be a few miles northeast of present-day Blue Ridge and northwest of Morganton, Georgia. The village of Galloway once existed near present-day Mineral Bluff.

FACT: Etowah and New Echota – These once major Cherokee villages were renamed Canton and Calhoun, Georgia, respectively.

FACT: Fannin County – When Georgia annexed the Cherokee Territory (1828), the entire area became Cherokee County. Cherokee County was then subdivided into several counties in 1832. Parts of Gilmer and Union Counties subsequently formed Fannin County in 1854.

FACT: Railroads – Georgia was a leader in building railroads beginning in the 1830s. The Central of Georgia Railway connected many cities within Georgia and Alabama, with Macon as its hub. In the late 1800s, Georgia encouraged railroad expansion by offering to lease state prisoners for a fee.

FACT: Atlanta – Decatur and Marietta were founded in the early 1820s. The village at the north end of the Western & Atlantic railroad became known as Terminus, then Marthasville, and renamed Atlanta, feminine for Atlantic, in 1837.

FACT: Toccoa River – All the rivers mentioned in the story are real. The Toccoa River runs north to Tennessee, where it becomes the Ocoee River, the site of whitewater events in the 1996 Olympics. The river was dammed in 1930 to form Lake Blue Ridge and is part of TVA today.

STRETCH: Values in the 1800s – The story stretches some customs that people followed more strictly in the nineteenth century, such as the eldest son inheriting all estate assets, parents limiting the courting activities of their teenage daughters, and families having many children.

FACT: U.S. immigration – was wide open until quotas were imposed in the late 1800s. Large groups of Asians migrated mainly to the West and Europeans to the Northeast.

FACT: U.S. epidemics – Yellow fever, influenza, smallpox, cholera, scarlet fever, and other diseases plagued Georgia towns throughout the 1800s.

FACT: Depressions – There were major economic depressions in the U.S. in 1838 and 1873, consistent with the financial challenges the Bowers faced in the story.

STRETCH: Travel times – in the story are approximations. A man on a good horse might ride fifty miles in a day, horse-drawn wagons might average twenty miles daily, and an old steam train might go about 30 MPH.

FACT: Georgia capital cities – Savannah in 1776, Augusta until 1786, Louisville until 1796, Milledgeville until 1864, Macon temporarily in 1864-1865, and finally, Atlanta in 1868.

FACT: Mexican War – The U.S. annexed Texas in 1845, but disputes

WILLOW *and the boys*

over lands north of the Rio Grande River continued. The Americans captured Mexico City in 1847, and the War ended in an 1848 treaty ceding the Southwest to the U.S.

FACT: V.P. Andrew Johnson – Republican Lincoln chose Democrat Johnson, a Tennessean loyal to the Union, as his running mate in 1864 to attract the votes of Democrats.

FACT: Copper Basin devastation – The acid rain produced by smelters at multiple copper mines in the Copperhill, Tennessee, area caused massive destruction to the local environment. Reclamation efforts begun in the 1940s have slowly restored the flora, fauna, and quality of life.

FACT: Civil War battles – All references to generals (Sherman, McClellan, Lee, etc.) and battles (Kennesaw, Cleveland (TN), Atlanta, etc.) are based on historical accounts. Any dialogue of generals is imaginary. Sherman's March through Georgia is based on historical accounts.

FACT: Antietam cemeteries – The account of CSA soldiers being buried in an unmarked common grave in Hagerstown, Maryland, is true.

FACT: Age of Fraternalism – Social clubs grew rapidly after the Civil War. The desire to socialize also led to exclusive hotels in cities, resort lodges in remote places, and opera houses in almost every American town.

FICTION: Historic lodges – The vision for Turkey Hollow was inspired by the Grove Park Inn (1913) in NC, Skytop Lodge (1928) in PA, and the Greenbrier Inn (1778) in WV. The Marshall House (1851) still exists in Savannah. The Jekyll Island Club (1888) and the historic cottage district have been open to the public since 1987.

STRETCH: Railroad to Bowerton – The railroad from Atlanta to Blue Ridge (near the fictional Bowerton) was not completed until 1886. The story has the tracks coming to Bowerton in 1877.

STRETCH: Slate in Georgia – There are no accounts of slate mining in the Fannin County area, but the existence of slate in the ground is possible. The largest slate operation in Georgia is in Rockmart, located between Atlanta and Rome, Georgia. The sandstone used to build Turkey Hollow could exist adjacent to a vein of slate in the fictional open pit.

STRETCH: Electricity – Atlanta introduced streetlights in the 1880s. Towns like Ellijay and Blue Ridge (fictional Bowerton) probably did not get electricity until after 1920. The Federal Rural Electrification Act of 1936 extended power to rural farms and communities. Having locally generated power in a town like Bowerton in the 1880s was possible but highly unlikely.

FACT: Innovation – The design and application of steam engines evolved throughout the 1800s. Samuel Morse developed the telegraph in 1837; telegraph lines were built throughout the country over the next forty years. Larger cities began providing water and sewage utilities for residences in the late 1800s.

FACT: Fires – were common in the 1800s due to open flames and before fire codes were enacted.

FACT: Henry Grady – the publisher of the Atlanta Constitution in the 1880s, was nationally celebrated as a champion of the New South era. His many accomplishments in promoting Atlanta have been tarnished by what are now considered racially insensitive perspectives. His trip to Bowerton, however, is fiction.

Rick Maier

Made in the USA
Columbia, SC
15 January 2024

29789204R00209